UNCLE PIPER OF
PIPER'S HILL

Tasma was born Jessie Catherine Huybers in London in 1848, of Anglo-French stock on her mother's side, and of Belgian descent on her father's. In the early 1850s the family migrated to Tasmania – hence Jessie's *nom de plume*. She was married in 1867 to the well-connected Charles Fraser, but within six years they had separated and young Mrs Fraser travelled in Europe for two years with her formidable mother and several of her brothers and sisters. By the late 1870s, Jessie was publishing a steady stream of essays, stories and travel articles, at first in Australian and then also in European journals. She returned to Europe in 1878 and lived there until her death in 1897, paying one further visit to Australia in 1883 to secure a divorce. In 1885 she married Auguste Couvreur, a well-known Belgian politician and journalist whose role as Brussels correspondent of the London *Times* she took over after his death in 1894. *Uncle Piper of Piper's Hill* (1889) was her first novel; she published five more and a volume of short stories; her work in journalism, both fiction and non-fiction, remains uncollected.

Margaret Harris, Associate Professor in English Literature at the University of Sydney, has published on such English nineteenth-century novelists as George Eliot and George Mere-dith. She is currently working on a study of woman novelists of the late nineteenth and early twentieth centuries, and a critical anthology of the work of Christina Stead.

AUSTRALIAN WOMEN WRITERS:
THE LITERARY HERITAGE

AUSTRALIAN WOMEN WRITERS
The Literary Heritage

General Editor: Dale Spender
Consultant: Elizabeth Webby

Pandora is reprinting a selection of nineteenth- and early twentieth-century novels written by Australian women. To accompany these finds from Australia's literary heritage there will be three brand-new, non-fiction works, surveying Australian women writers past and present, including a handy bibliographical guide designed to fill in the background to the novels and their authors.

The first novels in the series are:

A Marked Man: Some Episodes in His Life (1891) by Ada Cambridge
Introduced by Debra Adelaide

An Australian Girl (1894) by Catherine Martin
Introduced by Elizabeth Webby

The Incredible Journey (1923) by Catherine Martin
Introduced by Margaret Allen

The Bond of Wedlock (1887) by Rosa Praed
Introduced by Lynne Spender

Outlaw and Lawmaker (1893) by Rosa Praed
Introduced by Dale Spender

Lady Bridget in the Never-Never Land (1915) by Rosa Praed
Introduced by Pam Gilbert

Uncle Piper of Piper's Hill (1889) by Tasma
Introduced by Margaret Harris

The companion books to this exciting new series are:

Down Under: Two Centuries of Australian Women Writers
by Dale Spender

A lively, provocative overview of the history of the literary scene and the position of women writers in Australia which shows that any image of the country as a cultural desert was not based on the achievement of Barbara Baynton, Ada Cambridge, Dymphna Cusack, Eleanor Dark, Katharine Susannah Prichard, Christina Stead and the many other Australian women who have enjoyed tremendous international literary success.

Australian Women Writers: The Contemporary Scene
by Pam Gilbert

There are a number of outstanding contemporary Australian women writers about whom relatively little is known. This book fills that gap with a comprehensive discussion of the work of Helen Garner, Kate Grenville, Elizabeth Jolley, Barbara Hanrahan, Robin Klein, Thea Astley, Jessica Anderson, Jean Bedford, Olga Masters and Antigone Kefala

Australian Women Writers: A Bibliographical Guide
by Debra Adelaide

Covering over 450 Australian women writers, this invaluable sourcebook outlines their lives and works and puts rare manuscript collections throughout Australia on the literary map for the first time. A comprehensive guide to the articles and books written about these women is also included.

UNCLE PIPER OF PIPER'S HILL

TASMA
(Jessie Couvreur)

Introduced by Margaret Harris

PANDORA

London, Sydney, New York

First Published in 1987 by Pandora Press
(Routledge & Kegan Paul Ltd)
11 New Fetter Lane, London EC4P 4EE

Published in the USA by
Routledge & Kegan Paul Inc.
in association with Methuen Inc.
29 West 35th Street, New York, NY 10001

Set in 10/11½ pt Ehrhardt
by Input Typesetting Ltd, London
and printed in Great Britain
by The Guernsey Press Co. Ltd
Guernsey, Channel Islands.

Library of Congress Cataloging-in-Publication Data

Tasma, 1848–1897.
Uncle Piper of Piper's Hill / by Tasma (Jessie Couvreur);
introduced by Margaret Harris.
p.   cm. — (Australian women writers)
ISBN 0–86358–222–2
I. Title.   II. Series.
PR9619.2.T38U5   1988
823—dc19

British Library CIP Data also available
ISBN 0 86358 2223

CONTENTS

———————•———————

INTRODUCTION

The woman who took the pen-name Tasma had made a living from her writing for a decade before the publication of her first novel, *Uncle Piper of Piper's Hill*, in 1889, and had developed a shrewd sense of popular taste and trends. Twice married and living in Belgium, Jessie Couvreur nonetheless looked to her childhood and early womanhood in Australia for a setting when she turned from essays and short stories to the novel. In choosing to write a kind of colonial romance, she was pursuing further the possibilities of exploiting the exotic aspects of Australian life which had provided the substance of her earlier stories such as 'How a claim was nearly jumped in Gum Tree Gully'. But in *Uncle Piper of Piper's Hill* she moved away from the conventions established by other writers of romances set in the Australian colonies, dwelling neither on the challenge of making a new life in the bush nor on sensational aspects of colonial life like the transportation of convicts and bushranging. (Rolf Boldrewood's *Robbery Under Arms* achieved book publication in 1888, with the one-volume issue in 1889 establishing its huge success.) The original edition of *Uncle Piper of Piper's Hill* had a monochrome frontispiece depicting Australian flora, which together with the subtitle 'An Australian Novel', and the author's pseudonym, suggested its affinity with other late nineteenth-century Anglo-Australian romances. The book broke new ground, however, by focusing comically on the affluent bourgeois milieu in the city.

The accuracy of Tasma's professional appraisal of the market was proved by the reception of her novel. Its publication late in 1888, in time for Christmas (though dated 1889), was well judged also. *Uncle Piper of Piper's Hill* was extensively and enthusiastically reviewed. The weighty *Athenaeum* declared that it was

... A well-written story in one substantial volume equal in subst-ance to an ordinary two or three. It is full of commonplace incidents: the love-making of average young men and women; the inter-ventions, conferences, and domestic diplomacy of their elders; influences of wealth and poverty upon character, with an accident or two introduced to effect what character cannot. But Tasma makes himself interesting, both by himself and through his personages.

The author drily observed in her journal that this was 'faint praise, but not sufficiently faint to damn.' It is notable that the *Athenaeum* reviewer did not stigmatise the novel as a woman's work, while other reviewers gave a livelier account of it: 'The tone throughout the book is pure and healthy, the narrative brisk and cheerful, and there is every indication that "Tasma" will some day take her place among the first and best of Australian writers of fiction' (*Pall Mall Gazette*); 'A capital sample of the novel of character. ... The story is very clever, very natural, full of satire without spite, of knowledge of human nature without cynicism' (*World*); 'A work of considerable promise' (*Academy*).

The book went quickly into a second edition, and there were further English reprints as well as unauthorised American ones. To cash in on the success of *Uncle Piper*, the publisher Trübner almost immediately brought out Tasma's collected earlier pieces (*A Sydney Sovereign and Other Tales*, 1890) and a second novel, this time in three volumes (*In Her Earliest Youth*, 1890). Tasma subsequently changed publishers, moving to the new house of Heinemann, set up in 1891, for *The Penance of Portia James* (1891), *A Knight of the White Feather* (1892) and *Not Counting the Cost* (1895); and her last novel, *A Fiery Ordeal*, was published by the reputable Bentley in 1897.

Such a profile presents a real if modest literary success. How then did Tasma's fiction come to be relegated to museum status in literary histories? For a start, she died relatively young, at the age of 49; and she was an expatriate. More potent in effecting her eclipse however has been the version of Australian literary history which sees the emergence in the 1890s, especially in the Sydney weekly *Bulletin*, of a tradition of authentically Australian writing. This male-oriented bush realism claimed to offer unadorned presentation of themes like mateship, the pioneering spirit and epic venture in the bush as against the pernicious mannered conventions of Anglo-Australian romance. Comparable American works have been described as 'melodramas of beset manhood' – an epithet which pungently exposes the assumptions underpinning these exclusive claims to authenticity. The irony is that *Uncle Piper of Piper's Hill* explores material as distinctively Australian as any, from a perspective which in its own way is aggressively nationalist.

The dominant concern in *Uncle Piper of Piper's Hill* is with the social consequences of the period of affluence and expansion which followed the gold rushes of the 1850s. The time is the 1860s, the place the phenomenal city of Melbourne, a city whose population increased fivefold between 1851 and 1861. Not only did the city centre expand (and Uncle Piper's shrewdness has enabled him to make profits in real estate to add to those made in meat), but the suburbs spread rapidly also. In areas like Toorak and South Yarra – the site of Piper's Hill – many mansions were erected from the 1860s on, a good number of them featuring a tower like the one by which Mr Piper sets such store at Piper's Hill. The poor of the city are not in evidence, as they are in Fergus Hume's *The Mystery of a Hansom Cab* (1886), for instance, but it is clear that the British class system, transplanted along with the convicts, does not survive the changed climate. The shift in the basis of power from old blood to new money is nicely played out in the contrast of Mr Cavendish, impoverished bearer of the name of the Dukes of Devonshire, with his rich plebeian brother-in-law Mr Piper. Uncle Piper is quite literally establishing his house. By building Piper's Hill he makes an ostentatious display of his wealth and claims social status. Further, Piper's Hill is designed as a family seat, and Uncle Piper means to generate a dynasty by the right marriage of his son.

And George does in the end make the right choice for the right reasons, as his father comes to accept. It is significant that his bride Laura is the character most in touch with European intellectual developments and most able to challenge cultural and social orthodoxies. Although she is punished for her pride, Laura's intellectual independence survives to modify the Piper philistinism. Mr Piper's notions of mixing the breeds are upset – he intends to strengthen his line with an infusion of the Cavendish blood of one of his nieces – but new forms of colonial life evolve, as the fittest adapt and survive (it is notable that Sara, the selfish beauty who embodies the worst Old World snobbery, is left unmated). The breakdown of English social barriers is indicated at every turn: Uncle Piper's family as a matter of course is invited to the Governor's 'At Home', and he claims a high place for them at the New Year's races. The novel is optimistic about the possibilities of growth and change, and of achieving happiness, in the New World. In its depiction of New World innocence and energy taking over from the exhausted Old World, Tasma's work has affinities with Henry James' investigation of such tensions in transatlantic contexts, and with his fascination with the power of wealth. Tasma is less equivocally committed to the virtues of the New World than James is, however, in her working out of some aspects of authentically Australian experience.

Uncle Piper of Piper's Hill is, then, an innovative work. It is also a first novel, and its early uncertainties of tone, particularly, betray the inexperience of the author writing at full length, while some unevenness of construction may be traced to its serialisation in weekly parts in the *Australasian* early in 1888. For these reasons, and also because of shifts in taste over the century since the book was written, readers may need to exercise a little patience as the novel gets under way. But by the time Mr Cavendish burns his fingers on the candle at the end of Part I, the gentle wit of the narrative is in the ascendant, and the point of comparisons of Tasma with Jane Austen evident.

The novel opens rather pretentiously, with a quotation from Milton and some laboured facetiousness about shipboard life. The citations of eminent authors and quotation of French and Latin phrases become less frequent as the book proceeds, and similarly the caricatures of the Irish emigrant family, the M'Brides, and of the priest, Father M'Donnell, yield to much more subtly observed characterisations of the principal characters. The first six chapters, Part I, introduce the Cavendishes and Francis Lydiat on board the ironically named *Henrietta Maria*, and bring the emigrants within sight of the Australian coast. Then, in a parallel exposition, the four chapters of Part II introduce the Pipers and Laura Lydiat at Piper's Hill, indicating Mr Piper's opposition to the understanding between his son George and his step-daughter Laura, and taking Mr Piper and his adored younger child Louey to the point of their departure to meet the boat. This kind of strategy, involving converging sets of characters, was one which Tasma used again, for example in *Not Counting the Cost*, with the same effect of presenting characters in others' perceptions of them, and of contrasting expectations and images. Mr Piper is not described by the narrator until the seventh chapter, but already in the opening pages he has been delineated in letters to Francis Lydiat. His mother's courteous expression reveals her character and situation as it offers her version of her intended: 'I have consented to marry Mr. Piper.

He is a kind, though a self-made man ... your sister's welfare is my chief motive for becoming his wife.' The thirteen-year-old Laura's letter telling her brother of their mother's death in childbirth actively establishes her precocious defiance as she proposes to claim her baby half-sister from her 'coarse and contradictory' father. The Cavendishes' conjectures about Mr Piper's appearance and character also anticipate the authorial version of him. Accordingly, though the novel is almost one-third advanced before the two sets of protagonists meet when the emigrants are landed, the respective characters and relationships have been well-established and the plot – which depends so heavily on the conflict of temperaments – begins to move.

It doesn't seem sporting to spell out the turns the plot takes: I've no wish to anticipate a reader's pleasure in following out the ways and means by which those young people who so deserve are properly paired. *Uncle Piper of Piper's Hill is* a Victorian novel, though, and there has to be at least one major calamity: watch out for Louey's premonitions of platforms and streetcrossings. The calamity, when it comes, is not simply a contrivance of plot. The accident in Part V, chapter 6, provides a moral testing for all the characters. The selfish ones, Mr Cavendish and his younger daughter, the beautiful Sara, definitely fail the test, the one complaining of being inconvenienced, the other expediently accepting a new and more prestigious suitor. By contrast, for Mrs Cavendish the time of trial provides occasion for further demonstration of her gratitude to her brother and of the Piper goodness of heart as she triumphantly produces copious quantities of good broth and jellies. For Louey along with her suffering comes fulfilment of some of her dearest wishes.

Various kinds and degrees of awakening are required of the other characters, each of whom must in some measure set vanity aside. George is enabled to discover his better self; Laura painfully learns humility. The saintly Francis comes to terms with some aspects of this-worldly existence, and the similarly saintly Margaret finds a vocation and requited love. The most severe trial is reserved for Mr Piper, whose belief in his own infallibility has been at odds with his goodness of heart. The possibilities of social equality in Victoria are aligned with the equality of all before God, and the saving grace of humour is apparent even in the more fervid passages of moralising.

In an inversion of the usual antithesis of the idyllic rural world with the wicked and dangerous metropolitan one, the accident occurs out of the city – not quite in the bush, but in the country town where

Francis is performing parish duty. Barnesbury affords no pastoral bliss: it is hot and dusty, with the elements providing no challenge beyond those of keeping clean and cool. Tasma's description of the town's seeming to have 'been brought to a sudden halt in by-gone years, and of having never been set going again', implicitly endorses as preferable the pace and progress of Melbourne.

The title of the novel puts Uncle Piper in pride of place, and its course gives him fuller warrant for his pride in his place in the world. The character is essentially a stock one, shamelessly sentimentalised: the common man made good, who despite his roughness has a code of honour equal to any, and whose generosity of spirit comes to match that of his purse. The narrator works hard to show what is estimable in Piper, and why Cavendish's patronising is so misplaced, thus heading off condescension on the reader's part. Elements of caricature are invoked in his very name: there is explicit reference to Peter Piper and his pickled peppers, and implicit reference to the nursery rhyme pig stealer and to the saying that 'he who pays the piper calls the tune'. The whole question of the Piper name is canvassed at the end of Part I, chapter 3, in a way which well demonstrates Tasma's lightness of touch. For all the superiority of the glorious Cavendish name to that of Piper,

> the young husband and wife were placed in very similar circum-stances. Both were poor, both orphans, both acknowledged an elder brother – with the difference that Mr. Cavendish could say, 'My brother the bishop;' while Mrs. Cavendish was constrained to say, 'My brother the butcher.' The benefits conferred by the bishop, though priceless, no doubt, considered from a spiritual point of view, had hardly the solidity of the tokens sent by the butcher.

Mr Piper, of course, sends his sister a timely gift of one hundred and fifty pounds just after Mr Cavendish has begged a loan of fifteen pounds from the bishop on the security of the silver teapot. The passage enunciates a moral theme on which variations are to be played, of honesty and sincerity as preferable to affectation and hypocrisy. In due time Mr Cavendish finds compelling material reasons for revising his opinion of the Piper name, and there is a very amusing exchange when he announces to the bearer of the name:

> 'In fact, my dear sir, I am engaged in a work of no less moment than that of reconstructing your family tree.'

'My what-do-you-call-it tree?' exclaimed Mr. Piper aghast, with a hazy idea that Mr. Cavendish had been trying some unwarrantable experiments upon his lemon and orange bushes. 'Don't you take and put any rubbish in the garden. I've got a new lot of guano, and I don't want it meddled with.'

There is a particular piquancy in Piper's having earned his money as a butcher. Tasma could have made her point about social mobility by allocating him a different trade, but his being a butcher directly erodes an element of the pioneering mythology. To have made a fortune in cattle is one thing, but the cash value of the beast on the hoof has to be realised by dressing it as meat for the table. There may also be a reflection on the staple outback diet – unrelieved mutton, damper and tea – as one of plenty.

In addition, it is emphasised on several occasions that Piper's fortune was won by his honest toil. He is guilty of no shady dealings, and he has no secrets to hide – by contrast, for example, with Thomas Longleat in Rosa Praed's *Policy and Passion* (1881) who is concealing a convict past. Piper's nearest brush with the taint of transportation is through his first wife, George's mother, who came to the colonies as matron on a convict ship. In Tom Piper, then, the ethic that hard work brings its due reward, is presented in its purest form.

The other characters are in various senses subordinated to Mr Piper, and many of them are also stock types deftly drawn. The non-conformist is Laura, who prefigures Tasma's later heroines, the women who crave independence and identity but endure their penance, often within a misguided marriage. Tasma's subsequent novels are frequently described as more autobiographical than *Uncle Piper of Piper's Hill*. Such a judgment overlooks both the extent to which firsthand experience informs *Uncle Piper*, and the ways in which autobiographical material is used later as the author engages in the debate about the 'New Woman' which so occupied much of English fiction of the 1890s. Although in the later novels there is more active exploration of the limits of women's freedom, inevitably the texts present an almost superstitious reinforcement of those limits until the spell is broken in *Not Counting the Cost*, which ends with Eila Frost and her family permitted a second chance. *Uncle Piper of Piper's Hill* is undoubtedly more radical in relation to class than to gender. The insistence on traditional women's roles is strong, and the women are subservient to the men whether as good housekeepers, ministering angels or flirtatious beauties. Even Laura is in bondage to the male through her financial dependence on Mr Piper and her passion for George. Nonetheless it must be recognised that the women in the novel can exercise some effective control, and certainly they are necessary for producing the fullest enjoyment of wealth and success, not only for reproducing.

The mellow comedy of *Uncle Piper of Piper's Hill* has been damned for what it is not. The acuteness of its registration of a particular period in a particular colony should be recognised for the achievement it is, and its unabashed celebration of Australian possibilities simply enjoyed.

Margaret Harris

PART I

CHAPTER I

———— • ————

The Rev. Mr Lydiat's Reverie

'All my evasions vain,
And reasonings, though through mazes, lead me still
But to my own conviction.' – MILTON

That celebrated appeal from Philip drunk to Philip sober might have been made with almost equal effect from the Rev. Mr Lydiat on board ship to the Rev. Mr Lydiat on land. I don't think his ingenious theory of the necessity for the due development of a sea-brain as well as of sea-legs could account quite satisfactorily for those uncut volumes on his cabin shelf, or altogether explain the lack of zest he had felt latterly with regard to the process of induction, as shadowed forth by Bacon. A passing glance at him, as he stands with his elbows on the bulwarks of the vessel, looking across at the watery clouds that fleck the margin of the horizon, would impress you very probably with his listlessness.

A tall young man, in a plum-coloured vest, and a coat whose clerical cut seems to demand an absence of all triviality, with a fair complexion, becomingly browned by the tropical sun, a jaw slightly underhung, but square and clean-shaved, a general squareness of forehead and shoulders, typical of an unyielding English framework, and eyes, if you take them under their present aspect, of more latent than active power. You would hardly credit him with having gone through twelve and fourteen hour days' work in the most villanously crowded parish in the crowded East of London – to the point, in fact, of bringing very dark rings round those somewhat deep-set eyes, and making it a matter of imperious necessity that he should abandon the miserably multiplying souls in the afore-mentioned crowded parish.

Perhaps this enforced rest was partly accountable for his present air of dreamy inquiry. Hitherto that constant dedication of active thought to the service of others, which more than art or literature, or any self-evolved occupation, has the power of lifting man out of himself – and which, thank Heaven! is within the reach of the merest nullity in creation – had left no room for questionings or musings of any kind. But then how had this new unsatisfactory communing with self been brought about?

Could it be that the influence of the great unpeopled space around, following upon the constant pressure of the burdens of overplus humanity, had shaken his proper parochial views? It is one thing, certainly, to learn that there is a Pacific Ocean, truthfully represented in your atlas by a speckled blue patch, and another to spend days and nights, and weeks and months in crossing it, to be engulfed by it sometimes, or maybe never to reach the shore you are steering for. And it is one thing to know that there is an ocean of doubt appearing in your theological charts as a parti-coloured patch called heterodoxy, and another to embark upon it on your own account, and to find it just as treacherous and just as unfathomable as the great Pacific itself.

But I have no warrant for referring Mr Lydiat's abstracted air to a voyage upon such ever-explored, and yet ever-unexplored seas. I daresay, seeing that he is a young man, and just now undeniably an idle man, and – despite the clerical coat and the self-renunciatory mien it implies – a man of quick sensibilities and responsive enthusiasm, there is some human agency at work, after all, in the impressing of his sea-brain with its present sea-perplexity.

It is so evident that Bacon's directions for phenomenal research have not solved his present problem, and again, the problem is apparently of so mixed a nature – half-delightful, half-unsatisfying – as would appear from the changing expression in his deep-set grey eyes, that I feel sure it would be useless to look for it either in the *Organum* or the ocean. For the sea, if it can be commonplace, is commonplace to-day. A regular work-a-day sea, of uniform indigo, neatly ridged over with little white curves of foam, quite at one with the wind. As for the sky, it is as uniform as the sea, only becoming a little indistinct and watery where it seems to merge into the circle around. Taking it altogether, a useful sea, but of a sort that, seen for the fiftieth time, could scarcely arouse any particular impression of sublimity.

Failing the sea, there is nothing left for it but to go below. In that little commonwealth lining the saloon are varieties as distinct as any you will find in the vast world itself; jumbled together as oddly as sometimes happens in life, though journeying in company, it is true, towards a more definite end.

From cabin No. 1 a dreadful family aroma of babies' partially-sucked biscuits, orange-peel, and linen drying in eight feet square of space – a scale of the cries of human young, graduating from the quavering clamour of a six-weeks-old baby to the patient chant of an elder sister. This is the cabin of the M'Brides, Irish, improvident, and impoverished. 'And it's in Australia they'll make their fortune, sure!' is Mrs M'Bride's unvarying hopeful assertion. This fund of hope is common to the tribe of M'Bride, being, in fact, the only thing Mr M'Bride will have to bequeath them. But it is a fund that on board ship, where the dinner for the day is not a matter for forethought, seems quite inexhaustible, and by means of which every sturdy juvenile M'Bride is already appreciated at the parental rate of estimation in free Victoria.

Two doors from the M'Brides' cabin, which it may be as well to leave just now to the sanctity of its torn curtain and its privacy, is a little cabin of very different appearance – more like a boudoir, indeed, than a cabin. The berths are covered with fine white quilts. The pillowcases are frilled. On the miniature floor is spread a soft white rug. The shelves are filled with women's toilet nick-nacks, arranged in ship-shape fashion. It is all so tiny and so tidy. You think of birds in a cage or squirrels in a trap. Some faint suggestion of perfume, such as escapes from a chest of lavender-besprinkled linen, seems to detach itself from the clothes. It is a cabin that links you with the air wandering about an English garden more than with the warm brine-laden breeze from without.

But cabins are only a makeshift at best. I will spare you an inventory of the boxes and the books – passing over the little gilt keepsakes on the shelves, and even the open novel on the swing-tray – and come at once to the living presences. We are still in quest of some tangible cause for that unexplained reverie on the part of the Rev. Mr Lydiat. And though, so far, it is only possible to assert hypothetically that there is any tangible – that is to say, any flesh-and-blood – cause at all, a scrutiny of the inmates of this fragrant cabin may help to throw some light upon the quest.

For one of them is ready to bear a very close scrutiny indeed. That sage who once defined women as one of 'Nature's agreeable blunders' would have granted that Nature had seldom blundered more agreeably than in the framing of Sara Cavendish. Look at her as she lies in her berth, with half-shut eyes, and heavy hair pushed back from her delicately-veined temples. You are reminded of the Magdalen in the wilderness. Her head, a little thrown back, in a pose that would be fatal to any but faultless nostrils and well-curved lips, is the daintiest, shiniest head conceivable.

That is the real test of beauty, to come upon it unawares, with loosened hair and undiscovered bust. For I maintain that it is only spurious beauty at best which needs gaslight and a French dressmaker to bring it into prominence. Genuine beauty needs nothing but health, of which Sara is blessed with an inordinate share. Perhaps, under the board-ship *régime* of perpetual meals, with a little too much, as shown in her full-blooded red lips, and that faint foreshadowing of a double chin, determined by a tiny crease. But then the skin itself reflects such an opalescent light. If Madame Rachel could have approached within the most distant imitation of it, she might have found fresh victims to roast and to rob to the end of her days. That texture of skin is the purest accident, as we all know; but such accidents may sometimes alter the destiny of a kingdom. Yet Sara is by no means high-coloured, despite the redundancy of health to which she is subject. The general hue of her face is rather colourless, and just now, as the mingled green and yellow light streaming through the open port-hole travels over her uncovered neck and arms, you would almost suppose her to be plastered. Though such an illusion only helps in another sense to deepen the impression of having come upon a very fine piece of statuary, and gives a strange air of sculptured reality to the line called by artists the *collier de Venus*, clearly traceable where the neck merges into the shoulders.

Sara's eyes, as I have said, are half closed, and as she is not likely to open them so long as her eldest sister, Margaret, continues to read Macaulay's *Essays* in a cheerful monotone, I must explain what they are like. In the first place, because, as somebody has said, 'Eyes are the windows of the soul,' and it is possible to take a peep through a window as well as out of one; and, in the next, because I have not forgotten that the Rev. Mr Lydiat, of ascetic principles – of almost superhuman renitence, where the affections are involved – and of a determined bias respecting his mission in life – is still standing on the forecastle, with the *Novum Organum* opened at the same place, and his face still full of thought. To come back to Sara's eyes. It might have been nothing but their dark setting of lash and brow, or the peculiar colouring, that almost seemed like a reflection of the sea;

it might have been a something subtle in their expression, like the piercing of a mind through mere crystalline matter; it might have been none or all of these that gave them their special charm. The effect of fine eyes is often felt, like colour or music, neither of which can be analysed as to the emotions they produce, however wisely we may graduate their component parts. Sara's eyes were invariably the first attraction which lured you on to the inspection of her charming face.

But how it comes about that I enter into such a minute description of them, following the portrayal of Mr Lydiat's attitude on the fore-castle, requires thus much of an explanation.

Some few weeks ago there had been tropical Sundays, when even the vessel lay at rest, fretting, as it seemed, at the delay. For she was wont to creak complainingly all over, her sails slapping the air petu-lantly, her ropes stretching and straining themselves unaccountably. Metaphorically speaking, she yawned all over like a tired woman in the sulks. It is true that at these times the sea was usually of most seductive smoothness, giving vent once in a way to a long uniform heave, as if it were content that the sun out west should flatten himself in a broad warm sheet upon its treacherous surface before wishing it good-night.

But the passengers, for the most part, were more influenced by the humours of the ship than of the sea. When she grumbled because there was no 'getting on' they grumbled too. The captain, I may surmise, was chief grumbler, and being very much in the position of that pedagogue whose frown was enough to set all the little boys in the class whimpering, helped to depress his passengers proportionally during these tropical calms. Yet it was on Sundays such as these that Mr Lydiat's sea-brain seemed to awake. You would have thought sometimes that it was the only active element on board. To begin with, he read prayers beneath the awning on deck in orthodox clerical garb. No longer the indolent young man in the plum-coloured vest, but a grave curate, with a little infusion of High Church sentiment in his priestly mien, with face clean shaven, allowing full scope for the play of his well-cut flexible mouth, with light brown hair, brushed in a broad sweep away from his square white forehead, with much sweetness of expression in his deep-set grey eyes. He seemed to find a fund of imagery in the grand desolation around. Even Father M'Donnell, the apple-cheeked Catholic priest, found it in his heart to regret that such power of exposition could not have been enlisted under the banner of the Pope. And later on, towards sunset, when all the children on board claimed him for their Sunday hour, and a little horde of M'Brides and others hedged him in, he never failed or flagged. The cadence of his voice blended so harmoniously with the subdued swish of the tired waves, that he seemed to be speaking to the measure of a music that it was only given to him to detect.

Like St Augustine haranguing his congregation of fishes by the seaside, it would sometimes befall the Rev. Mr Lydiat to find himself addressing a little audience of a comprehension not greatly beyond the standard attained by the fish-brain. At such times he could be marvellously succinct – simplifying each short illustration, yet driving the moral home. Any one who has seen that old picture of the saint, standing with outstretched arm by the sea-shore, must remember the open-mouthed interest of the fishes. It would seem that St Augustine was telling them, from a fish point of view, of the deadly danger that lay concealed beneath the appetising wriggles of the agonised worm. Mr Lydiat, in the same way, could deduce examples without end of the deceitfulness of appearances, pointing to the beautiful, treacherous sea, and instancing his meaning by stories that made the children as round-eyed and open-mouthed as St Augustine's fish.

But somehow these arguments of his never took more definite shape than when the younger Miss Cavendish stole into the group of children that surrounded him. What if a mermaid, with sad oval eyes of beautiful human comprehension, had suddenly regarded St Augustine from the midst of his staring fish congregation? Don't you think he would have fortified himself by affirming with fresh ardour that the hook lay surely concealed behind everything that was graceful – whether worm or whether sweet feminine eyes. And the more pleading the mermaid's glances, the more strenuous, I am convinced, the saint would have become.

Now, with regard to eyes, such as are potent to lure away a man's immortality, any mermaid might have envied Sara Cavendish. Sunday after Sunday – with an expression that made them look, according to Tennyson's beautiful simile, like 'homes of silent prayer', Sara would fasten these speaking eyes upon the young clergyman, as he discoursed to the listening children. Sunday after Sunday the young clergyman, with inflexible resolution, would look steadfastly before him. That a woman's gaze should move him to eloquence, instead of that ardent consciousness of his Christ-given task, which had carried him unflinching through the slums and pollution of the thieves' alleys of London, was abhorrent to him. But now these Sundays were nearly at an end.

Tokens of the nearness of the Australian coast had already drifted past the *Henrietta Maria* as she sped to the eastward before a southerly breeze. And the Rev. Mr Lydiat, looking from the forecastle across the blank before him, saw with his mental gaze the great blank of his life to come, stretched with equal clearness before him too. He could not see where it would be absorbed into the life to come, any more than he could see where the boundary-line of the ocean – obscured, as I have said, by a watery haze – merged into the horizon above. He could see nothing clearly, either here or there. I doubt whether Sara, lying in sleepy contentedness on her berth, could have had any notion of the tumult she had raised in his soul. The greater tumult that he had forced back all expression of it until now – and now, seeing the inevitable separation surely approaching, the truth had confronted him, defying him to gainsay it. A brief outline of his life hitherto is here called for, if only to prove that it was no shallow mind that this new emotion had stirred to its depths.

CHAPTER II

———————•———————

Chiefly Explanatory, But Brief

'Every step in the progression of existence changes our position with
respect to the things about us.' – JOHNSON

Francis Lydiat had found himself fatherless at the age of ten, in the
safe keeping of a practical mother, who was pleased to take prompt
advantage of a means which offered itself for placing him in the Blue-
coat School, and enabling him to cram his bare brown head with the
knowledge he coveted. She herself, with an infant in arms – a little
girl of whom Francis had retained ever since a sort of idealised
remembrance – took a post as travelling companion to a rich widow.
Emigrating after a short time to Australia, she continued to send him
letters replete with maternal cautions. The boy's heart was always
going out to his mother and sister. His recollection of his father as a
consumptive clergyman, kindly, weakly, learned in his son's eyes in
learning more profound than the Magi's, was beginning to diminish
in intensity. Nevertheless, it came upon him with the force of a first
wound to learn that his mother was about to marry again. She gave
him the news curtly enough, as was her fashion.

'For Laura's sake,' she wrote, 'as well as out of regard for my future
husband, I have consented to marry Mr Piper. He is a kind, though
a self-made man, and will give me ample means for the education of
my little girl; in fact, your sister's welfare is my chief motive for
becoming his wife. Laura promises to be very handsome, but she is
strange and self-willed to a degree. There are times when she literally
alarms me; I tremble for her future. You, my good son, give me no
fear, but the one of seeing you sacrifice yourself through life. I always

8

predicted you would enter the Church' (Francis was now in orders), 'and am content for my own part that you should follow in your father's steps. But I must tell you that it is one of Laura's oddities to detest clergymen; so don't expect her approval.'

This strange assertion was literally true. A year later Francis received a letter (not black-edged, albeit it contained the news of his mother's death) addressed in Laura's handwriting – a hand, for a girl of thirteen, of astonishing squareness and firmness of stroke. It was dated Melbourne, 185-, and ran thus:

'Our mother is dead, Francis. She had a baby and died. The baby, a girl, is alive. I intend to bring it up. Mr Piper is grieved. He is accordingly more coarse and contradictory than usual. I show no grief in his presence. The child is to be called Louisa. In my own heart I have called it Hester, after Lady Hester Stanhope, you know. I shall make it answer to that name to me.'

And when Francis, at this time in his twenty-fourth year, and already entering upon that long struggle against the degradation of his fellow men in the corrupt parish under his care, wrote such a letter of sympathetic tenderness and love and brotherly solicitude as might have set an ordinarily forlorn sister crying as she read it, Laura returned such a cold answer that her correspondent, disheartened, addressed himself to his stepfather. No notice was taken of his letter, and after a time the one-sided correspondence came to an end.

I am not sure that anything short of the quality Thomson has called a 'godlike magnanimity,' could have enabled him to cherish – as he cherished after this – a vision of a small rosy sister, whose mutinous baby mouth he had liked so well to kiss. He had been so clearly spurned, and the quarter whence the blow came lent it a poignancy that would leave an inward bruise for ever. As for that new sister, she was most probably kept in ignorance of his existence. Yet what was there left for him to do? How could he save her? Intense in belief as in action – the one essential he held to be faith in the Faith that was a reality to him. If Laura abjured clergymen from a transcendental conception of Christianity – then he would still have taken comfort and bided his time. Had she been floundering in pitfalls of doubt, he was prepared to write reams of controversial reasoning, giving a digest of all the works on divinity published by the Parker Society, and coming down to Hugh Miller's *Testimony of the Rocks*. But she would not even read what he might have written. What, in point of fact, was there left for him to do? Nothing, in so far as the healing of his own

sore was concerned. Everything in respect of the sores that gaped
around him. Thenceforth he renounced, like the early anchorites, the
want inherent in every man, from the savage to the sage, of continuing
his race. He resolved that the scourings of the back lanes of London
should hereafter constitute his family – the pickpockets become his
brothers, the harlots his sisters. And he kept his vow.

I do not want to depict another Abbé Myriel. Habit, perhaps, as
well as a natural energy which would have made him equally indefati-
gable in any other career, may have helped the Rev. Mr Lydiat in his
work. He had entered upon a certain groove, and found no time for
resting or thinking, or even pausing. His salary would have been
scouted by an Australian boundary rider. Yet even out of this he
straitened himself, and kept a few wretched lives going.

Eight years of such a life. And at the end of it all what a drop in
the bucket his labours represented! If from out of the slime and the
squalor a few souls had been lifted, there were still struggling multi-
tudes left behind. His impassioned preaching had in no wise changed
the cast of faces procreated by vice and cunning. The soul-sickening,
work-annulling 'Cui Bono' was confronting him with spectral impor-
tunity. If he had remained he would probably have succumbed in
mind. Gaunt in person at this time, with the strange air that a mind
matured by contact with the old misery of the world, new born in
every generation, imparts to a youthful face, he looked fit subject for
Wordsworth's description of 'A noticeable man, with large grey eyes.'
Looking thus, and carrying besides in his thin cheeks a colour that
betrayed the existence of the germs of consumption – of which, as I
have said, his father had died – he made application to be sent to
Australia. It was now imperative that he should take a sea voyage.
Curates of his stamp were wanted in the colonies. He was promised
clerical work in Victoria, and took passage for Melbourne in the
Henrietta Maria. This is how he comes to be standing on the forecastle
this afternoon, and how it happens that on the eve of a new life he is
reviewing the old one.

For the voyage in more than one respect has revolutionised his
being. He can see himself, three months back, creeping on board with
the burden of his fruitless toil still weighing him down, apathetic as
to his recovery, dimly conscious only of a longing to find that little
sister to whose image he still clings, that she may look at him
perchance with his mother's eyes before he dies. He can see himself
a month later, amazed at his own increasing bulk, not comprehending

aright the new zest for life that stirs his pulses, as he wakes after his blissful nights of unbroken sleep. He can see himself again famished at breakfast-time, hungry at lunch time, unblushingly hearty by the time the first dinner-bell rings, and almost shamefacedly searching for a ship-biscuit before turning in for the night. Remembering the rank atmosphere he has left behind him, and the poor souls still steeped in it, his sense of well-being brings a pang in its wake. He would fight off this gross content were it possible. Yet it assails him in a fleshly sense, notwithstanding. Compared with his erewhile meagre exterior, the Rev. Mr Lydiat is actually becoming plump. He has some trouble in recognising the handsome stranger who looks at him with lathered cheeks from the glass before which he is accustomed to shave.

Only contrast, as he is doing now, these two pictures! The picture of red-rimmed, blear, vice-haunted eyes, bestowing grudging glances upon him for eight dragging years, as he pours forth the eloquence of a heart big with compassion, and the picture of an assemblage of innocent child faces turned towards him, and (for it is beneath you to stoop to self-deception, Mr Lydiat) the picture above all others of a pair of eyes that overcome him with a sensation of heavenly martyrdom, because he still looks away from them – believing that they are absorbing his meaning into the soul of their possessor. He was not only reviewing his past life now – he had faced the truth at last, feeling that the time had come for him to decide upon one of two courses.

The *Organum*, I need hardly say, lay by this time with fluttering leaves at his feet. Rules that may be applied with wonderful precision for the establishing of natural phenomena are impotent in their dealing with that most unsearchable phenomenon of all – a human heart. The first of these two courses was prompted by an instinct that for a short space gained the mastery over him. It told him that it was no mere blind adoration of a fine pair of eyes and a well-moulded figure that held him in thrall. It was a sentiment that seemed, on the contrary, interwoven with the nobler part of his being. You see he had reached a ripe age for the experiencing of a first love, and it is a matter of fact that any visitation of the sort deferred beyond its legitimate epoch gathers proportionately in intensity. Measles, chicken-pox, and calf-love are apt to assume forms that leave no lasting scars – under age. But they may shake a matured frame very considerably; and calf-love especially – retaining nothing of the calf-period but the desire to worship the divinity that has stirred it – may be prolonged into a love durable as life itself, with all its exaggerations, its short intervals of rapture, its checks, and its aspirations. Following his instinct, the Rev. Mr Lydiat would put an end to this purgatorial phase of a first passion in the simplest and most natural way. He had hitherto avoided Sara. Now he would find means to talk to her often. He would not let her leave the ship without telling her how dear she had become to him. It was true that he was poor; but he had barely reached his prime. And how he had increased in vigour! What power he seemed to feel! What! He had worked almost from boyhood among influences so depressing that, save for his religion, the world might well have appeared to him one lump of sentient depravity; and now should he not strive for some of the sweets in his turn! Imagine those eyes always in front of his as he preached to his new congregation in Australia, with no longer a necessity for shunning their inspiration with the ferocious determination of St Augustine. I think he pressed his hand upon his eyes at this point. There was a radiance in such a vision that made his temples throb to contemplate. It could in no wise be associated with the world as he had hitherto known it.

No, he could not promise to pluck this human love out of his heart – but he took Heaven to witness that it should not enervate him, his enthusiasm should not slacken. He would train himself from to-day to the anticipation of beholding Sara, beloved, rich, and magnificent here below, bearing as his cross the certainty that his devotion could never be of benefit to her. He had, besides, an object that, in relation to his human affection, he would never rest until he had achieved. He must find his sister, and move her heart – towards him if it were possible; but beyond and above all else, towards Christ. Still, for instinct gave him one parting thrust, he felt as if the merest sign that his love *might* have been in part returned would have enabled him to turn more resignedly into the course that he had resolved to follow. It could not but be pardonable to hope for such a sign before the end of the voyage, but then there could be no possible justification for seeking it.

I am afraid his cogitations made him heedless of the bell that clanked for the second time below, despite the promptitude with which he had obeyed its calls during the early part of the voyage. While he had been thinking out his position, the fleecy haze that obscured the border-line of the ocean to the westward had been gathering a pale rose-colour, that was fast tinting the watery atmosphere. He had been standing all this time with his elbows leaning on the bulwarks, and his hands covering his face. Now, as he removed them, a sudden stream of amber light enveloped him, and softened his resolute expression into a radiant calm. The clouds fronting him were turning from pink to salmon-colour, and from salmon-colour to the purest gold. Small wonder that their glory transfigured him for the instant, though I am inclined to think that inward act of renouncement invested him with a luminousness which would remain long after the sunset had quite died out of the sky, and which was dependent for its intensity upon no refracted beams of mere solar light.

CHAPTER III

———•———

Family Confidences

'Who that should view the small beginnings of some persons could imagine or prognosticate those vast increases of fortune that have afterwards followed them.' – SOUTH

The green door of communication between the Misses Cavendish's cabin and the adjoining cabin, occupied by their parents, was hooked back. The girls were on their knees before their trunks, inspecting the creases in black cashmere dresses that were to be brought out fresh for the arrival in Melbourne. Mrs Cavendish's voice, from the neighbouring cabin, was heard ejaculating at intervals, but as the coherence of her exclamations was somewhat marred by the fact that she was embedded among some house-linen she was 'turning over', and as her words seemed to be directed at no one in particular, but appeared simply an outlet for strong feeling with reference to some mildewed pillow-cases, they continued their conversation unheeded, with only such breaks as were absolutely necessary to enable them to give vent to an interjection of acquiescence or sympathy, when the voice from within their mother's cabin took a more decided inflexion.

'Shall you be pleased or sorry that the journey is over?' asked Margaret, not looking directly at her sister, but intent upon the crumpled cashmere that she was now shaking vigorously with both hands, as she knelt before the trunk.

'Oh! glad! – but I don't know, either. Why do you ask?' said Sara, with something of a questioning suspicion in her glance as she turned her head.

Margaret began to rummage among the lowest layer of clothes in the bottom of her trunk. She had a face that was given to flushing

14

upon the very shortest notice, and probably the blood had rushed to her head now. Her cheeks had reddened considerably before she replied, 'Oh! for a reason. I wish I knew how you felt about it. Aren't there *some* things you'll miss?'

'You'll miss them more, I think,' said Sara curtly.

'Perhaps so; but my missing them won't matter to anybody,' rejoined Margaret promptly.

'Nor will mine, that I know of.'

'Oh! Sara!' ('Yes, mamma – a *dreadful* pity.') A deplorable cry of 'Just think – your pa's collars all green – there's a pity for you,' called forth this irrelevant exclamation. 'Oh! Sara!' reiterated Margaret.

There's a way of saying 'Oh!' which simply amounts to giving the lie direct, as you may easily find out by noting the inevitable remonstrance, indignant, or self-defensive, that such an 'Oh!' invariably calls forth.

'Well, it *won't*,' said Sara, with unnecessary emphasis. 'It won't matter to anybody. I don't know what makes you think it will. I do wish, Margaret, you wouldn't hint at things. . . . I might talk at *you* – if I chose!'

'Not in that way,' said Margaret quietly. 'I don't think it'll make the smallest difference to anybody on board how soon the voyage comes to an end – as far as I am concerned.'

It was impossible to detect even a flavour of bitterness in her voice. From the time when Margaret was eight years old – an old-fashioned little girl, with bright cheeks, and a chin whose upward tendency had given her even then a resemblance to a quaint little old woman – from the time when she had received her baby sister into her arms – she had taken, as it were, the second place herself.

Sara coaxed or coerced her from the beginning, her beauty carrying, even in her own family, a sort of dominion with it that was yielded to with astonishing readiness, considering the slender reasons apart from it that she could most often advance for getting what she wanted. Yet Margaret never dreamed of revolting against her own secondary position. The delighted pride with which she had first heard Sara lisp the inane little rhymes she had taught her took new forms as Sara grew to womanhood; but a form tinctured with jealousy, or a begrudging of the triumphs that Sara's beauty and witchery were always gaining her, never once poisoned Margaret's mind. I am sure that sort of fate is always to be deplored – self being, no doubt, the most engrossing, but at the same time the most tormenting subject for solicitude in existence.

Away from Sara, Margaret would hardly have been called plain – any one might have conceded that she was pleasant-looking. The oddest thing was to trace the family likeness between the girls, and see where Margaret's face stopped short of beauty and Sara's blossomed into it. Sara, it is true, was hardly twenty, and Margaret might have been anywhere between twenty and thirty. But with regard to the family likeness, one might almost have supposed the sisters to have been cast in the same mould at birth and handed over to a magic artificer – who would have tried his ''prentice hand' on Margaret, and turned out his finished achievement in Sara. That fatal little upward curve of the pointed chin gave Margaret, from the days when she was in short frocks, an old-maidish air. Her figure was neither so tall nor so finely developed as her sister's, and, despite her kindly blue eyes and soft brown hair, a susceptible skin, that was apt to grow unduly heated and to make her feel nervous in the sun or after dinner, was in itself a foil to Sara's faultlessly clear complexion.

If ever so wild a wish as the possibility of arraying herself for a few short instants in Sara's body had occurred to Margaret, it would have been when the children's service was over on Sunday afternoons, and the Rev. Mr Lydiat turned, with the look she knew so well, to the place where her sister was sitting. His way of saying, 'I am so grateful to you for helping me, Miss Sara,' with reference, perhaps, to the closing hymn, or because Sara had held by the skirts the particular M'Bride that always fell off the skylight while the text was being read, seemed to call for a rejoinder that Margaret would have liked to make. Besides she *felt* every word that had been said. In Sara's place she could have followed up remarks that opened a vista of ideas such as Margaret could comprehend and discuss. But then the remarks were not addressed to her, and not being in Sara's body she could only sit with flushed cheeks, a little apart, and wish that she might prompt her sister's replies. It is certainly among the unfair advantages that beauty takes to itself that a pair of fine eyes should be credited with volumes of meaning, and a little 'yes' or 'no,' pronounced in a tone that asked for more, accompanied by one of those sweetly encouraging glances that came from Sara without any conscious artifice on her part, seemed quite enough to convince Mr Lydiat that she had penetrated the very depths of his meaning.

'There's mamma again,' said Sara, not wishing to agree in too direct a manner with her sister's inference that the end of the journey could give any one on board a pang. 'It's the shirt-fronts now! Never mind, mamma,' in a key that long board-ship practice had pitched to the exact carrying of the words no further than the next cabin; 'papa can get new ones in Melbourne, I suppose. Uncle Piper won't examine his shirt-fronts directly we land.' Then in her ordinary low-toned voice, 'Isn't it deplorable, Maggie – I wish we could begin the journey over again. Oh no, not for the sentimental part of it, but one's things are so villainously packed. I can't call it anything else. Only look at the back of my cashmere polonaise.' She held it up in front of her, frowning. Even a frown did not seem to affect Sara's face as it does more homely countenances, imparting rather a masculine semi-tragic air to her handsome profile. 'And I can't put on my jacket' (plaintively). 'It makes me look about as old as mamma. What do you think – eh? Can't you make a suggestion, Maggie' (impatiently); 'you're looking at your own things as complacently as if you were the only passenger on board ship that had to be landed at all.'

'I wasn't thinking of my clothes,' said Maggie, her colour rising as usual; 'but I wouldn't make such a trouble of it if I were you, Sara. Captain Chuck says we can't get in before to-morrow night. We're only off that cape – what is it called – oh, the Otway, he said, and the wind might change; and, anyhow, if we hang up our things some of the crumples must come out.'

'Well, we'll try it,' said Sara discontentedly, rising at the same time with effort, and quietly hanging her polonaise on the only two available hooks in the cabin; 'I suppose it's out of self-respect one doesn't want to look as if one's things had been tied in a bag. I don't care a bit what Uncle Piper thinks. I don't believe *parvenus* ever know whether women are properly dressed. What a pity for us, isn't it, that it should be mamma's brother instead of papa's who made the money. I know beforehand I shall hate him, and I dare say our cousin and all his set are just as bad. Oh dear, why are some people so unlucky in their relations?'

The ill-luck perhaps was too heavy a burden to be borne standing. After spreading her polonaise on the hooks with elaborate care, Sara stretched her finely turned arms, unbuttoned the front of her board-ship dress of dark-grey cloth, and clambering on her berth, propped up the pillows and settled herself back with hands clasped behind the back of her head, in an attitude of luxurious ease, looking, with her polished throat uncovered, like a beautiful Bacchante who was on her proper behaviour.

'You're such an unsatisfactory person, Maggie,' she went on; 'I believe it's a mania with you to like common people. You don't seem to understand the least bit how hard it is to go to a new country and find yourself dragged down by a whole heap of vulgar relations. I suppose there *are* some people worth knowing in Melbourne – but you'll see! We'll be swallowed up in the Piper set. I shall be *accaparée* by the cousin. And papa – oh, *won't* he hate it! Papa'll have to toady to Uncle Piper, and pretend to be enraptured with his fine things all day long.'

'I'd like papa to hear you say so,' retorted Margaret, who was scanning the cabin in the vain search for a place wherein to hang her dress.

'Well, isn't it true? Isn't papa the gentleman and poor, and isn't Uncle Piper the *parvenu* and rich?'

'It doesn't follow that he wants to be toadied to.'

'Yes, it does. All those self-made people are bumptious and stuck-up. They wouldn't care for their money if they couldn't make a display with it. Really, I almost wish sometimes I'd stayed behind and trusted to my wits.'

'That's the penalty of being so exceptional,' said Margaret, advancing the statement as a plain truth, without a shade of irony. 'You ought to have been born in a palace, Sara – you always put your surroundings in the shade. Now, *I* feel rather pleased to think we're going to a homely old uncle, who'll treat us, perhaps, to a share in his good things for mamma's sake. He *must* have a kind feeling for us all, or he wouldn't have offered to find papa a post in the Government, or have sent half our passage-money, or anything.'

'Oh, I suppose he wants somebody to show off to. His wives are dead, aren't they?'

'Wives? Uncle Piper isn't a Mormon!'

'Well, he's had two, at least. Mamma said so herself. I suppose one died first – Oh dear! there's mamma exclaiming again! Do pacify her, Margaret. Tell her to come in here and tell us about Uncle Piper. And just give me the pillow off your berth, will you? My head's quite in a hole.'

Margaret was accustomed to be ordered about in this regal fashion. Had she not said in perfect good faith that Sara should have been born in a palace? And if you imply that your companion is a queen by nature, can you be astonished if she occasionally mistakes you for her subject? She shook up the pillows and re-arranged them behind her sister's head, moving her tumbled hair out of the way as tenderly as if Sara had been a victim to rheumatic fever, instead of a young woman of almost plethoric exuberance of health.

In the meantime, the ejaculations in the neighbouring cabin were gathering in intensity, and Sara had the ill grace to laugh as her mother came breathless through the door of communication, staggering under the weight of the injured clothing.

'It's shameful!' said poor Mrs Cavendish, gasping. 'Your pa's guernseys! did you ever see the like? I knew all along the water was coming in. I said so; now, didn't I say so? I said so to the carpenter with my own lips, I said' –

'Yes, mamma, you said so!' interrupted Sara, not lifting her head from her pillow. 'We know you said so.'

It was Sara's invariable way of checking any plaints on her mother's part to agree with her tersely, and nothing short of unusual exasperation could move good-tempered Mrs Cavendish to resent the implied rebuke.

Margaret, meanwhile, had taken the heap of linen out of her mother's arms, and laid it on her berth.

'It *is* a shame, mother!' she said, in that full voice of sympathy that strikes so gratefully on the irritated senses, as proving that one's feeling of injury is at least entered into, and one's just indignation shared. 'I think the captain should be spoken to about it, or at least we'll show the carpenter what it's come to. I remember he wouldn't believe the sea worked in at that place. But don't you think' (spreading the things out with a hopeful air) 'it'll come out with the first washing? *Do* let me help you with the rest of them by-and-by, and stay with us a little now; we want to ask you ever so many things about Uncle Piper.'

Mrs Cavendish was especially fond of what she called 'a little family confab.' She already saw the mildewed stains fading away in an imaginary lather, as she sat herself comfortably down on the square trunk that Margaret had covered with a shawl and pushed against the cabin partition for her mother's greatest comfort.

The first glance at her was sufficient to determine the source of Sara's beauty. She was verging at this time upon fifty, and if you could have studied her head alone, you would have found a model for the countenance of a goddess. It was from her mother that Sara inherited the delicious tone of her healthy pallor, her eyes of deep blue, and eyebrows marked by a single arching line. I suppose the lastingness of their beauty was one of the chief attributes of the charms of a goddess, and I should imagine that there were certain lines in Mrs Cavendish's face that must remain beautiful to the end. Such, for instance, as the peculiar cut of her narrow nostrils and small mouth that curved downwards on either side, the finish of the firm chin, of which the perfect shape, full and slightly advancing, as if it had been boldly chiselled by a master hand, had developed in Margaret's case into a form that caricatured it. Mrs Cavendish affected a cap, of the jaunty make known as 'Dolly Varden' – a mere little knot of dark blue frippery, surmounting a square of white net. An antique goddess in a 'Dolly Varden.' Her daughters should have saved her from such vandalism. She never looked better than when she was going to wash her face, and had screwed her still abundant black hair, faintly marked with grey, into a knot at the back of her classic head. But you must be content to stop short at her head. The torse was much too ample to serve as a celestial model. The solidity of her mother's bust and the amplitude of her waist were often a matter of secret alarm to Sara, who was inclined, as the trainers say, 'to put on flesh' with a facility that caused her many a qualm in the enjoyment of board-ship tarts.

And another quality at which you must stop short was the voice. No after association can give an educated intonation, a thing which must be acquired, like a foreign language, when the human being is in the initiative period that marks its nearer connection with an earlier form of being. But it was a voice that had sounded melodious enough in Mr Cavendish's fastidious ears nearly thirty years ago. Perhaps it was the recollection of that early wooing, conducted on his part with a kind of old school gallantry, which had touched with a wondrous charm the simple heart of the plebeian girl – that helped to maintain her inviolable loyalty to her husband through ups and downs innumerable. The girls were accustomed to look upon 'your pa' as their mother's watchword. If the poor thing happened to be laid up for a day, her first warning was, 'Don't neglect your pa!' When small domestic privations, consequent upon a forgetfulness on the part of Mr Cavendish of the claims of vulgar tradespeople, were submitted to in the little household, her one fear was, 'Your pa'll be taking it to heart!' Mr Cavendish's aristocratic nature was not devoid of the commonplace tendency I once heard attributed to husbands in general – a tendency to look upon their wives very much in the light of fetishes

– to be treated as the savage African treats his little idol – that is to say, to be petted and made much of when things are going well with him, and to be severely knocked about when anything goes wrong.

But though the girls had frequently seen their mother harassed, and had even detected an irrepressible quivering about the corners of her down-curved mouth, they had never heard her say a word that savoured of resentment towards 'your pa.'

Yet hers was the better brain, the sounder heart. Only clear common sense and womanly devotion, unsupported by self-assertion, are like unset gems. The setting that brings them into prominence may be little better than dross, but without it any other than a skilled lapidary would assuredly pass them by.

The only defensive weapon Mrs Cavendish ever flourished when the fetish had met with especially rough treatment was couched in an allusion to 'brothers.' There could be no question that, without her brother Tom, those little domestic lapses already alluded to would have stretched into very yawning gulfs indeed – whereas Mr Cavendish's only brother, of whom he found occasion to say at least twenty times a day 'my brother the bishop,' had not scrupled to take the silver teapot as security for the loan of a very trifling sum, which, as a precaution that had stronger associations in Mrs Cavendish's mind with a pawnbroker's shop and three gilt balls than with an episcopal palace and a cross of gold, had led her to make the unpardonable surmise 'that the church was a poor business, after all.'

Now, Tom Piper's business had not been a poor one – albeit he had started in life with just three pounds seventeen and sixpence to his credit. His father had been a small shopkeeper who had failed, paid his debts, and died – a career so much more ignominious in Mr Cavendish's eyes than the life of a defaulter in a wholesale and respectable way, that he never alluded to his father-in-law, in conversation with his wife, without stigmatising him as 'your unfortunate father.'

Tom had much more than his father's shrewdness, and perhaps not quite so much of his scrupulosity. Finding himself in this impoverished plight, at the age of five and twenty, with his beautiful sister Elizabeth dependent on him, he called up his energy bravely. These two were the only representatives of the struggling Piper family. Tom housed his sister as nursery governess with some people that he described as 'good marks,' in the sense that her wages would be punctually paid every quarter. But 'good marks' constituting a very impersonal recommendation, Elizabeth did not find that she had fallen among kindly souls. Tom had worked his way to Australia, where, as he wrote to his sister, 'he had started butchering, and saw his way to make a good thing of it. In the meantime, she had better stick to the old game of teaching, and stay where she was.'

Elizabeth's docile nature would have led her to follow this well-meant advice to the letter had not a sudden and delightful change offered itself. Young Mr Cavendish came to stay as a guest with her employers. His vapidness was so hidden under his air of distinction that it often passed current for depth. His good family tone, as unattainable without certain associations as the sinewy shininess of a racer without a long course of training; his courtly deference to women; the very set of his clothes, never brand-new, like Tom's go-to-meeting suit, or worn at the seams, like his working one; the way in which he pronounced the very commonest of words, make him something distinct from all other men, even from those whom she had heard Tom call half-jeeringly the 'nobs.' And this Eros actually came down from his height to worship *her!* How it might have ended there is no saying, for Elizabeth's beauty was a kind to take a strong and instant hold upon the imagination. But her innocence was so transparently palpable, and her unprotectedness so remarkable, that Mr Cavendish succumbed to the one chivalrous and unalloyed impulse of his life, and married her. That in so doing he was a renegade to his race – of the house of Devonshire, according to his own showing (though it must be allowed that his particular branch of it had never been in a very flourishing condition) – he was fully and completely convinced. Yet, if there is a nobility distinct from the possession of a genealogical tree, I think he was never truer to it than when he 'lowered himself' by his marriage.

It was an odd coincidence that with the one exception of birth – the Pipers, exclusive of that celebrated individual who performed the feat of picking the peck of pepper which afterwards disappeared so unaccountably, never having made much of a name for themselves in England – the young husband and wife were placed in very similar circumstances. Both were poor, both orphans, both acknowledged an elder brother – with the difference that Mr Cavendish could say, 'My brother the bishop;' while Mrs Cavendish was constrained to say, 'My brother the butcher.' The benefits conferred by the bishop, though priceless, no doubt, considered from a spiritual point of view, had hardly the solidity of the tokens sent by the butcher. In fact, distant and powerful connections, whose influence, seconded by the happy chance of his preaching before a prince, had raised Mr Cavendish's brother to the rank of a spiritual lord, absorbed such family regard as he had to dispose of. Whereas, his own brains and hands being the only helps to which Mrs Cavendish's brother owed allegiance, he found room for taking to his heart in a substantial way 'his sister Bess, and that fine husband of hers, whom he hoped to set eyes on one of these days.' How ungrudgingly he had acted upon this feeling, during his rise to wealth and power in Australia, the Cavendish family in England best knew. If Mr Cavendish had not been strongly tinctured with the aristocratic failing of imagining that in the world's economy grosser clay should work for pedigreed humanity, he would never have spoken other than with grateful warmth of his distant brother-in-law. Poor Mrs Cavendish's tenderest point, with the one exception of 'your pa,' was Uncle Piper – his goodness, his constant and generous recollection of her. It was with the adroitness prompted by love that Margaret had touched upon the theme of Uncle Piper, as a salve for the contemplation of the mildewed shirt-fronts; her mother desiring nothing better than to hold forth upon his deserts.

CHAPTER IV

Retrospective

'My generous brother is of gentle kind.' – POPE.

When Margaret declared that her sister should have been born in a palace, she might have added the proviso that the palace should be under an Eastern sky, and that it should be provided, moreover, with the silken hangings, the arabesques, the perfumes, the gold-fretted lattice-work so wrought into our imagination by Eastern tales. The house of Devonshire can show, as history has already attested, more than one princely vagrant among its ancestors, whose wanderings among the Moors and Turks three centuries ago may have had a remote share in tinging Sara's blood with an infusion of the lymph of an Eastern odalisque. Another trait that savoured of Orientalism was the pleasure with which she listened to anything conveyed in the form of a story. There was the secret, in the first instance, of her rapt attention on deck when Mr Lydiat had recounted to the children, through the best part of a tropical afternoon, how Joseph rose to greatness among the swarthy Egyptians, and justified the somewhat egotistical dreams of his boyhood. For Sara was given to dreaming too. And what pleasant dreams she fostered, what dimly outlined shapes of all that is costliest and loveliest floated through her brain as she lay on her berth with half-closed eyes, the green-hued light playing about her bare shoulders, her body gently swayed by the dip of the vessel when the wind blew stronger. Ah me! Where is the physiognomist whose discernment has not been set at naught by a quality altogether superficial? Here was Mr Lydiat convinced that you might have looked into Sara's mind as into a crystal, and seen your sublimest inspirations reflected, with the lustre of her own purity upon them besides – and all, I firmly believe, because she had well-cut eyes – whereas, no one would have been more disconcerted than Sara herself had the dreams in which she did the fullest justice to her own power, and applied it to the most thoroughly practical purposes, been rendered public and handed down, like Joseph's dreams, to posterity.

But now the time for dreaming was drawing to a close. The future, that is so plastic in our hands until the time approaches when it becomes a reality too solid to be kneaded, was stretched before her in the guise of the Australian shore she could already discern in the distance. Margaret was folding away the shirt-fronts with reassuring words, and actually talking as if the maltreated linen would be washed, starched, and ironed within a week; and all the time that she was reassuring her mother, she continued to ply her with questions.

'Three hardly touched! I think, mamma, you took alarm at this one, and it's so frayed it's hardly worth washing. Besides, I know papa will go back to his old extravagances now. *Two* white shirts every day! I wonder whether Uncle Piper wears white shirts. I've got a sort of idea that everybody in Australia, except the natives, goes about in top-boots and a red shirt. How long *is* it exactly, mother dear, since you last saw Uncle Piper?'

'Oh, my dear!' said Mrs Cavendish, glancing at the berth where Sara was lying in luxurious languor, 'it's many a long day. It was before I married your pa, so you can tell! I was only a slip of a girl, as you might say – not so stout as Sara there!'

Sara lay immovable, but her eyes flashed as she raised her lids. It was evident that the odalisque was wroth. Indeed, if anything roused Sara's ire, it was the suggestion that the word 'stout' could fittingly be applied to what in French would graciously be termed 'opulence' of the form – the more so, that she had an uneasy dread of its becoming strictly appropriate.

'Did he go away before you were engaged to papa?' persisted Margaret.

'Stop a bit,' said Mrs Cavendish, narrowing her eyes in the effort at recollection, like short-sighted people who aim at bringing a distant object within range of their vision. 'Was I keeping company with your pa at the time?' A charming colour rose to her still unwrinkled cheek as she spoke. 'No,' triumphantly. 'I hadn't so much as met your pa. That's why your Uncle Piper never saw him.'

'But I suppose you wrote and told him as soon as you were engaged. He was like a sort of guardian, wasn't he?'

'He was father, mother, and brother all in one!' said Mrs Cavendish warmly. 'I wouldn't hurt your pa's feelings by saying so, but there's brothers and brothers. It didn't take me long to find that much out. Why – after we were married – your pa had an invite to go over and stop at *his* brother's for a couple of days. He was to stay over the Sunday, I remember, and he was to bring me along with him, and, oh dear, what a preparation and a drilling I did have, to be sure! Well, my dear, I'd as lief have been with strangers. Your pa bid me mind and remember I was to call his brother "My lord!" Fancy that to a brother! And I wasn't to forget the bishop's house was a "palace." A pretty palace, to my mind! There was plenty of show for anybody who's taken with that sort of thing, but not much else, and the quality of the meat such as I wouldn't like to set before my brother, if I were twenty bishops.'

'What did Uncle Piper say when he heard you were married?' asked Sara, from her berth, to whom her mother's impressions of the hollowness of episcopal magnificence were not new enough to be interesting.

'He sent me a letter like a brother who was fond of you might be expected to write to a person,' replied Mrs Cavendish, the slight confusion of persons apparent in her answer resulting from the strength of her sentiment. 'He couldn't be sending me money, you see, for he hadn't begun the butchering just yet.'

Sara's eyes opened wide with disdain.

'Mamma,' she exclaimed, with the first inflexion that spoke of animation in her voice, 'do you want to turn me against Uncle Piper before I see him, and make me hate to hear his name? Because, unless you do, you won't allude to that disgusting part of his life again!'

'Why, my dear,' answered Mrs Cavendish, unruffled, 'I might have remembered that you took after your pa, if I'd thought of it. You see, I was brought up to think no manner of work a disgrace. Never mind how you soil your hands, so long as you keep your heart clean.'

'I think with you, mother, in my heart,' said Margaret, patting the shirt-fronts pensively; 'but I'm not so brave as you. I'd far rather Uncle Piper had never kept a butcher's shop. It's not that I don't respect butchers – *as* butchers – but to be on visiting terms with them seems such a different thing. And it's such a long time since Uncle

Piper kept a shop of any sort. I'd rather forget about it if I could. I dare say it's cowardly, but I can't help it!'

'I'm sure, my dear,' said her mother, 'I don't want to rake it up against your wishes. But I believe it was the butche – it was *that*, *I should* say – that brought him his money. For after he had been two years at it he gave us a lift that was the saving, as I might say, of your pa.'

'How was it, mamma?'

'Well, we'd been married close upon two years, and your pa had a little work in the post-office. It always went against me to see him work. I'd have waited on him hand and foot, to save him from it; but folks must live, and I didn't see the way to make both ends meet. *You* were on the road then, Margaret; and what with joy at thinking of what was coming, and grief that I had to look twice before I could lay out as much as a penny in a little frilling for your caps, I was nearly out of my mind. And then there was your pa to be kept in the dark. I made sure he was fretting his life away, and one day there wasn't actually enough to eat in the house! So he went to his brother, the "bishop"' – Mrs Cavendish could always point the delivery of this word by a finely ironical intonation – 'and he got the loan of fifteen pounds; but I know where our silver teapot went the very same day, and my time drawing near as well. I was so down-hearted, it came to my thinking whether it wasn't selfish to be rejoicing over bringing a helpless little body into such a cold world. And if I should die and leave it! I could have broken down then.' Margaret detected a tremor in her mother's voice, and caressed her head furtively as she passed by with the shirt-fronts. 'But it wouldn't do to lose heart, and while I was thinking it over comes a knock at the door, and the postman gives me in a letter all covered with postmarks. No sooner did I open it, with my hands all shaking, as you may guess, than out drops a draft for a hundred and fifty pounds!'

'How you must have jumped!' said Sara, the odalisque part of her too much interested in the story to allow her to sulk any longer at the former offence to her susceptibilities.

'I didn't feel like jumping, so much as like going down on my knees,' said poor Mrs Cavendish. 'To think a bit o' paper like that can make the whole world different! I never cried for joy but that once in my life.'

'And what did the letter say?' asked Margaret.

'Well, it was all a surprise from the beginning. Your Uncle Piper made the butche – I mean, he was getting along finely; but what gave me the biggest start of all was to hear that he'd got married. And his wife was the same way as me. I'd wrote your uncle word about myself some time back, and here was his answer. He was feathering his nest for the little one that was to come, that was what he said; but he had it in his mind that my little one should have as fine a christening cup as his, so he sent me the hundred and fifty in that sort of way, you see. He didn't know we were more in the way of wanting bread than christening cups!'

'So I am about the same age as my cousin George, mamma; is that it?' asked Margaret.

'That's it,' said her mother; 'turned seven-and-twenty last Michaelmas.'

'Poor old Maggie!' thought Sara, in the superb insolence of her nineteen years – an age apt to look incredulously upon the power of attractions verging upon thirty. 'She's much too good to be considered on the shelf, and she's never had an offer!'

'Seven-and-twenty!' repeated Margaret, the ready flush spreading itself over her face. There was nothing unmaidenly in the involuntary regret expressed in her tone. She did not even translate such regrets as a more self-absorbed person would have translated them, or perceive that they were the inevitable consequence of finding the few years which mark an ordinary woman's period of power slipping away without any of the tribute which seems of right to belong to them.

'Your cousin's a bit older than you, though,' remarked Mrs Cavendish, hopefully. 'He takes after his poor mother, your Uncle Piper says – an ailing body, from what I can make out. She never had but the one child all the years they were married.'

'And when did she die?' asked Sara, to whom this picture of her cousin George did not present itself in a romantic light. A puny little fellow she could imagine him to have been, playing around the blue block on the sanded floor of his father's shop. It was many years ago, it was true, since the shop and all its associations had been swept away. Yet she had no doubt that her cousin could still remember how he had watched his father chopping the meat in one of those shocking blouses that butchers seem to affect by way of bringing into relief the universal red of their surroundings.

'She died the same year your pa was down with the fever,' said Mrs Cavendish, accustomed to make a sort of ready-reckoner of domestic visitations of all kinds. 'It's a good ten or eleven years back. Your uncle took it to heart sadly' –

'But he married again very soon,' suggested Margaret.

'It's *my* opinion,' said her mother, oracularly, 'he was worked upon to marry again. I've never had much opinion of widows myself. When I heard how your Uncle Piper had found a *real* lady to do his house-keeping, I said to your pa, I said, "We all know what *that'll* come to"; and sure enough, before the year was out, he writes me word he's married.'

'What was the widow's name?' inquired Sara.

'I don't rightly remember just now; your Uncle Piper was pretty close about it at the time. She didn't keep her new name long, anyhow, the poor thing! Married and dead, all in ten months!'

'And she left a child, didn't she, mother?' asked Margaret.

'Yes; she left a child to your uncle. She had one, besides, to her first husband.'

'Shall we see that one?' said Sara, in a tone that did not promise much cordiality. 'She's no sort of connection of ours, I'm glad to say. Is she grown up?'

'She might be two or three and twenty, I should say,' said Mrs Cavendish, with another contraction of her eyes, induced by the effort of making a calculation to which no family affliction could be affixed as a guide. 'Now just to show you what a good heart your Uncle Piper's got! It's my belief he's provided altogether for that girl, and I don't think he took to her from the first, somehow. He was very short in his letters about her all along. "Right enough outside," he said, "but a queer lot within." Those were his very words, just as he wrote them down.'

'Right enough outside!' echoed Sara, the idea of possible rivalry never once having intruded itself as an unpleasant possibility before. 'What *could* he mean, mamma? Why, she was a child, wasn't she? She couldn't have been more than eleven or twelve when Uncle Piper first saw her. How could he tell what she would be like?'

'He hasn't said much about her since, anyway,' replied Mrs Cavendish; 'nor yet about his own little girl!'

'Another relation!' exclaimed Sara, disconsolately; 'I'd forgotten all about the child. Uncle Piper – and *two* cousins – and that other strange girl. I *wish* we hadn't come.'

She turned round on the pillow and prepared herself for a doze, as if nothing short of instant sleep could fortify her against the crushing discovery of the number of her kin in the antipodes. She would have found it difficult, nevertheless, precisely to define her discontent. Uncle Piper, perhaps, in consideration of his wealth and of his good age – the most graceful accompaniment to wealth possible to a *parvenu* uncle – was supportable. And her cousin George – though she could not divest herself of the unpleasant impression she had conceived of a full-grown sickly man, inured during his infancy to a discriminating taste in butcher's meat – as the only son of the *parvenu* uncle, was worth some share of cousinly regard. But further she would not go.

The presence of that interloper, whose 'fair outside' had been so remarkable at an age when a girl's appearance is rarely noticeable, was clearly uncalled for; and the juvenile cousin, the legacy of Uncle Piper's second wife, was a disagreeable and tangible reminder of Sara's own connection with the interloper. She established the relationship with painful exactitude as she closed her eyes, reminding herself that the interloper's half-sister was her own cousin. It was *hateful*, looked at in any light. And Margaret had no comprehension! She would 'cousinise' with them all, Sara knew – as though Uncle Piper had never weighed out steaks and chops, and the Cavendish crest did not belong to the house of Devonshire. An indistinct vision of the place she should rightly have occupied began to shape itself to her vagrant imagination. She could hear her mother saying, in a voice that seemed to come from the other end of the ship, 'Your pa'll miss his rubber, I'm afraid!' Then she fell to regretting, after a sleepy fashion, that her father or her other uncle, the bishop, had not thought of emigrating, instead of Uncle Piper, when gold was found in Australia. Before she could find any satisfactory reason for this almost culpable oversight on their parts she fell into a doze, and, carrying out in her dreams:

> 'Which are the children of an idle brain,
>   Begot of nothing but vain fantasy,' –

the ideas, too vague to be defined, that had just assailed her, fancied that the little ship presented itself to her as a type of the great world without. Only Captain Chuck, who, without conscious disloyalty to a substantial spouse in London, was foolishly helpless under a glance from Sara's eyes, became in her dreams the Lord High Admiral. And Father O'Donnell, whose proselytising zeal it was, perhaps, that made him so eager to lose his '*Bonjour*, Philippine,' to the younger Miss

Cavendish, as an excuse for presenting her with costly miniatures of saints and martyrs, became converted into the Pope. As for the grave-eyed and reverend Mr Lydiat, the plum-coloured vest made way for the pontificals of an archbishop. I don't know that Sara shared the primateship with him in her dream. She was a princess now, and the Lord High Admiral, the Pope, and the Primate were just as amenable as the skipper, the parish priest, and the curate; and through them Sara was conscious of holding sway over millions of souls. It was more of a yielding to fancies suggested by the universality of her power than of a dream that Sara experienced, and I for one am not prepared to say how much might have been inspiration and how much folly, seeing that that part of man's nature to which Sara's charm appealed is much the same in the loftiest and the lowliest, and if chance had brought her into contact with the head of an empire, instead of the head of a small merchant-ship, she might have swayed the destiny of a nation.

CHAPTER V

---•---

The Result of the Reverie

'The coquette is indeed one degree towards the jilt; but the heart of the former is bent upon admiring herself, and giving false hopes to her lovers.' – STEELE.

'I think the cloth has a leaning towards whist,' said Mr Cavendish, authoritatively. 'My brother – I believe I have mentioned him to you before, Mr Lydiat – was very fond of a double-dummy game – he wasn't a bishop *then*, by the bye – and one of the best players I ever knew was a prebendary of Westminster.'

It was to the Rev. Mr Lydiat that this remark was addressed, following an allusion from Captain Chuck to the good cards Father O'Donnell invariably seemed to hold.

'Faith!' the priest had replied, 'they tell me, "Lucky with carruds, unlucky with a wife!" Now, as I'm debarrud from trying me luck with the one, 'tis but fair I should have the benefit of the doubt, and get it the one way at laste. Now isn't that the truth, Miss Sara Cavendish?'

Sara considered a smile of acquiescence answer sufficient to Father O'Donnell's query. She was conveniently placed for the position of umpire, being seated to the right of Captain Chuck and next to the communicative father. The last board-ship dinner was over. The chief steward, like a dame on breaking-up day, had unearthed dainties from the depths of his *lazarette* that gave an air of Sunday festivity to the dessert – notably the ginger, stringy and lack-syrupy, and a pyramid of shrivelled apples, sacred hitherto to Sabbath indulgences.

The mild Australian spring air was circling round the saloon. Table and passengers reflected the mellow light of the last yellow sunbeams. At the same hour on the morrow what a revolution would have been brought about in the lives of each! It was natural that they should linger a little longer at the table than of custom. For reasons, too, apart from the sumptuousness of the dessert, though Sara smiled as she noted the abstracted air with which Mrs M'Bride drew into some unseen receptacle walnuts, almonds, raisins, and biscuits for the regaling, at future unseemly hours, of Terence, and Larry, and Corny, and Kate, and Mike, and Baby M'Bride.

The Rev. Mr Lydiat did not attempt to confute Mr Cavendish on the question of the partiality of prebendaries for whist. He was thinking of something so widely different, being seated, in fact, just opposite to Sara, who, fresh from her afternoon sleep, was looking adorably pensive in her black dress edged with a soft white frill that took a heart-shaped curve in front, just wide enough to show the exquisite hollow in the lower part of her throat. She was still carrying on the same train of thought. Were there cliques in Melbourne? How terrible if she should find herself hopelessly submerged among the second-rates! What preconceived pleasure could she possibly take in the idea of impressing such a person as her cousin George? – and to Sara the impressing of strangers was a delight of daily renewal. Hardly anybody hitherto had been quite stolid under the first surprise of her beauty. But her sphere on the *Henrietta Maria* was a very restricted one. Yet what a harsh fate it was that made her loth to leave even this restricted sphere, lest in that unexplored one she must enter upon to-morrow her world should be peopled with *parvenus!*

Her meditations, it is clear, were thoroughly practical. But, as her expression gave her the air of thinking out an unwritten poem, Mr Lydiat could only see in her a being to be enshrined in the holiest sanctum of a man's heart. The only side of woman's nature he had studied so far was that debased side of which the better impulses are at most erratic and simply emotional. What other study, in point of fact, had his drink-sodden parishioners in the east of London afforded him? It was natural now that he should err simply from want of experience in what may be called the conventional-young-lady side of woman's nature. It was natural that, having known for eight years violent extremes of perversity, he should imagine in so opposite a type a corresponding extreme of purity. Sara was absorbed for many instants of every day in the contemplation of subjects certainly not criminal, and no less certainly very far from elevated – following the Rev. Mr Lydiat's conception of elevation. She had a fancy for imagining becoming dresses. She would build up a delightful wardrobe in the air, entering into as many details of her airy outfit as though it could be instantly materialised. And she liked to imagine a becoming background for her own beautiful person, in which a husband with the essentials of good birth and unlimited money, and the desirable qualifications of an air of distinction and great devotion to her, filled a reasonable space. In his walks up and down the main deck Mr Lydiat had often seen her lost in daydreams, such as it would have seemed to him almost sacrilegious to disturb; though it is probable that the only notion he would have been guilty of upsetting had reference to the shape of an imaginary velvet train. Still, with women as with creeds, it matters little what particular kind we profess, provided we invest them with the attributes that make them answer our needs. it is true that if a shorthand writer had taken down for Mr Lydiat's edification every word uttered by Sara in the course of a day, he would have found it hard to extract therefrom a single sentence that he might have treasured away. Yet, if it pleased him to ascribe to her silence a sweet and modest comprehension, and to perceive in her lowly uttered replies a virginal reticence of sublime ideas, the delusion, at least, was a pleasing one. And when – for the old promptings were stronger than ever to-night – *when* he should have fought down his love into its proper state of subjection to his duty, how it would help him through his work to think of Sara's eyes! Was ever so ingenious a self-deceiver? For if he was now content to worship woman's purity in the abstract for the remainder of his days, why did he pass so entirely by Margaret – unobtrusive Margaret, reading with heated cheeks, under the awning, to her mother of an afternoon? Not so suggestive, certainly, of a travelled Saint Cecilia as Sara, but so full of thought for others that day-dreams bearing upon vandyked flounces could find no room in her busy brain. And why did he neglect to bestow a part of his immaterial adoration upon Nora M'Bride – an untidy, whole-hearted little maiden of fifteen, with skirts pulled out of shape by the chronic dragging they underwent from younger brothers and sisters in the juvenile clawing stage – with hair '*crépe*' into tangled frowsiness by a long succession of Baby M'Brides, and nose that never rested sufficiently from the attacks of baby finger-nails to allow itself to assert its pretty pertness – with mouth always opening into a laugh at the eccentricities of the latest and most adored baby of all – and the sweetest voice in a lullaby that tired ears might wish to hear? Why did he long so restlessly, on this last night of all, for just the smallest sign of personal interest from Sara – a look only

– provided he might recall it to the end of his life, and say, 'She read me aright'? He would have been ashamed this evening, even in his own eyes, to attempt so transparent a fraud as the study of the *Organum*. Hitherto it had been his custom to leave the table earlier than the rest – knowing beforehand the succession in which Captain Chuck would tell the same stories, and Mr Cavendish would make mention of his brother the bishop, and Father O'Donnell would contradict Mr M'Bride on the subject of the true nature of Irish grievances. To-night he could not go away. Moreover, what faith was he to place in the reality of his victory over self if he must shun Sara's presence lest he should be betrayed by the strength of the feeling against which he believed himself to have struggled so successfully?

I am inclined to think, however, that Sara's astuteness in such matters was greater than even Margaret had inferred, and that the Rev. Mr Lydiat would have learnt with surprise that he had betrayed himself at least a hundred times already. If nothing short of a declaration in a few set words could apprise a woman that she was foremost in any one man's heart:

> 'Love – the secret sympathy,
> The silver link, the silken tie' –

would be much too prosaic a theme for poets and novelists to descant upon through centuries innumerable.

'Madam, will you have me?' 'You surprise me greatly, sir.' 'Yes – or no,' and all would be said. It is the mysterious beginning, the tracing of the mutual sensation, with reference to which Shakespeare has bidden us 'Let every eye negotiate for itself' that fills the poem and the romance. Not many women are really taken by surprise when the proposal comes at last. It is the inevitable crisis in a series of symptoms they have been studying and experiencing for more or less time, according to the bold or timorous disposition of their lovers. Of course, I am referring to unhampered love, of the which either board-ship love or pastoral love are very fair examples, the sea, indeed, having even more potency than has been ascribed to bucolic influences in leading the mind to defy worldly trammels, which may account for the unconsidered marriages a long voyage has so often been known to bring about.

I wonder whether such a voyage as those old explorers were wont to make, setting out with no surer goal than the westerly sun before them, might have been long enough to diminish to Sara's view the magnitude of the terrestrial objects she prized so much; whether, after two years' sailing through strange seas, thick as soup in parts with weeds, reflecting in others unsubstantial pomps and glories, she might have imagined before the end of her journey that there was something within her reach better worth living for than the dresses she was to wear at the end of it, the position she was to assure herself by her marriage, the dread of being hedged in by *parvenus*. No such imaginings had arisen as yet, perhaps because the voyage by the *Henrietta Maria* was hardly a four months' affair at its best, perhaps because it was not the time but the imagination that Sara lacked. Such imaginings at least would have failed of their effect with Melbourne so close that the Queenscliff lights were already clearly discernible in the distance. Margaret pointed them out to her sister as the two girls ran up the zinc-lined steps that led from the saloon to the main-deck overhead.

'Yes,' assented Sara, wondering whether the dim lights in the distance could represent the Queenscliff that had been described to her as the resort of 'the wealth and fashion of Melbourne;' 'the humdrum life is all but over, and now for a worse one, I'm afraid. Do you know, Maggie – tedious as it was – I'd almost pledge myself to go straight back again in the *Henrietta Maria*, if I could only escape that hateful family meeting to-morrow.'

'Why?' said Margaret, surprised.

'Because it's all so incongruous – can't you see? What's Uncle Piper to us? If he'd had the grace to die and leave us his money, I could understand it. But to send for us twelve thousand miles, and expect us to be in a constant state of effusiveness – I can't tell you how I hate it. I'm sure papa abominates it! And an old butcher, too! Maggie, I never seem to have realised the full *horror* of it as I do now – when it's too late.' A pause. 'Do you think I'll have to *kiss* them?'

'I wonder whether you care for mamma at all, Sara,' was Maggie's irrelevant answer, made in a somewhat constrained voice.

'That's right,' said Sara, with the air of a person who has been unjustifiably attacked, 'take it the wrong way, as usual!'

'You weren't asleep, were you,' pursued Margaret, thoughtfully, 'when mamma was telling us all about her early life in the cabin yesterday afternoon?'

'Oh! I've heard it all before. So have you,' retorted Sara. 'He could have gone on sending money if he was so anxious to help us – or he could' –

'I think it's a hundred times kinder,' interrupted Margaret, 'to promise papa an appointment out here. I wonder, if you are so proud, that you like the notion of having us all pensioners upon a person you would feel ashamed to thank.'

'I wouldn't feel at all ashamed to thank him – in a letter.'

'But you think it a frightful humiliation to be brought into contact with him.'

'Not a humiliation, exactly; but it's a coming down – you can't deny it. And the terrible part of it is, that I don't see what's to rescue us. We won't begin life in Melbourne as the *Cavendishes*, but as connections of *Mr Piper*.'

'That's better than being his hangers-on in England, at least.'

'Maggie!!!' with three notes of exclamation in her tones. 'What a temper! Don't charge me with being undutiful to mamma, or I shall retaliate on behalf of papa. It's cold. I suppose you want that woollen thing of yours, don't you?'

'Here, take it; I'll get another,' said Margaret, subsiding into her accustomed position the moment anything tangible was to be sacrificed to Sara. It was only a principle, or a point involving her affections, that Maggie would not sacrifice. She threw her wrap around her sister's shoulder, who, bending her stately head that overtopped Margaret's by at least a couple of inches, expressed her thanks by rubbing her cheeks caressingly against the hands that were swathing her. Margaret was more than repaid. She ran with a light-hearted sensation below to find herself another covering. On returning a few minutes later with one of those mazes of white and scarlet wool known as 'clouds' to the initiated, she found Sara had gone. Maggie looked anxiously round, and scanning the deck by the uncertain light of the stars, descried her sister's figure, with its back towards her, standing against the opposite bulwark, and facing the Victorian coast.

'Still deploring Uncle Piper's connection, I'll be bound,' thought Maggie. 'Poor Sara! If any one has a right to be fastidious, it is she. I wasn't half consoling enough.'

She was advancing primed with words of sympathy and reassurance, when suddenly she stopped short. Sara was not alone. Standing close by her side in the shade Margaret recognised the outline of a man – tall, square, breathing even in the half-unreal illumination on deck a something of earnestness and intensity of purpose. Sara's head was slightly inclined towards it, but her statuesque outline was immovable.

Was it pain that Margaret felt? She would never have admitted that it was pain. And can that be called so that we do not recognise as such? Besides, had she not foreseen this from the days when the vessel lay becalmed in the doldrums, and she had noted the Rev. Mr Lydiat's expression, transfigured, as it were, at the close of his address to the children? Yes; she had known it from the beginning! Just as we often know, when there is sickness in the house, that Death is waiting at the bed-head; yet start, as though he had taken us unawares, when the moribund gives up his being. There was only one fear. Would Sara feel that her lot was above all others a favoured one? True, Margaret had allowed she should have dwelt in palaces; yet even in the 'divinity' that 'doth hedge a king' there did not seem to be the power of inspiring such joy as in the divinity that surrounds a being wholly worthy of belief. Margaret, it must be opined, reasoned according to her nature, essentially woman-like in its proneness to worship. She had long ago passed through the early stage of hero-making, having often smiled since at the ineligible qualifications of her heroes; but she never relinquished her fundamental and romantic principle that there can be no blessing equal to the finding of an anchorage for the affections in a heart worthy of entire and unreserved confidence. Would she, then, have grudged Sara the first of blessings, when from the time of receiving her within her childish arms a blessing of any sort would have had no meaning for her that could not be transferred to her sister? Anything but that! Yet how overcome an uncontrollable misgiving that a blessing of this nature had not the same value in Sara's eyes as in her own? Her step lacked the buoyancy of tread it had possessed erewhile, as she descended the saloon-steps for the second time. The irradiation of the phosphorus seemed to have been transformed into a very feeble glimmer, and she went quietly below to her cabin, where, more than half-an-hour later, Sara found her, busying herself in packing those overlooked odds and ends that seem to accumulate at sea almost as marvellously as they accumulate on shore. She was finding available corners in portman-teaus, and fitting books into vacant spaces with extraordinary nicety; her eyes shining, her cheeks – not burning, as of custom – but almost white. The unusual pallor was so becoming to Margaret that she might fearlessly have walked abroad with Sara, not as foil now, nor as owing every stray glance that rested upon her entirely to the reflected lustre of her sister's beauty.

Sara did not fail to notice the change.

'Why, Maggie, how long have you been here? I've been looking for you everywhere. You look like your own ghost. Has anything happened?'

'Nothing, dear,' said Margaret, turning her back as she knelt before the open trunk. 'But, oh! Sara, do tell me dear – are you happy?'

There was something in the tremulous utterance, in the almost vehement manner, as coming from quiet, collected Margaret, that made Sara look at her with astonishment.

'Because,' continued Margaret, confused, 'I think – I don't know – isn't it *that*, Sara?'

Being still on her knees, though she had turned round as she said the last words, the anxious expression in her eyes as she looked up at her sister for a response gave her the air of a pale petitioner waiting for a reprieve.

'You're too wise, Maggie,' replied Sara, laughing. 'Do you want to hear all – *all* about it?'

'Please,' said Margaret resolutely – '*all*.'

'In the first place, then,' said Sara, taking a pillow from Margaret's berth and patting it into a seat for herself on the floor, 'I must pay you a compliment upon your discrimination. Oh, don't be modest! You read faces *wonderfully* – I always said so.'

'Some, perhaps,' said Margaret, rather sadly; 'but this was reading an expression more than a face. Any one might do that.'

'And what did the expression tell you?' asked Sara, her eyes animated with feminine triumph – an excusable triumph, because so natural. The craving for power in some form or another is almost an instinct, and the sense of its possession that must needs follow such an avowal as Sara had just heard on deck might well fill her eyes with triumphant light.

'Well, what did it tell you?' she repeated. 'Say what you think – do, Maggie – and then perhaps I'll tell you the truth.'

'It told me,' said Maggie, with effort, 'that you had filled up a good man's heart and soul – yes, you may smile, Sara, at my way of expressing it – but that is what I mean. The expression you want me to interpret does not take a bit from that other expression. It is *goodness*, nothing else – not Sunday-school goodness, but the sort of goodness that must come from having a strong mind, and bending it all to the carrying out of one's idea of what is noble.'

'What a flow of eloquence, Maggie! And you used to sit like a mouse in the corner, at Madame Thonon's debating society – do you remember? But, *ápropos* of the strong mind. If it was all full of noble purpose, where was the space for poor me?'

'I think he had idealised you, Sara! I don't mean to say anything uncomplimentary, dear – you know that I consider you worthy of a throne! – but I think he blended this ideal conception somehow with his other high aims; and – well – I don't think he was in love with you in an ordinary way.'

'I've never admitted that he was "in love" with me at all yet,' said Sara. 'You must know, Maggie, all this happened quite by chance to-night. I was looking over the side of the ship at the lighthouse, you know, thinking of those hateful Pipers, and wondering whether we'd be at their mercy by this time tomorrow night, when a voice – I knew whose it was directly, though it sounded rather muffled – said, close to my side, "You are taking leave of the phosphorus, Miss Sara?" I wasn't thinking of the phosphorus in the least, as it happened. "I wish all leave-taking came as easily," I said, never dreaming that I was going to explode a mine. But, Maggie, you should have heard the change in his voice! It almost terrified me! "Do you mean it?" he cried. The way in which he said it sounded almost fierce, if you can understand. And before poor I could say a word, or do anything but simply *stare* at him in astonishment' – a smile from Margaret, who knew of old the witchery of glance implied by Sara's 'stare' – 'a torrent of words came out – I can't remember half of them – but really I almost felt as if we were acting a play. I wish I had them written down!'

'Give me the meaning of them, if you can, will you, Sara?' said Margaret gently.

'Oh, you know the meaning, Maggie, well enough. I think he began by saying that he had determined to keep his secret to himself – a fine secret when even *you* guessed it – and that to have met a "perfect type of womanhood" – I remember those words, because no one ever called me that before – should be encouragement, or support, or something of the sort enough all one's life. You see he mixed up his faith with it in a way that bewildered me. But now, he said, the faint hope my words had given him – I am sure there wasn't any meaning of the kind in them, but I didn't like to disappoint him by saying so – the faint hope my words had given him broke down all "prudential considerations." Isn't that well remembered? And, at least, he would tell me that henceforth – by which he gave me to understand that he meant to the *very* end of his days – he would cherish, next to his religion, of course, his recollection of me, or my image, at any rate. I really can't remember how he said this part of it. It's the funniest sort of love-making, if you come to think of it, for the upshot of it seemed to be that if at any time of my life I had a sort of *penchant* for him, he'd come from the other world to marry me. And in the meantime I'm his "lady," and he's my knight, or, rather, he's like one of those good-natured people you can always fall back upon at a party if somebody you don't like asks you to dance; in fact, if one were *frightfully* unlucky in all one's offers he'd always be there as a *pis-aller*.'

A *pis-aller!* When poor Margaret would have cut off her feet or walked upon knives, like the little mermaid in Andersen's tales, if thereby she could have testified to her longing to serve him.

'And you didn't say you cared for him, Sara!'

'Why should I?' said Sara, open-eyed. 'He's very well! I like him in a way, but you wouldn't have me live like that dissenting minister's wife at Highbury, with darned chairs and no tablecloths. We're going out to "better ourselves," aren't we! I'm sure I don't know what else we're going for!'

'But there are such different ways of bettering oneself,' pleaded Margaret, as if she were wooing her sister by proxy. 'What would it be to you to wait for a little!' Then, in a voice of which the intonation sounded broken to Sara's ears, 'Tell me – I could advise better if you would tell me, dear – you don't care for him *rightly*, do you?'

'I don't know what you call *rightly*,' said Sara, in offended accents. 'If things were different I might have said "Yes,"'

'Do you mean if he were rich?' asked Margaret, with an inflection of something that grated on Sara's ears.

'Yes I *do* mean it, if you will put it in that way. I know what I like, and how I should feel towards any one who couldn't give me a single thing I cared about. Besides, what better arrangement could I make? I haven't bound myself in any way.'

'But he's bound, you say?' interrupted Margaret quickly.

'That's because he chooses to be. I don't think he's like other people in that way, I must say. He told me, Maggie,' dropping her eyes, 'that he could not understand caring about more than one woman in a lifetime. Well, I should say he must be thirty, at least, by this time, and as he's never cared about any one before, I don't suppose he's likely to change, even if he wanted to.'

'To change! Oh, no!' said Margaret.

She turned to her trunk again, and went to her packing with a will, her fingers trembling a little as she smoothed out the top layer of all. What a world of misfits it was. How one creature might spurn what another would have treasured so rapturously! For what was it but the spurning of proffered love to speak of it as a *pis-aller* – a something to be held over for use if nothing better offered? And it was as fruitless to look for any responsive sentiment in Sara as to look for enthusiasm regarding the sunlight from a mole. Even the foundation for it was lacking in such a nature as hers. Margaret doubted whether Sara was capable of feeling any kind of love beyond that purely instinctive family regard common to such as do not hate their belongings. To enjoy bodily luxury and be treated with consideration, these, then, were all her desires. Still, had Margaret any right to quarrel with her sister because she did not see the Rev. Mr Lydiat through another's eyes? Surely not; and Margaret told herself that had Sara attested her inability to love him as a reason for her coldness, she could have respected the reason without entirely comprehending it. But how could she respect the calculating, worldly reasoning advanced so transparently by Sara? Mr Lydiat, she had admitted, was not distasteful to her. She might have been bought at a price, had he wooed her with gold in his hand. Failing which, he might lavish his heart's store of devotion upon her through a life-long stretch of years unavailingly. If Sara had seen in him the tenth part of the qualities that Margaret saw, she would have had no fear as to the future. His wife would want neither for food nor clothes, nor decent habitation, nor lack the necessaries of life. Though heaven only knows what different meanings may attach to that simple word – all arising, I sincerely believe, from our different conceptions of the universe. For Sara, with the cravings of an odalisque, it was a very solid world – capable of affording happiness only through its tangible parts. Whereas for Margaret, though she had found it, indeed, a working-day world, its material good seemed trifling compared with a good wholly independent of it. But Sara studied her sensations only.

'Margaret!' she said, after a long pause, during which Margaret had been thinking all the things I have recorded.

'Well!'

'Margaret, don't put away that tin of preserved milk. I asked the steward for some dessert biscuits on my way down; and if you'll get a plate from the saloon, we can have a feast. Don't look so cross about it! I suppose I'm not to be hungry next, because I've had an offer!'

CHAPTER VI

———————•———————

Mr Cavendish Makes A Difficulty

'Come, give us a taste of your quality.' – SHAKESPEARE.

I do not know that there is anything more irritating to a placid temperament, convinced of the futility of 'kicking against the pricks,' than the constant companionship of a carping spirit, or a mind prone to indulge in what has been happily designated 'harking back' upon grievances. In the first place, the process appears almost as foolish in the eyes of an onlooker as the worrying of an unsound tooth, that would not be aggressive if it were only let alone; and in the second there is a terrible sense of impotence in the good-will with which one applies the oft-used salve. Small wonder if faith in its healing power becomes less and less every time it is called upon to act. A trouble of this kind is almost invariably a woman's trouble. Men would not dare to inflict it on one of themselves. A man has been scripturally commanded, it is true, to forgive his brother unto 'seventy times seven,' but nothing was said as to the number of times he must submit to hear a repetition of his old grievances. I doubt whether the most forbearing of brothers would not indulge in a little pardonable profanity long before the seventy-seventh repetition had been reached. But for women there is no such outlet for justifiable irritation, and unless they are hysterically inclined there is no escape.

Perhaps the cultivation of such a spirit as Mrs Cavendish possessed would be the best resource after all, though I admit, at the outset, that it is not within the bounds of every one's attainment. This stout, classic-featured, comely wife was constrained to sit still and listen –

every time her lord had lost at whist, or was reminded of the existence of his liver – to a sort of synopsis of the fatalities that had attended the House of Devonshire from the moment of his birth. And she listened without detriment to her matronly portliness, or even much diminishing of her wifely affection. 'Your papa,' she would tell the girls, after Mr Cavendish had worn his voice to the pitch of a rasp, 'your papa wants a little cheering up. See now, to talk lively to him, Sara!' – an injunction that Sara generally interpreted by keeping carefully out of her father's way until he had been 'cheered up' by other means than hers.

Mrs Cavendish had heard less of the catastrophes that had overtaken the House of Devonshire since she had embarked on board the *Henrietta Maria* than at any former period of her life. She had battled through a weary phase before Mr Cavendish could be induced to accept her brother's offer and emigrate with his wife and daughters to Melbourne. Nothing short of necessity made him yield at last. He had all Sara's antipathy to being forced to acknowledge his humbly-born connections. With half a world between them he could condescend to be benefited by his wife's brother with a charming affability, but it was quite another thing to come to Australia at his bidding, and almost entirely at his expense. The *parvenu* butcher might prove insufferably familiar, and the unfortunate circumstances of the case left him without defence.

I believe this feeling was inherent in him. In virtue of his episcopalian belongings it may be inferred that his theological views were sound, and that he would have acquiesced in the gospel views of equality generally. But in virtue of his instinctive prejudices – stronger than any orthodoxy consequent on the possession of a bishop in the family – he was one of a race as distinct from the plebeian Pipers as though blue-dyed blood had actually run through his veins, and common human blood through theirs. His definition of evil, if he had been forced to think out his conception of it, would have been the unaccountable oversight in the arrangement of the universe that left patrician humanity open to the same wants as grosser clay, and neglected to endow it with the means of supplying them.

It was in this mood that he had come on board, though once there, to his wife's surprise and delight, 'your pa' took a turn. The pastime of posing for Lord Byron, whom he had been said to resemble in his youth, wrapped in a long cloak that had protected a Devonshire of the last generation from Peninsular breezes, sufficed to amuse him until the Southern Hemisphere was reached. Moreover, there was his favourite whist, in which even the antiquity of his family was sometimes forgotten in his cordiality towards a partner who held five trumps; there was the sympathetic M'Bride, who, as showing an unbroken descent from a king contemporary with St Patrick, was eligible as a deck chum; there was an absence of the perplexity of beholding the flourishing condition of his tradesmen as compared with own; and there was, in a physical sense, an inability to keep awake when he sought his wife's cabin at night that gave her an immunity from the familiar narratives of his ill-usage.

But the inevitable reaction occurred on the last night of the journey, as was evident to Margaret, lying wide awake in the adjoining cabin, while Sara slept soundly as a child. The sound of her father's voice, that reached her ears like a continuous unbroken grating, filled her with anxiety for her mother. She longed to knock at the door, to say a word only that might stem for an instant's space the monotonous flow, hardly interrupted by the soft rejoinders that she could not hear. But old experience had proved to Margaret that a pretext of the sort was invariably detected, and only served to add a parental grievance to the ancestral list. She sat up, feeling sadly helpless and full of commiseration, until a hearty 'Bother papa!' from the opposite berth proved that Sara had been aroused.

'Poor mother!' said Margaret. 'Don't you think I'd better say *something*, Sara? It might do some good.'

'Oh, ma's used to it!' said Sara sleepily, and carefully doubling down her soft pillow over her free ear, was soon drawing regular breaths that were not far removed from snore. Margaret, meanwhile, continued to listen with a feeling which in a less filially disposed daughter would have borne a close resemblance to exasperation. She knew that her mother had been toiling through the greater part of the afternoon, and that, thanks to her care, every article of her father's clothing was in a condition of immaculateness that might have satisfied even the head of the House of Devonshire himself. She knew, too, how sorely rest and sympathy must be needed by a mind almost painfully strained with the anticipation of the morrow's meeting. And, knowing these things, she could have wished it was not so horribly undutiful to ponder on the relief it must have afforded her mother if her father could have been instantly gagged.

Nothing, in point of fact, short of gagging, could have restrained Mr Cavendish once he had entered upon the subject of his grievances.

Did you ever see a man thoroughly convinced that the world has been ill-using him from his cradle? There is something almost touching in the naive egotism with which he puts his case, and expects you to see it solely and entirely from his own injured point of view. If all the universe had only taken shape from nebulous chaos for the purpose of thwarting him he could not show a more profound conviction that he had been singled out for ill-treatment. For an evangelised Christian who may be possessed of such a delusion there is the comforting reflection that he has been selected for chastisement as an object of Divine favour. But Mr Cavendish was not an evangelised Christian – only an orthodox one – and could have foregone with great resignation any of the striking marks of 'Divine favour' that made the subject of his plaints.

I am sure his wife could have foregone with equal resignation the recapitulation of them to-night. The brush almost dropped out of her hand – so weary she felt – as she prolonged the brushing of her hair with seraphic endurance all the time her husband was speaking; sitting right up in her cabin-chair, lest it should appear she was not wide-awake to his troubles, while he, too excited to rest, walked up and down the confined length of their cabin, wrapped in his flowered dressing-gown.

Even under his present fretful, undignified aspect – for there is nothing more undignified than the attitude of a grumbling man, not an inveigher against fate, but a carper against petty ills – Mr Cavendish asserted his deprivation. He was a slight man, with a generally pinched but thoroughly refined set of features, not unbecomingly bald about the temples, and graceful, even to his manner of extending a slender taper forefinger upon the occasion of haranguing his wife or daughters. He had never had a beard, and was almost whiskerless, a fact which, coupled with his slight figure, made him look like his wife's son in the distance. But on a closer inspection her face was found to be smooth and youthful, with the enduring youth of a perfect texture of skin, and a chiselled nose and chin, while his was seamed with the grievances of his five and fifty years of life. I do not think he had omitted to emphasise a single one of these life-long grievances to-night. The cabin candle – alight in defiance of Captain Chuck's printed regulations – was burning low – upon ordinary occasions it would have lasted for a week – before he had half exhausted himself, and poor Mrs Cavendish's eyes were blurred with something which made the candle throw out long quivering darts of light as he said,

'It's most unaccountable – most unaccountable; indeed, I might say – most extraordinary – your brother's conduct. In fact, it's not far short of presuming. By what earthly right does he suppose the Cavendish family is to be at his beck and call? I shouldn't wonder if he were to send for my brother the Bishop next. Upon my honour, I shouldn't be in the least surprised. To say the least of it, it's a gross piece of officiousness on his part. I never objected, that I'm aware of, to your receiving his little presents in England! Can you charge me, I say, with every offering an *objection* to your receiving them?'

His wife shook her head – and indeed, considering that the 'little presents' had signified their daily bread to the Cavendish family, an objection on the part of Mr Cavendish would have been a somewhat unlikely proceeding. 'No! I'm not aware, I repeat, of offering any obstruction to his communication with you. What did he require? More facilities for correspondence? Had you ever to complain of a delay in the delivery of your letters? No!' He stood before his wife and extended the inevitable forefinger, marking off each phrase with it, as if he had been delivering the heads of a discourse. 'I can see his motive, *of* course! He never considers what it is to *me*, at my advanced age' – nothing would have irritated Mr Cavendish more than a hint of the sort proffered by any one else – 'to leave my country, my kin, my ancestral associations, and die in a country of convicts and gold-diggers.' Nothing could impress Mr Cavendish with the fact that Botany Bay was *not* in Victoria. 'To die there, I repeat,' solemnly, 'and why?' – the forefinger took a prolonged swoop – 'Yes, why? Only because your brother mistrusts me! He cannot believe his paltry benefits are fittingly bestowed. Good Heavens! what a want of consideration – of delicacy. I am well aware that it is useless to look for delicacy from people of a certain class – no one need tell me that, I have had sufficient experience of it, unfortunately. I don't expect *you* to sympathise with me. I see it all clearly enough, and I must repeat what a want of good breeding, of proper feeling, to extort, as it were, a sort of guarantee in my presence – a guarantee, evidently, of the way in which I dispose of his money! But it is useless, as I said before, to expect anything else – quite useless.'

He stopped short to give vent to a profound sigh. Mrs Cavendish had the silver teapot on the tip of her tongue, but she refrained.

'You ain't fair to my brother, Mr Cavendish,' was all she said. When scenes of this nature took place, the poor woman betrayed her emotion by relapsing into early untutored expressions, and above all,

by calling her husband 'Mr' Cavendish – at other times he was 'Pa.'
'You don't give him his due. I'd like to know where we'd be now, if
it wasn't for him.'

'Be now,' said Mr Cavendish sharply; 'in England, of course.' Mrs
Cavendish forbore again to observe that *England* might have many
meanings, and that a poorhouse in that favoured country need not
display any singular advantages over a poorhouse in any other part of
the world. She returned to the defence by remarking –

'Tom 'ud take it to heart sadly, Mr Cavendish, or I don't know
him. Do you think I can't say what was his main thought in bringing
us away? It wasn't to see how we were spending his money, as you
said, awhile ago, nor yet to set eyes on his sister again, though, trust
my heart, that 'ud something to do with it. It was all so as we should
"better ourselves," nothing but that – or he's not the Tom that I
remember – when I hadn't a friend but him in the world!'

'Better ourselves!' objected Mr Cavendish scornfully. 'I do wish,
Elizabeth, you would make use of more appropriate expressions. A
valet "betters" himself! A chambermaid "betters" herself when she
marries the butler. Your brother, I am quite willing to concede, has
"bettered" himself, taking into consideration the circumstances in
which he was left by your unfortunate father. The House of Devonshire can have no motive for bettering itself. Pray remember that!'

He was so irritated as he began to pace the cabin floor again that
his wife would not risk a rejoinder. All thought of personal hurt was
merged into pity for him. What if it were only 'proper pride,' after
all, that made him seem so hard? For he had always chafed against
the sense of being under obligations, and surely it was natural for a
man so well born to feel it out of place that he should come for help
to those below him. Thus she argued, resenting in no wise the fetish
régime by virtue of which she was morally belaboured so severely –
but feeling tired, and sick at heart, and desiring nothing so much as
rest.

That peculiar sensation of anticipation, that affecting some people
physically produces an actual sense of internal strain, had well nigh
worn her out.

All pleasure in the morrow's meeting was gone. The zest of
presenting 'your pa' to her brother Tom – of bidding her beautiful
Sara and Margaret, of the sweet manners, kiss their Uncle Piper; nay
– for she had not forgotten Tom's blunt appreciation of her girlish
charms – the pleasure of greeting him again with her own comely

visage still smooth and recognisable – had all been destroyed by her husband's remarks. The whole aspect of the meeting was changed. Mr Cavendish would make it plain that he had no intention of being 'friendly' from the first. And what more natural than that Tom should be 'short' with him, if that was all the return he was to get for his kindness? He was a 'plain-spoken' man, as she remembered him. She could not even picture him as living in other than a plain way, having but vague ideas of colonial life and its near approach, among the wealthy, to the luxury indulged in at home. But that was the more reason for refusing to be 'put off' with mere cold civility. How could she possibly soften her husband's heart before the morrow's meeting? How lead him to pardon, as it were, his benefactor, for having dared to benefit him? Not, it was evident, by twitting him with the lavishness of his brother, the well-born bishop, and the episode of the silver teapot. Not by saying to him, 'You married me, believing you were lowering yourself; you have often hinted as much to me since. You thought it a piece of condescension to let me write to my own brother; you would hardly as much as believe that I had any feeling for him. Yet who, when your brother played the Jacob to you, and took our only piece of plate before he would save you from starving – who, when your child might have been born in a lying-in hospital, for all you could have done to prevent it – who, I ask, came to your help then? Who has sent us money time after time without being asked for it? Who after pretty well *keeping* us at home all these years, wishes to have us come to him, only that he may see better what more he can do for us? Who is it that you are abusing, after taking his presents? It is true you may have a crest of your own, and may talk about ancestors who cut people's throats three hundred years ago. It is true my brother Tom can remember no farther back than his father's counter, and that he began his life by "butchering," but which of you can hold his head the highest now? You whose gentle blood would not have kept your wife and children from the workhouse, or he whose honest hands have made him independent of all the world; who has never wronged a man of a penny; who has not only provided for his own family and his wife's daughter (who had no claim upon him), but for you and your family to boot?'

Without entering upon so exhaustive a method of reasoning as the above, Mrs Cavendish was aware of the futility of 'speaking her mind,' even a mind so lenient and charitably inclined as hers. But she apologised for the slight offered to the House of Devonshire.

'I didn't mean it that way, Mr Cavendish – you know I didn't. I'd only money in my mind when I was talking o' bettering ourselves.'

'Bettering ourselves, indeed!' repeated Mr Cavendish, in whose mind the expression apparently rankled; 'you call it "bettering ourselves" when you force me to sell my birthright for money? This is what my ancestors fought and died for, I suppose – that I may be transported to a land of upstarts and convicts – this is what you call "bettering ourselves."'

His voice failed him in his choking indignation. And it was the more embarrassing that, even granting he had had the best of grounds for posing as a martyr, there was clearly nothing to be done, the family fund being represented by £27, together with a few odd shillings left over from Uncle Piper's *largesse*, a sum insufficient even to take Mr Cavendish back in the *Henrietta Maria*, should his aversion to being 'bettered' by his wife's relations make him refuse to leave the ship when the moment for landing had arrived.

The point of the discussion was now reached at which a right-minded woman, in Mrs Cavendish's place, knowing what was due to herself, would have sobbed loudly and continuously. Noise has in all times been the weapon of weakness – force, for the most part, working silently – and the acknowledgment of weakness that tears bring with them has sometimes a mollifying effect on the tyrant, especially where they are accompanied by some nicely pitched moans. For of two results, one. Either the man is flattered by the commotion he has aroused or fearful lest some sympathetic soul should hear it. In either case he is quieted for the time being. Therefore, despite those misleading theories which would have you believe that a man is goaded by a woman's tears, and that a 'soft answer' is the surest means of disarming him, I counsel all young wives starting in life with a grumbling helpmate, or hindermate (as the case may be), to cultivate a facility for crying instantaneously, distinctly, and perseveringly.

But Mrs Cavendish, as I have said, had never been taught their value in a crisis of this sort, and spontaneously they could hardly have come to her aid, seeing that her life from its outset had been developed in a school of self-restraint. She sat perfectly still, with all foretaste of gladness in the morrow's meeting crushed out of her – while the candle, which, I think, must have been her ally, spluttered significantly. 'You may well sit like a log,' said Mr Cavendish, in bitter allusion to her crushed quiescence; 'if you had a spark of sensibility – a spark of womanly – of lady-like feeling' – there was such a disclaimer from the candle at this point that he turned to pull the wick up – 'if you were not a "Piper,"' extending a delicate forefinger towards the flame – 'if you were not a "Piper," I say – Damn –' the flame had gone out, while the wick held fast to Mr Cavendish's finger. Four bells, faintly repeated by a ghostly peal from the distant forecastle, sounded in the pause that followed – during which Mrs Cavendish inferred from the solemn stillness that her husband was nursing his finger. It would have been dangerous to advance any sympathy. She felt her way almost noiselessly to her berth – so wearied out, that it was only reserved for Margaret in the next cabin to know that her father had gone to bed under difficulties in the dark.

Meanwhile the *Henrietta Maria*, as unheeding as Jonah's whale of all the fretting ambitions, the hopes, the despondencies, the passions that she held massed for the last time between her bulging sides, was slowly making her way up the bay. Already the stars that had encrusted the sky all night, like so many pale precious stones of enduring brilliance, were effacing themselves in the deepening pink – the fore-runner of a light before which they must all obliterate themselves. And two watchful souls among the passengers who were aware of this first early summer sunrise over the Australian coast were Margaret lying quietly awake, with sad sleepless eyes, and the Rev. Mr Lydiat looking from his port-hole at the distant scrub-enfolded hills, whose black outline he could trace distinctly against the brightening sky. For it was not only in Shakespeare's age that:

> 'Some must watch while some must weep,
> Thus runs the world away.'

PART II

CHAPTER I

———————•———————

Why Mr Piper Looked, Like Sister Anne, From His Tower

'I know my price: I am worth no worse a place.'

– SHAKESPEARE

Mr Piper was one of those whose thousands had turned into tens of thousands, yet I have no intention of ranking him among either the mighty or the petty usurers. In his own estimation it was 'hard work' and the 'keeping of his wits about him' that had put him into the proud position of being able to 'snap his fingers' at the rest of the world.

Foresight, or shrewdness, which is only foresight in its most practical form, was the quality upon which Mr Piper specially prided himself. 'Where would he have been now,' he used to ask, 'if he hadn't kept his eyes open through life?' and as nobody was ever known to hazard a direct answer to this question, he would look across his flawless garden from his arm-chair in the verandah, or cast his eyes round about his expensively furnished drawing-room – by way of leading you to infer that he might have been in many worse places than 'Piper's Hill.' Of this nobody but a Diogenes, who was partial to restricted accommodation, could have had much of a doubt. Piper's Hill, with a little of the toning down that Time's fingers only can bestow, and a few of the associations that mark the distinction between a house and a home, would become the type of a dwelling-place in which success might rest content and take its ease. If to-day it flaunted its tower, its summerhouses, its outbuildings, in tints that the French

52

so well call *criard*, one might be sure that to-morrow the dark Murray
pines, the broad-leafed Moreton Bay fig tree, the inevitable *Pinus
insignis* that dotted the lawn in front of the house, would interpose
their rich sombre green between your vision and the brightness of
colouring that offended it.

There was something touching in the aspect of Mr Piper among
his trees and shrubs. He would have liked to live long enough to see
them surrounded by garden-seats enveloped in shade. It seemed to
him that in the matter of growing old he was leaving them all behind.
Every morning regularly he would tell the gardener 'to see and hurry
up them pines' after looking at them wistfully as he made the tour of
each separate tree. For family matters, to be made clear by and by,
prevented him from feeling unmixed satisfaction in the idea that the
trees which were so tardy of growth to his age-infected eyes would
spread their great knotted branches over his son's head, and shelter
perhaps a 'posse' of grandchildren. Having a passion, now that his
money-making days were over, for dictating absolutely to every one
about him, a possibility that his son should presume to look for
happiness in a direction that he himself had not pointed out was
marring the enjoyment, from a paternal point of view, of the future
of the trees.

Mr Piper would not have been an unkindly autocrat, but a very
uncomprehending one, and if you had dared to be happy in any way
but the one which he had indicated, he would not have let you enjoy
your self-evolved happiness long. No one could spend two minutes
in his society without seeing that he was not a man it would have
been safe to contradict. On principle, he contradicted every one
himself, because it stood to reason that people who had not made
'their way in life' could not speak authoritatively like those who had.
Success had not altogether engendered this failing, but by giving scope
for full play to latent qualities, it had helped to develop it. In some
people it brings out good humour, in others self-indulgence; in some,
who, like Mr Piper, have always had a faith in their own infallibility,
it confirms the tendency to lay down the law. What better proof that
they have always been in the right would it be possible to advance
than the proof that they have 'made their mark' after starting in life
with nothing? The self-evidence of such a proposition was so clear to
Mr Piper that it was in perfect good faith that he contradicted every
member of his household, and flew into a rage consistently if any one
contradicted him. The only person who did so impolitic a thing in an

open way was his step-daughter Laura, and the fact that he could not always talk her down, and that she was the only being who had ever given him a vague, uneasy sense that his reasons were occasionally more blustering than convincing, did not tend to mollify the resentment he felt for her in consequence. Even to tell her 'she was a fool,' which he did every time he could think of no sounder argument wherewith to confute her short, pithy rejoinders – did not always bring an entirely satisfactory assurance that the rest of the world agreed with him. Laura had always been a thorn in his side; and latterly his suspicion that in his son's eyes she wore more the aspect of a rose than of a thorn increased a hundredfold the smarting sense of her presence.

Perhaps it was some reflection of this nature that was souring his expression as he sat in his tower before breakfast on the very morning which saw the *Henrietta Maria* tacking in a light land breeze up Hobson's Bay. It is not the best of moments for introducing him to your notice. The light is shining upon his face, and there is no gainsaying that for all its shrewdness the cast of the face is plebeian. That would be your first impression of it. After you had allowed for a little redness of the skin, you would begin to see that there were traits which spoke of a kindly, obstinate, limited nature – a nature not to be driven, but coaxed – above all, not to be reasoned with. The lips were slightly coarse, the grizzled beard and moustache cut close all round against the face. It was in the general spreading more than the wrinkling of the cheeks that Mr Piper's sixty-five years of life were discernible. There was still a covering of coarse grey hair all over his head. His eyes had still much sharpness of expression. Strip him of his accessories, and substitute for his easy-fitting grey suit and gentleman's linen the blue blouse and coloured Crimean, and you would see much of the huckster left. But take him as he has appeared for the last ten years at least, with the stamp of assurance that the possession of wealth has given him, and you would admit that he might pass muster with many a middle-aged, fleshy, grizzled gentleman of unimpeachable uncommercial antecedents.

Besides, when the outcome of wealth is the background against which you examine a new face for the first time, it is next to impossible to form a judgment entirely independent of it. And when this outcome has taken the form of a crenellated tower, with four plate-glass windows, a Persian rug, and painted panelling, the chances are more than ever against your coming to an unbiased decision on the impulse of the moment. As for the decision of the inmates, if I were to give you the one Mr Piper's step-daughter Laura had arrived at years ago, you would think Mr Piper hopelessly pig-headed and vulgar. His son George would see him as a 'governor who had his good points if you took him the right way,' but who 'was apt to turn rusty without cause,' and was not altogether 'good form.' His youngest daughter – the child that in the bequeathing him his second wife had yielded up her own life – saw him simply as '*dear* papa.' This was the baby about whom Laura had written that tersely expressed note at the age of thirteen to her brother in London. The child had lived, but the mother died. Before dying, the child being brought to her, she had made a mother's appeal to her husband. 'I don't ask you to be good to *our* little one, dear,' she had said, in the earnest, weak tones of a voice that is framing its last prayer; 'I know you will cherish it; but be good to *my* girl, too! Do the same by both, promise me. I can't die in peace if you don't give me your word you'll be good to Laura.'

Mr Piper had promised, and so solemnly, and in such good faith, that his wife had died with broken words of gratitude on her lips. He could not gather the purport of what she said. Mingled with her thanks there had been allusions to her son in England – fears lest Laura should give trouble, entreaties that she should be tenderly dealt with. Through the incoherence Mr Piper recognised the main point, that he must look upon his step-daughter as upon his own. I think he held to that fact, and tried hard to act upon it. His marriage with her mother, a widow, and a 'real lady,' as he had called her in his letter to Mrs Cavendish, had been brought about more, as Miss Edgeworth would put it, through 'propinquity,' than through spontaneous sentiment. As his housekeeper, her refinement and good sense had won upon him. He would have been better pleased had there been no grown-up clerical son in England – or rebellious, bright-cheeked fast-growing daughter here. But the English son was a drawback of which nothing but mail-day could bring a faint reminder; and the daughter, despite her peculiarities, was, as Mr Piper had expressed it, 'right enough outside' to marry, within all probability in a very few years' time. As for Mr Piper's own son George – then a youth going through his last term at the grammar school – there would be no injustice done to *him* by the match. Mr Piper could have provided for a dozen children. He would like to receive wifely amenities at the hands of his ladylike housekeeper. He had 'pulled' very well with his first wife for ten or eleven years, and he had no doubt he would 'rub along' all right with another. He had liked the way in which this Mrs Lydiat had 'shaped' from the first. After a recapitulation to himself of these cogent reasons every evening for a fortnight, Mr Piper made his proposal. He was unhesitatingly accepted.

I cannot say that he was not troubled by misgivings before the wedding took place. He never woke without a start of consternation, and the sense that something unsettling – perhaps ruinous – was hanging over him. He felt as in former days, when he had given large credit to a house of business about whose security he had no absolute certainty. What if second matrimony should turn out as irremediable an evil as an unredeemed bad debt? I think he hurried on the match in defence against himself.

But once in the haven, I must admit that his misgivings vanished at once and for ever. Laura was sent to school, and, in so far as it was possible, made to 'keep her place' when she was at home, a position hard to define precisely, in consideration of the different limits it assumes from the different points of view of the parties interested. And as for the amenities he had looked for, Mr Piper had nothing to complain of. A show of perfect submission to his superior judgment was all he wanted. His second wife deferred to him in everything, and, as a consequence, she was allowed to exercise her own taste. He looked upon these eleven months of middle-aged married experience as the part of his life that had been most to his taste. His first wife's delicacy had been a drawback; his second one was always ready to put on her hat and come outside to acquiesce in the improvements he was making, or placidly approve his taste in garden-planting. This peaceful epoch promised to last through their united lives, and so tenderly considerate did Mr Piper become to his wife as the period of his child's birth drew near, that she found herself thinking less of the 'tact' she had hitherto employed than of the dawning affection that was developing itself for her husband.

But there was short space left for the appreciation of it. She died, as I have said, and he could not bring himself at first to look upon a puny, wailing infant, albeit his own flesh and blood, as worthy substitute for an intelligent companion, who had understood him, and rated him at a *just* valuation – signifying, of course, his own. His heart ached for her sympathy, even when it was for her loss that he was grieving. Failing the satisfying acknowledgment her manner had always conveyed that 'whatever Mr Piper did was the right thing to do,' he became more positive and overbearing than before. He satisfied his conscience by providing for Laura, settling a thousand pounds upon her immediately after his wife's death, which, being invested in some property along the Alma Road that increased considerably in value, yielded her a settled income of something like two hundred a year at the present time. But the claims of his conscience and his temper by no means accorded. There was something in Laura's presence alone that seemed mutely to negative his own estimation of his brains.

Can anything more irritating be conceived to a man who believes himself, and would have the world believe him, capable of accomplishing anything he sets his mind to, than a sort of palpable protest against this belief in the shape of a little schoolgirl? It mattered little whether Laura sat silent or spoke in her short, condensed fashion. Mr Piper felt, and the feeling goaded him, that she had opinions of her own, that probably she had already formed her own estimate of him, that there was a lurking sarcasm in a rejoinder of which the very simplicity gave you distracting suspicions as to the meaning it veiled. He would have liked to see her whipped, or to have an archangel declare that 'she was a fool, and knew nothing,' and that 'Mr Piper was *always* in the right.' If there was one aspect in which she was more bearable than another, it was when, by some unforeseen chance – for she restrained all demonstrations in his presence – he had seen her caressing her little half-sister. Though even here her peculiarity asserted itself. She persisted in calling her sister 'Hester,' when both upon the baby's silver cup and the baptismal register it was patent to every one that she had been lawfully christened Louisa.

But whether as 'Hester' to Laura, as Louisa, 'Poppet,' or 'Squirrel' to her father, as 'Chick,' 'Mouse,' or 'Little Redhead' to her half-brother George, this little one was the go-between that served to keep the rough edges which the rest occasionally presented to each other from scraping into dangerous friction. It may be that the tact employed by the mature mother during the short year of her married life was inborn in the child. It seemed at least inherent in her. Before she could speak she had shown an impartiality worthy of an ancient mistress of ceremonies in her bearing towards George – her brother on her father's side – and towards Laura – her sister on her mother's side. To her father – who was *all* her father – she had shown the most marked of her baby attentions; inheriting, it may be, along with the tact, a portion of transmitted tenderness such as her mother had felt for him latterly. In this she could not have displayed more courtier-like sagacity had she been an old-world changeling with centuries of experience respecting rich fathers of uncertain testamentary inclinations. She was beginning to be what any being that is truly loved must become sooner or later – a *necessity* to the elderly man. It is all very well to talk of self-sacrificing love that will rejoice in the welfare of the beloved object and sit calmly down with the certainty that it is prospering thousands of miles away. Real love, be it marital, motherly, or otherwise, hungers for the *bodily* presence, and cannot rest without it, or if it be constrained frets itself into the rest from which even the love it has yearned for cannot arouse it.

CHAPTER II

———————•———————

And What He Saw Therefrom

'Oh, what a world is this, when what is comely
Envenoms him that bears it.' – SHAKESPEARE

Mr Piper, you may be sure, had not been long at his tower-window,
where he was standing on this particular morning, like a corpulent
Sister Anne in a Blue Beard extravaganza, before small feet were
heard toiling up the tower stairs; and with an old-fashioned sigh, as
testifying that the journey had been a laborious one in parts, his little
girl opened the door. At first sight you would have taken in nothing
but a general impression of small features, freckles, and curling red
hair. But the least scrutiny of something more than the mere colouring
(which is all the eye is apt to catch at first) would have shown a pair
of very sweet grey eyes that could assume a comical reflection of Mr
Piper's shrewdness at times, and again – when their owner was
thinking hard – an expression of dreamy abstraction that brought them
wonderfully close to the eyes of the Rev. Mr Lydiat, during his
noonday reverie on the forecastle. At first sight, too, you would have
supposed you were looking at a child of seven, but the moment after
you would have put her down for a small creature of twelve. It is
probable she was somewhere between the two ages.

Mr Piper, you may be certain, feigned to know nothing of this
diminutive presence in his tower, until his hand was caught from
behind, and, following the kisses that it was made aware of, little teeth
made the tiniest of dents upon his thumb, as though some small
animal were nibbling at it.

'It's the squirrel, papa, wants to know why you didn't call it this morning?'

'That's never the squirrel!' said Mr Piper, turning round as though he were quite overwhelmed with astonishment. 'Squirrels up at this time o' day! I don't believe it!'

But he seemed to believe it all the same, and to be very glad of it, as he took the little being up in his arms, and set her down on the broad window-sill in front of him, where she stood after smoothing down her pinafore like a bird whose plumage has been ruffled, with one arm round his neck, bestowing intermittent little kisses upon the tip of his ear, and pretending to rub them away, so as to make a fresh place that wanted kissing over again.

'There'll be a lot of folk'll want kissing to-day,' said Mr Piper; 'but you mustn't give 'em *my* sort o' kisses, eh? That's the sort you keep for your old father!'

'I'll kiss them like this,' said the child. 'Now, say you're my aunt – "Oh, aunt, I'm so glad to see you!"' (very primly). 'Oh, but you must give me your cheek, papa, or I can't show you how I'll kiss her.'

'That'll do, I expect,' said Mr Piper, after Louey, with great gravity and demureness, had kissed him precisely on the cheek-bone; 'but mind you, you've got to be very fond o' your Aunt Bess! There's no better girl in this world, nor a finer – I don't care where the next is!'

'Do you call big, grown-up ladies "girls," papa?' asked the child, not as if she were cavilling at the use of the word, but simply as one who wanted enlightening.

'Well, they ain't boys, are they?' said Mr Piper, with the air of a person who has said something smart.

Louey would have liked to inquire how that proved they were girls, but seeing that her father continued to chuckle with the consciousness that he had said a good thing, an expression of almost womanly consideration came into her grey eyes, and she stroked his face and told him he was a 'funny papa.'

When Mr Piper had chuckled to himself three minutes longer, he grew suddenly serious.

'I'm too old a bird to be caught, eh, Poppet? You'll have to get up in the middle of the night if you want to catch *me!* You never saw any one yet who didn't get the worst of it, did you?'

'No,' assented the little girl, with something in the manner of her assent that made her seem, for the second, much the older of the two.

The distant sails had been gathering distinctness while this discussion was going on. Still mere jags against the horizon, they were at least jags which the imagination might more readily fill with ships than with anything else. Mr Piper had filled one in with a ship, which following his predetermined idea could be none other than the *Henrietta Maria* – his predetermination being assisted, it must be confessed, by the contents of a telegram he had received from the vessel's agents the night before.

'That's her, squirrel,' pointing a broad-tipped finger at something that seemed to Louey like a little dark triangle that was trying to climb over the distant water's edge. 'That's the ship that's got your Aunt Bess on board. I'll be bound she's feeling queer to-day. It's close upon thirty years since I set eyes on her, and I've buried two wives and got a son bigger than myself. And I mind the same as if it was yesterday the day she walked alongside of me in her cotton gown, when I was going to catch the Plymouth coach.'

'Is she like you, papa?' (ponderingly).

'Like me! that's a good one! I've been a rum 'un to go, in *my* day, Poppet, but I wasn't a beauty to look at. She was the sort o' girl folks 'ud turn round and have a good stare at. She was as handsome – as handsome' –

'As handsome as Laura?' suggested Louey with perfect simplicity.

'Now, I've done with you,' said Mr Piper, in a tone of severe disgust. 'You can take and go! I've had enough of you for this morning.'

He pushed away the arm that had been encircling his neck. 'I won't have my sister talked about in the same breath with Laura! She wasn't a painted Poll! She was none o' your brazen-faced hussies! When the people kep' on looking at her, she'd be none the wiser for it.'

'Don't you like me to think *my* sister pretty, too, papa?' with a pathetic stress on the 'my.'

'What do you know about what's pretty and what isn't?' retorted her father. He nevertheless allowed the small arm to creep back into its old position. 'It's handsome is as handsome does, that's what it is; it wasn't only by reason of her pretty face folks made so much o' your Aunt Bess, she was sound all through, that's what she was, and fond o' me. Why, bless you! I've seen that girl cry fit to cry her eyes out when I was talkin' o' leaving!'

'And why did you leave her, papa?'

'Why did I leave her! Do you know where she'd 'ave been now if I hadn't left her? Do you know where I'd have been if I hadn't come straight out here, and worked, and slaved, and kept my eyes open, and never missed a chance? It's fine times for you youngsters that think the world's nothink but a big playground. Fine times! Fine times!'

He stopped short, to go back fifty years at least, and see himself at Poppet's age, carrying his little sister up and down a dingy London street. In those days people who could have pudding every day in the week seemed to be bloated with riches. But if he could have had a foreshadowing of the change that half a century was to bring – have seen himself inviting this sister and her children across twelve thousand miles of sea to a grand house, with a magnificent tower, that he had built himself – a house wherein the very scullery-maid and stable-boy might have eaten pudding all day long, and did eat it, too, for all he knew to the contrary! – what would he have said? What would he have thought? What would his father – whose summit of ambition would have been reached could he have lived to see his son foreman in some well-established grocer's shop – have said or thought? There were moments when Mr Piper half doubted his identity with the toiling boy-nurse of fifty years ago – moments when it seemed that either the present or the past must be a delusion – so impossible did it appear to connect the two.

Louey knew what was coming when her father's eyes proved that his mind was given up to this inward retrospection. She knew the grumbling protest that was sure to follow. It was not that Mr Piper begrudged his children one rose in their flowery paths, one feather in their couches of down. He would have surfeited them, figuratively speaking, with both had they told him their road was not scented, their rest not luxurious enough. But it was their taking these things as such a matter of course that presented itself to him in so aggravating a light, after a reviewing of this kind. Though it is hard to say what he wanted, whether he would have had them express constant surprise and delight, whether he was tormented by an apprehension that they had no proper appreciation of the miracles he had worked. A man whose own earliest impressions are all of a battling with some uncomprehended oppression called life – that has betrayed itself to his perceptions through a hunger never quite satisfied, through chilblained feet and aching bones – finds it impossible to allow for the difficulty creatures born among kindlier surroundings must find in sympathising with his self-gratulation.

Could you accuse a pet lap-dog of heartlessness because he had no comprehension of the sensations which accompanied the baring of the ribs of a starved mongrel?

Moreover, it must be admitted that Mr Piper was inclined to cavil at much that he was responsible for himself. There had been times without end when he had encouraged boyish extravagances in George's schooldays, secretly half-amazed, half-gratified, and in a measure pleasingly tickled, at the natural way in which his son could 'lord' it, as though to 'the manner born.' But as the lad grew older, and continued to appropriate in the same natural way everything that a passing fancy inspired with a momentary value in his eyes, his father's appreciation became tinctured with irritability. He did not quarrel with him for his choice of companions; the sufficient reason that they were either 'club fellows,' or 'in society,' carrying a patent of their worthiness. For Mr Piper was not devoid of that inevitable ingredient in the character of the best of *parvenus*, that feeling by which the gratification of associating on equal terms with a better-born class is none the less keen, that it brings an unacknowledged sense of being condescended to in its wake. And he did not actually quarrel with him for his desultory turn of mind, which made him decide upon choosing a profession, upon going to Europe, upon taking up a block of country in Queensland, upon settling down on one of his father's stations, and led to his doing none of these things, though this desultoriness, apart from George, and as an abstract quality, was not one to be leniently looked upon by the man who had stuck to the 'butchering,' as Mrs Cavendish expressed it, through the early years of colonial settlement, working unflinchingly, during a succession of burning summers, in a purgatory of flies and dust. Though his reward had come, it is true, accompanied by the inevitable alloy – the alloy that, measuring itself by the fulness of the cup whose sweetness it tempers, helps so much to bring the inclined scale of human lots to one common level. What this alloy had in common with Mr Piper's grievance against George, and how its influence was the more baneful that the grievance was of the subtly-tormenting description of an undefined ill (for the mind has its interior and un-get-at-able organis-ation as well as the body), can hardly be made clear without the transcribing of some of Mr Piper's impressions. I say 'impressions,' because he was conscious of their disturbing influence, yet lacked the power of analysing them, and elevating them into thoughts that can be classified.

The first of these impressions, then, was a general sense of not being properly estimated, none the less disquieting for its vagueness.

Large self-approval is very sustaining, no doubt, but even the most stolid of self-approvers cannot subsist altogether on themselves. And to a man of Mr Piper's temperament even the evidences of what he had accomplished that cried out to him from his tower and his verandah were only witnesses to the insensibility of his human belongings.

There was George, now, a young man who 'kep' his racehorses' – his father had been carrying dry goods round to his master's customers at George's age – who had his 'bottle of champagne to his dinner every night' – his father had never tasted champagne before he was five-and-thirty – who smoked his Havannahs before breakfast of a morning – his father could not afford to spend sixpence a week on tobacco at George's age – and what store do you suppose 'my gentleman' set by it all? How often did it cross his mind that he'd have been no better than a 'nobody' if it hadn't been for his father? For as to his book-learning – apart from their low commercial value – Mr Piper was inclined to look upon the classics with dubious faith; not wholly sure whether they were in any way answerable for what he called the 'jargon' in which George would sometimes talk to Laura – a jargon Mr Piper nevertheless strained his ears and his mind to their utmost stretch to catch the meaning of – baffled and incredulous of his own interpretation of the drift of it, when he could make out nothing more than this, that George, with what Mr Piper called 'the ball at his feet,' didn't hold much by life altogether. He'd 'set along with Laura' at the breakfast-table, when they'd nothing to do but to think how they'd enjoy themselves, and 'he'd talk' and 'she'd talk,' and 'they'd spout their scraps of poetry, that hadn't an ounce of the sense any good, honest, old rhyme could show; and you'd think, to hear them, they were doing their Maker a favour by condescending to go on living at all!'

At such times, if Mr Piper could have been invested with the authority of a Chinese parent, he would have threatened to knock them on the head, both as a salve to his own irritation, and by way of making them 'change their tune.' As it was, he could only find an outlet for his perplexed indignation by sarcastic allusions, containing broad references to the good appetites of the arguers. For a very strong ingredient in the alloy I have referred to – stronger, perhaps, than Mr Piper had any conception of himself – might have been

traced to the depressing influence of that *cui bono* philosophy of which
George and Laura, as was consistent with their perfect physical health,
and general flush of pleasurable distractions, were the natural
exponents. Its incomprehensibility, too, made it none the less
oppressive. It might be the right thing, by what he could learn of these
'new-fangled notions,' to call the Deity over the coals at the breakfast-
table, but to Mr Piper's mind the bringing of His name in at all, out
of church, or perhaps, once in a way, at a burial, was depressing and
uncalled for. What people wanted when the whole thing was 'cut and
dried for them beat him altogether!' There was a good kind of a place,
to which he and other people who paid their debts were bound – and
whose reconnoitring he was anxious to defer as long as possible – and
there was a place in which murderers, and people responsible for bad
debts, would 'catch it hot.' What more could any one want to know?
All the rest was the parson's business. If other people would only
mind their's, and learn to do something useful – something that would
put the bread into their mouths – there'd be less of this folly in the
world. And when he considered how George – who'd never earned
a sixpence in his life; and Laura, who'd never done a hand's turn of
work worth a red cent – would 'cotton' to each other, talking their
'gibberish' in his presence, and 'smiling' – actually smiling – when he
gave them '*his* opinion for what it was worth,' Mr Piper had some
ado to refrain from making use of the 'knock-down argument' which
is 'but a word and a blow.' Indeed, if George had not been his only
son, and endowed, besides, with a something that carried off even his
nonchalant treatment of his father and his father's wealth with grace,
and if Laura had not been a kind of sacred trust, of which his little
Poppet was a reminder, Mr Piper would have turned them both out
'neck and crop' long ago. But separately, not together. The reflex
action of pessimism, the tormenting apprehension, that he and his
belongings were undervalued, these, indeed, had their part in his
share of alloy. But the bitterest compound of all – the trouble that
would have made the alloy outweigh the good a thousand-fold – was
the possibility he dared not even contemplate – the possibility that
George should 'make up' to Laura with any serious intent, and thus
make common cause with his enemy.

Taking this dread into consideration, it will be easy to understand
that it was not entirely in obedience to the dictates of brotherly
munificence that the Cavendish family were now sailing up the bay
in that indistinct speck Mr Piper had detected from his tower window.

The moral support he might look for from four recruits, whose allegiance he counted upon as a kind of purchased right, would make him strong in his self-assertion again; and if it could only chance that Laura should be cut out by one of his nieces, Mr Piper felt that the maintaining of his sister's family for the rest of his days would be a small price to pay for such a triumph, for his views for George were free from a mercenary bias. He did not hold by marrying money for money's sake. If he could keep what he had in the family, so much the better. And if it came to birth, you couldn't want to look much higher than a Cavendish. Though even birth Mr Piper subordinated to wealth, as a kind of accessory that had very little weight in the money market, and, indeed, was only to be tolerated matched with means, seeing that the longest pedigree in the world would never give you credit at a cookshop.

If, in thus communing with himself, Mr Piper had been silent for as long a time as it has taken me to interpret his mood, Louey, you may be sure, would not have played the *rôle* of a mere passive little squirrel. As old as any changeling in detecting the signs of an inward brooding on her father's face, with wondrous intuition of the place which needed the balm, she would have acted her part of the caressing and admiring squirrel, full of cajolery, but avoiding the faintest mani- festation of anything like pity – as a feeling not to be considered possible in relation to him; soothing (as she had so often soothed before) the chafed susceptibilities by making him feel that here, at least, was a soul who saw him as he was. If she, like George, took her everyday life as a matter of course, handling the big illustrated volumes, whose green-and-gilt magnificence even now raised an old respectful awe in Mr Piper's breast, with just as much unconcern as though they had been the Sunday-school penny tracts of his boyhood, at least she showed appreciation when he gave her a present. And if Mr Piper had a weakness almost as strong as the afore-mentioned weakness of wanting to be held in proper esteem, it was the importance he attached to the fact that his presents should be made much of.

You will see that his exultation in his wealth was not that of a wholly selfish nature, the making people happy with it in his own way, and the being constantly reminded by them of the happiness he could give and did give, constituting almost an essential to his due appreciation of it. Your people who couldn't show more gratitude than to prate about 'the good of living' were not to his taste, but he would 'bring them to their bearings' when he had his own belongings about them.

So thinking, Mr Piper directed his little girl to give him the field-glass from the side table, and adjusted it to his sight, scanning the horizon again for that vessel which was to contain so much healing might (it was as well that he had no inner vision of the cabin scene of the night before), which was to bring him all the appreciation his soul craved, and read undiscerning people a lesson they would not forget. But while he had been weighing his grievances a light haze had obscured the distant bay, and Mr Piper was fain to leave the *Henrietta Maria* in its shadowy meshes. But travelling his glass about, as one who would not be foiled of seeing something that his everyday eyesight might have failed to bring before him, he brought his own lawn, with its surrounding shrubbery, directly in the range of his vision. And with it a sight that put for the moment all thought of the *Henrietta Maria* out of his head.

It was the sight of his own son George, who, seen as Mr Piper was seeing him, through his glass, from a height of nearly a hundred feet above the ground, showed nothing more remarkable than the top of a white puggery, two well-defined shoulders, and a figure that seemed to narrow gradually to the ground, where it was finished off by what might have been passed off for two sharp, little painted supports, but were, in truth, the brightly broidered slippers he was treading down upon the closely-cut turf. He was strolling across the lawn with the easy, half listless saunter peculiar to a man who has nothing particular to do, and more than sufficient time to do it in, walking with his eyes directed towards his slippers, which he was probably admiring, in the perfect unrestraint that implies a belief in one's freedom from all observation. For the lawn, it must be explained, was on the side of the house that looked upon the bay, and being hedged in for three parts of its circuit by a thick plantation of carefully-trimmed pittosporums – those sentinels of the choicest and the humblest of Victorian bowers alike – and facing on its undiscovered side only the still drawn blinds of the drawing-room and library bay windows below, further screened by the broad verandah in front of them, and a balconied bedroom window immediately above, seemed to give full assurance of its unassailable privacy. That a hundred feet above, from the tower's broad loophole, a field glass should be betraying all his movements, and betraying them moreover to two paternal eyes agog with carping curiosity, was an idea that could never have suggested itself to George. Or he might possibly – I do not say certainly – for it was his conviction that he regulated his life with an entire disregard of what he called his father's 'prejudices,' have continued his saunter across the lawn, and so, disappearing into the path that bordered it, have given Mr Piper no greater satisfaction than was to be found in a last examination of the top of his puggery. But seeing that he could have no suspicion of the scrutiny directed towards him from above, nor any means of hearing Mr Piper say, 'What the devil!' and 'What's my gentleman up to now?' or of hearing Louey's piping rejoinder, 'He's been out to the stables, papa' – he acted with the inconsequence that was the natural fruit of his delusion.

Arrived in the middle of the lawn, he stopped, looked harder at his feet than ever, and turned abruptly towards a flower-bed, whence it seemed to Mr Piper that he gathered sand and pebbles instead of flowers.

The glasses were now becoming dim to the old man's eager sight. He rubbed them impatiently, and held them to his eyes as before, pushing away the little hand that sought his shoulder caressingly. 'You sit still; do you hear, my girl?' he said, with an impatience the squirrel seldom aroused. 'Stables! – fine stables he's after! He'd better let me see that jade trapesing after him – that's all!'

'Papa, *please* don't lean out so far. Why mustn't George go out on the lawn? Oh, papa! I *do* wish you wouldn't! See, he's going in now!'

'*Is* he going in?' Mr Piper's scorn seemed to crush the child into silence; but as she knelt, mute, by his side, her grey eyes grew large with wistful meaning.

For the answer was not of the kind her oppressed little soul was praying to witness. George was standing still in the middle of the lawn, with the pebbles in his hand, and aiming them with nice precision in the direction of the balconied bedroom above the drawing-room. There was an assurance in his easy manner of swinging his arm round, and flinging these missives in the same unswerving line, that spoke of long practice. He was as dexterous as the ruddy stripling David, and, putting Mr Piper into the place of the raging, blundering Goliath, he was wounding him with his smooth pebbles as deeply – aye, more deeply, it may be – than David wounded the giant. For the throwing of a pebble, or the very wave of a hand, may still leave its impress on the brain, and I am not sure whether the pebble which enters by the temples and stills all brain throbbings for ever be of so much crueller import than the pebble which is directed through the heart, and lodges itself in that poor, irritable, dependent incomprehensibility we call the affections.

So George's pebbles were carrying a twofold message, and the one they bore to Mr Piper was not received with welcome.

'So that's your game, is it!' he said. 'You're going to fetch 'er down, are you? Just let me see you do it – that's all! I only want you to let me see you do it.'

As if by way of obliging Mr Piper by an instant compliance with his earnest request, a woman's figure emerged at this moment from the path that skirted the house, and advanced swiftly towards the centre of the lawn. Bareheaded – with fair hair drawn up in the fashion of the day – all that at first sight met the angry gaze behind the field-glass was a twisted layer of bright fair plaits, disposed like a Minerva's helmet. It is probable that they covered a pile of padding, but they covered it honestly at least – that is to say, all that met the eye was genuine hair, with its roots on its owner's head and not on some pauper's skull. There was nothing classic, but something, I must admit, that was infinitely becoming to fair hair in this regal adjustment of its soft profusion. Provided always it approached to the hair at which Mr Piper was scowling through his glass, that is to say, was lustrous, not dank – strokable hair, that would slip through the fingers like pliable spun silk, and leave no impress of grease or roughness behind.

But Mr Piper was not in a mood to detect the beauties of light-reflecting hair. The field-glass in his trembling hands took another turn, and swept over the woman's figure; and now it might be seen what justified his applying to her that sourly-emphasised epithet of a 'painted Poll.' For brightness – the brightness of a Watteau on porcelain – the brightness of a parterre – the brightness of anything in nature made up of delicate, variegated colour – seemed to cling around her as she walked. With the tender green of the turf and the polished green of the shrubs as a background, she would have been a gem on a Dresden vase. Even to Mr Piper's spiritually detracting and actually contracting vision, a something of radiance – the radiance that might surround:

> 'A daughter of the gods – divinely tall,
> And most divinely fair' –

seemed to emanate from her as she trod.

And wherein lay the secret of it all? In the French dressing-gown of pale pink and blue, she was trailing in a line of colour behind her on the grass? In the blue satin shoes, with heels only permissible on china? In the flesh-tones so admirably contrasted on her face, in their blending of pink and white, as betrayed to Mr Piper, when his glass was wandering over her? No! Yet I think it must have been that all these things were such perfect complements to a woman in the flush of youth and health. Drape the dressing-gown around other than firm white flesh, dispose the flaxen wig about a shrivelled face, and then look, if you will, for the light-diffusing potency.

Failing which it must still be allowed that French dressing-gowns and satin shoes are amazing helps to a pretty woman, which, I may add, for the comfort of all who are not modelled upon the Greek goddess type, it is very possible to be without in any way competing with a Diana. And to Laura they were more than helps – they were almost props, her main charm, as I have said, lying for the most part in her colouring. 'As handsome as a picture,' men say, implying that it is in the warmth of tone, as well as in the grace of the outline, that handsomeness – properly speaking – has its domain. 'As *handsome* as a statue,' no one would say, because the beauty breathed by passionless marble is less of the kind that paints itself on the eye than of the kind which touches some inward sensibility. '*As beautiful* as a statue,' we say of that beauty which, following Victor Hugo's idea, is the embodiment of the absolute, and may reach, like an eternal truth, even the perceptions of the colour-blind, or of one groping in the dark.

Laura's handsomeness, then, took you by storm through its glow, like one of Turner's later delicious jumbles. There was no stopping to object to the size and derisiveness of the lips in view of their redness. You were hurled past a suspicion that the cheek-bones outlined a little too prominently the shape of the skull beneath by the perfection of the bloom that overspread them. How take objection to the undue width of space that divided eyes of such decided violet? There was such a feast of colour for your regaling in the shining hair, light brown against the face, but gathering gilt as it narrowed to an end, in the soft transparency of nose and forehead, in the rose on the cheeks, and the crimson on the lips, that you no more thought of picking to pieces the parts which presented such a banquet to your eyes, than you would think of asking, when viewing some inspired tossing of his palette against his canvas by Turner, whether you were looking at it right side up. But put Laura's tall, slight body into a dowdy wrap, on a frosty morning, and your eyes, less intoxicated, might find the substance hardly in accordance with the exterior; you might even wonder, in your more critical mood, whether when the *beauté du diable* of a virgin's painted skin had abandoned her, there would still survive in the unabashed eyes and mocking mouth much of the captivating influence of to-day.

Comparing Mr Piper's field-glass to a burning-glass, and he himself to the sun pouring smouldering beams upon the object it is held over, it may be said that the point which concentrated all his burning rage into a focus was reached when this gaily painted figure was espied by his son.

'The hussy! the painted hussy!' said Mr Piper, purple, as George took two forward steps, from which all the listlessness seemed to have flown.

But words (which even in the mouths of poets and blasphemers still leave the acutest emotions unexpressed, betraying more the *strength* of the feeling than the feeling itself which has given rise to them) – words failed Mr Piper as the top of the blonde head and the puggery seemed to merge into one; and for some long-drawn instants, during which nothing but a feeble shaking of his field-glass was indicative of Mr Piper's frame of mind, George and the painted figure presented a duality that might have merited a place on the frieze of a column in the alcove of an 'Œil de Bœuf.'

The searching testimony of the field-glass betrayed no coyness in the embrace on either side. And when it might have appeared that each, like Fatima, had 'drawn the other's soul' in one long kiss through the other's lips, the pair walked, hand in hand, with an air that suggested the unabashed reciprocity of feeling of mythological lovers, to a sort of couch of flexible steel that stood on one side of the lawn. Then it could be seen that the surface of the puggery overtopped by about a couple of inches the summit of the fair plaits.

Mr Piper, choking by this time with impotent wrath, for he was in the uncomfortable position, at once so elevated and so helpless, assigned by modern spiritists to their disembodied and defenceless friends, was aware of the imploring touch of small fingers between his shirt-collar and the back of his neck. A little palm carried piteous entreaty as it wandered furtively at the base of his skull. Louey's grey eyes were big with a want she would almost have surrendered her small soul to satisfy, the want of doing away with discord among all who were so dear to her! It was not to establish a harmony between herself and the outer world, in their seeking for which we owe such inspired beauties to the sublime egoism of poets, that the poor child

aimed. She was in harmony with everything in Piper's Hill, even to a
huge and carefully tended doll. The rest were, as I have said, in
harmony with her. Yet, I think, though to so acutely sensitive a
temperament severity of regard would have had almost the effect of
physical ill-treatment, she would willingly have borne the scowls Mr
Piper directed at Laura, the shrugs George hardly pretended to
conceal when his father's conclusive 'You are a fool' put a stop to
some argument, the scornful ring in Laura's laugh, have borne them
all in her own unobtrusive little person for the dear delight of seeing
her father, her brother, and her sister in unison.

There is an oppression to a small person like Louey in manifes-
tations of ill-will towards each other on the part of grown-up people,
that even parents sometimes can hardly realise – a something that
puts their 'world out of joint,' a foretaste of the lesson that soon
enough surely will be thrust upon them. That bitter lesson, which is
to explain how the delusions that have fooled them are sure to be
unmasked, and how of joys here and hereafter they cannot fail to find
out, sooner or later, that these and those are vanities alike! Reflections,
it may be, that strike some responsive chord in us all, but which
insisted upon to every fresh generation, oppress it unduly with the
accumulated gloom of every later experience of life, until we might
wonder that the heart is not taken out of it at the outset. Indeed, I
sometimes think if, in lieu of the protest so often made at the close
of a life that seems to have been a failure, there were a little thought
of mercifully deceiving such hopeful youth as is still left in the world,
we might have had a race of less penetration, perhaps, but of greater
buoyancy, more akin to the beings that sprang, so the legends tell us,
from the unreflecting, joyous life of the forests and fountains of a
golden age.

It is a question whether the mere accident of an agnate kinship
with George would have made Louey so anxious to screen him from
her father's wrath, if her childish sympathy had not been so powerfully
stirred in the cause of his attachment to Laura. The holding on to
those whom she was so fond of, the binding of them still closer to
her and to each other, was a sort of desire inborn in the child, having
its far-reaching roots perhaps in that longing expressed by the mother
who had died in giving birth to her. I don't know either what dim
distrust of the world beyond Piper's Hill, in which street-crossings
and railway platforms presented themselves to her in the light of
shocking and mysterious man-traps, may have haunted her childish

fancy. But it is certain that the wistful, yearning look that gave her eyes so touching an expression in the setting of her small freckled face, never gave place to such a fulness of satisfaction as when her father, her brother, and her sister were all, as it were, under her eye, and safe to remain indoors for the night. And when, in addition to this delicious sense of their security, it fell out, by some rare and joyful chance, that Mr Piper had a mind for a rubber, and offered to take 'dummy' against George and Laura, saying he would 'take the conceit out of them,' and Louey had the bliss of surveying the loved trio, all at the same table, out of the reach of carts and trains, all absorbed in something that gave them a 'together' look, as she called it – her cup of joy was full to its very brim. Sitting on a stool between her father and Laura, and transferring it noiselessly from time to time to her father's other side, lest George should feel himself overlooked – with the big doll brought into a sort of partnership in her bliss – Louey's nervous little face wore an air of contentment that it may have been as well there was no mother at hand to witness. I think, following her expression at such times, her notion of a real heaven must have been a place in which a celestial whist-table and an impalpable celestial dummy would never-endingly have prolonged these rare moments of perfect peace.

The establishing then of the earthly permanence of such a paradise, by seeing her brother George and her sister Laura become her twofold brother and sister, the heavenly complication of more closely riveted ties, which would result from making George her brother-in-law as well as her brother, and Laura her sister-in-law as well as her sister, seemed to Louey one of those perfect arrangements which it might almost behove a deity to put himself out of the way to further. What night fabrics she spun, lying awake in her bed, that all tended to this completely happy ending! But the bringing about of complete happiness nearly always involved a sacrifice somewhere, a deduction drawn from theological showing, as well as from the tales in her book of folk-lore. Oh! if she could only be the victim! If she might only have a bad illness that could enable her to plead with her father for Laura, and with Laura for her father! If she could only have a vision of the three, Mr Piper in the middle, George on his right, Laura on his left, all smiling at her, and at each other! She could almost have braved the black abyss that separated her from her mother, and left them in the strength of a trinity in unity to the pitfalls of platforms and street-crossings. In pity to the extreme misery this morning's experience was calculated to bring, Mr Piper might have dissembled some of the intensity of his fury; but his anger, like all passions which get the upper hand, was wholly selfish for the moment, and incapable, therefore, of considering anything out of itself. He turned such a face of swollen rage towards his little girl, the eyes seeming actually to throw out sparks at her, that she drew back her hand from his neck, and uttered unknowingly the sort of half shrill, half suppressed scream, a sudden horror or a sudden change in a face we know startles out of us – 'Papa! Papa! Papa!'

It was as if she had been imploring her father to come back and replace this dreadful effigy of himself in front of her. The vehemence of her terror shook Mr Piper's first expression of mere savage vindictiveness. The face was her father's again, but her father, puffed out and purple as she had never seen it before.

Still shaking his field-glass in the direction of the steel couch, he apostrophised the bright-hued pair upon it with the incoherence of a rage that uses speech only as turkey-cocks do their gobbling capacities, that is to say, as a mere outlet for offended spleen. But, as his threats took shape, the natural predominant conviction that nobody could get the better of *him* lent its colouring to their import.

'That's the way, is it? I'll show 'em who's master here! I'll show them what's what! I'll be even with them! I knew their little game! Think I didn't know it? Oh – you – ' with a splutter of helpless fury, as a fresh merging of the plaits into the puggery gave evidence of some nearer communion – 'Look you here, Louey' (turning upon her with trembling fingers that had almost lost their grasp of the glass), 'you take and tell 'em' (very impressively) – this old mid-county idiom, caught from his mother, who was not a Londoner, was always used unconsciously by Mr Piper in the moments of his strongest emotion – 'you take and tell 'em from me, mind you, that I'll turn the pair of 'em out of doors! Never you fret! I'll turn 'em out of doors, right enough! He shan't have a sixpence, you can tell him – not a sixpence! You take and tell him *that!* We'll see what my gentleman's good for once in a way! You tell him to come up here and I'll tell him so myself!'

All this time he was pushing the child in front of him to the door, such a white-faced, shrinking mite of humanity, with every freckle brought into relief by her bloodless skin, so wondrously altered from the trim little creature who had toiled up the tower stairs to recruit

herself by those old-fashioned sighs at the top, that in any other mood
Mr Piper must have had her in his arms forthwith.

'You tell him to come! Tell him to come up here! Tell him *I* want
him' (he was fumbling for the door handle with his shaking hands).
'She'd better keep out of *my* way, that's all! You can take and tell her
that! You can tell her she's a shameless hussy, do you hear, and that's
my opinion about *her*' (he almost drove the cowed child across the
landing at the top of the tower stairs). 'Tell her she's a shameless
jade,' he reiterated, 'and *I* said so.'

Outside the tower window red sunbeams were already bronzing the
distant mist, bringing a warning of what was to be expected from the
sun when he should have scattered the heavy, low-lying haze. At
Piper's Hill it would be an ideal day for the welcoming of sea-tossed
travellers, a day of calm repose. But the calm was all without. I wonder
there is no name in pagan mythology for the malevolent demon, the
oppressor of every domestic circle, whose influence is so remarkable
in bringing about our catastrophes on the very days of all days when
our minds are attuned to the expectation of some blissful or disturbing
event; who gives the baby convulsions on the morning of a dinner-
party, who waits with fiendish intent, through months of an uneventful
daily routine, the more surely to entrap us the instant we step out of
it. Every family recognises the existence of such a demon. We have
all been caught in his grip. He had fastened his cruel claws already
upon two victims, taken unawares at Piper's Hill this morning, of
whom the one, whom you may recognise as Mr Piper, was again
standing at his old post by the window, now making efforts to steady
the glass before his eyes with his shaking hands, anon rubbing it up
with a sort of mechanical frenzy, as if he defied it to translate such
sights any longer. Whereas the other, whom to recognise by aught
save the downcast red head would be a matter of difficulty, seeing
that the hand which is not clinging to the balustrade is pressing a
square-inch handkerchief over the childish face with a sort of piteous
apery of adult self-control, is descending the tower stairs to the garden.
But with a gait so unlike a child's – with such a forlornness of matured
grief in the very manner of holding the miniature handkerchief to the
quivering mouth – with such a submissive intercepting of the large
salt tears that seem to tighten her cheeks as they dry upon it. That is
no conventional child's giref:

'Like the dewdrop on the rose,

When next the summer breeze comes by,
And waves the bush, the flower is dry.'

That is the grief which has power to set materialists wondering
whether all is said when the physical well-being is secured. For here
was no question of bodily pain to anybody, yet the manifestation of
an anguish beside which mere bodily suffering would be as nothing.

The child had come into a world of cross-purposes, instinct with
a craving to hedge herself round with the blended loves of father,
brother, and sister; and her magic circle had turned into a ring of
torture, with spokes directed inwards that pierced her soul. That was
all. A fanciful grief, if you will. Yet it remains a question whether the
grief which first changes the cry of 'Where is God?' into 'Is there a
God?' can ever be truly called fanciful, though it reach only a child's
immature perceptions. We feel for a musical ear upon which a never-
ending discord sounds its jarring notes; but what can we say in behalf
of the soul's impalpable nerves, when their keenest sensibilities are
violated? What after rapture can ever atone for this first initiation into
the irremediable hitch as to whose origin such blatant doctrines are
sounded even now? Is there indeed fit answer 'behind the veil,' or
such answer only as a 'Nirvana' can offer – which silences for ever
the questioner and the question?

CHAPTER III

———————•———————

The Meaning Of What He Saw

'For aught that ever I could read,
Could ever hear by tale or history,
The course of true love never did run smooth.'
— SHAKESPEARE

It was now the turn of George and Laura to feel the demon's claw. He had done Mr Piper a bad turn that morning. All springtide influences, all promise of harmonious family meeting, seemed to have fled from the tower, thanks to the demon's venom; and he had torn at a most innocent little heart besides, and transformed its small world into one vast chaotic misery. But what would it have to say to the couple on the garden bench of pliable steel below? You have had a bird's-eye view of the pair already. You have seen what an idyllic pair it is – what lending and blending of mutual radiance – what an occasional confusion of plaits and puggery, calling forth some very ugly words from Mr Piper on his vantage ground. But come a little nearer, and have it all confirmed! You will see such an assurance in the very attitude of the lovers as might make the demon pause – something that, even from a hundred feet below, carries to Mr Piper such an assertion of his impotence to harm them as helps, perhaps, to make his fury so apparently extravagant and ungovernable.

For there seems little doubt that their pursuit of philosophy has not stood in the way of their prosecuting with equal industry their other pursuit of love-making. Indeed, I am not sure that it has not aggravated it, some philosophies – the philosophy of pessimism especially – tending to the grasping of every compensating sensation, than which, it is almost universally allowed, none more compensating for the moment have been discovered than those evoked by love-making. And

the deeper George and Laura go, the more the demand for this kind
of compensation seems to occur, until, as you have seen, to support
the burden of existence on a morning of perfume-breathing, bud-
opening balm, and to support it under the dismal conditions of a
French dressing-gown on the one hand, and gold-embroidered slippers on the other, it has become necessary for the philosophers to
meet and embrace with that unabashed ardour which, as Moliére
would put it, raises Mr Piper's bile.

After which an adjournment to the steel bench for the exchange *à
discrétion* of fresh compensating potentialities, or the renewal of a
discussion, perhaps, on such a topic as the overplus of humanity in
the civilised world. Though George's last remark, as he draws the
edifice of plaits to the more particular neighbourhood of his collar-
bone, hardly seems to tend in that direction this morning.

'For I see no other way out of it,' he is saying earnestly. 'You may
call marriage a folly if you will. I grant you it is a folly in the abstract,
and suicidal, and anything you like. But we must commit follies for
the sake of expediency. Up to a certain point we are always committing
them. And then ours is such an exceptional case. Don't you think
ours is an exceptional case, Laura?'

'I've heard hypochondriacs say that,' says Laura. 'I suppose lovers
say it too. I suppose everybody says it of his own case.'

'Well, and he acts accordingly. He applies an exceptional remedy.'

'You call *marriage* an exceptional remedy? It's horribly common,
George, and – well – I suppose it *is* a remedy. A very effectual one
sometimes.'

'Don't use that tone, Laura,' George says very gravely. 'Remember
it's of *us* I'm talking.'

No one knows better than George how to throw a whole world of
tender reproach into his inflection upon the '*us*.' No one better than
Laura how to make him feel her instant interpretation of it – by the
slightest additional pressure of her fair head against his neck.

'So that,' continues George, acknowledging that mute atonement
by stroking the delicately-veined wrist dependent from the dressing-
gown sleeve, 'there is no alternative, my darling. We must do like that
politic old fellow – Naaman – was it? We must bow ourselves down
in the House of Rimmon!'

'What is it you propose – *just?*' asks Laura.

She speaks with the usual curtness of expression, but the manner,
the intonation, the very ring of the notes of her voice – somewhat

hard and metallic in its everyday use – are indescribably attuned to some overmastering sentiment whenever she addresses herself to George. Her utterance, so short and sharp to the indifferent world, becomes almost tremulous in its tenderness when it is employed for him. Each is aware of the transformation of being that the presence of the other seems to bring. The complete dropping on George's side of that well-bred apathy so galling to Mr Piper – on Laura's side, the melting away of the asperity, the sarcastic rejoinders, the uncompromising disregard of feelings with which she does not happen to sympathise. And it is all the same, whether they sit for an hour without exchanging a single word, or whether they think aloud, as is common to them in each other's company. The personal presence is all-sufficient in itself, the mutual sense of well-being is complete. That either should have a fancy, a dislike, an interest not known to the other, would seem like employing artifice towards oneself. Not that Laura sees entirely through George's eyes – not that George entirely endorses all Laura's demolishing tendencies. Simply that each mind is perfectly transparent to the other – a result not always arrived at even when actual love and no semblance of him has linked a couple of souls – and arrived at sometimes without the intervention of love at all – as when some strong sympathy lends a clairvoyant power of the sort to friends or brothers.

To Laura's question of what he proposed doing, George, for all reply, draws her closer yet to his side, and propounds the following question –

'You love me, Laura?'

'Why do you ask?'

'And you know that I love you?'

'Well?'

'Well now, I ask you, can it affect a love like ours to swear it in a church? Shall I be less "George" because I'm your husband, or you less "Laura" because the world calls you "Mrs Piper." It's not a pretty name, I know, but I suppose you won't hold me responsible for *that*, any more than for the other shortcomings of my progenitors. Don't we know each other through and through? Could we find "mates" if we looked for them all our lives, excepting in each other? You know whether I'm an advocate for marriage or not. But the objections to it don't hold good in our case, I only live a sort of half-life when you're away. And you, do you feel so independent of me that you can look forward to a time when we shall live together no

longer? You don't answer. What sort of idea have you, Laura? Do you
suppose the exchanging of a few promises before a man in a white
gown must be so damaging to our love? We shan't be able to help
acting up to them, as you know. Take our position into account for
a minute. There's my father dinning into my ears the names of all
the unmarried girls in Melbourne from morning till night. There are
you – in a position to listen to offers of marriage from every stranger,
as if you had not put your heart into mine long ago. It's not to be
borne any longer. And think what it'll be when the Cavendish horde
descends upon us! One of my cousins is meant for me. What! you
didn't know? Of course she is. The youngest. A "plum!" that's the
word I was telling you about. A regular plum! And you're going to
expose me to all the equivocal intimacy of cousinship with a "plum,"
when a little word would set matters straight at once; and enable me
to stop all the persecution – fathers, aunts, uncles, cousins, all the
boiling – and say once for all, "Laura is my *wife!*" Oh yes, you may
smile! I can feel you're smiling' (passing his hand round her chin);
'but call it old prejudice – anything you like. There's something that
takes my fancy about the sound of "my wife." It seems to put anybody
else's meddling with you so entirely out of the question. Now, what
have you to say? You can be eloquent sometimes, Laura, but you'll
have to make the most of your eloquence to convince me that I'm
wrong.'

'You *are* wrong, nevertheless,' replies Laura with decision. She
paused for a few seconds, as though the better to weigh her words.
'You're wrong, because you're arguing against only one of my reasons,
and that the weakest one. I believe you think I hold out against your
new crotchet of making me marry you because I won't be inconsistent
– because I won't belie all I've said so often. But, you dear donkey!'
– a lapse, accompanied by a fresh agitation of the field-glass at the
tower window – 'who would be such a fool as to let a general theory
interfere with individual happiness? I'd like to see all the paupers in
the Benevolent Asylum swept into the Yarra – no, chloroformed and
burnt – but I'm not going round to do it myself and be hung for it!
Well, then,' with great deliberation, 'though I abominate the system
of marriage, though I think the yoking of two people together without
a chance of release – as if the yoke mightn't gall them any day –
perfectly barbarous and absurd – still, in view of our "exceptional
case" – there, don't be demonstrative till you've heard me to the end
– in view, as I said, of our "exceptional case," I'd have gone off with

you to the registrar's any morning – no, *nothing* would induce me to go to church – and have signed myself Laura Piper, instead of Laura Lydiat! I'd have done it to-day as far as that goes, *but* you must hear me out, George, for this *but* upsets all the rest. There are the best of worldly and practical reasons for refusing point blank, under any circumstances whatever, to marry you for the present.'

'You will tell me these best of reasons, I suppose?' says George. His voice is constrained. Laura's last words sound like the outcome of the reflections, matured and positive.

'Reason number one, then, is your father. He's not a bad nature, but fearfully *borné*. I *can't* help rubbing him up the wrong way! He irritates me so inconceivably. In return for which – he hates me! That's the only word, George; it's downright hate. It really almost makes me laugh sometimes to see his face. If you were to marry me he wouldn't let us have a penny to live upon. And, George dear, we say life's a poor look-out, but think what it would be to you if we'd nothing to live upon! It's bearable, you say, *now*. My little income keeps me in clothes, barely' (adjusting the lace within her sleeve with a sigh). 'Now, just suppose he turned us out of doors! What could we do? Go and select on one of his stations? That wouldn't be a bad notion; but even *that* we could do better without being married. We'd have a selection apiece then, wouldn't we?'

'I know where we'd select,' says George, laughing. 'We'd peg out an allotment near the main line of rail – But I fancy I see *you* working, Laura!'

'I fancy I see *you*!' retorts Laura; 'you'd turn it into a training-ground, and take me out to see the horses gallop in the morning. That would be work enough for *you* for the day! We'd drive, and read, and play duets the rest of the time, eh?'

'I fancy I see the governor's expression!' says George, his mind still running on the subject of the selection. 'It's the cheek of the idea that fetches me. I believe he'd tell his manager to hunt you out with the stockwhip!'

'Well, I'm afraid I don't mean to give him the chance,' she replies. 'You grant he would make us paupers if we married in defiance of him. Is that established to your satisfaction, sir?'

'N-no; not entirely. If you were only a little more politic.'

'But as I *can't* be politic?'

'Well, do what I want. Marry me privately.'

'How would that alter our case,' objects Laura, 'if it were a marriage we dared not declare? Besides, this brings my other reason against it to the front. You said just now your father intended you for one of your cousins. Now, I know, George, when you hear what I am going to say, you will think, "That is one of Laura's extravagant notions;" but if with so little money on my side, and the prospect of so much on yours, I would still have ventured to marry you without a suspicion of your supposing there to be any question of inequality between us, I deserve to be listened to, when I tell you my motives for wanting you to be entirely free just now. I am all yours – am I not? And I believe you to be mine. Don't be vexed, George, I *know* you are all mine, but if I thought a signing of deeds or a swearing of oaths were necessary to keep you to me – if I thought, when your cousin, the "plum" one is here, any legal claim I might have on you had one hair's weight of restraining power – I should let your love go through mere distrust and misery. As if a sentiment could be of the least value that requires to be kept in its place by law. No; look at your cousin, if you will, with indifferent eyes, because you have found the woman you want already, but don't be debarred from looking at her for any other reason in the world. I shall like to see you together. Do you know, George, I've never seen you in the everyday society of another woman yet. But I am not afraid, my love; I am not afraid.'

'It's poor justice you do me, all the same,' says George, responding to this effusion by raising the pretty wrist to his lips. 'You speak as if I urged a marriage upon you as a guarantee against myself. Don't you see, I only want to be able to fall back upon it in case we're driven into a corner?'

'But you can't fall back upon it while your father's alive. It would only make things worse.'

'But what do you mean to do, in Heaven's name? Never marry me at all? Hurl the gauntlet in the face of the world? Don't you know that you'll be worsted?'

'I mean,' answers Laura, with quiet determination, 'to let things take their course while Mr Piper lives, or while he remains of the same mind. I won't have you disinherited, and through me, upon any pretext whatever. Don't worry about the future, George. I like going out, though I don't care much about the people, and I won't keep house with you, and not take your name first, I promise you; because it's not agreeable to be a target for all Mrs Grundy's store of stones. But let that be for the present. As things are I will not marry you now. I won't have anything but our mutual love hamper you when your cousin comes, and I won't run the risk of making you a pauper. Why can't you let things remain as they are?'

'Because they *can't* remain as they are always; you don't take into account all sorts of risks. If I allowed you to be compromised it would be too late. You don't think, you don't consider, Laura. How do you know what my father may know? How do you suppose' –

'Nonsense!' interrupts Laura, the pink on her cheeks deepening until it seems to reach the very roots of her hair. 'What right has Mr Piper, or any one else, to *suppose*? Hasn't it always been so? Usen't the very servants to say of us, long ago, "What one says the other'll swear to!" You want to frighten me, that's all.'

'I wish I could, my darling, if I frightened you into prudence. What safeguard have we as it is? Why, even this morning – we'll only suppose now that my father had been behind the pittosporum hedge all this time, and that' –

'But as I can't suppose anything so ridiculous!' interposes Laura. 'O George, sit up, and look demure. Don't look at *me*! Look anywhere. Here's somebody coming! Ah!' with a breath of relief, 'it's only Hester.'

'What, the dreamer?' says George; 'the Joseph, the trimmer! Here you are, red-head, come over here! Laura and I were just saying we would put you into a pit. We can't have you cutting us out any longer. Come along, Chick! Why, what's the matter? What's up now? You look as if you had been put into the pit already, and never fished out! I never saw such a Godforsaken expression in my life.'

'Hester!' cries Laura, with the sharp ring that precedes the slap a frightened mother will give an offspring who alarms her unnecessarily. 'What *is* the matter? A pit, indeed! Why, you looked bleached, child, and ironmouldy, like a washed-out rag! Has anything happened?'

'Come, little woman, and tell me all about it,' says George, holding out his arms.

The tenderness of his voice has the inevitable effect of all sympathy in its action upon pent-up grief. Most of us can remember how, sitting silent and resentful under a severe rebuke, an extenuating word, interposed on our behalf, has made the sudden tears start out, despite our struggling endeavours to swallow the lump in our throat, and 'not to cry,' just as at other times, in places where laughter signified an outrage upon the powers that be, a ghastly ludicrousness seemed to cling round the most ordinary of acts. George's endearing tone naturally resulted in his bringing a sobbing child within his sheltering arms.

'Why now, Chick!' he says in a deprecating voice, fondling back the red curls with brotherly caresses as he draws her on his knees, 'I don't know you in this watery state! Your grave, grey eyes are washed away. This can't be *our* little sister, Laura, can it?' reaching out for Laura's hand, and clasping it in his own behind the child's neck. 'What's to be done, do you think? We must turn off the Yan Yean, I can see. Stop, I can see your eyes. There, give yourself a final mop with my handkerchief. And now for the moral of it all; what is it all about?'

'About you,' says the child, 'and Laura.'

The emphasis imparted to her words by the effort to give distinct-ness to them, for she could not stay at once the intermittent gasps that oppressed her after the drying of her tears, brought a sickly hue into Laura's brilliant cheeks. George's sallow face flushed. Apathy, as I have said, was its dominant characteristic. A kind of chronic indifferentism was stamped upon its every feature. His deep-set eyes seldom reached their legitimate limit of openness. Even in the down-ward droop of his moustache, which formed a perfect arch above his long clean chin, you might trace the lack of the buoyancy that gives the moustaches of so many men a self-asserting turn, especially at the age when the development of a becoming twist at the corners is a matter inviting some little consideration. 'My gentleman,' as Mr Piper called him, half ironically, half under compulsion – for George's torpor during its most irritating phases was never anything but the best-bred torpor imaginable – seemed, in fact, to keep only one-half of his brain awake in the general way. He had admitted to Laura that his life was only half a life away from her. Consistently with which it would appear that the inert half of his brain only wakes to action in her presence.

But all is on the alert now, touched to the quick by some sudden alarm. Nevertheless, he makes no betrayal of his fears. Only Laura, who can read an uneasy suspicion in his eyes – who can feel the involuntary tightening of his grasp upon her wrist – knows that Louey's words have given him a qualm.

'About Laura and me, eh?' There is a studied carelessness in the tones that only Laura's acute ears can detect. 'Well,' with a forced laugh, 'I daresay we *are* in a bad way, but I haven't found it out yet. Have you, Laura?'

'What do you mean, Hester?' says Laura, with less firmness of tone than usual. 'George and I are quite well, I think. There's nothing to warrant you're going into hysterics about us that I can see.'

'It isn't *that* (hesitatingly). Oh, please, Laura; please, George,' with a sudden recollection of the direction of the field-glass, and the expression of the face behind it, on perceiving that she had gone over to the enemy. 'Let me down! Indeed, I can't tell you sitting here!'

'Put her down, George, can't you!' cries Laura vehemently. 'Now, then, quick. What's the tragedy?'

A dread of making matters worse – a longing for words that may soften in the telling those messages of wrath and vengeance she bears from the tower – fill the childish face with distress and perplexity. Nor does George's keen reading of her expression assist her in the finding of softening phrases.

'Papa,' she begins, whereat the hearts of the pair on the steel bench give a simultaneous bound; 'papa was so sorry – at least I think he was a little angry too – because you called Laura on to the lawn this morning.'

'How did he know I called Laura on to the lawn?' interrupts George, his thoughts reverting to his suggestion of an ambush behind the pittosporum hedge, and Laura's scouting thereof.

'We saw you out of the tower window quite plainly. Papa saw you through his field-glass.'

'What did he see?'

'He saw you kissing Laura – you seemed to be a long time kissing her,' the child replies with the utmost simplicity. 'Then he grew vexed – rather. He made me come. O Laura, I didn't want to, you *know!* But I *had* to, and he wants George – immediately' – the lips were beginning to quiver again.

'Wants me!' exclaims George, with a sensation that recalls a summons to the private study of Dr Birchem fifteen years ago. Then, in a hurried aside to Laura, 'This is the turning-point, Laura. I have made up my mind. Do you decide, darling. Tell me – quickly – supposing I say we're engaged, that we're going to be married, will you support what I say?'

'How *can* I say? so much depends on it. Stand aside, Hester. O George, listen one minute. Don't lose your head when he's pumping you. I don't think you will, but find out *just* how much he knows. And don't think of me. Promise! If' – Laura pauses – 'if you see a faint prospect of reconciling him to it you might say there's a chance of our being married some day, that we mean to, if we can. But there isn't any hope of your reconciling him, is there? I know him too well. And, George, you *must* think of your interests. Don't irritate him. *I'm* beyond redemption, but it's not altogether my fault nor altogether his. We're like two chemicals that can't come into contact without making a commotion. You'd better go now, George. And promise again – you won't consider *me*.'

'But I *must* account somehow for our intimacy.'

'Oh, say I ran after you – say anything. I won't have you disinherited for me. And do go now, quickly.'

'Remember!' cries Laura, with all the solemnity of the murdered Charles, as George turns away from her; the interpretation of which George understands to signify that his interests must come first and her character second. He is to figure, it would seem, in the undignified position of a new Adam, and attest the eternally perpetuated male excuse of 'The woman tempted me;' while she – most self-effacing of Eves – has no Devil left in her creed to fall back upon.

She watches him until she has intercepted his last longing, lingering look, and then, with a sudden recollection of the field-glass, her face assumes a new expression.

'Here, Hester!' said Laura, suddenly recovering from her abstraction, and turning into the everyday imperious Laura, whom the child loved and dreaded, 'I want you to tell me something. Who did your father abuse most – George or me?'

'He said *they* nearly always,' answered Louey in a low tone, tracing imaginary patterns on the skirt of the dressing-gown.

'They *what*? They should "pack and go"? He'd "take and turn them out"? Was that it – eh?'

'No; but (reluctantly) a little like that.'

'And you stood and whimpered, I suppose, instead of dropping the glass out of the window?'

'The *field-glass*?' with wide open eyes.

'Or done anything (impatiently), it does not matter what? Do you think I came to say "good morning" to George on the lawn for Mr Piper's amusement?'

'N-no. But, oh, Laura (flutteringly), do you mean I was to break papa's new field-glass?'

'You're like all children,' said Laura contemptuously. 'No wonder one hates having to talk to them, they're so idiotically matter-of-fact.

This is what I mean. If I were writing a letter, and went out of the room, would you let any one go and read it?'

'No one would' (promptly).

'That isn't answering! It's just as bad to stare at people when they think they're alone as to read the thoughts they only mean for each other.'

'But (very hesitatingly) people mightn't think people think they're alone on the lawn.'

'Then they ought to think it! Would you choose a time when everybody was looking to – to – kiss George?'

'I don't think (reflecting) I'd mind.'

'Well, with grown-up people it's different, remember that!'

'Yes (very humbly). Won't you kiss me, please, Laura?'

'I think we've had enough of family demonstrations for this morning! Your father will be sending for you, as he sent for George, to keep you from being contaminated.'

She said it bitterly. Nevertheless, her arm had somehow found its way round the little girl's shoulder. Louey belonged as much to George as to her.

And the demon went his way, having succeeded in upsetting an entire family to his satisfaction. And the morning mist vanished from the sea, like the breath from a shield of polished steel, and the English thrushes in the Piper's Hill garden, having no fear of Mr Piper's glass, courted each other with responsive thrills from the pittosporum hedge on a morning of mellow sunshine. And the long shadows of Dianas of the chase, and piping Fauns, like the soft shades in velvet folds, lay across the turf at Laura's feet, as the Australian sun began his upward journey across a field of unclouded blue.

CHAPTER IV

———•———

Father and Son

'He draweth out the thread of his verbosity finer than the staple of his argument.' – SHAKESPEARE

I remember a Frenchman who, by way of airing at the same time his sympathy with the human race and his perfect familiarity with colloquial English, used to speak of mankind generally in an easy way as 'poor d'ells.' His pride in the expression made him bring it to the front perhaps a little oftener than the occasion warranted, but the sentiment was not a misplaced one. And the conviction that we are all 'poor d'ells' is forced upon me whenever I come to think seriously of the matter.

Do any of us deny, for example, that it is quite a truism that 'happiness is our being's end and aim'? Do we not, most of us, believe, on setting out in life, that we are keeping this end in view? And might not most of us acknowledge, when we come to the end, that we have been industriously frustrating it all the time? And if we were given another start, and carefully skirted all the rocks we had split upon before, we should only find that we had arrived at the same result by a different path. As to there being any free-will in the matter, the ingenuity with which creature after creature is his own undoing should be proof sufficient that his goal is marked in the map of the eternal – albeit he may seem to select his own road to it.

Let us consider for a moment the family at Piper's Hill. Did not each inmate, down to the youngest, find that something just unattainable was wanted to make him happy, beginning with Mr Piper in his fine tower – who, as he walked between the window and the door, listening, with the sense of exasperation that the very footfall of a person who has irritated us seems to bring, to the sound of George's slippers leisurely ascending the staircase, was comparatively speaking, a most miserable man? Stubbs, the milkman, who was just then measuring cream out in the back verandah of the Piper's Hill mansion, and whose son was courting the greengrocer's daughter with his approval, was a happy man compared with Mr Piper. And young Stubbs, who was wont to kiss his 'girl' with unabashed satisfaction beneath the paternal eye, was a yet happier man compared with George, who felt, as he slowly climbed the eighty steps, that his conduct in turning Laura's philosophical bias to his own ends would have laid him open at the hands of an unthinking world to the meriting of a title less euphonious than that of philosopher.

The thousand several tongues of his conscience cried out to him with every step. They affirmed that the only manly course open to him was to meet his father's remonstrances by the simple statement that he had been embracing his affianced wife. George could not silence these clamorous tongues. Therefore he engaged them in argument. The course they insisted on was the right one, he told them, had he been any one but George, and Laura any one but Laura. But expediency was the measure of their right. It was not expedient to enrage his father and succeed in being turned out of doors. It was not expedient to leave the coast clear for the working out of the designs of his aunt and cousins. It was not expedient to relinquish his racehorses, and throw over his only prospect of making something for himself – something which he might hold independently of his father's bounty. Hence a course that might bring about any or all of these catastrophes must be clearly the wrong one to take. Besides, had he not pleaded in behalf of this obviously wrong and Quixotic course with Laura herself – though whether he was especially desirous that Laura should yield to his pleadings was another question. Still, he *had* pleaded. Whatever might happen in the future, it was evident that he was not to blame. And what could happen, after all? That his father should esteem Laura more lightly than before? Well, that was a matter of small moment, provided he kept his doubts in the background. But let him only so much as hint or look them – and George looked fierce at the very possibility – and he would carry her off by force, and marry her in spite of herself. Things, as at present arranged, were a great bore. So were fathers, generally speaking. So was the world, that meddlesome abstraction that seemed to turn into a hydra-headed personality, and soil you with its venom, if you dared to establish that you lived for yourself, and not for it. Life itself was an infernal nuisance, if you came to that – being only another sort of world in the arbitrary conditions it attached to the enjoying of it. It was at this cheerful stage in his reflections that George had arrived as he landed on the top of the tower steps, and composed his face to its expression of laziest indifference before walking into the turret chamber.

This expression was the shield against which Mr Piper had broken so many of his heart's lances in vain. George's imperturbability had the effect of a goad upon his father's temper. His face never changed colour when the old man's was purple. His voice never lost its measured drawl. No fiercest agitation on his father's part could raise its pitch one semitone in feeling. When father and son were at issue, Mr Piper was like the bull who charges a stump, and splinters his horns as he butts at it; or, like the surf, that fumes and thunders with fruitless force against a wall of granite; and George's resistance was passive in its nature, and slippery on the surface, like that of any granite wall. He had all the advantage of an object that presents no unevenness whereon the assailant may leave his mark. After a contest with Mr Piper, George was accustomed to stroll with a half concealed yawn out of the room, while his father was wiping his face with trembling fingers, or stuttering a final malediction upon him in an impotent fury of incoherence. Yet George never quite forgot that his father held the purse-strings. If he angered him by the displaying of his negative qualities, he was careful not to outrage him, as far as his actions were concerned. He knew exactly how to regard his father's threats, and knew that he was secure so long as threats were the safety-valve by which Mr Piper's wrath might escape. But there was a point at which the safety-valve might prove an insufficient outlet, and the wrath, instead of expending itself in windy threats, might blow the restraining pressure of paternal sentiment to the winds. And it was within this point that George had been diplomatic enough so far to keep himself. He gave his father nothing to remember against him. Mr Piper could not disinherit an only son for 'biting his thumb at him,' nor allege the irritating effect of his half closed eyes as a reason for turning him adrift; but in a marriage contracted in defiance of his orders he would have found a plea for treating him with all the severity so justifiable in a disappointed parent, whether tried by the standard of antediluvian times or our own; and the sympathy of the world –

excepting, perhaps, the youthfully romantic part of it – would have been with him; even modern fathers adopting unconsciously the patriarchal view of self-perpetuation through remote generations to come.

George reached the landing with an idea of sounding his father upon this dangerous subject as cautiously as might be, but the aspect of Mr Piper's back, as seen through the open door, made him hesitate. It was not a back that would lend itself to a compromise. Any one who has tried to soften a school-girl with shoulders that tell of the sulks will understand George's feeling of hopelessness at sight of his father's back. Besides, he knew how to interpret it of old – looking upon this bodily manifestation, indeed, with a curious sensation, half pitiful, half contemptuous. Pitiful, because he knew it betrayed the deepest chagrin and resentment – contemptuous, because in his quality of man-of-the-world he abhorred all outward demonstrations of a mental state. He forgot that, between the perfect self-control of a man of culture and the equally perfect stolidity of a Red Indian, there are gradations of feeling common to an intermediate class – such a class, for example, as that whence Mr Piper had sprung, which catches enough of the quickening influence of civilisation to have its sensations sharpened and intensified, yet is not put through a training that may school the expression of them. He made scant allowance for the flushed face, the trembling hands, the raised voice. 'Mere bluster!' he said to himself every time he had words with Mr Piper. 'I wish I could convince my father that bluster is no argument.'

But to attempt to convince such a back of the propriety of conducting an argument 'politely' seemed so hopeless a task, that George advanced quietly to the front in his broidered slippers, and, saying in his suavest voice, 'Good morning, governor! you wanted to see me, I believe?' leaned his back against the window-sill, and pulling out his penknife, became absorbed in the work of paring his finger nails with an elaborate attention to their ovalness.

As Mr Piper turned and faced him, you would never have traced the sonship in George. There was nothing in common between the sallow, indolent face of the younger man, and the spreading, heated face of the elder. George looked like any club lounger – not unwilling to let it be seen that he is slightly bored, yet ready, with perfect acquiescence, to go through with an hour, or a forenoon, of the infliction of boredom, as conveyed by a father's presence. Whereas Mr Piper looked as though the matter in hand were of more moment than the adjustment of the balance of European power – which, indeed, it was to him, and feeling which, he showed what he felt, a disadvantage, at the outset, that George would have no compunction in turning to account. There was nothing, in fact, that George would not have turned to account for the gaining of his ends, no weak point betrayed by his father, of which he lost the import, as he sat balancing his penknife in his long white fingers. Beneath his immaculate waistcoat – for from the chin downwards George had much of the *petit maitre* in his outward man – his heart was beating with the strongest desire it was capable of cherishing. Could he by concession of coercion bring his father to 'hear reason' – could he, at·the close of the interview, go straightaway to Laura, and taking her aurora-like radiance to himself, tell her that henceforth he might wrap himself in it in the eyes of the world, instead of regarding it like a thief, who watches the sun rise from behind his prison grating – he would accomplish the only wish he had ever framed with a feeling that savoured of intensity. Laura might rail against marriage to her heart's content, provided he might make her his wife first. He would prove to her that if she wanted toleration for her theories she must act in exact contradiction of them. When does democracy ever gain so fair a hearing as from the lips of a titled apostle? Do not all allusions to the wallet and scrip come with most force from the princeliest of church dignitaries? Laura, cavilling at matrimony, with a husband who gave her ball-dresses, and a carriage, would be 'eccentric' and 'charming;' but Laura, expressing views against marriage, with a lover only to endorse them, would be simply an abandoned young woman. George must rescue her from herself. For his own part he liked the flavour of the extremest Nihilism, provided there was nothing to be sacrificed for the enjoyment of it. But Laura was imprudent! She showed an inclination towards the courting of martyrdom which he must check. Imagine his allowing her to stand in a pillory for his sake, and seeing her pelted by the world's mud until she became all draggled and brazen. Such a result, thought George, follows inevitably if a woman acts in avowed defiance of the world. She may break its every rule with careful concealment of the fact, and while it believes in her she may carry in genuine earnest the chastest of expressions as she traverses it. But once let it look at her in a certain way, and she will answer the look as those do who have arrayed themselves against it. She will be more honest, perhaps; but in the gaining of her honesty she will have lost all her other womanly qualities. For while the mask she wears is the safeguard of her modesty, she cannot afford to let the world pull it aside for an instant.

Thinking all these things, George waited for his father to speak, not, it is true, 'with filial confidence inspired,' but as prepared to deal with an uncertain, and it might be an unmanageable opponent. Mr Piper watched him as he continued tranquilly to pare his nails, the baffled sense of helplessness that exasperated him at the outset of an interview with his son creeping over him as he watched. If George could only once have lost his head and sworn – or only once implored or threatened! But he never did. The apathy and unconcern of his attitude – the veiled disrespect it implied – spoke of an indifference that was worse than the most open revolt. But surely he would be made to feel now! Mr Piper had never tried to reach 'my gentleman' through his 'young woman' yet. In this respect there was a mixed feeling in the paternal mind. Although Mr Piper was resolved that his son should give up Laura, although he had sworn that George should be an outcast unless he promised to relinquish all thought of her, he felt that in the event of his submitting without a struggle he would be bitterly disappointed. Not that he wanted to hurt for hurting's sake – only to feel that he was dealing with a flesh and blood offspring, who would be capable of undergoing something like a pull at his heart-strings when he himself should come to his last hour. A man who could throw off a sweetheart whose arms he had just left without making an effort to keep her would be capable of looking upon a father's face pinched by death with just the expression that George wore as he continued to pare his nails. And it never seemed to change! A slight elevation of an unruffled brow just gave evidence that though his eyes were looking critically at his almond-shaped finger nails, his ear took in the sense of his father's word. Otherwise he might have served for as perfect a model of intentness upon his hands as the statue of the boy, who to all eternity will be absorbed in the task of extracting a thorn from his foot. With Mr Piper it was different. In his agitation the field-glass travelled between his eyes and the window-sill, where his trembling fingers deposited it. He twisted the barrels until the horizon was nothing but a blue blur, unheeding of the distorted nature he was bringing before him. I doubt whether his eyes even knew that it was distorted. The effort to adjust the sight to his liking was purely mechanical. He was talking the whole of the time.

'I'll see and put a stop to it,' he threatened. 'I'll take and pack her off, and you at the back of her, "my gentleman."' George knew that the use of this expression signified especial bitterness on his father's part. 'I'll have an end of this nonsense – a painted jade like her!'

'Wait a minute, please,' said George, shutting the knife with a little snap, and settling himself back upon the window-sill; 'you are a little hard to follow, or I am slow at catching your meaning, perhaps. I understand that you had some object in sending for me. Are you explaining it to me now? I am quite prepared to listen, as you see.'

'You're very condescending, I'm sure,' said Mr Piper, with such withering sarcasm that George stroked his moustache and smiled. 'You put yourself about for your father a deal too much, "my gentleman," there's no doubt of it.' Then, with a sudden break in his voice – 'No, George, it's not much of a son you've been to me, and no one can say I've stood in your light. I'd like you to show me another young man who could carry on top ropes like you. There's not many fathers 'ud have stood it. Most fathers 'ud made you turn to long ago.'

'Do you want anything done for you?' interrupted George, with the air of a man who is laying himself out to oblige – 'another tour of inspection in the north?'

Whenever Mr Piper made allusion to George's want of occupation, it was the young man's policy to refer to this tour of inspection, a memorable tour, seeing that it had given him employment for at least three months. But there were circumstances attached to it which had served to show that under his coating of sybaritism George possessed a great measure of his father's shrewdness. And it had proved that, put to the test, there was as much manliness beneath his effeminacy as beneath the roughest exterior of any fire-eater who swears 'strange oaths.' Indeed, if Laura's faith in this quality had not been as unquestioning as her want of faith in other directions, no sympathy of taste would have held her to George. Manliness is such an essential in a woman's estimate of the male that she hardly counts it among his merits. Without it, he is worse than nothing. Indeed, she is inclined to credit every man with it, until she finds an instance where it is lacking. For a woman's interpretation of it does not demand an absence of laziness and self-indulgence on the man's part, or even the display of much moral worth. It simply requires that he should never flinch before bodily risk or danger, and, if the occasion arise, he should 'dare do all that may become a man.'

But Mr Piper could hardly be expected to see mere passive manliness from a woman's point of view. There was something more than this that he would fain have infused into his son. The lack of energy and ambition on George's part filled him with a kind of helpless desperation. Unwilling to see the cause of it in his own system of bringing the lad up, which would have been a tacit denial of his axiom that 'whatever he did was right,' he attributed the evil to some foreign influence – naturally a woman's, and, as a matter of course, Laura was that woman. Mr Piper was no more unjust in this than is any man of little education, whose self-love has been wounded, and who has been provoked in consequence into regarding some member of the other sex with special dislike and distrust. No harsher interpreter of her actions could be found. He sees artifice under her most unstudied gestures. He gives a meaning that she was innocent of to her most natural remarks, and all because she has failed to appreciate *him*. Yet the same man, in the hands of an intriguing woman, will see a touching artlessness under the most transparent wiles – once she has impressed him with the belief that she looks up to him.

Gratitude on Laura's part might have made her defer to the man who had provided her with all those good things she counted as compensations for the penalty of living. But habit makes us singularly obtuse. Her mother's marriage with Mr Piper seemed the price that had been paid for the establishing of her own rights, and if she thought about the matter at all, when her quarterly allowance was due, it was to reflect that the price paid had been a goodly one. She was almost devoid of sensitiveness, though keenly alive to anything that touched her personally. Her antagonism to Mr Piper never discommoded her as she sat at his table. She would finish her dinner with a smile, when some argument in which she had sided against him had irritated him to the point of leaving his food untouched on his plate. It was Louey who, at these times, would lay down her knife and fork and watch her father with a yearning towards him in her grey eyes that made her look as though her mother's soul were shining through them. George was neutral, or languidly smiling behind his moustache when Laura made a 'hit.'

But such things rankle until the mind is abnormally sore, and chafes at imaginary offences. This was the stage at which Mr Piper's mind had arrived. There was such unappeasable bitterness in his accents when he alluded to Laura that George turned the conversation upon himself, lest he should yield to the temptation of retaliating in a quiet rejoinder that might be damaging to his interests, and Laura had enjoined him to think of them first. He must remember that, for her

sake as well as for his own. Still it might be difficult to keep them in
view if his father persisted in calling names. With his neck still warm
from the pressure of Laura's silky head, he could not bring himself
to remain stolid while his father called her 'a jade.' So he courted a
personal attack, which was more easily parried, and sat caressing his
moustache, as was his wont, with his eyes bent on the floor, while his
father exposed his grievances in a crescendo key.

If there was anything humiliating in being rated as an 'able-bodied
young man who wasn't worth his salt,' as a loafer who was hardly fit
to 'jackaroo' on a station, as a 'lazy lubber' who would 'go to the
dogs if it weren't for his father,' George never betrayed that he felt
humilitated by so much as the twitching of an eyelid. Persistently
stroking the ends of his moustache with an air of profound abstraction,
he made it apparent, as soon as Mr Piper stopped to take breath, that
he was suppressing an inclination to yawn.

'I daresay it's all very true, governor,' was all he said in reply. 'It's
very nice and complimentary, I'm sure, and I ought to be very much
obliged to you. But, *apropos* of your compliments, may I ask if it was
only to treat me to them in full that you brought me up those
confounded tower steps this morning? Because in that case I wouldn't
have minded waiting, you know. It's hardly fair upon a man, is it, to
put him to the treadmill before he's well awake in the morning?'

'If you were like other young men,' retorted Mr Piper, 'you'd be
up and down them steps twenty times a day (George shuddered); but,
oh no! my gentleman can crawl on to the lawn and carry on with a'
–

'Stop there!' cried George, in a tone that made his father silent
through sheer astonishment (George had never been known to raise
his voice before). 'Do you know the relation in which Laura stands
to me?'

He looked Mr Piper full in the face as he said it, and seeing the
ghastly change that came over the face as he looked, he felt that he
had been over-hasty. For the glass through which Mr Piper had made
a feint of looking dropped from his quivering fingers; his lips worked
in a distorted fashion over his discoloured teeth; the blood rushing
away from his florid cheeks left them streaked with thready sanguin-
eous veins, mottling the ash-coloured patches; and rushed back again
with a force that seemed to swell the veins around his temples to
bursting. It was the second time that morning he had succumbed to

an access of rage, against yielding to which full-blooded persons like
Mr Piper are cautioned by their medical men.

'What's the matter, father?' said George at last, not with any of
Louey's vehement alarm, but eyeing him rather gravely and curiously.
'Do you object to my looking upon Laura in the light of a – *sister?*'

'Eh?' said Mr Piper. His power of articulation was slowly returning,
but his breath as yet was only equal to the monosyllable.

'Of a sister,' repeated George slowly, 'and a friend?' He added the
last clause in a voice that was almost inaudible. His hope of making
his father 'hear reason' was abandoning him. Laura was right after
all, but through his acknowledgment that she was right, the young
man was conscious of a faint feeling of irritation. It was true that his
father was obstinate and unmanageable, but she need not have brought
him to such a pitch of exasperation as this.

'Your *sister*,' said Mr Piper, as soon as he could speak distinctly.
'That's as you choose to take it. She's none o' mine, thank God! But
you take and make her more than your sister, and see how soon you'll
come to repent it. It's down in my will. I've sworn it. Dead or alive,
I won't have the jade in my family. If you've got a fancy for her, you
may take her, but never you come anigh Piper's Hill again.'

'You mistake the position of affairs,' said George calmly. 'Laura
wouldn't have me if I wanted!'

'Ho, ho!' Mr Piper's laugh was more insulting than mirthful. 'That's
why she comes and hugs you on the lawn of a morning, is it?'

George winced interiorly. The vulgar interpretation of the whole-
hearted kiss Laura had bestowed upon him was hateful in his ears.
Yet what could he say in her behalf that would not render them both
ridiculous? His father's English might be coarse, but if the fact was
undeniable, to cavil at the manner of expressing it might only elicit
something still harder to bear. What would he have given for the
courage to say, 'Turn me out, disinherit me! I shall take Laura away
with me as my wife.'

But the folly of it! Laura and he with a list of debts – no credit at
the shops – and no means of providing themselves with a meal. No;
he must lay his plans a little more wisely first. It might come to his
taking her away some day – and toiling for her perhaps! George sighed
– the work-a-day world had no allurements for him – but in the
meantime his father must be reassured. Still, he felt that it was an
ignoble part that was thrust upon him.

'Laura would not have me,' he reiterated, with slow emphasis. 'She looks upon me as a brother. You must not misinterpret – a – morning greeting.'

'Why don't she marry?' growled Mr Piper. 'There's fools 'ud have her' –

'Perhaps she *may* be induced to marry some day,' said George jesuitically. Mr Piper detected something like an indication of feeling in his low tones. 'I wouldn't advise you to force her, though. You're bound in honour, I think, to give her entire freedom. She's very friendless – very helpless – very much at our mercy!'

As he reminded his father of his duties to Laura and of her unfriended position, George's subdued voice rang with a didactic virtue that imposed upon himself. Nothing is more remarkable than the action of the mind in the moral labyrinth into which sophistry conducts it, whence it dictates with clear-seeing fervour the straight course for another mind to take, and retires with perfect self-approval and no misgivings into its own devious paths.

But Mr Piper was not of the school that might call a spade the first violator of Mother Earth, or any other equally euphonious and ambiguous name. With him a spade was a spade – and right was right – and wrong was wrong.

'It isn't for you to take and preach to me, George,' he replied shortly. 'She's a hussy – and she'll come to no good end. But I'm the best friend she's got. I don't pretend to understand your new-fangled way of talk, and I don't want to – what's more! It's a way of calling black white, that's what it is. When I was a young man I called things by their right names. Sisters were sisters, and them as weren't sisters didn't go on like you and Laura without there was something in it. In my day young women didn't go and take young men round the neck for nothing. *You* take and talk to me – eh! I'd like to know who's spoiling 'er for an honest husband – you or me?'

A gleam of hope came into George's mind. It might be that he had given up his chance too soon. What if he were to feel his way again with all the caution in the world?

'As to that,' he said, stroking his moustache, as he looked down and carefully weighed his words, 'my interpretation of an honest husband is not altogether one who would condemn a girl for anything Laura ever did. After all, we have been brought up like brother and sister. Your child is alike my sister and hers. And you must remember, you were watching her this morning from a hundred feet in the air. No wonder your judgment is not very clear – no wonder you saw' –

'I saw quite enough,' interrupted Mr Piper bluntly. 'I don't want any o' your fine talk to tell me my eyesight ain't as good as yours.'

'Well, that isn't the point,' rejoined George. 'You concluded more than was called for from what you saw. However, perhaps it's as well we've been forced into a sort of explanation. I meant to speak to you in all cases soon.'

'It's no use, George,' said Mr Piper, gasping again. 'I'll take and turn the pair of you out.'

'You are premature,' said George, in his most measured accents, tinged with a slight inflection of scorn, 'and just a little illogical. You lose your temper when I speak of Laura as my sister – yet you become simply furious when I hint at regarding her in any closer light. I wish you could control yourself while I could put the case before you. There is no question of marriage between Laura and me. I don't even know whether she would like me for a husband, but I know' – his words fell with a kind of dragging emphasis as he looked straight into his father's angrily expectant eyes – 'I know that she is the only woman I shall ever feel the least inclination to make my wife.'

'Then I've done with you!' said his father, turning away.

'No! Stay a moment, please. The only woman I should ever feel an *inclination* for, I said. It doesn't follow that I'm going to act upon that inclination. And yet – by the by, father, you've never told me what motive you have for objecting so strongly to my pleasing myself in this matter. Laura mayn't be altogether congenial to you – but as a daughter-in-law you needn't be ashamed of her.'

'I won't have her at any price,' declared Mr Piper doggedly, 'and you shan't have her without you want to be a pauper. A nice helpmate for a husband she'd make! Why, she's taken the heart out of you already with her talk. What's the good of you? What are you fit for? If it wasn't for her you'd be making up to some nice girl with good principles, and her mother's church to back her up – ay, and making your own way, too, as I did mine – 'stead o' danglin' at a showy woman's skirts, and mooning after her like a great simpleton, and pretending you're going to put the world straight by turning it topsy-turvy. It's a very good world for them as knows how to do their duty in it. I think I managed to get along in it, anyhow. I've been in worse places than Piper's Hill.' Mr Piper instinctively glanced round his tower as he said it. 'But don't you put it into your head, George, that I've spent the best years o' my life, slaving and saving, for a pair of useless idle do-nothings – who won't even give me a thank you for my pains. You may take and turn your nose up at somebody else's things.'

'He has been touched upon a tender point,' thought George, 'and I'm afraid it's too late to retrieve our position. What fools Laura and I have been! We should have made use of systematic flattery.'

George made no allowance for his father's sense of injury. It did not occur to him to consider that something of affection or gratitude might have proved an efficacious substitute for flattery. From this point of view, the smoothing of the path that he and Laura were fain to follow was the task that devolved upon the rest of the world. According to the degree in which this might be carried out, he considered his relation with it. For individuals who wanted to be ministered to, as well as to minister, he had no sympathy. Such a lack of comprehension is sure to follow any abandoning of the mind to its natural self-centring proclivity.

He made no further effort in behalf of this cause that morning. The Piper's Hill breakfast had been hurried on, that Mr Piper might set out early to meet the *Henrietta Maria* in the bay. And the four sat down to it, with the spring sunshine glazing the interior of the beautiful dining-room – throwing patches of brightness upon the grand mahogany sideboard, creeping in little streams of light across the satiny tablecloth, dimpling the flesh in the paintings on the wall bought on commission for Mr Piper by the artist who had furnished his house, and travelling over the living faces with strange betrayal of their separate dissatisfactions. If it were only all that appears on the surface which need be taken into account in the world's economy! In that case, there would have been nothing to learn in the Piper's Hill dining-room from the sight of a crusty old gentleman, a languid young man, a somewhat disdainful-looking, well-favoured, pink and white young woman, and a grey-eyed freckled, solemn child, any more than a lesson could have been drawn from the sight of four other faces twenty miles away, in the saloon of the *Henrietta Maria* – the face of a spare gentleman with the air of a peevish court gallant of fifty years ago – the face of a large matron, with sweet, sad eyes, swollen-rimmed and heavy – the face of a lady called by courtesy a 'girl,' with pointed chin and flushed cheeks, betokening an excitement half pleasing, half painful, and the face of a girl, really a girl, who, save for the life hues in her transparent skin, might have descended from any pedestal in a gallery of antique goddesses, to sit in maiden meditation among the passengers on an emigrant ship. But what lay beneath the surface, or how one quartette was to influence the other, is another thing. Supposing there is a little penetration allowed us of these merest externals! Supposing under the grizzled head of the testy old gentleman we discover a brain given over to all the contending influences of wounded self-love, and resentment, and brotherly affection – and under the dark head of the young man and the fair head of the girl we discover a common impulse to combine against the grizzled gentleman and his new relations, and under the red curls of the grey-eyed child we chance upon nothing but one heart-whole longing for the binding of all, those present and those to come, closer to her and to each other – will this insight assist our predictions, or will it only serve to show how seldom ostensible motives are real ones? But that we know already. Still, I believe if one half of the family meetings that make hearts to throb daily could lay bare the motives and impressions that underlie the effusion, there would not be half the attendant enthusiasm that characterises them now – as even the neediest of relatives might object to being regarded in the light of means to an end.

PART III

CHAPTER I

———————•———————

Family Greetings

'To say you are welcome would be superfluous.'
– SHAKESPEARE

'I have a presentiment, Maggie,' said Sara, 'that the next boat will be for us. There's a red-faced old man in it – *that's* Uncle Piper – and a red-haired child! I suppose that's our cousin. Dear me! I wonder what I can do to make the captain take me back to England!'

But Margaret did not answer. She was gazing abstractedly at the wide-spread city in the distance.

'And now for family effusions!' Sara went on. 'Call mother, will you, Margaret! That dreadful man's getting out of the boat – I'm certain he's going to kiss us.'

There was little occasion, as it happened, for calling Mrs Cavendish. As the 'dreadful man' came ponderously up the ship's steps, with a nervous little girl, pale-faced and freckled, holding his coat-tails, she had come from the cabin below and looked over the ship's side, and now she was turning to her daughters with an expression that almost brought tears of sympathy into Margaret's eyes. There was something that spoke of such yearnings towards her brother – of such half-apologetic pleading for him withal! 'And yet it is we who ought to feel the most humble, I am sure,' thought Margaret.

The next minute was what Sara referred to afterwards as 'something to be remembered with a shudder.' To her it seemed to be nothing but an indiscriminate and very objectionable kind of 'kissing-all-round' ceremony. It was all 'most uncomfortable,' she declared. Her mother

cried, and protested to the red-faced man that she 'had never thought
to live to see her brother "Tom" again.'

'And live a sight longer yet, my girl,' Mr Piper said, looking at her
with the old fraternal admiration. 'You've worn better than me – got
a bit stouter maybe, but that's all! There's the living image of you,'
he added, turning to Sara. 'Yes, Tom!' said poor Mrs Cavendish,
bethinking herself of wiping her eyes. 'I hope you'll take kindly to my
girls, Tom!'

'Take kindly to 'em! We're going to be one 'appy family; ain't we?
Blood's thicker than water – as I tell George! None o' your interlopers
for me!'

What hidden meaning might be veiled under this dark allusion was
uncomprehended by the Cavendish family; but Sara did not like to
have it emphasised by another kiss from her Uncle Piper. She wished
he would not single her out so specially. Margaret, perhaps, would
have minded it less, but Margaret did not signify all that Sara did in
her uncle's eyes. Mr Piper used to say of himself that 'he had an eye
for a woman;' and his belief that he had transmitted this tendency to
George made him see in Sara's beauty a hopeful assurance of Laura's
future discomfiture.

'The painted hussy!' he said to himself, thinking of her by the name
he always gave her in his own mind. 'She can't hold a candle to *my*
niece. We'll see where she'll be in another six weeks – with all her
airs!'

The prospect of seeing Laura's beauty completely thrown into
the shade by Sara made him unmindful of something in his niece's
expression, which at that minute bore a strong resemblance to her
father's, when the recollection of his brother, the bishop, was at its
height.

'Take kindly to 'em!' Mr Piper said again. 'I'd like to know who
I'll take kindly to if it isn't my own flesh and blood! And, now, where's
your good man, my girl? Why didn't you take and bring him along
with you, eh!'

'He's coming,' said Margaret nervously, with a flush of apprehension dyeing her cheeks. 'Papa, here's our Uncle Piper at last, and our
dear little cousin!'

Louey, with a child's fine instinct, had nestled close to Margaret
from the very outset of the family meeting. Always sensitive on her
father's account – accustomed to wince at the very inflexion of Laura's
voice when it was addressed to him – she had detected intuitively the

feeling in Sara which Mr Piper's coarser nature had not penetrated. The lovely lady, with the mouth and chin like those of the statues to be seen all along the walls in the Public Library, did not kiss as Louey understood kissing. She seemed to be only anxious to get it over, and to be a little ashamed of having to do it.

The other lady, with the red cheeks and pointed chin, who looked as if she would cry that moment if there had been nobody to see her, had kissed in quite a different way. Here was some one who would never wound her father, nor make him leave the table with his plate still full, and his eyes worried and shining with anger. Louey stood next to her, a little behind the group, unspeakably anxious for the appearance of Mr Cavendish. This great addition to the family might mean so much happiness – if people would only find happiness in all being fond of each other, and fortifying themselves mutually against the dangerous world of noisy railway platforms and street-crossings. But oh! what misery it might mean, too, if some of the new-comers took part against her father. That they should supersede her in his affections never even occurred to Louey. Her love was of the lofty kind which implies utter self-effacement, and which indeed is attainable only by a few rarely constructed souls. Mr Lydiat, to be sure, had proved himself in possession of this quality, until he had learned to gauge, on board the *Henrietta Maria*, the overruling power of a more egoistic love. Louey gave herself up to it in obedience to an instinct – heaven-born, it may be, – for if there exist a heaven that can approve such sweet self-effacing affection as her mother had shown to her father during the year of their wedded life, Louey's altruistic nature was surely traceable to its approval.

The meeting between Mr Piper and Mr Cavendish was followed by a gasp of relief on the part of Margaret and her mother. They had never dared to hope it could have been half so cordial. The truth is, that Mr Cavendish, having bravely browbeaten his wife the night before, having flung the whole ancestral House of Devonshire and the episcopal palace into her face, and having made her feel the height from which he was descending in allowing himself to accept her brother's – *a ci-devant* butcher's – hospitality, was by no means prepared to quarrel with a well-appointed house and its accessories. Besides, wealth was an acknowledged power, even though pork-sausages should have been its alleged first cause; and politic members of the great ruling houses in the old world had been known historically to make concessions to trade. Mr Cavendish was prepared to make concessions, too. The remainder of the loan that Uncle Piper had advanced was represented by a few sovereigns in a pocket-book stamped with the Devonshire crest. It certainly behoved Mr Cavendish to be magnanimous, and it was with a return of the old courtly urbanity that had made him such a god in Elizabeth Piper's eyes, that he came forward in the Byronic cloak, and held out his hand to his wife's brother.

Mr Piper's feelings respecting his brother-in-law were hardly clear, even to himself. Mingled with a half contempt for a man who could not 'make his mark' in the world, was the kind of uneasy deference which, despite all his wealth and his consequence, Mr Piper could not mentally control in connection with the class he had been used to call 'nobs.' Yet, in his position of benefactor, he was hardly prepared to 'stand any nonsense' from Elizabeth's husband, a 'beggar, if you came to that, for all his fine breeding.' He bestowed, you may be sure, one of his shrewdest glances upon his brother-in-law, as he approached.

But there was no resisting Mr Cavendish, when it pleased him to adopt his *air de grand seigneur.*

'This is a real pleasure, my dear sir,' he said, with ten white fingers, the fingers of a thoroughbred hand, closing round Mr Piper's plebeian knuckles. No onlooker could have supposed for an instant that he had come with the whole of his family, in an entirely destitute condition, to live upon his wife's brother. Besides, we know that among well-bred people to receive a favour is virtually to oblige a man. You only accept cordialities from people you esteem. A witness to the meeting would have imagined at once that Mr Cavendish had left England for the special purpose of conferring a benefit upon his humble colonial connections.

'You're welcome, sir,' said Mr Piper.

Then there was a pause, during which Mrs Cavendish wiped her eyes, and Mr Piper said again very heartily, 'You're welcome, the lot of you.'

Thereupon ensued one of those disconnected conversations in which nobody says anything for the sake of being listened to, but simply from the dread of the uncomfortable pause that seems inevitable. Margaret had stolen below, with her newly-found cousin, to bid a last farewell to the cabin in which she had dreamed out the one romance of her lifetime. She begged the little girl to remain in the saloon, on the plea that the cabin was full of packages, and going within by herself, she stood next to her dismantled berth, and gave herself up to her reflections. It was here that Sara had recounted all the circumstances of Mr Lydiat's avowal, with no greater emotion than the small triumph of knowing that she had enslaved a heart. Had such an avowal been made to Margaret, what a different hue the sad-looking houses in the distance would have assumed! Melbourne or London, it would have been all the same then! The dull weight that seemed to have been pulling at her heart-strings all the morning would have been transformed into a burden of joy that it would have been ecstasy to carry. The time for self-deception had passed away from Margaret, as well as for Mr Lydiat. She confessed to herself that it was for something more than the sight and the sound of those restless green waves that she would have given her all to begin the passage again.

Louey meanwhile waited patiently on the bench without, shrinking a little from the noisy children who tumbled in succession from the cabin of the M'Brides. Mrs M'Bride's hopefulness had received its first shock at the discovery that the stock of family linen had been all 'used up,' and that the future legislators of the colony must land collarless and sockless at the antipodes. Perhaps if she could have known how many of the legislators had been known to disembark in a still worse plight, she would have drawn hopeful auguries from the out-at-elbows appearance of Tommy and Biddy.

While Louey was wondering whether she might find her way back to her father alone, a cabin door a little way down was suddenly opened, and a gentleman holding a copy-book in his hand came out and sat beside her. He had not even noticed her, the child thought, for his eyes were fixed upon the pages of the copy-book; more as though it reminded him of something else than as though he had been reading what was written there. He had a face that Louey liked. She thought Laura would have liked it, too, despite her antagonism to clergymen, and although George and she always laughed together in exactly the same tone whenever there was any mention of them. Louey would have liked her brother and sister to see what grave, kind eyes, and what a serious, sweet expression this clergyman had; like nobody Louey had ever seen before. She wondered, for a moment, whether he had any little sister whom he had left behind, and, so wondering, gave vent unconsciously to her old-fashioned sigh.

The clergyman turned round at the sound. One would have supposed that the sigh had chimed in with his own thoughts, and startled him. He saw, on turning round, a carefully-dressed little girl, with light-red curls falling from beneath a fashionable hat, surrounded by a large fluffy feather. He would have returned to his book at the sight, but there was a wistful expression in the blue eyes, that shone out of the freckled little face, which arrested his attention. One cannot be – like Mr Lydiat – a curer of souls for many years without learning to read expressions.

'She looks like a motherless child,' he thought, and it was with this thought uppermost in his mind that he addressed her. 'Was she waiting for any one he could find for her? He knew all the people on board.' Louey thanked him demurely in her old-fashioned way. 'She was not tired of waiting at all, thank you, provided papa was not looking for her. Her cousin Margaret was in there.'

'Miss Cavendish, was *that* her cousin?' asked Mr Lydiat, immensely interested. This little girl would see Sara every day. It seemed like a wonderful coincidence that the first friend he should make (for he was sure that this little girl and he would be friends) should be of the same blood as Sara. 'I know your cousins better than any one on board,' he continued. 'I am waiting to say goodbye to them now. Have you come to take them away?'

'Yes,' said Louey; 'they are going to live with us at Piper's Hill.' The name caught Mr Lydiat's ear like a long-forgotten once-familiar sound. Nevertheless, when he remembered his relations with it he never thought of connecting it with the name of the little girl's home. Piper's Hill must be a place like Stamford Hill, and possibly, as his stepfather was a rich man, the name had reference to him. Still, that there should be any personal interest for him in the fact, did not as yet make itself clear to Mr Lydiat.

If it should seem strange that people may travel for three months together, and seeing each other every day, should still fail to know anything whatever about each other's destination, I must explain that Mr Cavendish and Sara had stipulated at starting that the name of Mr Piper should never be made known on board.

'A hundred casualties may occur,' Mr Cavendish had said.

'We may all be drowned,' declared Sara.

'We may be greeted by news which will prevent our having recourse to Mr Piper's hospitality,' said Mr Cavendish.

'Of course,' said Sara, 'a bishop and seventeen Devonshires might die in three months; mightn't they, mamma?'

And considering that there was always a possibility, if not much reasonable hope, of some such contingencies as these, the desired counsel had been kept by Mrs Cavendish and Margaret.

Mr Lydiat, for different reasons, had been equally reserved. He was going out in obedience to a summons. The Bishop of Melbourne was to find him work. Of what avail to speak of a stepfather who might close his doors against him – of a sister who had turned her back upon him, or of a half-sister who in all probability had never heard of his existence? It had, therefore, so fallen out that the moment of parting had come, and that until now Mr Lydiat had not known that Sara had relations in Melbourne. The name, too, of Mr Piper's second wife was almost unknown to the Cavendish family. The girls knew that their uncle had a stepdaughter, who was bound by no ties of blood either to his family or to their own. But they had forgotten, if indeed they had ever known, that her name was Laura Lydiat. So it happened that Mr Lydiat continued to talk to Louey, as he might have talked to any other strange little girl whom he had chanced to find left by herself in the saloon.

'Piper's Hill! that must be near Melbourne, I suppose,' he said, with the vision of a colonial Stamford Hill still uppermost in his brain.

'Yes, at South Yarra,' said Louey, looking down the saloon, and contrasting its narrow length with her own beautiful broad verandah and garden at home.

'Would you like to make a long journey, like your cousins?' asked Mr Lydiat, following the direction of her eyes.

'N – no,' replied the little girl, hesitatingly, and unconsciously plagiarising the great Doctor Johnson's words – 'It must feel like being shut in prison; and, besides, I should be so frightened.'

The clergyman inquired whether she was never frightened on shore, and, little by little, the child was led on to unburden herself of some of those terrors that were ever present to her. She was not capable of formulating them, as an older person might have done, under the influence of the relief of talking to some one who seemed to understand all about them. But Mr Lydiat was learned in translating expressions of face and tones of voice. He had not talked for many instants to Louey without feeling that he was in the presence of a nervous, sensitive organisation, whose balance of suffering was greater than its balance of enjoyment. Louey's very affections were a pain to her, because of the anxiety she suffered in behalf of those she loved. Yet it was clear that she kept those trials pent up within her childish brain. It was abnormal, and moved Mr Lydiat to pity. I daresay in his own case he would have been quite willing to accept, as a truth, the sentiment enshrined by Cowper in a melancholy little couplet, addressed to an afflicted Protestant lady:

> 'The path of sorrow, and that path alone,
> Leads to the land where sorrow is unknown.'

But in the case of frail little children it was different, and Mr Lydiat, with professional promptitude, bethought him of spiritually prescribing for Louey's relief.

'But you know there's somebody much wiser than we are – who is sure to do what is best for us, my child,' he said gently. 'When you say your prayers, at night and in the morning, and ask Him to take care of you, why don't you feel certain He listens to you? Then there is nothing to be frightened of.'

'I don't say prayers,' said the child simply.

The clergyman started. Could it be a colonial custom to bring up well-dressed little girls with thoughtful faces and drooping feathers in utter ignorance of religion? Then, indeed, there was a field for him in Melbourne, compared with which even Thieves' Alley offered scant labour. 'Not say prayers?' he inquired aghast.

'No,' repeated Louey. 'I used to, but Laura says it's no use. She says if there's anybody who knows better what's best for us, it's only like telling him what to do to say prayers to him. So it's no good, and only silly.'

Mr Lydiat grew pale, but not, as might be supposed, on account of this unexpectedly Voltairean sally on the part of the shrinking little girl. That, indeed, would have taken him somewhat aback under any other circumstances, but now the name of Laura, in connection with such a sentiment, striking him as something more than a coincidence, he inquired eagerly –

'Laura, you say! Is that your sister?'

'Not *all* my sister. But then, George is not *all* my brother, either!'

'Not *all* your sister?' repeated Mr Lydiat, ignoring George for the present. 'She is your mother's daughter, is she not?'

'Yes,' said Louey wonderingly.

'And her other name is Lydiat?'

'Yes!'

'And your name *is* – let me see,' he put his hand to his head – 'ah, your name is Louisa Piper?'

'But how do you know?' said Louey, bewildered.

'Only your sister Laura sometimes calls you Hester, doesn't she?' he continued; 'or she used to when you were a baby.'

'But how do you know?' insisted Louey.

If the clergymen had not had such very kind eyes – eyes that looked at her as tenderly as those in her mother's portrait in the locket round her throat – she would have run away from him. It was like magic, and Louey, like certain older people who call themselves agnostics, believed there was something in magic.

'How do I know? Because' – and the clergyman did a very strange thing – 'because you are my own dear little sister,' and then he bent down and kissed her. 'See, shall I show you our mother's portrait? It is all I have of her now.'

Louey, feeling the ship turn round with her, under this stupendous revelation, watched the clergyman draw a black silk riband from under his clerical vest.

She felt awed when he opened it, and showed her a grave sweet face with her mother's eyes, that seemed to look earnestly into her own.

'But mine is not the same,' she said.

Mr Lydiat opened her locket as it hung round her neck. The face was older than the one he had shown Louey, and, to the son's thinking, the gravity of the expression was softened by an air of pitiful pleading. He looked at it long, and when he closed it again, his voice seemed to Louey to tremble a little.

'Has Laura never spoken to you of me?'

'No, never.' There was no thought of suspicion in the child's mind. She was happy and bewildered. It seemed as though, in the midst of the family reunion, a special brother had been miraculously raised up, who would make all the others good to each other, and soften Laura's heart towards clergymen for ever. But the right apportioning of the relationship was a thing to be deferred.

'I must run and tell papa,' she cried. Then the cabin door opened, and Margaret came out, with tired eyes, troubled and apologetic, because she had forgotten her little cousin. She started on seeing Mr Lydiat. 'I have found a little sister, Miss Cavendish,' he explained. Margaret thought he must be alluding to a kind of Christian fellowship of souls.

'I am so thankful to you for taking care of her,' she said. 'It was unpardonable to forget her, but – but – we are just going away. I must bid you good-bye, Mr Lydiat!'

It was the moment for which Margaret had been nerving herself since the morning. And a second later it seemed as though that moment were miraculously averted for ever.

For just then, the whole party came down from above, in search of the two absent ones, and Louey ran forward, and seized his father's hand, with a cry of 'Oh! papa, dear papa! I've got a brother on board.'

'Eh – what – what's that?' said Mr Piper, quite unable to disentangle a brother for Louey out of the new family that had accrued to him.

'My name is Francis Lydiat,' said Mr Lydiat, stepping forward. 'I had not thought to chance upon my mother's family on the instant of my arrival, but I had intended seeking you out; you are Mr Piper, are you not? I had intended to seek you out, and to ask your permission to see my sister – my sisters rather;' he laid his hand on Louey's shoulder as he spoke.

There was quite a scene. Margaret's breath came and went spasmodically. It was so wonderful that she could not help thinking of 'special providences' in connection with it, and she looked at Sara in a kind of ecstatic delight. But Sara's expression was hardly rapturous on the occasion.

Mr Piper was the quickest to arrive at an understanding. A shrewd glance – the glance of a man who had measured his customers, and read his short credit and his long credit accounts in the very air with which they entered his shop, reassured him instantly as to the Rev. Mr Lydiat's honesty of purpose. He was by no means cordially inclined towards Laura's belongings, but in the young man before him he saw something that recalled Laura's mother. He held out his hand warmly. 'So you're Laura's brother?' he said slowly. 'I knew she had a brother knocking about somewhere. I'm glad you've come, sir. She wants looking after a bit.'

'Does she live with you?' inquired Mr Lydiat.

'She's never lived anywhere but at Piper's Hill. It's a good thing you've come,' he said again; then, as though dreading lest he had said too much – 'We ain't always o' the same way o' thinking, that's about it, but you take and talk to her, Mr Lydiat! I make no doubt but what it'll all come right.'

CHAPTER II

───────────●───────────

A Home At The Antipodes

'Whose merchants are princes.' – ISAIAH

No persuasion on the part of Mr Piper – pleased, perhaps, to show that Piper's Hill might have held any number of unforeseen guests – had induced Mr Lydiat to accept his invitation to take up his quarters there. To be under the same roof with Sara was too dangerous a delight – apart from which consideration Mr Lydiat was determined to owe nothing to Mr Piper's bounty. He promised to go to Piper's Hill the same evening, but resolutely refused to dine there first, on the plea that he made it a rule never to go out to dinner. Mr Piper was puzzled. It was evident that Mr Lydiat, in his way, was quite as resolute as Laura was in hers, albeit, as Mr Piper mentally expressed it, 'he seemed to have gone off on quite another tack.'

But there was too much to be done in the way of landing his own especial belongings for Mr Piper to find much time for reflection upon this topic. The boats were crowding round the vessel, there were directions without end to be left respecting the big baggage and the little baggage of the new-comers, and ways and means of transporting them to Piper's Hill to be taken into account. And first Mrs Cavendish expressed some anxiety as to the kind of 'flies' they should find in Melbourne, surmising, with some trepidation, that 'they would fill a couple of them.' Whereat Mr Piper chuckled, and told his sister he hoped he had carriage-room, as well as house-room, for the 'lot of them.' A family carriage of magnificent size, drawn by a pair of horses that might have trotted with credit through the Marble Arch, was waiting for them at Port Melbourne railway pier.

'We can all stow away,' said Mr Piper, 'you see, but you must make up your minds for a squeeze.'

Poor Mrs Cavendish was over-awed. Her expression of timorous delight and surprise was a source of the keenest possible delight to her brother. She could have reckoned up with ease the number of times it had befallen her to drive in a carriage. She never remembered sitting other than with her back to the horses in the whole course of her life. Now, as her brother Tom helped her in, and she took her seat upon the luxurious dark green cushions, while he pulled back a tiger skin of a kind she had seen in the windows of the Oxford Street furriers, her thoughts seemed to sweep her back over a space of nearly half a century. She saw herself sitting on the back of a costermonger's cart in a narrow, dirty London street, with Tom walking behind, holding the edge of her little cotton dress. How proud he had seemed, and what a fine thing she thought it when he gave the costermonger a halfpenny at the corner of their lane, while the man nodded at her kindly as he turned the donkey round. Now, instead of the coster-monger's cart, there was a beautiful carriage for her to drive in, and instead of the costermonger to nod his head at her, there was a coachman with silver buttons on his livery to touch his hat to her. Instead of the poorly-dressed errand-boy she had known as her brother, there was a stout, red-faced gentleman, of whose grand surroundings she felt herself almost terrified. The only thing that remained unchanged was the expression in Tom's eyes as he looked at her. For the minute, it made him seem almost young again – and, indeed, when a sentiment is appealed to of which the recollection remains fresh and pure for more than half a century, it is hardly to be wondered at if the emotions which re-awaken it re-awaken for a transient space the air of youth and ingenuousness which first saw its birth.

So many other feelings had moved Mr Piper since! Before he could make his 'mark in the world' he had learned to mistrust his kind, or to gauge them by the trader's estimate of their marketable worth. His son had disappointed him. His wife was dead. The only affections that could give him the highest satisfaction in the possession of wealth and power – the highest, because the nearest to our conception of certain divine attributes – were those which he cherished for his child and his sister. It was only natural that, seeing him look thus at her mother, Margaret should forget that her Uncle Piper's face was red, or that his h's were misplaced, and remember only that his heart was waiting for affection and gratitude, and that she, for one, would give him her share plentifully and ungrudgingly.

The Piper's Hill carriage seemed as elastic as Cinderella's pumpkin. Mrs Cavendish and her daughters were placed in a row upon the back seat; the two gentlemen, with the little girl between them, sat opposite. Mr Piper made his coachman drive the new-comers through the whole length of Collins Street on their way from Sandridge to South Yarra.

'I've seen it go up stone by stone,' he told them; 'I've seen it grow from the time that it was nothing but canvas, like a big fair. A few shanties and stores – that was the beginning. The best day's work I ever did was to buy that bit o' land at the corner. You wouldn't ha' given me a thank you for it then, and just you take and look at it now.'

It was about eleven o'clock in the forenoon, and the street was very full. The part Mr Piper pointed out was the most crowded of all. It was a space on the broad pavement under a verandah in front of a row of offices and hotels – a kind of open-air Exchange in which the new-comers were assured that 'big fortunes were built up and pulled down daily.'

It was evident from Uncle Piper's tone that he was prepared to look upon his nieces as his children. Every word he addressed to them made the tears start to Mrs Cavendish's eyes, but how would the position affect 'your pa?' Accustomed to interpret every passing expression in the pale peevish face, she glanced at her husband as the happy bumptious voice continued to assert itself. But there was nothing but condescending urbanity to be seen in his countenance. Between her husband and her brother Mrs Cavendish could not fail to notice that there was a great gulf fixed as the two men sat opposite to her on the seat of the Piper's Hill carriage.

Now, Mr Piper in all his letters had purposely referred but little to his home. The Cavendish family was prepared to find abundance, but abundance of a coarse description. In all their confidential talks upon the turning and retrimming of dresses, Margaret and Sara had never taken into account the possibility of finding themselves in a place where the very surroundings seemed to demand that they should be dressed with fashionable elegance. The Piper's Hill carriage had suggested the idea to Sara for the first time; and, truth to tell, she had been pondering upon little else while her uncle was pointing out the buildings.

It came upon her with fresh force as the carriage turned suddenly off the main road through two wide-open gates of wrought iron, and rolled swiftly and smoothly up a broad and perfectly-kept avenue. To the right lay a lawn as soft as velvet pile, dotted with flower-beds. The first spring roses were already opening their pink and lemon-coloured buds. The orange shrubs, clustered round a fountain in the centre of the lawn, filled the air with wandering scents. The Moreton Bay figs and the Murray pines, which Mr Piper would fain have urged into speedier growth, looked to the unaccustomed eyes of the new-comers like rare tropic trees of rich beauty. At the foot of the flight of steps leading up to the verandah, upon which the great entrance-door seemed to open by magic as the carriage approached, stood two mighty marble vases, whence trailers of the scarlet passion flower, now little but a mass of light-green foliage, threw out long tendrils that twined themselves around the verandah balustrade, and disputed the space with roses and jessamine sprays.

The verandah seemed of great and marvellous breadth, notwith-standing the intrusion of deep bay windows on either side of the door. To the Cavendish family it seemed large enough as they approached to have held a whole row of London terrace-houses of the cramped kind to which they had been accustomed. Yet here, as everywhere else, flowers and shrubs caught the eye in every corner, and delicious lounges that looked fit place for the weaving of such fancies as 'youthful poets dream,' encompassed by 'Sabean odours,' stood next to the balustrade or against the wall. As the carriage stopped, being brought up with a kind of mathematical precision that spoke of long practice, at the very centre of the bottom step of the verandah flight, Mrs Cavendish looked at her husband for the second time. Surely there would be some little trace of surprise or amazement at such unlooked-for magnificence! For herself, she was in a kind of dazzling and happy dream, of which the splendour crushed her a little at the time. By-and-by, when the confusion was gone, she would wake to the knowledge that much of her dream was abiding. But, as yet, that old vision of the costermonger's cart, the halfpenny, and the narrow London lane, was so persistently obtrusive that she felt as many doubts about her own identity as the old woman whose 'petticoats had been cut round about' in her sleep by the wicked pedlar. Her hope of seeing something in her husband's expression that would speak of a corresponding state of feeling was a vain one. Mr Cavendish inspected the front of the house with his eye-glass, and turned affably to his brother-in-law.

'For coolness, I suppose,' he observed of the verandah, and indicating the view with a wave of his hand as though he had been doing the honours. 'Ah! a charming lookout – most charming! The *entourage* reminds me of the grounds around my brother's palace. It really does, I can assure you.'

'Surely, papa,' exclaimed Margaret, 'this is ever so much lovelier! I hope you don't mind our talking about it, Uncle Piper, for it *is* so beautiful. I never dreamed that Piper's Hill was such a lovely place!'

'It's well enough, as far as it goes,' said Mr Piper, doing the utmost violence to his feelings with a marvellous effort. 'There's a tower up there ain't a bad look-out, either. It was a good two thousand I got put in for there, I know. We'll go and 'ave a look at it by-and-by. Now I'm going to take and show you your rooms.'

All the time Mr Piper had been helping out his guests, standing at the door of the carriage to receive them, Sara had noticed that he turned his head every now and then with an air of nervous expectation. She had forgotten that there were yet some family greetings to be gone through, until, with her parents and sister, she followed her uncle into the house. Then, as they stood for an instant in a great marble-floored hall, from which a grand circular staircase rose at the lower end, and took in vaguely the impression of a soft stained light, streaming through a painted window over the landing – of statues in niches, holding candelabras in their extended hands, of gilded baskets filled with flowers, and porcelain vases filled with rose-leaves – Sara was aware that a door to the right was suddenly opened, and a figure that looked as though it might have descended from the very brightest of the vases, and grown into breathing flesh and blood, advanced towards them. Sara looked at her with prompt and critical curiosity, after the manner of her sex. Women are often more impartial judges of beauty than men allow them to be. Sara decided instantly in her own mind that Laura was extremely pretty. Query No. 1 – 'I wonder whether she is made up?' Query No. 2 – 'I wonder whether she gets her things from Paris?' Query No. 3 – 'I wonder whether she's engaged to our cousin George?'

Margaret looked at Laura too, classing her with the other marvels that seemed common to Australia. Nothing could shake the poor girl's loyalty to her sister. No one could be so really beautiful as Sara, but apart from statuesque and colourless beauty, there might be beauty of a warm and painted kind which harmonised wonderfully with such a setting as Piper's Hill.

Such beauty as this seemed to belong to Laura. Query No. 1 – 'Is she at all like Mr Lydiat?' Query No. 2 – 'Will she make him feel he has found a sister?' Query No. 3 – 'Will she make us feel our dependent position?'

Laura, in the meantime, had been unable to refrain from taking a comprehensive glance at the 'beauty.' Had George's heart been still a possession to be fought over, such a glance might have failed to reassure her, for there was something in the faultless lines of Sara's figure, as well as in her chiselled features, that seemed to speak of entire beauty – beauty of form, as well as beauty of face. 'But there never *was* any one perfectly beautiful yet,' said Laura to herself. 'I can't quite see her in this light, and I dare say she's dreadfully matter-of-fact and stupid – most English girls are.'

Women can appraise each other in so short a space of time that Laura had not reached the middle of the hall before these reflections were made. Mr Piper stopped to introduce her to the notice of the new-comers in a few constrained words –

'There's Miss Lydiat coming along,' he said. 'Poppet's mother took and left her to me. Ah! *she* was a good woman, Elizabeth! There ain't many left like her in the world.'

'If there were,' said Laura, 'it would be a delightful world, wouldn't it, Mr Piper? It would see everything as you wanted it. Here, George, aren't you coming to see your cousins?

The ring of familiar appropriation in Laura's tone, as she called to some one within the room she had just left, did not escape Sara's notice. Neither did the air with which she turned to a tall young man who came out at her call, with both hands in the pockets of his morning coat.

'Do come and speak for me, George!' said Laura impatiently. 'Mr Piper's introducing me in such an impossible way.'

'We'll both have to speak for ourselves, I expect,' said George, unwittingly betraying that he was colonial-born by the colonial termination to his sentence.

Then he shook hands with all the party, bestowed a keen glance upon Sara, and inquired in a general kind of way whether they had had a good passage.

'You're a nice sort of cousin,' said Mr Piper, who had been watching the meeting with the keenest anxiety; 'why don't you take and kiss 'em all round?'

'Nothing would give me greater pleasure, I am sure,' said George. 'Perhaps it's as well, though, not to remind my cousins that they're in a savage country so soon.' And so saying, George turned round, and went back to the room he had just left. The rest of the party went upstairs, but Sara, turning her head on the landing, had time to see the flowing train of Laura's dress disappear into the same room. Then the door was suddenly shut, and Sara's eyes grew reflective, as she followed her uncle upstairs.

'Well?' asked Laura, shutting the door and standing with her back against it, while George looked up from his seat at the table.

It was the most delusive room for a study that it would have been possible to conceive. There had been such an evident aping of severity in the beginning.

It was still visible in the stiff-backed chairs of plain oak, the massive and severely plain inkstand, the unornamented bookcase with its rows of works, scientific, historic, and philosophic, the maps, the rulers, and the heavy piles of manuscript-paper in the corner. But the effort to preserve it in this condition of primitive simplicity had been in vain. George and Laura had almost as many whims as in their childish days, and the outcome of them might be seen in every corner of the study. There was Laura's guitar in one – memento of a six weeks' interruption to a serious course of Comte and the *positive philosophy*. George's French horn lay in the other, next to a dainty box of fancy cigarettes he had persuaded Laura to smoke while he was practising. 'All the discord,' he told her, 'would resolve itself into the sweetest harmony under their soothing influence.' Laura liked the cigars even less than the horn, and many months' dust lay upon both since they had been abandoned. An invalid reading-couch, so arranged as to give the student the full use of his hands, stood next to the large table in the middle of the room. An easy chair, next to a smaller one, upon which stood a pot of lemon-thyme of delicious fragrance, spoke of studies carried on with a careful considering of bodily ease. There was an easel, with a half-finished picture in oils of a racer, and a Chinese workbasket, whence the edge of a saddle-cloth with a gilt-broidered rim depended, and on the top of a massive volume, entitled *Biology*, lay a well-used edition of Swinburne.

At one time the ambition of seeing themselves in print had evidently pressed the students hard. A complete miniature printing-press, with blocks and letter-type, occupied the whole of another side-table, and some sheets which might have afforded an industrious antiquary a whole evening's pleasing bewilderment lay scattered next to it. But it would seem as though the capsize of a bottle of printer's ink had brought the proceedings to an abrupt close. A large black patch, that looked like a map of Ireland, figured on the matting beneath the table, and upon it lay numerous sheets of paper apparently gummed together by a substance equally black and glossy. Yet that the 'poetic fire' had not been completely quenched by this disaster was evident from the closely-written pages that lay upon the middle table, and the torn scraps of manuscript in lead-pencil that filled the waste-paper basket in the chimney. Altogether, it was a room over which an orthodox demon might have chuckled, for the number of abandoned good intentions that declared themselves in its every hole and corner was infinite.

'Well?' Laura had said, looking down upon her lover.

George, with his hat laid aside, showed a pleasant brow. His eyelids matched his hair, which was pushed carelessly back in a dark glossy tuft from his forehead. Laura, in his schoolboy days, had compared his tuft to the crest of a cockatoo; as long as she had known him she could remember how he liked her to smooth it back for him when he had a headache.

'Well?' she repeated, more imperiously this time, for there was something provoking in George's silence. 'What do you think of them?'

'Of the handsome one, you mean, don't you?' said George.

'Yes, if you like – of the handsome one?'

'Well, I think she's handsome.'

'Is that all?'

'Not quite. She's a beautiful figure.'

'Anything more?'

'More? What more would you have? A woman can't have much more than a fine face and figure, can she?'

'Did you ever in the whole course of your life,' said Laura – 'did you ever see a finer?'

'Never so fine that I remember. Laura' – as the girl turned with a sudden movement to the door.

'What?'

'You can't think how pleased I am that she's here.'

'Yes,' drily.

'If she were even handsomer – though I doubt whether it's possible

– if she were something quite divine – a goddess outright, in fact –
I'd be better pleased still. But I *think* she's near enough to do. Don't
you think so, eh?'

'I don't understand you,' said Laura, only half turning round, her
fingers still playing round the handle of the door.

'It's the first time I ever heard you say so,' said George. 'Do *not* be
in such a hurry, Laura. All I wish for now is, that the very handsomest
man you ever saw – somebody quite inconceivably handsome, and
"quite too awfully nice," as you girls say of fellows – could come into
the house, too' –

'For your cousin?'

'I wasn't thinking of my cousin – I was only wishing that super-
excellent, imaginary, handsome man could be got at. The odds are
all against me now!'

'Really, George, I've plenty to do upstairs; I've no doubt it's very
clever' – and the handle of the door took a more decided turn.

George pushed aside his chair, walked across to the place where
Laura was standing, took her hand deliberately from the handle, and
imprisoned it within his own.

'Never, Laura, never in the whole course of my existence should I
have thought it possible to meet with any one so obtuse, so matter-
of-fact, and so dull of comprehension as you are this morning.'

'Thank you,' said Laura, but she was laughing. George's dark eyes
had never looked more tender.

'No, never,' with emphasis. 'So then, my darling, I must put all my
nonsense into plain English, must I?'

'Oh! it *is* nonsense, then?'

'No, my sense, I mean. Don't you see as things are *now* what an
advantage you've got. There's my cousin Sara with everything that's
perfect in a woman to show. Awfully handsome, awfully clever.'

'How do you know? I think she looks rather stupid.'

'Well, never mind, let's say "awfully clever," it sounds well; and
awfully everything else. What effect do you think such a paragon of
perfection could possibly have upon me? What do you suppose I shall
ever think about her excepting this – She isn't Laura? Now, don't you
see, if my imaginary handsome man would only come.'

'Really, George,' said Laura again. 'I didn't know you could be
such a baby.' But somehow, as Laura said it, her head seemed to
have found its accustomed place on George's shoulder.

'Does that mean that you'd say "He isn't George?"' he asked, stroking the fair head fondly.

'It means anything you like,' said Laura, in a voice that spoke of entire peace. And as such an admission might very naturally be looked upon as a preliminary to a repetition of the scene of the morning, and we have no wish to copy Mr Piper's indiscretions, it may be as well to betake ourselves to the apartments of the new arrivals upstairs.

CHAPTER III

---•---

The Thin End Of The Wedge

'Say wisely, Have a care o' the main chance,
And look before you ere you leap,
For as you sow y'are like to reap.' – BUTLER

Sara had installed herself, as a matter of course, in the bedroom with the prettiest chintz and the long glass mirror in the wardrobe. Margaret would never have dreamed of demurring when such points as these were in question, being the first to see that pale rose-coloured cretonne besprinkled with lilies of the valley, and Huon pine furniture as smooth and glossy as satin, formed the most suitable background for her sister's beauty. For her own part, she was delighted with her room; and, indeed, its disposition of soft white drapery over her bed and in front of the large plate-glass windows, its sofa and easy-chair, its foot-stools and *prie-dieux*, its charming little five o'clock tea-table, with its tea service in harlequin cups ranged upon it, made it look like an apartment too lovely for common use in Margaret's eyes. Sara had surveyed it with an air of indecision through the open door.

'It's more like a sitting-room, Maggie. You've heaps of things you don't want. That table, for instance, and that extra arm-chair. But perhaps it's better to leave it as it is; then mine can be my bedroom strictly; and, of course, this one does for us both to sit in when we like. It's easy to change if we want to later.'

Margaret was too happy to care how it was settled. She had just been called to see her mother's room, which was only separated from Sara's by a kind of half-boudoir, half-dressing-room that was to belong to Mrs Cavendish exclusively, and served as a pendant to a similar room on the other side of the apartment, which was to belong to Mr Cavendish. The suite of rooms prepared for their reception was the crowning surprise of the long list of surprises that had overwhelmed the new-comers' arrival. Mrs Cavendish felt almost diffident about treading upon so great an extent of Brussels carpet. She could have put her London home – kitchen, backyard, and all – into her bedroom at Piper's Hill; and when she turned to tell 'her brother Tom' what she thought of it all before he went below, excess of emotion seemed to have taken away her power of speech. Mr Piper stood with his hand on her shoulder as in old times (he was barely as tall as she was, but thirty years disuse had not destroyed the early habit), and answered in cheering words of welcome her incoherent expressions of gratitude.

'I put up this wing o' the house for you and yours, and I'm right down glad that you're pleased with it. Of course it ain't a palace; but there's worse places, you'll find, than Piper's Hill.'

Worse places! Why had Tom never told her? It was too much of a surprise, all at once. Did he remember – and then, half laughing, half crying, she reminded him in a half-frightened whisper of the dark London lane, and the drive on the back of the costermonger's cart. Remember! Why, of course, he remembered. This was what Mr Piper liked. There had been no one hitherto to relish the contrast he loved to draw between that very London lane and the emerald lawns at Piper's Hill. Even Louey, who would have imagined a Black Hole to please her father, could not remember anything that might assist him in this respect. Her solemn baby eyes had opened upon nothing more bare than the lofty ceiling of her Piper's Hill nursery. She had never known what it was to want even a visiting dress for her doll.

'Remember! Ah! *don't* I?' said Mr Piper. 'And I took and set you on the back o' the cart. Well, the carriage was a bit more to your liking, we'll say, just a little bit. And now mind, my girl, if you want to keep friends with me, you'll make yourself at home.'

'I'll try, Tom!' said his sister doubtfully; 'but everything's so grand!'

'Nonsense!' said Mr Piper, with delighted deprecation; 'it's comfortable, nothing more! I don't say but what it's the best you can get for the money. I didn't look at pounds, shillings, and pence when I sent for you. Let's have no two words about it. This wing o' the house belongs to you. I've told off a maid who's got nothing to do but to look after you. Mind now, you take and treat her as if she was your servant, and give her your things to brush, and your stitches to put in for you' –

'Oh, Tom! but we're so used to waiting on ourselves.'

'I ain't going to have my sister waiting on herself. You'd be keeping an idle woman on my hands if you don't give her plenty to do. And you'll soon get into the run o' things. Breakfast at 9, lunch at 1. Louey'll show you the ropes. And you take and ring for your maid.'

As Mr Piper went along the corridor which flanked the row of rooms given up to the new-comers, he chuckled to himself meaningly. Meeting his little girl on the stairs, he bade her come below with him to the back entrance, and see whether her aunt's boxes had arrived. As they crossed the yard together, Mr Piper saw his son at the stable-door in earnest consultation with a groom; and calling to him to know whether anything was the matter – 'Casserole put her foot into a hole this morning,' said George, turning leisurely round.

The extent of the catastrophe might be measured by the way in which the groom seemed to make himself small, and disappear into some recess behind the stable-door as Mr Piper came up. But the old man had apparently taken no notice of him. He came close to his son and looked him full in the eyes.

'Ah!' he said, 'so the mare's gone wrong, has she? I think I wrote you out a cheque for five hundred the day you bought 'er at the sale.'

'Yes!' said George; 'she was worth it, the brute.'

'That's as may be,' said his father. 'I give you another cheque for five hundred since.'

'Yes,' with sulky acquiescence. Even George's philosophy resented this inopportune reference to his debts.

'You've got outside debts – no end of 'em,' continued Mr Piper, 'you needn't take and deny it, George. I know all about 'em.'

'It's not the best of moments for discussing them, sir,' said his son.

'That's just what it is,' said Mr Piper. Then he hesitated, as though there were a difficulty in saying the words that he had in his mind. 'The finest creature I ever set eyes on, excepting her mother.'

'Her mother!' exclaimed George. 'She was a screw compared with her.'

'What do you mean, sir?' said his father aghast. 'How do you dare?'
–

'So she was,' repeated George. 'She's got all her good points from her sire. She's the living image of him.'

'I wasn't thinking of your blasted racers!' said Mr Piper, furious. 'I suppose you've no eyes left for a woman. A woman that's worth looking at, that's to say. Well, you can take and think it over, George

– that's about all you're likely to get from me next time you come and pull a long face over your debts.'

He turned away and recrossed the yard with Louey still by his side. But the little girl had withdrawn her hand, and was walking next to him with her eyes full of their old sad abstraction.

'I'll be even with 'em,' said Mr Piper. 'I'll be even with 'em, Squirrel!'

'Papa,' said the child, with a nervous tremour in her voice, which made it ring somewhat plaintively in his ears. 'What makes people fond of each other like George and Laura?'

'Because they're wicked!' said Mr Piper promptly; 'they do it to spite *me*.'

'But what makes them fond, like you and me?' clasping her small fingers round her father's hand.

'That's right and proper, Poppet; that's as it should be, they can't help it!'

'I think, papa,' tightening her grasp on the large hand nervously, 'if any one were to tell me I *must* love somebody else's papa, I couldn't bear it. It wouldn't make me love them, would it?'

'You've got your dolls to mind,' said Mr Piper after a pause; 'and mind, you mustn't let that parson brother o' yours cut out your old father, eh!'

'But nobody could, papa' (earnestly), 'and I'm so glad Laura's got a brother all to herself.'

'Ah!' said Mr Piper, as though an idea had suddenly struck him. 'We won't say a word about it. Wait till the parson turns up to speak for himself.'

Thereupon a solemn engagement was entered into that no one should mention Mr Lydiat's name. Louey must go forthwith and tell her aunt, her uncle, and her cousins of the plot. She had never felt so like a successful conspirator in her life as when she returned from this mission, and was swept off by her sister Laura, to whom she recounted with an air of constraint that rendered that impetuous young woman justifiably indignant, the narrative of how they had boarded the *Henrietta Maria*, and how the boat swung up and down, how the oars seemed to break when they went into the water, how silver sparks seemed to jump out of the sea, how her aunt and one of her cousins had cried, and the handsome one had looked cross.

Louey herself had gone below into a long place like a kind of passage with tables in it. It smelt like a store-room. And from this point her narrative was so disjointed and unsatisfactory that Laura became exasperated.

'You mustn't suppose I don't know that your father said everything that was nasty about me, Hester,' she said with some asperity; 'but of all silly ways of letting me know it. . . . Well, he can't do us all the harm he'd like – that's one comfort.' And in vain Louey protested that Laura's name had hardly been mentioned. Her sister insisted upon interpreting the mystery after a fashion that reflected upon Mr Piper.

Margaret and Sara had promised to keep the secret. They were still examining their new and magnificent possessions, with an appreciation sharpened by a long experience of poverty – and of that kind of shame-faced poverty especially which is the hardest to bear.

Their birth and education had prevented them from caring about the society within their reach at home – such as that of the music-tuner's family next door; their want of means had prevented them from seeking any other. They had been accustomed to see their mother look upon every object from the sad standpoint of 'Can we do without it?' Sara's only eligible offer had been from the chemist, who dealt in Windsor soap, at the corner of their street, and then the proposal had been made across the counter, and was only excusable because of the chemist's desperate and reverential worship of her. It is true that the actual burden of their struggling lives had pressed most heavily upon Mrs Cavendish and Margaret. 'Your pa' and Sara, more observant of their own feelings than of those of others, never quite knew how much had been spared them – by what sublime wiles, when the wolf was actually at the door, they had still dined and supped, while the other two had feigned, even to each other (but this, I am afraid, was a transparent artifice), that headache had destroyed their appetites, or that they had been making a substantial meal at the baker's, with some imaginary coppers left out of some imaginary change. And now Margaret was laying by her small store of clothes in a wardrobe that would have swallowed up all her worldly possessions in one of its partitions, and Sara was setting out Father O'Connel's philippines upon a dressing-table that might have come from a Rosamond's Bower in St. John's Wood.

'Oh, Sara – look!' Margaret exclaimed over and over again as she made the tour of her room. 'To think of having mother settled in such a lovely place! Now if only Uncle Piper finds something for papa, it almost seems as though one might hope for some happy days – for I'm *sure* to find work.'

'Do leave work alone for the present, can't you?' said Sara. 'I'm sure that girl – Mr Lydiat's sister – doesn't work. Did you ever see anything like the draping of her skirt? I couldn't have believed a dressmaker out of Paris could have draped a dress like that.'

'I didn't notice the draping; but she seemed beautifully dressed altogether. Still, if Uncle Piper were to look at *me* like that I don't think I could feel comfortable for an instant in his house. But whatever I may do, it needn't affect your position, dear! I'm sure to be better paid out here than I was at home – there can't be so many teachers in a new place. And as for you – I don't want to influence you in the least, you know, but if you only could look a little pleased when Mr Lydiat comes to-night! Don't treat him quite like a stranger, Sara; he must feel coming away from the ship, a little.'

'Is he coming to-night?' said Sara absently. 'By-the-bye, Maggie, George is about your age – isn't he?'

'Yes, about,' said Margaret, flushing a little.

'And Miss Lydiat – Laura – what's her name – she's about the same, isn't she?'

'Oh no!' replied Margaret, who inherited her mother's interest in the records of the family ages; 'three or four years younger at least.'

'She might be any age if she paints,' said Sara reflectively; 'of course it was hard to tell in that light, but her complexion seemed almost too perfectly white and pink to be real! She seems to be *au mieux* with our cousin George, doesn't she?'

'They've been so long in the position of brother and sister,' suggested Margaret.

'Rather a hard one to keep, I should think,' reflected Sara, 'when people aren't really related to each other. The only thing that makes me think that perhaps there's nothing in it is their not being married long ago!'

'Does it interest you?' asked her sister.

'No!' replied Sara shortly; then, after a pause – 'Our cousin looks nice – I don't suppose, though, his fascinations are quite too irresistible. Only you know, Maggie, how tiresome engaged people are – always thinking of themselves, and always making you feel *de trop*. An engaged man's worse than a married one. I only hope, if there really *is* anything in it, it won't be long before it comes off.'

CHAPTER IV

———•———

The Widening Of The Cleft

'Look here upon this picture and on this,
The counterfeit presentment of two brothers.'
– SHAKESPEARE

As so often happens in Victoria, a day of early spring-tide heat had been followed by an evening of chilly sea-breeze, and the great double drawing-room at Piper's Hill, with the folding-doors thrown open, had fire in each of the grates. The reflection of the brilliant red blaze played upon the walnut-wood legs of the grand piano, and fastened a hundred shining spots upon the polished backs of gilt and walnut-wood chairs. Mrs Cavendish had been brought in from dinner on her brother's arm. There could be no sitting over their wine for a father and son upon such terms as Mr Piper and George, and Mr Cavendish was nursing a headache upstairs. He had already explained that they were hereditary headaches, peculiar to every male member of his particular branch of the family, being distinctly traceable, as he assured Mr Piper, to the cleaving of the skull of an ancestral Cavendish, who had a posthumous son, by whom they were transmitted in an unbroken line down to the present era. The period of skull-cleaving was, of course, coincident with the period of battle-axes, and was in every sense a more glorious and more comfortable age; but I think Mr Cavendish was not sorry that his headache was the only part of himself that he could relegate to it when a dinner-tray was sent up to his room at Piper's Hill. Lined with spotless linen, and covered with small side-dishes, whence an appetising odour at once gamy and piquant seemed to emanate, and bearing, moreover, a small bottle of Lafitte, and a decanter of sherry that looked like a liquid topaz, the tray reconciled Mr Cavendish to a barbarous nineteenth century devoid of battle-axes, and he set to work to minister to his headache with a goodwill that even his ancestor could hardly have surpassed.

Louey was in the perfect enjoyment of one of her ideal evenings at home. No one seemed to think of going out. She had dressed her doll in its company-dress, trimmed with real point-lace, made for it expressly by Laura, and, sitting on the rug at her father's feet, with her aunt in the arm-chair opposite, and Laura and her two cousins, with their little tea-cups in their hands, all laughing and talking like sisters, while George held up some absurd photographs of a stout, round-faced little girl, with a strongly-curved mouth, which he declared to be portraits of Sara in her early youth, Louey felt that her world contained all she could desire, or nearly all, for Louey had not forgotten that a wonderful thing was to happen the same evening, which would make her happiness altogether complete.

It came at last – the ring at the front door that she had been waiting for so long. The bell, which brought forth pealing echoes at the lightest touch, rang with its usual clamour as the clock hands pointed to half-past eight, and Louey started up from her seat on the rug, her expectant eyes shining and hopeful. Mr Lydiat looked pale as he entered the drawing-room, and Margaret was reminded of the first day she had seen him on board the *Henrietta Maria* – when he came to take his seat at the upper end of the table, and she had been struck by the stamp of spirituality that seemed to distinguish him from the commoner types of hungry humanity all the way down.

His first glance rested on Sara, his second on his sister. But Laura saw nothing but a curate in orthodox garb, with an English air of distinction that did not seem to cling around the few colonial curates she had met, and she remained silent in her seat while Mr Piper came forward and shook hands with the new-comer. It was almost impossible to remain silent under the influence of sheer astonishment a moment later when Louey (the most self-effacing of old-fashioned little mortals, as a rule) came forward too, and, not content with shaking hands with the new-comer, held up her childish face to be kissed.

It was an embarrassing position for the Rev. Mr Lydiat – though Sara admitted afterwards that he had not 'lost his head' upon the occasion. 'In fact, Maggie,' she had added, 'if I didn't happen to know that he *could* be thrown off his balance a little, I should think he'd trained himself never to show what he felt; for I'm sure last night was trying enough for any one!' The trying part of it was his sister's unpreparedness to accept the fact that she had a brother who believed that the mere accident of sisterhood or brotherhood was reason sufficient for tenderness.

Upon Louey was to devolve the grand task of the introduction. Leading Mr Lydiat up to his sister, she had announced the great secret of the morning in her piping little voice, with a '*Now* you know what I couldn't say this morning, Laura, and papa said I wasn't to tell you.' Laura had only coloured, and exclaimed, 'What *does* she mean, George?' turning her puzzled face towards her natural protector. But George was in the dark as well. The others were looking on, and Mr Lydiat said nothing, contenting himself with looking at her with his eyes full of yearning affection.

Only Mr Piper had cried out, in tones that had a vicious ring, 'Don't you tell her, Poppett. I won't 'ave her told! We'll see if she knows a real brother from a sham one!'

There was much more in this than met the ear, as any one might have guessed who had seen the dark look that spread over George's face, but it served to let in a sudden light upon Laura. Mr Lydiat was still standing in front of her. She raised her unresponsive eyes, and looked at him. It would be hard to say whether the expression of longing tenderness that she encountered in his most pleased or irritated her. If he were sincere what could she hope from his presence but a living protest against her interpretation of life? And if he were not (Laura had the illiberality of judgment which is so often an accident of extreme liberality of opinion, and willingly attributed insincerity to professors of faith of all descriptions) – if he were not, why, then, what could she feel towards him save contempt? The result of her indecision made her give him her hand as one would extend it to a stranger upon a first introduction.

'You are my brother, I suppose? How did you find me out?'

Her tone was so curt that the hope died out of his eyes as she spoke. He answered quietly that his 'finding her immediately upon his arrival was owing to the happy accident of meeting *his* – no, *their* – little sister the same morning on board. But I had intended to seek you out at once, Laura,' he added.

'Well, I hope I shall be worth the finding – that's all,' said Laura; 'it's really coming on a mission to the heathen. We're all dreadfully wicked out here.'

'You needn't speak for any one but yourself in *this* 'ouse,' interrupted Mr Piper, poking the fire with a vehemence hardly warranted by the dancing red flames it threw out. 'You'd better ask your brother there, your rightful brother – that's to say, none o' your make-believes – what's he got to say to folks who never go to church from one year's end to the other.'

'Say they don't sail under false colours, I should think,' said Laura, flinging the retort at him with her sharpest utterance.

Mr Piper's retort would have been, probably, so far from courteous that George hastened to interpose.

'Red-head,' he said, 'I'm going to be very jealous. You've never presented *me* to Mr Lydiat. Aren't you going to bring your two brothers together, or are you going to leave me quite in the cold now that you've got a new mate, eh?'

The words were enough to bring the child at once to her old place next to George's side. She watched him shake hands with Mr Lydiat with a smile, proud to think she was the small sister of two such brothers; and when the clergyman had been made to sit down she crept back to her resting-place on the rug at her father's feet. Somehow she found a great many things to say to him in a little soft voice that interrupted nobody at the table – things to ask him about that long journey he had once made in a ship like the *Henrietta Maria*, that, it may be, she had heard many times before, but that somehow were made to take a long time in the telling to-night, sometimes in behalf of the doll's intellect, to whom they were evidently new, and sometimes in behalf of her own. And meanwhile the new brothers might be taken by the others into the family circle at Piper's Hill.

If Laura had been undemonstrative in her welcome, Mr Lydiat on his side had been outwardly very calm. He had pictured a thousand Lauras, all more or less impetuous, penitent, perverse; but still remembrances of the wayward baby sister, with the flaxen rings on her waxen forehead. A brilliant-looking, fashionably-dressed young lady – nay more, a magnificently-dressed one, for to Mr Lydiat's uninitiated eyes Laura's old blue satin ball-dress taken into daily evening wear seemed magnificence worthy of the stage – a young lady who looked at him appraisingly, and indulged in a sally of wit upon his holy calling, he had never yet imagined. How he watched for a sign of softening eyes – an inflection of voice, the very slightest, that might tell of a pleasure in his presence. But to-night he watched in vain.

'There have been demonstrations enough for to-day,' thought

Laura to herself, 'I suppose Mr Piper thinks I am to take this brother in the place of George.'

She looked reflectively at the clergyman as he sat by her side. Every line of his face seemed stamped by the rule of his life. 'Renounce,' cried the mouth with its impress of stern self-restraint and ascetic calm. 'Renounce!' cried the eyes with their penetrating spiritual glance, which seemed capable of piercing the fairest fleshly exterior, or of looking indifferently through the most shrivelled of skins in its quest for the soul in whose existence their possessor so firmly believed.

Laura shuddered as she thought of a life subjected to such an influence. Then her eyes wandered towards her lover. What a different signification existence would bear interpreted by such a face as his. The lips that were half hidden by the long silky moustache seemed made for a woman's kisses. If he opened his lazy lids, it was only because there was some pleasant object, whether sun-flecked landscape or woman's face, within the range of his pleasure-seeking eyes. Yet it was Mr Lydiat who thanked his Creator, with devout fervour, Sunday after Sunday, for his creation, his preservation, and all the blessings of this life, while George daily adjured his Maker, or the law that does duty for Him, and understood no higher form of appeal to the incomprehensible than a protest. Of these two interpretations, Laura inclined to the last, whereas Margaret would have found her joy in following the first – though whether she would have followed it in the strictest meaning of the term, seeing that if Mr Lydiat had directed her there would have been no effort in the following of it, I am not prepared to argue.

Sara never considered the matter of interpretations of life at all. She liked her ease and plenty of consideration. Admiration was too ordinary a flavour in her every-day life to be even desired. She had never opened the door to a tradesman without feeling that a tribute was paid to her mutely. One adoring presence was much the same to her as another. She had always been the object of the adoration, but since her arrival at Piper's Hill she had noticed for the first time that another might take what she had learned to regard as her right. Her cousin George was as cousinly to Margaret as to herself. He had plenty to say to them both, but he had eyes only for Laura. Sara had no intention of deliberately supplanting her, but the fact that another woman was the central object of George's admiration would certainly give a piquancy to any attentions he might direct towards herself. 'It's perfectly fair,' she reflected; 'if they're engaged, there's nothing to make a mystery about; and if they're not, I don't see why George should be monopolised by a stranger.' Sara had forgotten with wondrous rapidity her plaintive surmises respecting the sickly son of the *ci-devant* butcher in presence of the good-looking young man, with the lazy, pleasant face, and the prospect of such a possession as Piper's Hill and all its appendages.

I suppose it was in accordance with this purely feminine prompting that Sara what is called 'laid herself out to please' when the Rev. Mr Lydiat had seated himself among his new connections at Piper's Hill. She had never been more animated, and Margaret, who was too single-minded to dream of imagining that the smiles directed at the clergyman might be extended to have their reflex effect upon George, rejoiced at the thought that her sister might really have it in her mind to make her hero as happy as she would have had him.

Mr Lydiat explained his plans to them. That very afternoon he had called upon the Bishop. It seemed that his lordship had been apprised of his coming through a channel unknown to Mr Lydiat himself. But the interview had been eminently satisfactory. It was probable that he would be sent 'up-country' – 'that is the colonial way of expressing it, I find,' he interposed; but in the meantime there was work for him in the parish of South Yarra, to which his connections belonged. He would very likely be called upon to preach the following Sunday at Christ Church, 'a dark blue edifice standing in a garden; you must have passed it on your way,' he said to Sara. Sara had not noticed it, but she smiled as though she had; and while Mr Lydiat was asking George if they had sittings there, she exchanged a few words in an undertone with her sister. Then turning to the clergyman, she asked him, with the seraphic glance that had rewarded him so richly for those board-ship discourses in the tropic calms, whether he would not preach the '19th Sunday after Trinity sermon' they had liked so much? Mr Lydiat's cheek was faintly tinged with pleasure. Sara had always seemed to him like a kind of beautiful approving spirit; but the storing away of his words in her heart, among her own pure thoughts, would have shown a personal, as well as an abstract interest in them.

'It would be a happiness to me,' he said earnestly, 'to repeat any one of my sermons that you remember with approval. I don't exactly recall the subject of the one you mention, but perhaps' –

He paused, waiting for a suggestion. It was Sara's turn to colour now. Her transparent eyes grew troubled. 'Margaret, you know,' she began in some confusion.

'Yes,' said Margaret, promptly shielding her sister. 'We talked about it afterwards, Mr Lydiat. It was the definition of our real duty to God, and our duty to our neighbour, that we liked so much. It came into the gospel, don't you remember?'

Mr Lydiat remembered only too well. The younger Miss Cavendish had been sitting almost at his elbow. Under her broad straw hat he had seen nothing but the dark fringe of her eyelashes. Her eyes had been directed seawards. But all the time she had been drinking in his earnest words, the fruit of thoughts upon the signification of that word 'duty,' wrung out of emotions which had never found a place in her pure, unruffled soul! Had she remarked how he had insisted upon the personal sacrifice that was necessitated by a true conception of the first kind of duty, and did she understand –. Yes, she must have understood him from the first. But, perhaps, when he had found his work and his home, she might agree with him that the two duties could still be fulfilled, while the necessity for the personal sacrifice was done away with. He thanked her with his eyes, and Margaret, who, of course, had been simply the mouthpiece of her sister, put her hand before her flushed face and said no more.

Laura and George had exchanged more than one glance of understanding while this unblushingly orthodox conversation was being carried on. Time had been when Laura would have hurled an 'infidel lance' into the midst of the party, only George had taught her that it must never be used as an aggressive, but only as a defensive weapon. She contented herself with an effort to place the conversation upon a more mundane footing.

'I forgot to tell you,' she said to the two girls, 'that last time I went to Government House I put down all your names. There's an "At Home" there next week. What's your favourite evening colour, Miss Cavendish? I should think maize would suit your sister; don't you, George?'

'Margaret hesitated before replying. Sara found a readier answer than was prompted by the recollection of a 19th Sunday after Trinity sermon.

'I always prefer white,' she declared, looking straight in front of her. 'I think Margaret looks best in blue.'

Now neither of the girls had ever possessed a ball-dress in their lives, and such impressions of evening festivities as they were acquainted with were all drawn from a breaking-up party at their school many years ago. It was a school far beyond their means, but upon the one point of the association into which his daughters might be thrown Mr Cavendish had shown himself capable of resolution, and even of self-sacrifice. If he had had a son he would have starved himself, or, at least, left the baker's bills unpaid, to send the lad to Eton. Margaret and Sara had worn the usual black dresses which school etiquette required them to put on every evening (and all day on Sunday), Margaret being one of the eldest and Sara one of the youngest present. It was the youngest, nevertheless, who felt the mortification of having to appear among all her elaborately-dressed companions with no greater adornment than the addition of a little strip of her mother's lace, sewn round the collar of her Sunday dress. In those days she had been too young to understand why, even in this modest garb, she had attracted so much notice from the mammas of tall, weak-eyed young ladies – with curls crisp from the curling-tongs – and collar-bones of obtrusive prominence.

'They wear high dresses very much now, don't they?' said Laura, addressing Sara this time. 'And what kind of waltz are they dancing? Nearly every one from home seems to bring a different step.'

Margaret was longing to say, 'We never go out – we know nothing whatever about balls;' but Sara interposed with, 'I think waltzing is like the fashion of doing one's hair. People say there's only one step, but every one seems to follow the way that suits them best.'

There was something so oracular about this reply, that – notwithstanding its reckless disregard of all those rules of Lindley Murray that Sara had been taught to repeat – no one dreamed of cavilling at it.

'You must teach us *your* step anyhow,' said Laura; 'we'll have a practice some evening before the "at home." George waltzes splendidly. I suppose *you* only dance square dances, Francis?'

It was the first time she had called him by his name, and the half-mocking inflexion in her tones grated upon his ears. What a fool he had been to battle for earthly love. How often he had pictured to himself, after his weary round among faces old in vice, the rapture of greeting the innocent, frank eyes that he remembered under their setting of baby curls. They would be sure to soften a little when they saw him, for he had come prepared to love her so dearly. He would be so tender of her doubts and difficulties; she must have gone through such weary questionings, have been so sorely bereft of all spiritual guidance, before she could have brought herself to speak with scorn of the prayer her mother had taught them both – and even to turn it into ridicule before so timorous and trusting a soul as Louey. But he would bring her back into the only fold wherein safety and peace of mind are to be found, and he would bring her back through the channel of her sisterly love. All these hopes seemed chilled and driven back by the mere sound of Laura's voice as she repeated, 'You only dance *square* dances, I suppose?'

'I never dance,' said Francis, somewhat wearily; and soon after he took his leave. He remembered afterwards that Laura had never so much as asked him where he was staying, and that it was Louey who ran out after him into the hall and put her arms round his neck before he went away. Mr Piper had insisted, in his cordial, blustering fashion, that the clergyman should look upon Piper's Hill as his home.

'You'll find a knife and fork always ready for you at half-past six, and a warm welcome to boot,' he said; 'and there's *one* o' the party'll treat you properly anyhow. We don't always know our *true* friends till it's too late, but it's not come to the last word yet, Mr Lydiat. I can tell 'em *that!*'

The latter part of the sentence had been said in so loud a voice as to be more intelligible to the party in the drawing-room than to the clergyman, who was standing on the threshold, waiting for his host to finish, before he went into the moonlit verandah without. But the words recurred to Mr Lydiat some time after, and helped to explain a glance of understanding that had passed between his sister and the young man they called George, just as he was saying good-bye. They recurred to him perhaps more than was quite consistent with all those plans born of his interview with the Bishop, and certainly more than there would have been any chance of their doing had not that mention of waltzing unaccountably and unexpectedly filled his brain with a vision of Sara, in the pure white she had owned to preferring, floating through the mazes of that intoxicating dance in the arms of the young man with the silky moustache and the half-closed lids.

Who could have imagined that a long sea voyage and re-established physical health could have operated so perversely upon a nature that took for its motto 'the steep and thorny way to heaven'? Margaret would probably waltz, too. Laura's soul was in jeopardy. And Louey (whom Mr Lydiat looked upon as a kind of wonderful instance of Providential goodness, in that the sisterly affection taken from him with the one hand was restored with the other), Louey was waiting to be taught that she might lay her affections at her Father's feet, and that in submitting them to Him and giving them their rightful second place, she might look to carrying them joyfully through time and eternity.

'The Lord thy God is a jealous God' had its part also in the creed which Mr Lydiat professed, and if visions that he had not willingly evoked overcame him as he walked through the moonlight along the unfamiliar road, it must be allowed that he did his uttermost to beat them down by a mental insistence upon the meaning of the old formula.

CHAPTER V

•

A Shaking Into Place

'Pride, the never-failing vice of fools.' – POPE

Had Laura been a young woman accustomed to model herself upon the pattern of her elders, some spark of sisterly satisfaction in the unexpected presence of her brother might have been excited by the sight of the daily-renewed joy of Mr Piper and Mrs Cavendish.

No pair of re-united lovers could have had more confidences to exchange. For the first few weeks it almost seemed as though Mr Piper had forgotten that there were recalcitrant sons and superfluous stepdaughters in the world, in the happiness of telling his sister all those long stories concerning himself and his early career, to which George and Laura turned a deaf ear. Nay, worse than a deaf ear; for George looked half asleep when his father made an allusion that threatened to provoke a reminiscence of his bygone days, and Laura had a perverse way of looking so coldly intent upon anything but Mr Piper's early struggles, that the old man had been fain to repress the outlet so necessary to his nature, and to find vent for all his suppressed garrulity in bitter remarks upon the frivolity of the young people of the day. But now there was a receptacle of large capacity always ready for his 'experiences.' The ordinary routine of his daily life was flavoured by the certainty that in his sister's eyes it was incredibly grand and magnificent. Every time he gave an order to his coachman or consulted with his gardener about the 'hurrying up' of his Murray pines, he liked to feel that Elizabeth was on his arm; when Louey came to ask him for a shilling for a cover to her doll's perambulator, he purposely kept the little girl for a long time explaining her wish that his sister might come up to them in time to see him pull out half-a-crown and say, 'So you want to keep your doll from getting freckled, eh? Well, you take and get her a sunshade with *that*; if *that* don't keep 'er from being freckled I don't know what will!' Louey had thanked him with less rapture than might have been expected. And I think it is worth noting that the outlay for the cover by no means exceeded the necessary shilling, and that the extra eighteenpence was slipped into the pocket of one of Mr Piper's waistcoats, as it hung in his dressing-room, by some undiscoverable means.

There was something almost touching in the zest with which he mounted into his mail-phaeton every morning after breakfast, following the arrival of the Cavendish family. It was his habit to spend a few hours every forenoon in a handsomely-furnished room he called his office, in Queen Street, where he went through the work which the possession of wealth so unavoidably entails upon its possessor. His confidential clerk or agent was amazed at the good spirits he had brought with him latterly. Truth to tell, he was thinking that the same afternoon he would 'bowl his sister' down to Mordialloc, or show her the land he could call his own along the Dandenong Road. To have her comely face, with its sweet sympathetic eyes, close to him, and to know that, if he took five minutes or three-quarters of an hour in explaining how he got 'the best of a bargain,' or how wide-awake he had been when there was a depression in wheat, the eyes would still maintain their expression of alert and gratified interest, made the drive quite a new delight to him. And Mrs Cavendish was almost as fond of his little girl as he was himself. Louey, with her doll on her lap, used to sit between them, the groom (with his arms crossed) behind them, and leaving Mr Cavendish at home to write letters to his brother, the Bishop, or to ponder over the remarkable traits that had distinguished some of the ancestors whose names figured in his genealogical tree, the happy party spent whole afternoons in the open air, out among the white-blossoming bushes that border the Brighton Road, or following the rises that lead from Richmond to the park-like heights around Hawthorn and Kew.

Sara, in the meantime, was taken to the shops by Laura, and in the common interest of seeing the newest spring fashions in the show-rooms, secret surmises as to the sentiment that each might entertain towards George were left in abeyance. Sara continued to wonder, but found herself further from divining than ever. For Laura – partly to

show her confidence, partly from pride, and partly, it may be, from
caution – threw her lover and his handsome cousin as much together
as possible.

'What! Go to Flemington in the pony carriage? Sara'll go with you
instead, I'm sure, if you *must* have somebody, George' – or 'Make a
buttonhole for to-night? Sara can make you a perfect one. She'll do
it directly if you ask her.' These were the answers that George was
learning to expect when he came to Laura with his old demands. At
the inevitable introduction of Sara's name he laughed silently in a
meaning way. But Laura understood his laugh, and sent him away
with a perfect trust. Only when he came back, following his cousin
into the room, she could not refrain from darting a quick glance first
at his face, then at Sara's. It is to be supposed that the answer satisfied
her – though she flushed a little when George laughed again in the
same almost imperceptible way.

Upon this perfectly peaceable footing, however, a household that
combined so many discordant elements could not long be expected
to remain. And first, Mr Cavendish, who had been irritated to find
that the colonial bishop had not invited him to dinner after hearing
of his episcopal connections began to cherish a grievance of his own.
All the money that Mr Piper in his munificence was lavishing upon
his sister's family was either paid away directly by himself, or put
into Mrs Cavendish's hands for disposal. There had been a kind of
understanding arrived at upon this head between the sister and
brother, almost the day after the landing.

'We're just beggars upon your bounty, Tom,' poor Mrs Cavendish
had said, 'and it goes against me sorely – it does indeed! But my girls
can work – Margaret can, any way – and there's "their pa." Indeed,
Tom, he's never been rightly done by; his people have treated him
shameful. But there's nothing he couldn't do. If there was a secretary
of state now, or anything like that –'

But Mr Piper had interrupted her by taking her two hands and
shaking them up and down, telling her the while that he was never
'better pleased than the day he brought the lot o' them to Piper's Hill.
And I ain't going to part with you in a hurry – you're not going to
take and rob me of my new family.'

'Rob him! Tom knew that the girls loved him like a father; but he
must find them work.'

No; Mr Piper didn't hold by women 'slaving for themselves' when
they had husbands or brothers to keep them. He would find Mr

Cavendish a 'billet,' 'something light and genteel' in the Government; and meanwhile he wasn't going to let his sister and his nieces 'go about shabby.' They should have as good ball-dresses as Laura; they were his own flesh and blood, and what was she but a – a – Mr Piper finding nothing strong enough that might not sound *too* strong when it was said left the qualifying term unuttered. Supposing Louey had had a string of sisters and brothers – why, Mr Piper was ready for em! He wasn't afraid but what Piper's Hill would be big enough to shelter 'em all – ay! and his children's children too, if it came to that. And then Mr Piper had looked at his sister with a screwing up of his left eyelid that was intended to convey a hint of some design too deep for words.

Nothing more had been said at the time, but Mrs Cavendish noticed after this that Sara was the object of her uncle's particular attention. She was so grateful to her 'brother Tom,' that I believe if polygamy had only been in vogue she would willingly have made a second Leah and Rachel of her daughters, and given them both to their cousin. But Mr Cavendish, the prouder that he was penniless, and the less inclined to forgive his benefactor the more the burden of his gratitude was increased, might have objected to making *mesalliances* a kind of hereditary habit in his family. He was already objecting, in his querulous fashion, to the footing upon which he had been placed with regard to the receiving of money.

'It is perfectly clear,' he said to his wife over and over again, 'the clearest thing in the world – only you can hardly be expected, perhaps, to see it – that no gentleman would act in such a way.'

'Act in what way?' said Mrs Cavendish, her tones as indignant as her soft organ would allow of their being rendered. 'There's not a thing you can think of isn't done for us. If "No gentleman" 'ud do for us like my brother Tom, I can only say, thank God, Mr Cavendish, there ain't more gentlemen in the world.'

'It's hardly a matter you can be expected to understand, as I said before,' replied her husband. 'Of course, no gentleman would make presents in money to a man's wife and daughters before his eyes. He would make a loan in due form to the husband and father, to be repaid when circumstances allowed.'

'And take the only teapot in the house – thank you for such gentlemen!' interrupted his wife.

Mrs Cavendish had reached the highest point of exasperation that it was possible for her to arrive at before she condescended to refer to the teapot. But if she had hurled it actually, instead of metaphorically, at her husband's head, it could not have been a more effectual weapon of defence. Yet the registering of a small triumph of this kind brought more pain than gratification in its wake. She would have surrendered all her own share in the good things that had fallen to them to have him happy. Rather than have his feelings wounded by a suspicion that his wife and daughters were drawing comparisons between their life at Piper's Hill and their life in that sad little terrace-house in London, she would have abstained from a single expression of wonder or delight when he was there to hear. But the hard part of it was that, far from being contented, he seemed actually to feel himself injured. His wife could listen to his plaints about his unfortunate position. She could have soothed with gentlest consideration any fear that they were 'sponging' upon her brother; but to come in from the drives during which Mr Piper had been telling her of all he meant to do for them, to leave the table at which they had been eating of the best he could provide for them, and to join with her husband in abuse of the hand that was ministering to them – this was what Mrs Cavendish could not find it in her heart to do. Anything directed against herself she could bear with resignation, and, indeed, I am not sure that those rare allusions to the silver teapot were not made as much with the view of turning the torrent of her husband's displeasures upon herself alone as with the idea of proving that a 'gentlemanly' outlet for brotherly consideration is not necessarily the pleasantest of acceptance.

Although Mr Cavendish resented the necessity for feeling grateful, neither he nor Sara showed any desire to bring about a change in their present mode of life. Once in a way there would be an inquiry made as to the kind of Government post Mr Cavendish was to fill. 'My dear sir,' he would say to Mr Piper, 'you had better let me try what home influence will do.' And Mr Piper would look at his sister with something of an amused twinkle in his eye, and reply – 'Yes, yes; you take and write to the Bishop, and mind you tell him Melbourne ain't in New Zealand.' Mr Cavendish hated his brother-in-law upon these occasions with a cordiality of which his superficial nature seemed hardly capable, but he took care to wait until he had reached his private apartment before the explosion of his hatred found vent. Margaret was the only one who had shown an inflexible determination from the beginning to make a stand against the forfeiture of her personal independence.

'It would make me so much happier, uncle!' she pleaded, after Mr Piper had battled against her declared resolution of earning her own bread. The battle was renewed every morning. Nothing but the old man's threat that he 'would never forgive her,' prevented her from inscribing her name in the books of every registry-office in the place. In secret, Mr Piper liked her spirit – and what a good and submissive daughter she was besides! And never idle! Such a wife as she would have made for an early settler! He often found himself wishing that George's inherited 'eye for a woman' was a thought less keen, and that, looking at Margaret's sweet, eager expression, he might have forgotten the pointed chin and flushed cheeks, and made her the future mistress of Piper's Hill.

More than ever he wished it when the matter of Margaret's working for her bread was happily decided – decided in a way that hurt nobody's pride and made everybody happy. For Louey's daily governess having left her task of teaching, and gone away to marry a faithful civil servant and live at Emerald Hill in straitened splendour, and the little girl shrinking from the notion of going every day to a noisy school in the noisy outside world, Margaret timidly took her lessons in hand while the subject was under discussion.

Never was a more successful experiment. If teaching were always what Margaret knew how to make it – that is to say a gathering together and linking with each other of separate yet connected studies, instead of an administering of daily doses of bewildering parrot-lore – if it always aimed, as Margaret's did, at extracting the patent lesson of tolerance from the long record of fruitless feuds and struggles, the failures that were triumphs in disguise, and the triumphs that were worse than failures – and if the minds that were to receive such teaching were all as open to it as Louey's – as anxious for a happy interpretation of the 'dagger-drawing and the clapper-clawing' which have bewildered them so sorely from their first handling of a history-book – we should have heard the last of the drudgery of governesses and the perverseness of pupils, and the relations between teacher and taught would be as happy as between Margaret and her pupil.

Lesson-time, as it was represented at Piper's Hill, with its little table covered with books set out at the end of the great verandah, or carried into the summer-house, as the signal for its commencement, was a happy period for both. And perhaps Margaret was not sorry to find that Louey's theological ideas were of so chaotic a description that Mr Lydiat's advice might be asked, and his co-operation given, without any suspicion being aroused of the enormous value she attached to the privilege. The having a joint interest with him in a human soul, beloved by both alike, seemed to satisfy for the time all her longings. And Louey's was so plastic a spirit. As she had accepted, with a kind of mental chill, Laura's mockery of her unreasoning prayers, and had gone tremblingly to rest at night miserably assured that she was helpless to do anything for those she loved, so she drank in with delight the new assurance that Divine Might had incorporated itself in a frail little body like her own, that it might be the better able from its marvellous height to enter into fears about street-crossings and railway platforms. The being able to pray earnestly for the welfare of 'papa, and George, and Laura' once again, with a certain mental addition, by which she entreated that all the hurts that might befall them could be given to her instead, was the greatest comfort to her. It is a mistake to suppose that any other conception than a purely anthropomorphic one can have any meaning for a child. We can nearly all remember when it seemed as though little but the ceiling interposed itself between us and God, and the idea of an abstract force operating through everything would have sent us with a dreadful sense of being uncared for to bed. Children are no logicians, and logic after all is only worth impressing upon mortals with the temperaments of stoics. While Christianity can be presented under the form that Margaret and Mr Lydiat had agreed upon as being best suited to Louey – that is to say with the sacrifice left out, or only looked upon as a means chosen for the better experiencing of every kind of human suffering – it will always make heaven a tangible place for at least a few years in a young life, and who would rob an infant soul of so sweet an imagining?

Laura would have done so, because she was convinced that the awakening was only a matter of time. For herself she could not remember when she had believed anything beyond the evidence of her senses. That others should be so credulous was simply a proof that people were 'mostly fools.' As for the outcome of her conviction in her daily life you have already seen how much it had achieved for her.

Francis had tried to reason with her one day on the point, as the two found themselves alone in the Piper's Hill drawing-room. He had taken the habit of coming up on Sunday afternoons, while Mr Piper dozed in his armchair, and the girls, with flowers in their hair, sat with their books upon the lounges in the verandah. But Laura had put a stop to such advances at once. 'I'm past arguing with, Francis,' she declared. 'I tell you once and for all that there's no earthly form under which you can present any notion of faith to me that doesn't seem ridiculous. Keep it for Hester! You and Margaret are making quite a canting little creature of her between you –'

'I think she's happier than she was,' interposed Mr Lydiat gravely. 'And even putting the reason for accepting a belief that saves us from being mere beasts upon such a low ground as the one of happiness, it would be worth your while, Laura, to think a little before you reject it so utterly. I cannot conceive how a person with your views can understand what happiness means.'

'Nor I how a person with yours,' she retorted. 'I don't consider happiness a "low" ground either. It's the only one that anybody with any sense is likely to take into account. *Your* way of being happy seems to me only another name for making oneself miserable, so don't bring *that* forward as an inducement. Besides, I've thought it all out, I tell you. I never talk to any one about these matters but George.'

She rose as she spoke, to prevent the possibility of his replying, her long silk train rustling past him, with an almost aggressive sound. He was obliged to own that he had drawn her no nearer to him since the evening of her first cold greeting of him in the Piper's Hill drawing-room. She was never anything but the brilliantly coloured young lady, who would have reminded him of one of the bright birds of the country if she had not changed her plumage so often that there was none that could bear a constant comparison with her. A little laugh that was seldom uttered without producing upon the hearer an undefinable impression of discomfort, a deaf ear to the least approach to tenderness in his words, a hurried reply, and a quick escape if he entreated for details of his mother's last moments, this was all that the Rev. Mr Lydiat could associate until now with his sister. If she had been a woman of glass – reflecting all the rays of the sun, and warmed by none, she could not have been more resisting of softening influences. He sometimes wondered whether he were hateful to her, and the thought was so full of pain that he forced himself to ask her some inconsequent question that he might see whether her eyes gathered dislike for him as she replied. But upon this head, at least, he was reassured. There was no covert glance of hatred in their bright blue depths, nothing but an utter, unconquerable, unassailable indifference. Once, and only once, he had tried to interest her in his parish and his poor, for he was now established for the time being in a suburban

curacy. 'What a regular professional you are!' she had said. 'If I were
a poor person how I should hate to be meddled with. I'll give you
something for your poor if you like, but it's on condition that you
don't quote a single text, nor tell them they've got immortal souls.
When I give sixpence to a beggar, I like to see him make off with it
for a drink of beer.'

Louey was anxious to be made useful, and having pleaded against
her father's fear, 'lest she should take and fetch a fever into the
house,' was filled with delight when she set out with Margaret to carry
a basket of good things among her brother's poor. On their way back
they would turn into Mr Lydiat's lodgings. He had a modest little
sitting-room in a house of a dreary enough appearance outside. But
within, it seemed to Margaret as bright as the deck of their sailing
vessel. It was his pride to give his visitors tea on these occasions;
Louey pouring it out from a teapot that could never be persuaded to
keep all its feet on at one and the same time. How they enjoyed these
extravagant festivities, and how happily at home Margaret learned to
feel in the poor little room. Even her old flush had steadied into a
becoming glow before she left the house. And she and Louey talked
about children who were to be rewarded with gilt-edged cards, and
old men who had been so delighted with their tobacco, that they had
quite forgotten there were some tracts for them as well, as though
these were the most engrossing and entertaining topics in the world.

PART IV

CHAPTER I

———————•———————

Misgivings

'Men are the sport of circumstances, when
The circumstances seem the sport of men.'
— BYRON

'Then it's a settled matter, is it, and you give me your hand upon it?
If Casserole wins, and I pay my debts – the one being a consequence
of the other – you'll marry me straight off? We'll have no more
scruples about the folly of binding oneself, no more fears about love
and starvation. We'll marry quietly, rehearse how we'll drop upon our
knees before the old man, take a trip to Europe, and come out and
settle down at Piper's Hill, when – when –'

George did not like to say 'When my father dies,' but Laura knew
what he meant. She had gone out with him to the stables to see his
mare, whose hurt was not so serious but that George still cherished
hopes that she would be foremost in the great race. The girl was less
sanguine than her lover in the matter, but she smiled as she smiled
at no one but George. 'What a pity to be so helpless!' she said, as
they were crossing the yard to the house – 'to feel that wishing until
one strains one's brains can do no good even. You make me fancy you
want to be protected against yourself sometimes, George. Supposing
Casserole *doesn't* win?'

'It's a blue look-out, any way,' said George. 'I can't say what I may
have to do. I'm deeper in than I thought; if this chance fails me I'm
only fit to figure in the Insolvent Court. Mind you, I don't think the
governor would ever let it come to that, but it puts me quite at his
mercy. That's the devil of it.'

'How easily it might be all arranged if I could be put out of the question,' said Laura.

George did not contradict her. He would no more have parted with her than a mother would part with her last-born, albeit the task of providing food for the extra mouth be almost a matter beyond her powers. Yet it was allowable to remember that if Laura had never existed there would have been really nothing to hamper his carrying out of his theory of life. Without being vain he might feel assured that his beautiful cousin had no aversion to his society. If a man were to tire of her company he could hardly tire of looking at her. Besides, if Laura had not been in the way to spoil him for every other woman, by turning into such a double of himself, he had no doubt but that Sara would have satisfied all his aspirations.

'It's a pity I was born, isn't it?' said Laura again.

She was co completely a part of himself, she had accustomed herself from such very early days to judge their common interest from the point of view that most affected him, that she could feel a kind of irritation against herself for being there, to put a comfortable settling of the affair so entirely out of the question. Being there, of course, they could not help themselves. That it should be within the bounds of possibility for the one or the other to turn traitor or traitress never occurred to her. Upon the footing which existed between them such a thing could never happen. She was sympathising with George now as one would sympathise with a victim to some hereditary ill from which he can no more detach himself than from the constitution of which it is a part and which he is fain to carry to his grave.

'Where's the use of asking why one was born?' said George. 'You're not more likely to find it out when you're in a bother than at any other time of your life, that I can see. If I'm stumped this time I don't quite see what I'm to do. I know what I *can't* do, anyhow, and that's marry my cousin!'

The words jarred upon Laura like a note that makes a chord sound false. To protest against doing a certain action is to prove that it has presented itself to your mind as being possible of execution. Could it be possible that during those drives to Flemington in the pony-carriage, those expeditions after button-holes to the shrubbery, Sara's beautiful silhouette had impressed itself sufficiently upon George's fancy to make him feel that the gaining of Piper's Hill and his father's fortune would have resigned him to its possession – at the cost of losing that other himself without which he had declared even Piper's

Hill itself to be valueless in his eyes? Laura put the thought away from her almost before it had time to shape itself in her brain. No one had been severer than she upon the folly of jealousy – of all human frailties the most untenable (as she and George had often remarked) upon logical grounds. What an utter and humiliating inconsistency there was, then, in feeling an uncontrollable antagonism to Sara a moment later, because she came out to meet them with a light that made her look like an angel in her violet eyes. The subject which had kindled it was hardly one of great import to others, but to Sara it opened a vista along which she saw the day-dreams born under tropical skies dancing to the sound of ball-room waltzes.

'We're to go to an "at home" at last, Laura,' she cried. '*I* am at least – it's just been settled – and Uncle Piper says they'll make my dress at Moffat & Nunn's. And – what do you think? – some man's coming out by the next mail with a letter to Uncle Piper ... He's been in the Guards, and papa knows all about him. Do you often see people of that sort here?'

'People who want billets are always cropping up,' said George. 'The Guards! – that's nothing! We've had heirs to half the titles in England. My father said he'd done with jackaroos long ago. I wonder he lets himself be taken in again!'

'Taken in!' repeated Sara, with a pretty intonation of disdain. 'Papa knows all about Mr Hyde's family. Why, even the name speaks for itself, I think.'

'We're democratic here,' said Laura, in her short, quick way. 'The only use of a pedigree that I can see is that Mr Piper thinks it worth an invitation to dinner.'

'That's what he meant, I suppose,' said Sara, half to herself. 'He said, "Another of your good-family loafers," when the letter came. Then he gave it to Papa to read. Papa said directly he knew the branch of the Hyde family the young man belonged to. Then Uncle Piper said, "We'll have him to dinner before we pack him off," and then we got to talking about the "at home." '

'Yes, the "at home," ' said George absently. 'I hear – of course, you'll go, Laura!'

'I daresay. I've nothing in the world to put on, but perhaps I'll manage. You're coming, George?'

'If Sara promises me the first waltz.'

'*Do*, Sara,' said Laura condescendingly; 'and then it's settled.' Saying which she ran, as though struck by a sudden thought, into the

house and left the cousins alone. No one could have feigned more
complete unconcern as to the consequences. No one but Laura herself
could have told with what painful precision the long seconds, the
eternal minutes, were counted before George's voice was again heard
in the hall below. No one could have supposed when she came down,
pink-cheeked and radiant, at the sound of the dinner-bell, that she
had been haunted by a phantom whose power she had scoffed at until
now.

'It is softening of the brain,' she said to herself, as she came into
the drawing-room where Margaret and Louey were kneeling with
patterns of frocks for infant paupers, on either side of Mrs Cavendish,
'I must want a change, I think. George would never believe that I
could belie myself to such an extent.'

She sat herself at the table, and watched the group near the window
from behind her book. Could there be anything, she asked herself, in
kinship after all? Time was when Hester would have run to meet her
as she entered the room, instead of leaving her unnoticed as now. She
had always affected to despise demonstrations, but it was something at
least to have them to reject. It came upon her with a sense of some
great internal chill, that if she were no longer sure of George, Piper's
Hill would be a bleak place at best. What was Margaret but an amiable
and exasperatingly faultless young woman, whose immaculate mind
was as irritating as her sister's immaculate face? As for Mrs Cavendish,
it was clear that she saw through her brother's eyes, and Laura knew
with what kind of favour those eyes regarded her. Hester was a meek
little soul, easily impressed, but loyal at least. They would not get her
to forswear herself. 'Still what was a child after all?' said Laura. No,
there was no one but George, but then George was *all*.

Through all Laura's musings, the spectre that presented itself took
no other form than the fear that George's fancy should have been
momentarily impressed. But to what had not even momentary
impressions been known to lead? She had never known George so
depressed as now. It was a time at which he hardly seemed to know
where to turn for help. He had admitted that his debts were beyond
the power of payment, short of a chance against which half a hundred
other chances were mustered. He had literally nothing he could call
his own.

If it should seem impossible that the son of a millionaire should
find himself in such a plight, remember that George had nothing to
depend upon but his father's bounty. He had talked of professions,

had looked at properties Mr Piper had offered to buy for him, had inspected stations on rare occasions, and out of possibilities innumerable, had laid hold of none. How far he was involved he hardly knew himself clearly, for Mr Piper's credit might have been traded upon to an extent that had no bounds. And George never scrupled to say 'My father will take the risk of it,' when he entered into a racing transaction that required any immediate outlay.

Mr Piper was of opinion that a wife for his son of his own choosing was the only remedy that could be applied. He had yielded, in the first instance, to his fancy for horse-racing, on the promise that a limited sum only should be expended upon it. It was the old man's weakness to have his power of conferring favours acknowledged, and George had never humbled himself so completely as when he had wanted to run a horse of his own. But the horse-racing brought about no sign of reform. George still sauntered down to breakfast as though resignation to life were the most that a polite society could expect of him, still talked across his father to Laura, about matters that proved of how little account it was to have 'made one's mark in the world' in the history of the universe; still ate and drank of the best, and appeared to confer a favour upon the world in general by submitting to be fed and clothed. When the irritation became greater than he could bear, Mr Piper had sent for a host of supporters, who were to form, as Laura had said, his 'chorus' upon all occasions. And so far he had found no occasion to repent himself. If George and Laura still sneered at him under cover of scientific discussion, it was he who was in power, and they who were in the minority. When he went to church, out of deference to his wife's son whom he respected, with his comely sister by his side, Margaret and Hester behind, and sometimes Mr Cavendish – who venerated a church that made him the brother of a bishop – with Sara in their train, what mattered it whether George and Laura greeted them with a half-pitying smile on their return?

As to the covert antagonism manifested by Mr Cavendish, what could it matter while Mr Piper himself held the purse-strings? He liked to discuss politics in the evening with his brother-in-law, feeling that the latter was burning to denounce the degenerate times which put the control into the hands of vassals. Universal suffrage had not as yet had time to operate, the representatives of mobs had not felt their full power, and Mr Piper, who had not smarted sufficiently to give him grounds for belying his first democratic principles, took great delight in maintaining the right of every man who had not put himself out of the pale of the law to have a voice of some kind in the arranging of the laws under which he was to live. Mr Cavendish was violently antagonistic to the elevating of any human being beyond the grade which his family quarterings, or his lack of them, had been proved by a providential design to be the one for which he was fitted. The danger of such arguments lay in the risk of their becoming personal. When Louey heard her father's voice from the dining-room, 'I'd take and put 'em on the roads – I'd have none o' your fine-born loafers in Australia,' she knew it was time to run and tell him that his pipe was laid out ready on the little verandah table outside, and that she had put all his English mail papers next to it; and his footstool was waiting in front of his arm-chair, too. Mr Piper would push away his wine-glass at this summons, with a feeling that he had gone a little too far, and calling for Sara, ask her what she had been doing, and what the 'folks up there had said to her,' pointing to the tower of Government-house in the distance, by way of proving that he looked upon his brother-in-law's family as his own, and that those unfortunate allusions to well-born paupers were only to be generally applied.

But Mr Cavendish stored them all away, nevertheless; and if, from the little he could gather of George and Laura's principles, he had not found grounds for supposing that they were even more demoralising and subversive than Mr Piper's, he would have made himself the secret ally of those young people for the sole satisfaction of avenging his private grievances.

It was, as I have shown, a house divided against itself – to all outward appearance, a home of peace, of luxury, and of gratified desires. Yet who that could have looked into Laura's mind as she woke to every new disturbing day with the recollection of having shuddered at some fresh fissure the day before in the rock to which she was clinging – who that could have understood what those light allusions to Casserole's 'form' bore of heart-sickening anxiety to George – who that could have conceived how Mr Cavendish was railing at the fate that made him pensioner upon a *parvenu*, and Sara was wondering why her cousin remained unmoved in her presence, would have seen in Piper's Hill the realisation of the fair seeming? Yet, might the 'fair seeming' have continued indefinitely had not a disturbing cause from without come (like a stone that falls through a smoothly-surfaced pool into dark, conflicting currents below) to stir into activity the heart-burnings, the adverse desires, and all the cross-purposes which were born of these!

CHAPTER II

———————•———————

Sara's Triumphs

'Men some to business, some to pleasure take,
But every woman is at heart a rake.' – POPE

If you were to walk down the street any summer afternoon somewhere between four and five, and select the first tall spare Englishman whom you had reason to believe was abroad for his pleasure – the kind of man who might be going to his club, or to afternoon tea, but certainly to the performance of nothing more arduous than could be expected from a fashionable lounger – you would have a fair type of the gentleman who sat in Piper's Hill drawing-room one evening in December. Mr Piper sat opposite him, and, seeing that the tall gentleman was Mr Piper's guest, refrained, in his character of host, from making any of those remarks which, in his character of employer, he would probably think fitting to offer next day when he should again find himself *tête-à-tête* in his own office with Mr Hyde.

For instance, he might observe that, in the kind of 'swag' the latter should take with him to the bush, exquisitely glazed shirts and dress suits would be an encumbrance. He might point out – for Mr Piper prided himself upon 'calling things by their right names' – that people who were willing to travel with mobs of cattle could not expect to keep hands like a dancing-master. But there was a time when such observations would be more in place than now.

Mr Hyde's thin nose and military moustache – the line in his forehead which 'accused,' as the French say, his five and thirty years – his spare form, and his easy attitude – the attitude of a man who has stood against a ballroom door through a score of London seasons

153

– were all eminently in keeping with his position as a distinguished stranger – entertained by a wealthy colonist. No doubt, when his position on the morrow would become in no way different from that of any needy youth who might solicit Mr Piper for a 'job,' he would be found to fill it with equal dignity.

He was not the only guest at Piper's Hill – though, for the moment, he found himself alone with the master of the house. The Rev. Mr Lydiat, in view of his being obliged to take duty in a country parish on the morrow, and of his going away from South Yarra and Sara for an indefinite number of days or weeks, had broken through his self-prescribed rule, and consented to come to dinner with his relatives on *this*, his last evening. But just now he was walking about the lawn with Louey. It was the evening of the 'at home,' and the little girl was gathering the choicest flowers that the Piper's Hill garden yielded – to make bouquets for her sister and her cousins. She was greatly delighted with his help, but laughed gleefully at his promiscuous arrangements of his flowers.

'What *would* Laura say! Her's is to be all blush-roses – little pale buds – like these' (holding up a flower of a hue that was like the rosy reflection of sunlight on snow). 'I must make you pick all one colour, I think' (reflectively). 'Let me see – will you make Sara's bouquet? That's nice and easy. Nothing but white, all the white flowers you can find.'

Yes, that was just what Francis liked. He thought he could make a lovely choice now that his directions were clear. In London slums he had had but scant experience of scents and flowers, but with Piper's Hill garden before him, and the wonderful certainty that each beautiful bud he gathered with such tender handling would lie upon Sara's breast, he could not fail to succeed. And sprigs of almond-scented jessamine, delicate white roses, and even buds of the moss rose (which rarely attains to perfection in Australian gardens), clusters of deutzia exhaling an intoxicating perfume, and tendrils of maidenhair from the fernery in the greenhouse, were culled by the Rev. Mr Lydiat with a sense of happiness in the task that almost appalled him by its intensity.

The young ladies, he had been told by George, would not come down until dinner-time. They were dressing for the party, and dinner had been ordered rather later than usual that they might start as soon afterwards as they pleased. Mrs Cavendish was to chaperone them, and George explained that he could not 'very well get out of going himself.' He made this declaration in a way which implied that he did himself as great a violence by going to dance as by fulfilling any other of the agreeable actions that made up the routine of his daily life. Francis would have felt something like contempt for the young man if contempt had been compatible with the exercise of his Christian profession. George had made no confidences, and Mr Lydiat could not guess that there was anything in his position to excite pity as he went into the house to put on his dress clothes before dinner.

I don't know how long Mr Hyde had been sitting with his host in the drawing-room before Francis and Louey came in with their flowers. Long enough for him to wonder whom he knew at home who could by any rule of comparison be put into Mr Piper's place – a man with the home of a West-end magnate and the intonation of a groom. He allowed himself to wonder at the same time whether the ladies would also talk like grooms, when Mr Cavendish, Mr Lydiat, and Louey came in. Every fresh introduction necessitated the use of Mr Hyde's eye-glass. The dexterity with which he put it in, and was seen without it a second later, without its ever being clear to the keenest observer how it went in or out, spoke of long practice. Mr Piper made up his mind that he would tell the young man on the morrow that 'he might take and put his eye-glass along with his dress-clothes, when he was making up his swag;' but, as I have said, he did not make his intentions public to-night.

The eye-glass, however, was fast conveying a different order of impressions to its owner. The entrance of the clergyman with the high white forehead and the serene eyes, the fretfully-aristocratic expression on Mr Cavendish's sharp, refined features – above all, the sweetness that seemed to emanate from the eyes of the freckled child, as she stood next to her father with her arms laden with flowers, had all recalled his early English associations. Mess-room companions, days of sport, nights of play – all melted away. He was almost prepared now to see fair women with jewelled arms and bare necks, such as he could remember to have passed through his nursery, and kissed him in his little swing-cot, long before he grew old enough to be sent to Winchester, and then to Woolwich, and then to India, and to fall into extravagances that obliged him to sell out, and to look for his salvation to the Australian bush. He was prepared even to accept Mr Cavendish's insistence upon the fact that their families had intermarried.

'My brother's wife – my brother is the Bishop of Blanktown you know, and he married into the family of his predecessor – my brother's

wife had a great-aunt whose maiden name was Hyde. That brings it
to what I say, you see – the Hydes and the Cavendishes are one
family.'

It might have gone on until Mr Piper had been provoked into
proving, that all the 'human race was one family,' by an appeal to the
Church in the person of his step-son, but, before Mr Hyde could
find anything to say in refutation of 'the greatness thrust upon him'
by his alleged connection with the great-aunt of Mrs Cavendish's
sister-in-law, the drawing-room door was opened for the third time,
and his vision found its fullest realisation.

For here were bare necks, whiter than any he could remember, and
uncovered arms sparkling with jewels. Every one had come below, on
this warm December night, dressed for the ball; and as Sara and
Laura came into the room side by side, and Mr Hyde adjusted his
eye-glass with a precision that spoke of large expectation, even the
Rev. Mr Lydiat gave a sigh of admiration, and reminded himself with
surprise that it had once seemed strange to him that there should be
so much fervour in the worship he knew as Mariolatry. The girls were
as well aware of the effect they were producing as it is possible to
be, only to Sara the sensation of producing it among harmonious
surroundings was full of rapturous novelty. To drag a cloud of white
aerophane behind her over a thick, soft carpet, with three eligible
young men in full contemplation of her peerless beauty, was as
delicious as though she had been an actress receiving an overwhelming
ovation. It completed her loveliness by giving it the *entrain* (I am afraid
there is no English equivalent for that indispensable word) which it
needed under its everyday aspect. Her eyes gathered the light that
you may have remarked in the eyes of successful artists. She moved
forward to the chair that George advanced for her, with her head
erect, her beautiful shoulders displayed to the uttermost. She was
quite willing that Laura's 'Dresden china' beauty should be placed in
full evidence by her side. Perhaps the delicate pink of Laura's dress
served as a relief to the unbroken white of her own. But she felt she
had nothing more to fear from competition than a marble statue might
have had set side by side with a glazed portrait, smiling and bright,
on the top of a band-box. She could read the testimony in everybody's
eyes. She saw it behind Mr Hyde's eye-glass the instant she entered
the room. She fancied she saw it in her cousin's more animated eyes.
She triumphed to read it plainly in the Rev. Mr Lydiat's expression.

In point of fact, Sara's loveliness to-night almost alarmed him. What plea, excepting his constantly-increasing love, could he advance? And why did it advance so obstinately the more her beauty grew upon him? He began to feel a degrading sense of unworthiness; to reflect that he was falling flagrantly into the crime of creature worship, and then, Sara smiling and toying with her fan, asked him where he was going on the morrow, and whether he were leaving them for long; and the crime began to take such amazing proportions that the clergyman felt as though the worship he felt must be written on his face, and so become patent to all the world.

Nobody looked at Margaret, excepting Louey. Upstairs in her own room – when she had seen herself in the long glass, with her pretty evening dress of soft black material, setting off her slender white arms, and displaying the little bit of throat and neck that she had left uncovered, her brown hair glistening against the opaque white roses that Louey had fastened into it; her face not overflushed, but glowing with the anticipation of her first party; her soft eyes full of a sparkle she had never seen before – Margaret had been seized for a few moments with a new and wonderful hope. She hardly dared to confess it, but the reflection in the mirror seemed to accuse her of it, as she stood looking at it up and down longer than she had ever been known to look at such a reflection before.

'You are hoping,' it said to her, 'that people will think you pretty; you can hardly believe it is yourself that you are looking at. You are taken by a sudden longing to feel for once in your life the rapture of carrying a personal influence about with you.' Margaret almost trembled before the accusing shade. She believed she had found a refuge from all the harassing desires that the feminine instincts of wifehood and maternity repressed by civilisation bring into activity. She had felt sure of having heaped ashes upon the spark of self-love that is able to develop into such a consuming flame when it has but itself to feed upon. And now the first perception that her face was pleasing, her form graceful, made the hidden ember burn afresh, and her heart throb with a vision of the possibilities that life held out. Perhaps the best check she could have received came unexpectedly in the shape of a call from Sara, in a voice that vainly strove to repress an almost tremulous intonation of triumphant excitement –

'What an age you are dressing! Come and see how you like my dress!'

Margaret looked no more at the slender figure in the glass. She ran straight to her sister's room, and stopped at the threshold with an exclamation of admiration. It was all Sara wanted. She turned round to look at the end of her train, readjusted for the twentieth time the white flowers that garlanded her skirt, and said in would-be careless tones, 'So you like it. Well, you know, I believe in your taste; and mind, Maggie, I don't want any one but you to put my flowers in after dinner. We can come upstairs sooner if they're in a hurry to go. Where are you going? You're ready, aren't you? *Do* just knock at mamma's door, and tell her to come and see if I'll do.'

'My! my dear! I never saw you look so nice in your life!' Mrs Cavendish had said when Margaret entered her room with the message, and with this qualified approval and a kiss from Louey, who told her she looked like a 'lovely tame pigeon,' Margaret was fain to content the irrepressible craving born of her reflections in the mirror.

'It is *you* who look nice, mother dear – no, "nice" is not the word. You look like Sara, and Sara looks superb.'

There had been much contention with respect to Mrs Cavendish's presence at the party. She had insisted upon it that it was not 'fitting' she should go. 'I won't deny my girls the treat, Tom, but it isn't for me at my age, and upon our means – indeed, it isn't; and I won't hear of it.'

Then Mr Piper had consulted with Margaret, and shortly after one of Mrs Cavendish's dresses had mysteriously disappeared for two whole days, and had turned up at the end of them upon a peg, where it had evidently been hanging all the time. And the morning before the 'at home' the maid had brought a box to the Cavendish apartments with 'Mr Piper's respects, please ma'am, and I was to take and show you this.' 'This,' upon being disclosed to Mrs Cavendish's bewildered eyes, took the form of a black velvet dress, which gave the excellent lady the appearance of a ripe Norma. She did not, to be sure, upset her placid beauty by gesticulating like the unhappy priestess, distracted by domestic grievances, but somewhere on the satin lining of the black velvet sleeve Margaret detected a round stain with a blurred rim as she was folding the dress away. She told her uncle of this mute testimony to his large generosity, and Mr Piper, than whom nobody was more easily moved by appreciation of his presents, felt better paid than though all the contents of Buckley and Nunn's warehouse had been carted into his yard.

And now the evening was come for wearing the dress. It was the first time in her life that Mrs Cavendish had folded her hands upon velvet, as she sat by her brother in the Piper's Hill drawing-room. I think even his pride in his niece yielded on that occasion to his pride in his sister. If he could have seen – thirty years ago – when she walked with him to the coach office, and sobbed and clung round his neck as she bade him good-bye! – if he could have seen a vision of the room in which he was seated with her now – would he have believed it possible? Well, he had 'made his mark' for something after all. He had 'set his sister up,' as that knife-faced husband of hers would never have managed to do, 'with all his bishops and his crests.' He beamed upon her as he revolved these things in his mind. 'You ain't lost your looks a bit – not one bit!' he told her, in an emphatic whisper that made everybody look round. Mrs Cavendish blushed like a girl, and looked deprecatingly at her husband. If only he could have been made to understand Tom a little better! As things were now, it made her tremble when the two were left alone together. She knew that when the party was over she would be made to pay through the long-drawn hours of the night for the sin of delighting her brother's eyes by wearing his present, and setting it off to such advantage. And not only to-night, but for many nights to come, until some new grievance should replace the present one or an allusion to the 'tea-pot' should render her husband so indignant that he would declare her to be unfit for any society but that of her '*parvenu* brother' (his new name for Mr Piper), and would entrench himself in the silence that speaks of susceptibilities outraged beyond the power of retaliation.

If the alloy was large in the cup of happiness held to Mrs Cavendish's lips, in Sara's it was so faint that, for the first time in her life, she was drinking draughts of bliss, unflavoured by the miserable consciousness that her dress was too poor for the occasion, or that her gloves bore marks of too frequent cleaning. To-night she was sure of herself, and the assurance had for result the wish to test her power. Sara had had but few opportunities of flirting. It would be pleasant to prove her empire. Besides, the influence of a becoming dress, a moonlight night, and an approaching party, has stirred in pulses as calm as Sara's all kinds of vague desires. And for her, the influence was the more intoxicating that it had never fallen to her lot to experience it before. She had no definite notion of what she would like precisely to bring about, but she wanted to see some active expression given to the sentiment she was conscious of arousing.

Therefore, while Mr Hyde, talking to Laura in a slow, sleepy, English voice, about his journey in the *Somersetshire*, might have been observed to adjust his eye-glass every time Sara's beautiful profile

came within its range, Sara herself was watching George, and
wondering, perhaps, whether any stronger demonstration than the one
she had read in his expression would be forthcoming by-and-by. Was
it by way of provoking it that she seemed so oblivious to-night of his
presence? To all outward appearance she was wholly absorbed in her
conversation with the curate, and even Laura was startled when she
saw her leave the room with her brother, carrying his flowers in her
hand.

'They are beautifully arranged, Mr Lydiat,' she said, as they stepped
out upon the verandah and trod over the shadows of the leaves lying
in the moonlight. 'I only want a little more green to make it perfect.'

'There is plenty in the conservatory,' said Francis eagerly. 'May I
get it for you, or will you come for it? I wish you would come and
choose.'

'I will, if you like,' said Sara, and gathering up her cloud-like train,
she walked on by his side. The conservatory was full of scents, that
came forth freely at the touch of the evening air. Francis and Sara
stood silent in their midst, hedged in by green leaves and perfumes.
She looked dreamily at her flowers, conscious all the time that the
curate's eyes were watching her with passionate adoration, and her
strongest feeling was one of triumph that he should have put himself
so completely under her dominion. But now the question remained –
'How much farther should she put him to the test?'

Sara never forgot, even at such moments as these, that the income
of a curate was only elastic when gilt-edged cards were to be provided
at special seasons for Sunday-school pupils, and that long-buttoned
gloves, and diaphanous trains, such as the one that she carried to-
night, were among the worldly pomps and vanities that curate's wives
were expected to eschew. But a little amiability could do no harm.
That half-hour spent in listening to the assurances Mr Lydiat had
poured forth as they stood together on the moonlit deck of the *Henrietta Maria* had left a pleasing, disturbing impression that Sara was just
in the mood to wish renewed. He had told her so fervidly that whatever
might be her fate, he must love her for time and eternity. Supposing
she were to let him repeat the assurance. To listen committed her to
nothing, but it was nice to listen. The plants in the conservatory –
bleached under the rays that the moon was sending through the glass
roof overhead – made such an ideal background for a scene of love.
And he had a face that harmonised so well with the picture. What a
pity the chances of his becoming a bishop were so slender in the

colonies! Had they been in England, Sara could have found it in her heart to listen even longer than she intended to do now. As things were, the dinner-going would clang in another five minutes. She was like a child – eager to play with the forbidden 'edged tools' – fascinated by their glitter, and sure that they will forbear to hurt her, if she only handles them within a given time.

'I think if I were to put a little more maidenhair round it,' she says, holding her bouquet out to him, and looking up into his face from under those wonderful lashes, with eyes that seem to ask for so much more than his advice about the disposing of her flowers.

Francis had never encountered just such a glance before. His life among the outcasts of London had left him entirely ignorant of the class of woman to which Sara belonged. For him, such an expression as he saw in her eyes to-night could not mean anything but encourage-ment – and encouragement on the part of a wholly pure and beautiful being like Sara amounted to an assurance of some future fulfilment of his hopes that made him tremble with rapture.

'More maidenhair; yes, perhaps – I can't tell,' he replies, plucking the delicate sprays with feverish haste. Then, as Sara bends forward to stay his hand, and approaches her face so close to his that her scented breath seems to play upon his cheeks, she becomes suddenly aware that he has imprisoned her hand in his. 'My darling!' he cries, in tones of such intensity that she feels stunned and helpless, as though some torrent she could no longer stem were sweeping her from her feet. 'My darling, my darling!' – and all in an instant her eyes, her hair, her lips are kissed over and over again. She can feel the wild throbbing of his heart, as he holds her close clasped to his breast. 'God is my witness,' he whispers, 'that I will cherish you to the end. Tell me with your lips, darling, what your eyes have told me to-night.' And again the seal of betrothal is fixed upon her unresisting lips by her lover.

When Sara went into the house that night she was to all intents and purposes an engaged woman, though no word of consent had passed her lips. Her predominant feeling, indeed, was one of terror. What if the curate should really look upon her henceforth as his affianced wife? The idea filled her with dread. She had escaped from his arms at the sound of the dinner-gong and run past Laura to her own room above, frightened and trembling. Her dress was disar-ranged, her cheeks aflame. She dared not go below. The thought of seeing the Rev. Mr Lydiat and meeting his glance of assured happiness

under the searching light of the gas in the dining-room made her
quail. What had she done or said to authorise his making such a
mistake? Because – as was natural enough – she liked to be told of
her supremacy, she need not have had the smallest intention of
allowing him to say anything that was likely to involve *her*. She had
intended to bring about a repetition of a rather exciting scene. That
was all. Certainly she had resolved that nothing of any 'consequence'
should result from it.

It is true that to organisations like Sara's a few extra heart-throbs
of love or despair excited in a lover's breast cannot be looked upon
as a matter of 'consequence.' She asked herself now how she could
best escape from the equivocal position into which she had been
forced. Hitherto, Mr Lydiat's devotion had been of the mildly exciting
kind, which made her pulses beat a little quicker when he was present,
and added, perhaps, to the zest of putting a flower into her hair when
she knew he was coming. But now her feeling was altogether changed.
She shrank from the reflection that he believed at that very instant
that he enjoyed a kind of proprietorship over her, that he might even
presume to sit in judgment upon her at some future time in his own
mind, when he found that she had had positively no intention of giving
herself to him at the time that her eyes had drawn his very soul out
of his keeping.

Margaret came to her door while she was debating. 'Come in,
Maggie,' cried Sara, snatching up a powder-puff and recklessly
beflouring her face. 'Don't stare like that, for Heaven's sake! I tore
my dress on the conservatory floor. I can't come to dinner. It's no use
waiting.'

'Poor Sara!' said her sister, in grave, sweet tones, that trembled a
little in the effort to maintain their self-control. 'I know you are a
little unnerved, darling; but I'm *so* glad, all the same. I could see it
in his face when you both came in from the garden. Do you know, I
was afraid this evening, when I saw you dressed for the ball, that you
were farther away from him than ever.'

'*Will* you go?' cried Sara, turning almost fiercely on her sister.
'You're enough to drive one mad, Maggie, with your perpetual harping
upon that one theme. I don't think Mr Lydiat wants your help, or
anybody else's' (laughing scornfully). 'If you have his interests so very
much at heart, why don't you marry him yourself?'

'Oh, Sara!'

It was all Margaret could say. The recollection of the joy and triumph written in the curate's eyes, for her at least, who knew at a glance when he was downcast, when he was hopeful, when he was thinking of Sara, and coupled with it the image of her sister's wrath, made a contrast so impossible of connection that, in her pain and bewilderment, she looked as doubtfully at Sara as though she feared for her reason. But the laugh that greeted her alarmed expression of countenance might have reassured her on this score, at least.

'I'm not going to hurt you,' said her sister disdainfully. 'If anybody's gone mad to-night, it isn't I. But I want you to be my friend, Maggie, for once! Make my excuses downstairs. I can't face all those staring people below. I'll go to the drawing-room by-and-by, before we start – I promise!'

She almost pushed Margaret from the room. At the foot of the stairs Mr Piper's hoarse voice was making itself heard in tones of loud displeasure. 'If you don't come along quick, the pair of you, I'll take and fetch you down myself!' Then there was a rustling of dresses through the hall, the opening of the dining-room door, the mingled odour of curry and flowers stealing up the staircase, the sound of Margaret's voice in mild expostulation, and, finally, nothing but the far-away mingling of clatter and conversation, which proved that the excuse had been allowed to pass, and that she was free to hide her embarrassment away in shame-faced solitude.

It was more than an hour and a half later, at least, before she went to the drawing-room to await the coming out of the others – so calm, so collected, so superbly cold and beautiful – that it would have seemed more rational to imagine that Galatea in marble could have responded to the passionate adoration of Pygmalion than that this lofty creature should have ceded to the subtle influences emanating from the combination of her first ball-dress, a conservatory, and a lover, with nothing of love to sanction the impulse that had moved her. I think it is Pope who says somewhere that 'Woman, at best, is but a contradiction still.' And upon this plea only I can venture to affirm that Sara's conduct was consistent with her character, for out of many types of contradictions the one to which she belongs is not so rare as might appear on a first showing.

But, notwithstanding her calm exterior, Sara's heart was beating painfully as she waited for the reappearance of her lover. So much would depend on the manner in which her eyes might first encounter his, and when we are in a false position, moreover, we feel as though our eyes were revealing it to all the world. Sara dreaded the coming back of *her* world before she could make Mr Lydiat understand that he must forget her moment of weakness. Her heart misgave her more than once as she planned all kinds of means for undeceiving him. Henceforth, too, he would no longer worship her as his ideal of womanly purity, and it is disagreeable to forfeit an adoration of so exalted a kind that the very fact of having it paid to us is sometimes reason sufficient for making us believe that we merit it. There was the misfortune of having allowed herself to become involved in a flirtation with a clergyman! Sara instinctively disliked her admirer, as she reflected that he was going to apply his rigid standard of feminine virtue to her. She spent – as would be said of a French heroine under similar circumstances – a bad quarter of an hour while awaiting the opening of the dining-room door. She heard it at last, and as her mother and Margaret came towards her with anxious questionings and tender looks, Sara turned her uneasy glance towards the door through which George and the curate, who had left the dining-room with the ladies of the party were coming together.

That rapid glance was enough. A light, different from the faith-inspired radiance that always seemed to lie in the Rev. Mr Lydiat's calm eyes, was shining in them clearly to-night. To Margaret it seemed that the sons of God, who came down from their heights to woo the daughters of men, might have borne such an expression on their seraphic faces; but to Sara the betrayal of the intensity of the sentiment which could transform what she called 'the professional look' of the curate was almost as alarming as it was flattering. It made her task doubly difficult. She would have to write, perhaps, a long explanatory letter on the morrow, and Sara hated writing. After all, clergymen should not be authorised to fall in love. If she could only be in power, she would make them all take vows like Father O'Connell, who knew how to convey, in looks and 'phillippine,' a most fervid and stimulating admiration, but could not expose a confiding woman to the risk of being invited to share his income.

George's voice aroused her from the reflections. He was standing next to her with extended arm.

'One turn in the verandah,' he said persuasively; 'just to try whether my step will go with yours. Laura says I waltz abominably. I don't believe it. Will you be umpire, Sara?'

He was leading her out to the moonlit floor, stained with the shadows of the leaves and blossoms that garlanded the pillars. As Sara swept past the curate – seated next the open window – she carefully averted her eyes from his upturned face. She could hardly restrain a gesture of impatience when she perceived that he had followed her, and was standing against the balustrade watching her every movement.

'You don't mind obliging me, do you?' said George, in a kind of murmuring monotone, that was intended for her ear alone. 'I don't think I've ever asked you for a single cousinly privilege yet,' and he put his arm round her waist.

Sara made no reply, but the curate in the corner turned his head away as he watched the expression that seemed to grow out of the smile with which his betrothed listened to her cousin's whispered words.

Louey was playing for them inside. The musical sounds of an old-fashioned German waltz, taught her by Margaret, and imbued with the kind of weird pathos that Louey's fingers imparted to the most commonplace of airs, floated out into the moonlight. George and Sara glided round, with the harmony of movement that comes from perfect adaptation, and the Rev. Mr Lydiat stood motionless, like the skeleton at the feast, watching them with a strange regard. The longer George and Sara waltzed, the closer, to the curate's imagination, seemed to grow the mutual understanding that had sprung up between them. Sara, with a little smile of triumph on her lips, was listening to her cousin's whispered compliments. She was quite aware of a subtle change in his manner – something that only dated from the beginning of their dance – and he, on his side, found himself strangely moved at the discovery of the new sympathy existing between them. Hitherto he had looked upon his cousin's passionless loveliness as coldly and critically as though it had been embodied in marble. To-night she seemed suddenly to have sprung into sensuous life. Her soft, ungloved hand lay warm within his palm. Her breath was a caress. If she raised her eyes, it was to send out of their dreamy depths a glance that made his pulses throb. Heaven knows how many nations have bled because of such glances as these. In the chronicle of wars, in the annals of police courts, you may read of their fruits if you will. They emanate from a certain order of eye, in obedience to the same instinct which prompted the 'serpent of old Nile' to allure so many regal birds. It is their province to shatter allegiance under their baneful might, whether allegiance to God, such as Mr Lydiat had professed, or allegiance to His creature, such as George would have maintained towards Laura. And in return for the peace that they take away, what grace do they have it in their power to bestow? A tumult of feverish longing, moral degradation in that the victim is conscious that the higher part of his nature has succumbed to the lower, and at best rapturous illusions, unsatisfying and transient as the paradise of an opium-eater.

Sometimes the kind of power I describe has been known to lie inactive, like genius of a higher description, until the sudden discovery of the marvels it operates prompts its possessor to give it full play. Sara had never fully realised until this evening the potency of the wand she carried. The result of her first experiment had been disastrous, and now she was seeking to retrieve the disaster by making another experiment of the same kind which was to neutralise the effect of the first. George was less prompt of self-betrayal than the Rev. Mr Lydiat, but in spite of his loyalty to Laura there was something in his cousin's eyes which it was impossible to resist.

His own grew troubled. He left off dancing by a kind of sudden impulse, and passing her arm through his led her to a seat. But Sara would not suffer him to leave her. Laura had come outside under pretence of talking to her brother, and Sara was convinced that the quiet pair were suffering a real martyrdom. She was reading a lesson to her lover and her rival which should be useful to both alike, and she was determined not to spare them.

'George – I want to ask you,' she said, as he was turning away.

'Well?'

'Does my step suit you better than Laura's?'

'You dance like an angel,' he said, standing in front of her. 'I never felt any dancing like it before.' Then he turned resolutely away, and crossed over to where his betrothed and the clergyman were standing together.

'I'm never going to be modest again about my waltzing,' he said, with a little flush of triumph in his cheeks. 'I've been telling Sara she dances like an angel. Were you watching us, Laura?'

'Did you ever see such touching vanity?' said Laura, turning to her brother; but with her lips white, even while she feigned to smile. 'This is the man I call my "monster" at parties, Francis. His step, such as it is, is all my creation, and he is always victimising me to it. What a relief to think there's some one to take him off my hands!'

She hurled the last words at him defiantly, as she turned to her brother.

'You are going up the country to-morrow, Francis? Will you take me with you as far as Macedon? I am tired out of town!'

'Won't you come all the way with me?' he said, welcoming the change in her manner towards him with delight. 'There is an empty parsonage waiting for me where I am going. I should be so thankful for your society.'

Laura seemed to hesitate. George had heard her declare her intention of leaving him without a word of protest or inquiry. Should she find a refuge in her brother's affection from the torment that her present position was causing her – that torment which can only be compared to the martyrdom imposed upon ancient nuns? Though even they, shut out from the life-giving air, and compelled to watch the building of the tomb that was to encase their living bodies, as slowly with hideous regularity, brick by brick, the ghastly wall was upreared, might shriek out their own despairing dirge behind the murderous barrier. Laura must neither shriek nor protest, as day by day the impalpable wall that threatened to shut her away from her world of love and light received its daily addition. And what made it the hardest of all to bear was the constant terror that she herself was assisting to cement the bricks of her vault. Yes, she would take refuge for awhile in her brother's heart. He had known how to quiet the insatiable heart-hunger that he must surely have felt at times, and perhaps, if he would only spare her his theology, she might learn of him how human hearts could kill their egoism.

But it was an unfortunate moment for the fostering of Laura's promptings. As she looked at her brother, it happened that Mr Hyde stepped out into the moonlight, for the recess whence his eye-glass had been brought to bear upon the waltzers. He was petitioning Sara for 'one' turn before she went inside, and Francis could hear him declare, in his low measured tones, that he would live upon the memory of it through the long exile that awaited him.

Sara needed no pressing. With a dangerous light in her violet eyes, and the faintest flush on her pure cheeks, she floated in her partner's arms past the gravely-watching trio, while Louey, with the magnetic sympathy that made her rejoice with those that rejoiced, and weep with those that wept, without divining the cause of their joys or their sorrows, gave unconsciously a pathetic significance to every note she struck.

And now the carriage, with a due scrunching of the gravel under its sheels, drove imposingly to the front door. The footman jumped down with a rug to protect the ladies' dresses as they entered it; Mrs Cavendish's maid, with an array of fluffy wraps, followed in the wake of her 'young ladies;' while Mr Piper, with fussy kindness and a sense of triumph that he could not conceal, called to the loiterers to 'take and be off.' In vain Francis, with an undefined bewildering pain gnawing at his heart, sought Sara's eyes as she swept towards the carriage, including her lover in a farewell bend of her head as she disappeared from view. It was Margaret only whose handgrasp told of sorrow at his departure. In vain he tried to follow Mr Cavendish through the labyrinth that led to his connection with Mr Hyde. His brain was in a whirl, his soul in a tumult. It was only afterwards that he remembered how Louey had clasped her tender little arms round his neck as she bade him 'good-night' and 'good-bye,' with a whispered promise to write '*all* about *everything*,' and to send him news of Mr Smith's rheumatism and Mrs Jones's lumbago. Heaven knows what a storm of conflicting emotions assailed the poor clergyman that night as he walked like a restless spirit up and down his narrow room through the warm December darkness. Next day he and Laura were seated facing each other in the train that took them to Barnesbury, Laura pretending to be asleep, while the constant vision of a brilliant ball-room, through which George and Sara were for ever threading their way in each other's arms, floated before her mental gaze. Francis read *The Argus*, breathing quickly whenever an overmastering renewal of the scene in the conservatory burst in upon his forced perusal of Victorian politics. And Sara, meanwhile, sound asleep beneath the rose-coloured curtains of her Piper's Hill couch, was dreaming probably of the bliss of the night before.

'We won't wake her,' said Margaret to her mother, returning on tip-toe from her bedside, with a cup of tea in her hand. 'You know she danced nearly the whole evening through – and six times with our cousin George – without stopping.'

CHAPTER III

———— • ————

Laura Does Penance

'Brother, brother, we are both in the wrong.'
                                    – *Beggar's Opera*

The remark that Voltaire made about the great Russian Empire, when he compared it to a pear that was rotten before it was ripe, might be applied with equal truth to many a Victorian township. But the comparison, let me hasten to add, only holds good as regards the buildings and general aspect of these places. That 'peace and content-ment reign' therein, and that the small storekeeper and cockatoo farmer have nothing in the way of extortionate taxation or prompt knouting to fear in the land of democracy and universal suffrage, may be taken for granted. Nevertheless, as I said before, in the matter of their arriving at decay before they reach maturity, there are many Australian townships that might take Voltaire's remark to themselves.

Barnesbury is one of these. Its oldest inhabitants, still in their prime, look back with regret to the days when it was the railway terminus; when all the coaches, and buggies, and bullock-drays, and four-in-hands, and squatters and diggers made it their head-quarters; and money spending and money-making, and consequent joviality, were the order of the day. Then it was that the three banks were built, in front of the largest of which the cows and geese graze peacefully to-day. Those fine-sounding names were given to the broad tracks leading away into the bush, which a few years more (it was fondly imagined) would transform into bustling streets. The great bluestone public-house, designed for a monster hotel, was completed as far as its first story, but as it was never carried any farther, it naturally possesses at the present time a somewhat squat appearance, with a suggestively make-shift roof, and a general air of having been stopped in its growth. The church, too, was begun upon quite an ambitious scale, for to the credit, be it said, of Victorian country-folk, they pay as liberally for their religion as for their beer, and the Barnesbury spire was to be a 'thing of beauty' in the eyes of all men. But the church, unhappily, shared the fate of the public-house and the banks. The spire that was to have been a 'joy for ever' to the residents of Barnesbury shrank into a small wooden bell-tower, not unlike a pigeon house, and the incumbent deemed himself fortunate when a weather-board verandah, without a floor, was affixed to the modest bluestone cottage dignified by the name of the parsonage.

The same evidence of having been brought to a sudden halt in by-gone years, and of having never been set going again, clung to the commerce of Barnesbury. The one and only street ran down and up a hill, which is not the same thing as to run up and down one. In the hollow mid-way was a row of shops of the most casual order, in one or any of which you might purchase almost anything from a bonnet to a wash-hand basin. On race-days, or tea meeting evenings at the school-house, it was not unusual to see as many as three spring-carts, with a bush-buggy and riding-horses, fastened to the posts in front of the one bit of wide pavement that remained. On election days the crowd was even greater, but its chief scene of action was the aforementioned Junction Hotel, which made up in extent what it had lost in height, and which could have gathered almost all the population into its bar.

On the evening of the arrival of Francis and Laura, the main street of Barnesbury had been swept by a hot wind, which (water being precious in those parts) had performed upon the houses the disagree-able operation known to housewives as that of 'smothering them in dust.' The small parsonage, to which the new arrivals had been driven in the one hired car that represented the station cab-stand, was so full of dust that Laura was dismayed. The sitting-room struck her as looking appallingly dark and mean, with its common paper and single stiff window. She made a disconsolate tour of the bedrooms, and came back to the narrow entrance-hall where her brother was assisting a frightened looking maid to carry in the luggage from without.

'Francis – don't touch my box! Have you sent the man away? for I think I shall go back; they ought to have told you what it was like. I think the best thing we can do is to shake the dust off our feet – it won't make much difference, there's so much of it already – and go home.'

'This is *my* home, for the present,' said Francis quietly; 'and I'm sorry it doesn't please you, Laura. I thought it rather a pretty place.'

'Pretty!' Laura's laugh was the last expression of derision. 'Well, you approve of penances, don't you? If you'll put it upon the footing of my doing penance with you for all my sins – and yours, too, of course – I'll stay, but only upon that understanding.'

'Upon any understanding you please, so long as you don't run away from me,' said her brother. 'I thought I was in a fair way of finding the little sister I'd kept in my mind for so many years. Don't take her away from me so soon, Laura.'

'I never knew *her*,' replied Laura shortly, 'but I dare say she was a little idiot. Most babies *are!* Well, the luggage can go to the rooms, if you please. I've chosen mine. It's the smallest, but it's not quite so dark as yours. I never could exist without plenty of light. I hope you won't mind!'

'Oh, put me anywhere!' said Francis cheerfully. 'Your presence will be light enough, Laura; and I know this isn't Piper's Hill – so I'm doubly grateful to you for coming.'

Having once given in, Laura concluded to make the best of things. But how if George were in her brother's place, and this were their home-coming? How if she and he had been driven from the paradise of Piper's Hill to so sterile a world as this, to toil with the sweat of their brow for the common necessaries of life? Somehow she could not place George in her imagination among her new surroundings. It was hard enough to adapt herself to them. She scarcely recognised herself in the wry mirror in her little room, that exaggerated the dusty hue of her features with such disagreeable intensity. The flies were gathered in black clusters upon the ceiling. Already the ominous trumpeting of expectant mosquitoes sounded in her ears. Laura sighed impatiently, and rang a tin hand-bell for the maid.

'Turn on the bath for me, please,' she said, as the latter appeared at the door, more scared than ever at the unusual summons; 'and I should like a cup of tea afterwards.'

'Oh! please Miss, there ain't no bath; 'twasn't never fitted up, and Mr Marsh he goes now and ag'in to the river, which it's a long way from 'ere, and he don't go very often, please Miss.'

No bath! Laura's indignation against 'some person or persons unknown' deprived her for an instant of speech. The 'Oh indeed!'

that followed was sufficiently eloquent to bring the terrors of the servant to a climax. The Rev. Mr Marsh's factotum had never 'done for' any but 'plain-living people' before, and a modern farmer who should find Pegasus one morning standing with shining folded wings in his back yard would be hardly more discomposed than she at the advent of Laura in the unpretending parsonage.

When the cup of tea was brought at last, and the avowal of the existence of a tub and a pump in the back kitchen extorted from the servant, Laura bethought herself of sending some tea to her brother, and this duty accomplished, she gave herself up to her reflections. What was George doing now? Hot-wind evenings were not unknown at Piper's Hill, and signified, for the most part, hammocks, lounges, ices, cool Indian silks, and tea-gowns in the broad heliotrope-perfumed back verandah, with no harder work than the wielding of quaint Japanese fans, or the pressing of squirts of eau-de-cologne and white rose scents. Last summer George and she had engaged Louey in the service, and made her sing for them when they were too exhausted to continue their reading of Swinburne or Dante Rossetti. Now, probably, it was Sara who had taken possession of the hammock. Laura, tired, warm, and dusty, beating off the flies in the mean little room, could picture the superb figure that nothing seemed to discompose, lying draped like an antique goddess, against the screen of quivering leaves and flowers in this same verandah. And George? . . . It was too hard to bear! Why had she come away? She was a fool to listen to her pride. George was not different from other men, though no other man could ever exist for her in the world. But she must not try him beyond his strength. It was not too late. A word from her and he would give up everything – exchange his easy, luxurious life (and how easy and luxurious it was Laura had never realised until now) for penury, disgrace, and grinding work . . . But was she as *necessary* to him as he was to her, or is man so constituted that the constant presence of a beautiful woman must infallibly influence him, though his heart be irrevocably given to another? Laura shuddered at the questions she was raising. A few months ago and she would have dismissed them as the fancies of a sick brain.

'What! Doubt George? Doubt 'truth to be a liar?' But where is truth, and what is truth?

'Oh, I am tired, tired!' cried the girl, shaking her head wildly, as though she would free it from some great and unendurable pressure. Then, suddenly starting up, with a gleam of hard resolve in her eyes, she knelt before her trunk, unlocked it, and drew out a small pocket-book with feverish haste. Therein she wrote, in a firm legible hand – 'I bind myself not to see George until the New Year's Day races are over, nor to write him one single word that may remind him how we stand towards each other' – she hesitated; then, with a rapid pencil 'nor to make the least advance of any kind, now or henceforth. If he wants me let him take me, and if I could stand *this* for his sake,' she added mentally, with a glance of profound disgust round the room, 'let him do as much for me, and work in earnest.'

But even as she thought these words an expression of pity and yearning crossed her face. The idea of coupling George with hard work seemed cruel and ludicrous. But the fault was not his own. And then George was George. And, oh, to have him near her one instant; to put her tired head on his breast, and feel the dear hand steal round her neck! If he could only know how homesick and heartsick she was! In another minute the proud Laura was leaning her head in her hands, weeping the bitterest, forlornest, most scalding tears she had ever shed. I think if Mr Piper had seen her now his mind might have misgiven him that the 'painted hussy' had something that did service for a heart after all.

That we have each a separate world of our own is a fact that people living under the same roof often find it hard to grasp. Laura would perhaps have been drawn nearer to her brother had she had the least insight into the state of his mind during this first penitential afternoon. 'Of course, he's polishing up his sermon,' she thought impatiently; 'as though it mattered what one said to these country clods, and to a trouble like mine he could have nothing to say. I suppose he wouldn't understand the first letter of it.'

But there Laura was mistaken. From the time of his meeting with Sara Francis had learned to understand – he was learning still. But his path of discovery was beset with cruel surprises. While Laura was sobbing her heart out in her solitude he was wrestling in silence with a trouble that was exceedingly bitter to him. He had been lifted for one instant into heaven, and while his soul was still drunk with the bliss of his sense of the possession of the woman he adored, he had been cast into a kind of outer darkness, in which he was groping vainly for the light. What did it mean? How was it to end? If ever man loved with every fibre of his being then he loved Sara Cavendish. And if ever woman responded to love without affirming it in words, then Sara had responded to his. Francis had heard of coquettes; but surely this was beyond coquetry; or was he yet so ignorant that he mistook her meaning entirely? Did she intend to punish him for his too ardent seizure of her after her beautiful eyes had told him she was all his? And was it only because he was such an entire novice in all that concerned the social customs of his time that there had seemed to him something in her dancing so peculiarly intoxicating and unholy? Or was he to give heed to the voice that would have silenced all these specious pleadings, that told him he was a fool and worse than a fool, that convicted him of having surrendered himself heart and soul to a woman who would sell herself for gold, but never give herself for love?

As the latter thought passed through his mind, and the memory of the evening before thrilled him anew with its delirious sensations, Francis realised the state of feeling in which men have stabbed their mistresses and then themselves. Love and jealousy and madness were not mere words then, but plain and awful facts. But while the consciousness of madness exists the power to combat it must exist too. Then *he* would combat it, as though it were the devil in person, and pray, and starve, and fight it down. But first he would write to Sara, and put things upon a clear footing. And if after that he found his cross too heavy to bear he would ask for a mission to Central Africa, or the South Seas, or anywhere removed from the influence of Sara's eyes. Surely strength would be given him to conquer this infatuation if he resolutely tore himself away. And before he could lapse again into the dangerously sweet dream that the first hypothesis had evoked, Francis manfully wrote his letter, and went out to post it.

Brother and sister met that evening in the mood best described in the scriptural word chastened.

'It's all very queer and unhomelike,' observed Laura, as she sat down to the small, round table in the room that had been pointed out to the new comers as the 'best parlour,' and prepared herself to wield a teapot of the dimensions of a garden watering-pot. 'I suppose you have a soul above such considerations, Francis, but I do think eggs and bacon swimming in fat on such an evening as this, and fly-blown, glazed shepherd boys on the mantelpiece, are enough to depress the best-intentioned person.'

Francis smiled. 'It's all a matter of what you've been used to. If you could compare this with some of the homes I've seen' –

'Oh! I've seen pig-styes, too, with human pigs in them; but then there was no pretence about them. It's the pretension of this place that I can't endure. To-morrow I'll lock up every shepherd-boy in the establishment.

'I'm afraid you had an ideal rural parsonage in your mind,' said Francis, 'and that this doesn't harmonise with it; but I wish you could suggest how I might make your stay a little pleasant to you. We can hire a horse and buggy, if you will drive me about – you know I can only just distinguish a horse from a cow – and I've been making Jane tell me what points of interests there are in the neighbourhood.'

'Thanks,' replied Laura drily. 'I hope Jane doesn't suspect you of intending to lure her into one of them and murdering her – that is what she looks like at present – but I don't mind driving you about, and perhaps, Francis, if I make an arrangement about reading, a kind of give-and-take arrangement, you know, you'll agree to it?'

'Anything you like,' said her brother eagerly. 'I have so longed to get you to read certain books, Laura. Shall we read together?'

'Oh, I only read aloud with George. We like the same kind of books, you know, and you and I wouldn't!'

'How do you know? Won't you tell me what you read? Is your friend clever, intellectually, I mean?'

George her *friend*. Laura did not understand why the word grated upon her so painfully. She hesitated.

'*You* mightn't call him clever. He's awfully lazy, but he understands things more quickly than any one I ever knew. He seems to grasp a meaning, and see all round a subject before you've got the sense of the words into your head, and all the time you wouldn't think he was paying any attention. Oh! about what we read? I can't well describe it to you. It would be such a jumble. Bits of anything we like. We don't often read whole books, you know. Sometimes we go in for heavy reading, Bastiat, and Carlyle, and Spencer, and Tyndall, and sometimes for French novels, only we're always laughing at each other's accent, and sometimes we take a fit of poetry, only I can't stand Byron, and George will persist in saying he's such a great poet. But lately we've not been reading at all.'

'I suppose you've all been taken up with the new arrivals?' said Francis, longing to ask more particularly after Sara. 'Do the Misses Cavendish seem to like their home? It appears to be a most magnificent abode, and Mr Piper dispenses hospitality upon a truly lavish scale. What have I said that amuses you, Laura?'

'Oh, nothing,' said Laura; 'you're funny sometimes, without

knowing it. Yes, they seem to like it well enough. I shouldn't think they'd been very well off at home; Mrs Cavendish always seems astonished at the most ordinary outlays. But I believe she's really fond of that vulgar old brother of hers. And so's Margaret; but Margaret's painfully good, and she's making Hester just like her. She'll be the ruin of her, I know. But I can't help it.'

'And the younger Miss Cavendish?' Francis's voice sounded false and unnatural in his own ears as he put the question, but Laura did not seem to notice.

'Oh, Sara? As long as she has her ease, I don't think she cares much about the rest. I suppose she finds a resource in the contemplation of her own loveliness, but, of course, she likes a good setting for it. I think if she *has* any strong points, she gets them more from her father than her mother. I believe Sara's ideal of perfect happiness would be to marry some frightfully rich old man of title, who would die directly, and leave her a distinguished name and complete liberty to amuse herself with his money in the most aristocratic circles.'

Francis was silent. When next he spoke there was a kind of forced briskness in the tone of his voice that struck even Laura's insensible ears.

'I find there will be plenty work for us here, Laura – plenty – plenty! The more the better. Work is salvation.'

'I thought you people considered it a curse,' responded Laura, surprised at the vehemence of her brother's manner.

'That is quite a mistaken idea. Why, life itself is nothing but an opportunity for working in an upward direction.'

'Oh, don't let us begin to discuss things, Francis, or I shall tell you I would rather have been without the opportunity if I had had a voice in the matter. But don't let the work interfere with our plan. I'm going to make a list of two or three books I want you to read, and I promise I'll read yours, and even sit out your sermons – when it's not too warm. Is that agreed?'

'Is your list settled upon? Tell me that first. You're not going to set me to Voltaire and Tom Payne!'

'Voltaire! Payne! Oh, Francis, what centuries behind the times you are! Why, no one would think of reading them for that kind of thing, now. No! I have two or three names in my head. I'll give them you if you'll promise to send for the books to Melbourne to-morrow, and you can get mine sent up at the same time.'

Laura's list comprised a work of Greg, Draper's *Conflict of Science and Religion*, and a translation of Renan's *Life of Jesus*. Francis, on his side, was ready armed. He had brought a box of books with him, from which he extracted two volumes of Robertson's Sermons, attractively bound in black and gilt. These he handed to Laura, and an agreement was entered into between the brother and sister that neither should throw down the gauntlet for at least another fortnight. Laura pledged herself to read without prejudice, and Francis promised to approach the *Conflict of Science and Religion* with an open and unbiassed mind. To have Laura willing to interest herself in the subject of his convictions was, he felt, a great step gained. With an earnest and zealous adversary he might hope for all things, but before indifference he was helpless. What a glory and a triumph it would be to open her soul to the 'light from on high,' without which it seemed to him she must stumble on in the dark for all time. He had never engaged in polemics before. There had been too much practical religion to be taught in the miserable parish to which he ministered in England, and he was aware that, as Laura said, he was behind the times in his knowledge of modern theories. But he had not the least misgiving as regarded the effect of Laura's selection of books upon his own point of view. On the contrary, he hailed the opportunity of fighting for the good cause, being firmly convinced that the issue could only result in victory. After all, had he not Providence on his side, and was there not the precedent of the first mighty conflict between the heavenly hosts and the proud spirits who defied Heaven's might to point to? But he felt he must tread cautiously. When Laura was in a scoffing mood, he must answer gently. Enough that her heart had been softened to him so miraculously, for poor Francis was willing to believe that a spontaneous sentiment of sisterly affection had been the sole cause of her sudden resolution. Enough that he and she were nearer than they had ever been since the days when his mother had given him the 'baby-sister' to carry, and he had expended such a world of boyish tenderness upon her. If his heart must bleed in one direction, there was balm for it in another, and he earnestly resolved that no thought of Sara should render him neglectful of the precious opportunity that was given to him.

And Laura? Laura had said truly at the instant of their arrival that she had come to do penance. Reading and counter-reading were but a design for diverting her mind from the one invading absorbing thought that could never be shaken off. But it was well to let Francis suppose she was really interested in the subject of his orthodoxy. She

could not play her part becomingly without a pretext of the kind. Her
tired eyes and weary mouth must have betrayed her. As it was, she
set herself to work with feverish activity in all kinds of new and
uncongenial directions. She fed the fowls, and hoed the weeds that
had gathered under the Rev. Mr Marsh's verandah. Francis smiled
more than once, in spite of his trouble, as he perceived the Watteau-
like figure trundling a barrow out of the backyard. She took the
duster from Jane's nerveless fingers, and rubbed the cheap, common
furniture into new lustre. She substituted fresh flowers on the mantel-
shelf for the aggressive shepherd-boys, and sent to town for a cookery-
book. Only once a sudden and irrepressible burst of tears came into
her bright, hard eyes. It was when Francis, passing the dairy one
morning and looking in upon her among the milk-jugs, exclaimed –
'What a treasure you would be to a poor man, Laura, and a few days
ago I thought you almost a Queen of Sheba!'

Laura turned her back upon her brother at this compliment, and
he went his way, never thinking what a thrust of pain his simple words
had driven through her heart. What if George were the poor man for
whom she were toiling? And it might yet be so, if she chose. . . . But
then it must be George himself who demanded it – who *willed* it.
There must be no half-hearted petitions to her to save him from his
fate. And George was the only being who could render such toil
bearable to her. Poor Francis! How little he really knew her, or
suspected how every morning she longed for the night, and every
night she longed for the morning. The church-goers of Barnesbury
who came to pay their duty call to Mr Lydiat's sister did not know
what to make of her. The bank manager and his mother dared not
invite her to the 'quiet evening' they had projected, and the daughters
of the country doctor were full of misgivings as regarded their last
Cup bonnet, which had hitherto been considered as being beyond
criticism. Public opinion was more prompt in giving its verdict upon
Francis. It was generally agreed that Mr Lydiat was the 'right sort.'
His tall manly form and earnest blue eyes, his strong sonorous voice,
and unconventional large preaching were looked upon as a change in
the right direction.' No one was anxious for the speedy return of the
vacillating, weakly-smiling Mr Marsh, who piped his sermons with
such conscientious measure on hot Sunday mornings, regardless of
the fact that most of his hearers were asleep. Indeed there was already
a movement on the part of the church-wardens, encouraged thereto
by wives and sisters, to 'try to get hold' of the new clergyman for a

permanency; the fact that Miss Laura was only his sister, and that his real helpmate had still to be found, being a strong point in his favour.

CHAPTER IV

———————•———————

Plain Speaking

'But of what damned minutes tells he o'er
Who dotes, yet doubts; suspects, yet strongly loves.'
            – SHAKESPEARE

The day after Francis and Laura had taken their departure, Margaret, coming down early, as was her wont, to place a fresh rosebud among Uncle Piper's letters and papers on the breakfast-table, perceived an envelope addressed to Miss Sara Cavendish lying next to her sister's plate. She took it up, with the deepening colour that every reminder of the image she held so close to her heart was wont to bring into her cheeks, and resisting the evil suggestion that she should leave it in its place and watch how its discovery affected her sister when the latter should descend, as was *her* wont, after every one else was seated at table, she resolved to carry it upstairs. But first she sought for the freshest, sweetest, whitest rose that the warm December winds had still left intact, and laying it tenderly next to the letter, she carried the missive up to Sara's room. The space and magnificence of Piper's Hill were still sufficiently new to Margaret to make every run up or downstairs a delight to her. Her appreciation of the tower had given Mr Piper the keenest satisfaction, and this morning, as she passed along the great corridor in the upper story to the spacious wing that enclosed the Cavendish apartments and caught a glimpse of the beautiful distant view through the splendid painted window on the landing, her heart gave a throb of gratitude on her mother's account. Could it be the same world as that in which, during the very same month last year, they had shivered in their miserable, draughty, little terrace-house in London, and spent so forlorn a Christmas? Or was it not all, as Margaret was sometimes inclined to think, a beautiful dream, *too* beautiful and too enjoyable to last?

Sara had none of these misgivings. Margaret found her in an elegant morning wrapper in the hands of the maid (of whom Sara, by tacit consent, seemed to have the entire monopoly). Her long dark hair was falling round her like a cloud, and her face, fixed upon its beautiful reflection in the glass, was like that of a yet impenitent Magdalen.

Margaret laid the letter and flower softly upon the table in front of her.

'Oh, that's for me? What a lovely rose, but you needn't have been in such a hurry with the letter, Maggie. I'll look at it by and by. I know who it is from!' But in spite of her feigned indifference Margaret could see that her sister was agitated. 'Shall I finish doing your hair for you, dear?' she whispered gently.

'Oh yes, do! Goodman,' turning to the maid, 'you can go, thank you,' and as the maid disappeared Sara seized her letter with an expression that signified alarm rather than pleasure, and proceeded to read it silently.

But the very first words were reassuring.

'Dear Miss Sara,' it said. 'You allowed me to go away the other night in a state of the cruellest perplexity. You know what an absorbing love I have for you, and how ardently I had hoped I might win your affection. When I held you in my arms I believed before God that you were willing to become my wife, and the hope, the joy, the rapture of that momentary belief are beyond expression in words. But before the evening had ended my soul was filled with all manner of doubts, which no one but you yourself can explain or dispel. I have always believed you as worthy and noble as you are beautiful, and only my profound and passionate love and the possibility of your returning it could plead as an excuse for my presumption in aspiring to your hand. For I should have only a very modest home, and a life of holy toil to offer you. But I would so encompass you round with love that you should not have to descend from your own world of beautiful meditation for any vulgar ministrations. Am I to hope still, or have I been the victim of a wild delusion! My fate is in your hands. – Yours,

FRANCIS LYDIAT.'

Sara threw down the letter with a sigh of relief.

'There, bundle up my hair anyhow, Maggie. I want to write an answer directly. No; don't kiss me, please; it's so silly, when it's just the contrary to what you think. Answer me now, upon your conscience. Do you think I'm the right sort of wife for Mr Lydiat?'

Margaret hesitated.

'If you could only care about him a little, Sara!'

'I should care for him well enough if he were as rich as Uncle Piper. Don't look so shocked. I never intended to be a poor man's wife.'

'But I can't understand,' said Margaret, puzzled. 'Love doesn't depend upon money at all, and you speak as though you measured yours out at so much a yard. Would you marry Mr Hyde if he were rich?'

'To-morrow!' said Sara, and there was no doubting the sincerity of her tones.

'Or our cousin?'

'Perhaps; but I think he's done for. There, don't catechise, Maggie. I'm going to write at the davenport in your room. I can't find the key of mine.'

What Sara wrote was –

'DEAR MR LYDIAT, – I did not mean you to think what you did the other night. I am very sorry it happened. I think we had better both forget it as quickly as we can. I hope you and your sister are enjoying the change. – Believe me, very sincerely yours,

'SARA CAVENDISH.'

When Francis received this note he was writing a sermon on his favourite theme of renunciation. He held the envelope in his hands, not daring to open it. For an instant it seemed to him as though his life hung on its contents. After reading it slowly through he turned a curious ashen colour. The last hope had died out of his heart. Then he seized his pen afresh, and what he wrote will never be forgotten. For the sermon was the beginning of the series that sent the fame of his name throughout Australia. For it was as though he had written with his own heart's blood, and none could read or hear his words without being moved. And all the time he taught and preached he was as one inspired and possessed. For he was battling night and day with the love he still cherished for Sara. And the hardest to bear was the knowledge that she was unworthy of a loyal man's love, and that he loved her in spite of all.

PART V

———————————•———————————

CHAPTER I

Mr Cavendish Discovers His Mission in Life

'A successive title, long and dark,
Drawn from the mouldy rolls of Noah's Ark.'
– DRYDEN

Christmas at Piper's Hill had never been enjoyed with such a zest by its owner before. Mr Piper had prepared the inmates for a *largesse* of some kind by remarking, on Christmas Eve, that the 'Melbourne Father Christmas was worth a dozen of your old skinflints at home;' but poor Mrs Cavendish and Margaret felt literally overwhelmed upon finding near their plates, on Christmas morning, two small jewel-cases, containing monogram brooches in Australian gold, sprinkled with small brilliants. Sara had a bracelet, and Louey came running into the room with an apronful of the most captivating picture-books in the most gorgeous of bindings, to kiss her father over and over again, and to assure him that Father Christmas had given her what she liked better than anything she could have chosen for herself. Mr Piper replied that the squirrel was a 'humbug' and that she would 'sooner have had a box of chocolate;' but perhaps Father Christmas had thought of that too – which, sure enough, he had, for Louey discovered, hidden under her table-napkin, a box that might have come straight from Paris, full of the most astonishing snails and dormice in highly-varnished chocolate. Even Mr Cavendish had been remembered, as a Russia leather pocketbook with silver clasps testified. In short, such a Christmas it had never fallen to the lot of the Cavendish family to imagine, and the strawberries and cream and iced champagne that followed the great flaming Christmas pudding at dinner, helped to confirm the feeling that it was all a gorgeous make-believe, and that the dreary, dark, freezing, pinched face that Father Christmas had hitherto shown them, was lying in wait for them somewhere. Laura's absence was also a cause of rejoicing to the master of Piper's Hill. Free from the adverse criticism that he always seemed to read in her expression, even when her thoughts were otherwise engaged, he entered with great spirit into the preparations for the New Year's Day races, insisting on it that the whole family should 'take and come with him to the show.'

Though he 'didn't hold by racing,' as he took care to affirm loudly every time George was present, and would never give 'a day's credit to a bettin' man,' he was at heart too fond of display to miss the opportunity of showing off the Piper's Hill equipages. On the morning of the great day, which was full of a soft promise of unclouded beauty, he held forth on the same theme during breakfast time with renewed energy, casting side-long looks at George, and winking at Mr Cavendish from behind his paper, by way of explaining that in inveighing against the folly of racing he was only discharging a fatherly duty, and that his remarks were by no means intended to apply to the rest of the company.

Perhaps the person at whom they *were* directed was the one who paid the least heed to them. George sat in moody silence, a prey to the worst form of discontent – the consciousness of having acted badly, and of being about to increase the measure of his iniquities. The letters he had exchanged with Laura had been of the most unsatisfactory description. She had never alluded to his cousin, nor fixed a time for her own return. In fact, if he had not known her so well, he might have supposed that she was learning to become indifferent to him. Such conduct, he told himself, would have rendered most men excusable in acting as he had done – that is to say, in consoling himself by a flirtation with his beautiful cousin.

But even as he argued thus, George felt he was a coward. What might have served as an excuse in another case was meaningless in his. Every fresh advance in Sara's direction was an act of disloyalty to Laura, and then Sara was not a woman with whom a man could flirt with impunity. There was, indeed, only one escape for him, and that was in the possible success of Casserole. George was neither unreasonable nor superstitious enough to suppose that poetical justice *may* be on the side of a 'mare second to none,' as he held Casserole to be. And if this should be the happy result of to-day he was resolved that he would take the night train to Barnesbury. He would not even telegraph. He would carry the good news to Laura himself. With all his debts paid and a few thousands to the good, he would make Francis perform the marriage ceremony at once, and he would take the chance of being disinherited by his father. Perhaps in the vision of the meeting he dwelt more on Laura's joy than on his own, but the vision was very sweet to him nevertheless, for Laura's presence still meant home to George wherever he might happen to find it.

The contrary hypothesis was less pleasant to dwell upon, and was, indeed, quite sufficient to render him pale and downcast. His liabilities, as he had made them out the evening before, had startled him. Ruin irretrievable and complete dishonour stared him in the face, unless his father consented to come to the rescue. And that Mr Piper had no suspicion of the extent to which he had 'plunged' was another ugly feature in his case. Casserole's defeat, he told himself, would put him completely in the old man's hands, and marriage with his beautiful cousin would be the immediate sacrifice demanded of him.

Marriage with Sara a sacrifice! How many men are there, I wonder, thought George, who would look upon it in that light, situated as I am! The feeling was stronger than ever when his cousins came down, dressed for the expedition. Mr Piper had settled that they should go in the open landau with George and their father, while he himself would drive his sister in the mail phaeton, with Louey between them. The day was as perfect as an Australian summer's day can be upon occasion, with a far-away cloudless dome of shining blue, and an atmosphere that seemed to bathe every object in brightness.

The horses wore green and white rosettes – George's colours – a proceeding, however, which, as it had been carried out without previous reference to Mr Piper, might have disturbed the whole harmony of the day, had not Louey diverted the storm by holding up her doll at an opportune moment, and displaying its parasol, also of green and white silk, to the company. Mr Piper was so much amused that he forgot to swear at the coachman, and Louey, happy at having succeeded in making her doll the scapegoat, only laughed merrily when her father asked her if she wasn't ashamed to 'take and carry a fast lady like that in her arms to the races.'

Driving was Mr Piper's glory. As he gathered up the reins in one hand, and took the whip in the other, after asking Mrs Cavendish if she was 'all right and tight' on her seat, he bethought himself of his first apprenticeship more than thirty years ago, in his butcher's cart up-country. How proud he had been to have his name painted on it in gilt letters, with a flourish over the capital P! If it had not been for the groom sitting with folded arms behind, he would have liked to tell his sister all about that time.

Tom's driving was at once her admiration and her terror, though the latter feeling she carefully concealed from him, accepting it as the alloy without which all this newly-found happiness would have been too complete. Poor Mrs Cavendish was ready, indeed, to hail every passing ill that might fall to her share as she hailed in former days her rare moments of brightness. She was frightened at the period of prosperity that had come upon her. 'It's beyond me, my dear,' she would say to Margaret, the only one who understood her mother in these phases, 'and I hope the Lord won't visit it upon any of you. I *do*, indeed. I could find it in my heart to die, if he'd only take me now, and I might make sure your pa would never want for anything, nor you neither.' Margaret would soothe her mother at these moments as only she knew how to do, telling her that she had eaten 'her black bread first,' and she must not spoil the taste of the white now that it had come to her share. Nevertheless, the old instinctive superstition which the poet recognises who sings:

> 'And there is even a happiness
> That makes the heart afraid,'

the feeling that even the most reasonable of us experience when unaccustomed happiness falls to our lot, often drove Mrs Cavendish to impose unnecessary sacrifices upon herself of which even Margaret knew nothing.

She was the more prompted to this course that unless she devised some little penalty for herself her outer world had none to offer her. It really did seem as though the Fates had no more sad-coloured yarn left to spin, but only threads of brightest gold and silver. By way of saving the family pride and giving a sense of delightful stability to the present situation, Mr Piper had insisted upon giving Margaret a hundred a year for her education of Louey. In vain Margaret, with rising colour and tears in her eyes, had protested against such generosity. Her uncle had declared she would be worth more than that to an 'outsider,' and 'he would take and throw the money out o' the winder if she refused her honest wage.' The very next day he had told Mrs Cavendish, confidentially, that he had intended to look out for a housekeeper, and to give *her* a hundred a year, too, but he had kept the situation open for his sister Bess, 'blood being thicker than water.' The same ineffectual protests, with even more abundant tears than Margaret's, were Mrs Cavendish's reply. But Mr Piper was not be gainsaid, and the next day the poor woman was raised to the dizzy height of directing a household in which the item for trifling superfluities would have represented more than she had had to keep four lives going upon at home.

How busy, and energetic, and proud she was; with what keen delight she received from the cook the liberty of the wondrous underground domains; with what conscientious scrupulousness she balanced her accounts, wresting all 'sundries' from the vague regions to which they had hitherto been consigned, can never be told. But Mr Piper did not need telling. After the first fortnight he declared that his sister Bess was 'worth her weight in gold,' and by way of showing his appreciation of her services he fitted up a charming little office for her, with bewildering conveniences in the way of writing-table, armchair, and waste-paper basket, and a most astonishing cabinet, containing a mysterious secret-drawer, in which he placed a small bundle of blank cheques signed by himself that were to represent his housekeeper's bank. It is needless to say that Mr Cavendish reaped the principal benefit of the munificent salaries bestowed upon his wife and daughter. Mrs Cavendish had adopted the plan of placing a sovereign in her husband's purse every Monday morning, upon the 'clear understanding,' said Mr Cavendish, 'that a strict account is kept of every debt I may incur to your relatives. Upon no other terms could I possibly consent to take favours of them.' The promise was given, and Mrs Cavendish forbore to remind her husband that there was now no tea-pot to offer as security.

The government post was seldom alluded to now. Mr Cavendish had found an occupation which he confidently believed to be of the utmost value to his wife's family. As there was no longer any ignoring the fact that his '*parvenu* brother-in-law' had taken them all by the hand, the most graceful course would be to throw a veil over the unfortunate accident of his birth, and to redeem him from it, in so far as might be possible. The Chinese have ennobled the ancestors of many a man who has less means of conferring a lustre upon them than Mr Piper. Why should not the same plan be carried out in Australia? True, Piper is not a name of much promise, but there *had* been a Count Piper somewhere or other some centuries ago, and the very rarity of the name proved that every Piper must come from one common stock. Fired by this generous idea, Mr Cavendish gave himself up to its pursuit with enthusiasm. He would spend whole hours in the Melbourne Library, poring over books of heraldry. Every chronological or biographical document bearing upon the age in which Count Piper was supposed to have lived was made the subject of long and minute examination. When the monthly mail day came round, there was sure to be a budget of letters in Mr Cavendish's handwriting addressed to the different colleges and societies at home and abroad, who were to help in extracting all Pipers of any importance from the oblivion in which they had hitherto been suffered to remain. The happy change was first observed by Mrs Cavendish, through the dropping of the prefixes of 'unfortunate' and *'parvenu'* to the mention of her brother's name from Mr Cavendish's lips. But Mr Piper nearly spoilt all by the ignorant levity with which he received the first hint of the important work upon which his brother-in-law was engaged.

'I am – hem – I am pursuing a task of the utmost consequence to your family interests,' Mr Cavendish had told him one day. 'In fact, my dear sir, I am engaged in a work of no less moment than that of reconstructing your family tree.'

'My what-do-you-call-it tree?' exclaimed Mr Piper aghast, with a hazy idea that Mr Cavendish had been trying some unwarrantable experiments upon his lemon and orange bushes. 'Don't you take and put any rubbish in the garden. I've got a new lot of guano, and I don't want it meddled with.'

'Guano!' echoed Mr Cavendish, with a tone of the most withering compassion. 'I am afraid you don't quite apprehend my meaning. I am not alluding to coarse material facts at all. I am speaking of a genealogical tree – a ge-ne-a-lo-gi-cal tree, you understand? I am trying to rescue your ancestors from the dust of oblivion – I am . . .

'You'd better leave 'em alone,' interrupted Mr Piper with the sulky accent of one whose suspicions have not been altogether allayed. '*They* won't do you any good – no more than they've done for me. You've got some o' your own, I expect; that's enough for any man, I should think.'

Mr Cavendish had shrugged his shoulders and held his peace. If the matter had not become a hobby by this time he would have abandoned it then and there. As it was, he contented himself by deploring the sad effects of low association upon the possibility of introducing a hog in armour instead of a stag at gaze into the coat-of-arms that he foresaw would be the result of his researches, due notification of them being forwarded, as a matter of course, to the Herald's office in London.

But heraldry and heartburnings were alike in abeyance on this lovely morning of the New Year. While the mail phaeton took the lead, the landau rolled swift and close behind it over the long road to Flemington. Mr Cavendish rubbed up his recollections of the Ascot of the past, and astonished his daughters by reminiscences of the feats of legendary sires, whose descendants it was now the boast of the colony to possess. Whenever the occupants of the mail phaeton looked behind them, they were greeted by a laughing salutation from the landau, to which the doll with the green and white parasol was expected to respond. To please their Uncle Piper, the girls had come out in all the colours of the rainbow, with flower-spangled French muslins, and a perfect bouquet of variegated buds on their bonnets of blue tulle. It was Laura's practice on Cup Days and New Year's race days, to exchange her parrot-like plumage for the severest greys and browns, and Mr Piper, who was convinced that this was a manoeuvre to 'cross' him, had begged his nieces to wear 'something showy.'

The result was that the carriage looked, as George said, as though it bore 'a garden of girls,' and that while yet on the road it was made the theme of very outspoken admiration. Sara's was the kind of loveliness that made everything she wore seem the most appropriate at the moment of her wearing it, and George could not repress a feeling of exultation as he thought of parading his beautiful cousin up and down the lawn, under the gaze of thousands of admiring eyes. If fortune were kind to him and to Laura, he wondered who the lucky fellow might be who would carry off this prize. Somehow he could not think of any one who would be 'just the right fellow' as he passed the mental review of all his male acquaintances, and he ended by hoping that some abstraction in the shape of 'a swell from home' might be Sara's ultimate fate. But the speculation was not so agreeable as it ought to have been under the influence of a pure and unalloyed sentiment of cousinly regard, and George abandoned it for the more congenial resource of telling his cousins what to 'back,' and initiating Sara into the mysteries of 'hedging.'

And now the course was reached at last. The phaeton and the landau rolled into the carriage paddock with a delightful swinging motion that testified to the perfection of their springs. The coachman and groom, who had each their private venture on Mr George's filly, ranged the carriages in the front rank whence they could obtain the best view. The occupants descended – those who had never been to the races before a little bewildered as to what was to come next. But Mr Piper pointed to the grand stand, already thick with chimney-pot hats and Paris bonnets, as to the ultimate goal, and taking his sister on his arm headed the procession. Margaret instinctively fell back, leaving Sara to follow by the side of George. Only Louey, whose intuitive sympathy was ever on the alert, was by Margaret's side in a moment, walking between her and Mr Cavendish, and pointing out to them and to the doll, as to the three novices of the party, the various arrangements of the course.

'All that great place in front we may walk in, you know, but George says one sees the races better from the stand. He'll take us afterwards to the saddling-paddock, if you like, to see the jockeys weighed. And that funny little wooden house in front that's the judge's box. They can see the horses go by the winning-post from there. George has a watch that he can stop at half-a-second. And he has a glass, you can see the horses quite plainly through it on the other side of the course. But once I saw a jockey fall off through it, and he was all bleeding' – Louey gave a little shiver – 'and I won't ever look through the glass now. Most often I don't look at the races at all until the horses are all coming in.'

'Do you know whom you remind me of, Louey?' said Mr Cavendish, who had been won by the gentleness of the little girl, even before he had thought of conferring a pedigree on her progenitors; 'you remind me of a famous violinist I was reading of the other day, who used to play in the orchestra at the opera every night. But he never would look at the play, and even when all the ballet girls were dancing he never once raised his eyes.'

'Why not?' interrupted Louey, wonderingly.

'Prejudice, my dear child, prejudice! There's nothing so fatal as prejudice. I trust, Margaret, since you *are* so good as to interest yourself in the direction of our little friend's studies, that you show her the necessity of keeping an open and *un*-prejudiced mind.'

'Yes, papa,' said Margaret simply, with a little inward sigh. And as by this time the stand was reached Louey was obliged to defer asking for the explanation of the incomprehensible story, and the still more incomprehensible deductions she had just heard from her uncle Cavendish.

For the stand was filling fast now, and Mr Piper was not going to have his party 'put off' with any indifferent seats. It had never been his way to hide his light under a bushel, and to-day he had brought his 'family' out for the special purpose of having them admired. Margaret's cheeks burned in the midst of the strange throng, as she watched her uncle elbow his way about; but she could not help noticing at the same time how many people saluted him and shook hands with him.

If there was a furtive glimmer of amusement to be read in the eyes of some, as they looked after his broad back, after an exchange of civilities, there was nothing on the surface but the utmost politeness and cordiality. Whatever Mr Piper had been in the past, his dealings had always been honourable, and, perhaps, had they been even less strictly so than was the case, his present position, as one of the largest and wealthiest landowners in the colony, and a generous donor to charitable institutions besides, would have sufficed to procure him the consideration of the Australian world.

So, with a little more pushing and scrambling, Mr Piper procured himself the satisfaction his soul desired, and seated himself in fullest 'evidence' between his sister and Sara, while Margaret and Louey were relegated with the doll to the seat behind. George, whose face from the moment of reaching the course seemed to have acquired a kind of fixed pallor, had taken Mr Cavendish to the saddling-paddock, whither it is not our province to follow him. But one may be sure that a form unseen by mortal eyes was by his side. 'For Laura's sake,' he whispered in Casserole's ear, as she was led out for Mr Cavendish to admire. Ah, had the mare but known what she would carry on her back besides her jockey! As George scanned her with critical eyes, hardly heeding the encomiums that Mr Cavendish was lavishing upon her, he reflected that he had not perhaps done so unwisely in staking the chances of happiness of two lives upon her. More than one sporting friend had told him that Casserole was a 'red-hot favourite' already, and connoisseurs were gathering round her with knowing looks, and pursed-up mouths, and prognostications that she would make it 'pretty warm for some of them' before the day was over.

Meanwhile Sara, all unconscious of the influence that Casserole's 'form' was to exercise upon her destiny, was sitting by her uncle's side drinking full and intoxicating draughts of admiration. A whisper had already run along the seats, and the better-informed were telling those who were yet in ignorance that the beautiful and aristocratic-looking girl by Mr Piper's side was his niece. That, though you wouldn't think it, old Piper had very swell connections in England, and that you only had to look at the handsome woman on the other side of him to credit it. That Miss Cavendish had been *the* belle of the evening at Government House a fortnight ago, and that there was no one (this latter remark, however, was not uttered in the presence of marriageable daughters and their mammas), that there was no one in Melbourne to hold a candle to her at the present moment. Then eye-glasses were directed to her, and pretty necks were strained curiously, and guesses were made as to whether her dress had come from Paris; and the fragrant incense that Sara had breathed a few evenings ago seemed to envelop her once more, and the consciousness of her power quickened the warm blood in her veins, until, like another Galatea, she glowed with a beauty as sensuous as it was statuesque.

CHAPTER II

———————•———————

Casserole To The Fore

'What is worth in anything?
So much money as 'twill being.'
— HUDIBRAS

The great race – the race which was to decide the destiny of so many lives – was not to be run before three o'clock. Therefore, after Mr Piper had enjoyed to the utmost the sensation that his belongings had produced, he led them all back with as much stir as possible to the carriage-paddock, where an elaborate luncheon was awaiting them. Iced champagne-cup and mayonnaise, raspberry creams and trifles, were a very agreeable diversion, even to the triumph of the hour. But George felt as though the whole scene were an uneasy dream, from which he would only awake 'in his right mind,' when Casserole should pass the winning-post. More than one of his acquaintances had stopped him to ask the name of that 'awfully pretty girl' he had been seen walking with, and he was tired of answering 'my cousin – not long out from home.' He wondered how Sara really regarded him. But why should he wonder? What did it matter, after all? Laura was as 'good as his wife,' only he could not drag her and himself down into disgrace and poverty. And backwards and forwards, and round and round, the weary arguments, the pros and cons, the 'to be's,' or 'not to be's,' travelled through George's brain until he was hardly clear *what* he wanted, or *whom* he was suffering for; whether for himself, or Laura, or Sara.

Excepting for his sickly hue, no one of the party, however, could have divined that anything was wrong with the owner of Casserole. He wagered gloves against his own horse with his aunts and cousins with the best grace in the world, and instituted five-shilling sweeps as industriously as though the sovereigns of which Louey was made the treasurer would have served to recoup him if the day were to go against him. But when luncheon was over, and the hour of his doom had really arrived, George found that his nerve was failing him. He could not answer for himself if he were obliged to witness the race in the presence of others. He only waited to help to pilot his party to a good post of observation on the lawn, through the ever-increasing throng, reminding Sara to keep her eyes on the green and white, and then suddenly disappeared.

Whence George viewed the contest is known only to himself. He was seen for an instant in the saddling-paddock just before the race, as Casserole, with her little jockey on her back, resplendent in the green and white silk that Laura's fingers had stitched together, was dancing along towards the starting-point. He followed them with his eyes until they had found a place in the row of buoyant steeds that could not be held back, and then he turned away. That he was conscious of every minutest phase of the race, during the agonising moments that followed, is certain. Such instants are burned into the brain as though they were written there in letters of fire – that he knew exactly when Casserole was falling behind, and exactly when she was to the fore – that he was aware that she was fifth, and then fourth, and then third – that his heart stopped beating as frantic cries of *Casserole, Casserole* – 'I lay upon Casserole – ten to one upon Casserole' – told that she was first – that during the awful lull that ensued, he knew perfectly well that she was not keeping ahead, and that another was gaining upon her – that he felt in every nerve that she was half a head behind, and that she could not regain the same, and that the day was lost, irretrievably lost, even while her name was still being yelled aloud by vehement and disappointed backers, is likewise certain. But that George knew all this through the medium of his earthly senses, is by no means so clear. With a sick, stunned, dull sensation, and a sudden great longing to turn towards Laura, as a child turns towards its mother, for comfort, he took his hand from before his eyes, put his hat straight on his head, and walked aimlessly in front of him. Somehow he could not face his own people just now, and what was to be gained by going closer to the scene of his defeat.

But before he had gone far he heard his name called aloud. His father had come in search of him, and was gazing at his downcast face with unsympathising and calculating eyes. Perhaps Mr Piper was not really sorry at heart that 'my gentleman' should have had a lesson, and should have put himself at last so completely into his power. Now he could save him once and for all from the artifices of that 'painted hussy,' and bestow the money he had worked so hard to obtain upon his own flesh and blood, as he had always had it in his mind to do. He had come to make his own terms with his son, and any one who had studied the shape of Mr Piper's head would have seen that, having once made up his mind as to what those terms should be, he was not likely to change them.

But George felt too desperate to care whether his father was prepared to triumph over him or not. What mattered most just now was that he should know to what extent he had *plunged*, and that he should enable him to score off his debts then and there. Even in the midst of his misery he was conscious of a kind of malicious satisfaction at the idea of the unpleasant shock that the news of his losses would cause. If the old man were prepared to tyrannise over him, at least he would have to pay for the privilege. George was almost ready now to make him responsible for the whole disaster – by the ingenious kind of logic which people in his position are ever ready to employ. If his father had not refused to let him marry Laura, he would never have been driven to risk so much in order to obtain her. Hence, his father was clearly the cause of his losses.

But Mr Piper, it need hardly be said, was not prepared to view the matter in the same light. With the dread of a 'scene,' George had led his father to a comparatively deserted spot, where, without much preamble, he entered at once upon the subject of his losses.

At the first mention of the sum Mr Piper gave a prodigious start. Then he laughed uneasily and incredulously.

'You won't make me believe it, George! I didn't bring you up like a prince for you to take and ruin me in my old days. You won't make me believe it, my boy.'

'Father, I swear to you, every word of it's true.' There was a vehemence in George's tones that was not to be misinterpreted. 'I thought it was a certainty, and I went in heavily for once. If you want me to be treated as a defaulter, if you want me to be eternally disgraced, we'll say no more about it.'

For a whole quarter of a minute Mr Piper said nothing. When George raised his eyes he was alarmed at the change in his father's face. The cheeks were purple, there were swollen veins upon either temple, and the eye-balls seemed to protrude under the influence of some frightful strain.

'Father! What is it?' cried the young man, in an altered voice. 'Shall I call for a doctor?'

'Doctor be damned!' said Mr Piper, who had at last recovered his voice. 'You just listen to me, George. You've reckoned without your host. You think I'm going to be ruined in my old age by a – son?' Mr Piper did not measure his epithets, though the recipient of them showed no further emotion than a slight rigidity of the lips. 'But you're mistaken, I tell you. I'm going to do nothink o' the sort. What's your name to me? I made it what it is, didn't I? If you choose to take and disgrace it that's your own look out. You've no more right to rob me than any other loafer in Australia. I've done with you now, for good and all; you may go to the devil, and that's the last you'll hear from *me!*'

But as the infuriated man turned away his son laid hold of his coat-sleeve. George had never been in such a pass before, but he reflected that unless he were to blow his brains out, which would perhaps be the easiest way of adjusting the difficulty, he must drink the cup of bitterness and humiliation to the dregs. Whatever turn events might take Laura was lost to him. But he might sell his renunciation of her for better terms than these.

'Father, listen to me. I've been a fool, and worse than a fool – I know it – but I'll give you my word of honour I'll give up racing if you'll put me right this once –'

'What! pay three thousand down for you? I'd see you hanged first.'

'All right,' said George, turning away with a curious expression in his eyes. 'Good-bye, then, father; I think I'll go home.'

It was now Mr Piper's turn to lay hold of his adversary. 'Don't be a fool, George,' he said; 'you're quite enough of one already. What did you expect me to do for you? You didn't think I was going to take and throw all my money away to pay for your follies, did you? I've got a better use for it. But I'll tell you what I'll do – you'll take your Bible oath you'll never race no more as long as I'm above ground?'

'I'll give you my word of honour,' said George.

'And you'll go straight off *now* – yes, *now* – this very instant, and ask one or other o' your cousins to marry you before the month's out, and you'll take and bring her to me – there's to be no shilly-shallying, mind. You can do all your sentiment and spooning after the wedding.'

'Is it indifferent to you to *which* of my cousins I propose?' interrupted

George, with a shade of the old ironical inflexion in his accents; 'because perhaps they're not *both* so anxious to throw themselves away upon me as you seem to believe.'

'One or other of 'em,' said Mr Piper solemnly; 'I don't care which. Sara's the beauty, but if you don't make such a point of looks, you take and ask her sister to have you – that's *my* advice.'

'And Laura?' said George. The words were uttered before he knew what he was saying. If he had been a believer in spiritualism, he would have declared that her name had issued from his lips as from some passive instrument over which he had no control.

But the sound had reached Mr Piper's ears, who there and then swore that he would leave his son to his fate if Laura's name were mentioned again. 'You can take and turn out – the pair of you – and you can make a good start in life on your debts.'

George assured his father that he had no idea of dragging Laura into poverty and disgrace, and the following compact was made:

First the young man was to make himself certain of Sara's acceptance of him. He had no thought of insulting Margaret by an offer, but there had been passages between Sara and himself which rendered such a proposition possible in her direction. This accomplished, and the wedding-day fixed, Mr Piper bound himself to pay all his son's debts; further, to send him to Europe for a year's travel with his wife immediately after the marriage, and to settle enough upon the young couple on their return to enable them to live in Melbourne, or upon a station of George's choosing, as the case might be.

When these preliminaries were settled Mr Piper held out his hand, and father and son were united for an instant into the semblance of such friends as fathers and sons have been known to be. As George put his cold hand into the paternal grasp a sudden yearning impulse moved him.

'Oh! father,' he cried, 'you are using your power in a very dangerous way. Will you be responsible for the consequences if two lives are ruined?'

He might have said three, but he thought it wiser to leave Laura out of the question. It is doubtful whether his father understood the full significance of his words. The only reply he made was to advise George once more 'not to be a fool and to take and begin his courting at once.' And so the interview which sealed Laura's fate ended.

Sara had been wondering at the absence of her uncle and cousin during the moments of rest that followed the wild excitement of the race. She was tired of having no one to talk to but Louey – her own family had never counted as *society* in her estimation, though Margaret was agreeably convenient when there were confidences to be made – and surprised at the sudden disappearance of the male element in the direction of the saddling paddock. She had relapsed into a kind of dreamy reverie, her beautiful eyes apparently full of the 'high communings' with which Mr Lydiat had credited them – her mind full of future possibilities; in which the ardent desire for a life of the same luxury as her present one bore the principal share. To be always sure of the same surroundings, that was the paramount consideration. Sara did not quite see at the moment who was to procure her the certainty of their continuation, when George, with a face of most becoming paleness, came suddenly forward to propose a turn on the lawn.

'So your horrid horse didn't win after all,' said Sara, as she walked by her cousin's side in the direction of the carriage-paddock. 'Are you very much disappointed? You know you've won no end of gloves from us all. I was just asking Louey your size.'

'Disappointed?' repeated George, with a curious smile. 'No, not exactly that. A little knocked out of time; but it doesn't matter. Will you mind coming as far as the carriage, Sara? I've something important to say to you.'

'Certainly,' said Sara, with a slight inflexion of wonder in her tones. But when they had reached their destination George's first step was to order the footman to open a bottle of champagne. The place was comparatively deserted. It was easy to find a secluded spot under shelter of the mail phaeton in which the cousins might instal themselves, and when the bottle and glasses were forthcoming, and George had arranged carriage-cushions and rugs for Sara to recline upon, he sent the man away, and seating himself by Sara's side, filled her glass to the brim, and then proceeded to fill and empty his own.

'What an extravagant proceeding,' said Sara, but she drank her champagne nevertheless. 'Is it by way of forgetting your defeat?'

'My defeat? Oh, that's nothing,' answered George, emptying another glass as he spoke, and re-filling Sara's. 'Perhaps it's all for the best.'

'A philosopher!' said Sara, laughing. 'And then see what a number of gloves you've won!'

'I don't care about the gloves,' cried George, suddenly growing bold. 'What I want is this charming little hand,' and he took his cousin's hand and pressed it in his own.

'What do you mean?' said Sara, colouring violently, as much from surprise as from any other feeling, and inclined to think that the champagne had gone to her cousin's head.

'I mean what I say,' said George slowly, and somewhat as though he were repeating a lesson learned by heart. 'I want you to give me your hand. I want you to say you will marry me. I know it's a very awkward and a very – a – a – abrupt way of asking you – but – I can't help it.'

This was strictly true from George's point of view, and if Sara interpreted it as a tribute to the irresistibleness of her appearance in the French muslin and blue tulle bonnet, it must be admitted that most young women in her place would have arrived at the same conclusion.

Still she held her peace. A thousand calculations were flashing through her brain, and it was impossible to compass them all in such short notice. Her cousin, *with* Piper's Hill, and all that Mr Piper's wealth implied, was not to be disdained – though without these access- ories he did not count for more than any other good-looking, well- built young man of self-made stock and colonial bringing-up. But men like Mr Hyde were not likely to come to the colonies unless they were very hard-up indeed. And then George *was* very presentable, and, of course, he would be very rich. And he would be sure to give her her own way, and as much money as she wanted. But it was very sudden. Had he quarrelled with Laura, or had he never really been in love with her? And what would her uncle say?

While Sara was hesitating under the influence of these conjectures, George sat with his eyes fixed upon her, in a curious and utterly contradictory state of mind – a state of mind that he found it impossible to account for. Though her refusal would have saved him from a step that he loathed himself for taking, he was conscious that it would be disagreeable to him to receive it. She had never looked more beautiful than at this instant, as her breath came and went rapidly, and her colour rose and fell. George watched her from between his narrowing eyes, wondering within himself whether this superb creature really had any kind of sentiment for him, and whether her emotion arose from such a cause.

'Don't be so cruel, Sara!' he said at last. 'Don't keep me in such torturing suspense.'

There was such a ring of genuine feeling in the exclamation, that Sara turned her eyes upon him; and this time there was no mistaking the admiration in his look.

'It is so sudden, George,' she said at last; 'how do you know what my uncle will say?'

'What? The Governor,' exclaimed her lover; 'why, he – he'll be overjoyed – I can answer for *that*.'

'Then, of course, I must see what papa and mamma say!' said Sara. George's wooing was altogether so different from that of the Rev. Mr Lydiat's that Sara was still uncertain whether she ought to take it *au serieux*.

'Then I'll go and look for your father now, and ask him,' said George, rising.

'Will you – so soon?'

It was all Sara could say, for her cousin, in assisting her to rise, had kissed her ungloved hand and then her lips, and another race being on the point of coming off there was evidently no time for further debate.

So George and Sara walked away together from the carriage-paddock as two who have resolved to walk henceforth together through life, 'for richer or poorer, for better or worse,' in the closest, dearest, most sacred bond that can link two human beings to each other. Mr Piper's injunctions had been carried out. There had been no 'shilly-shallying.' Sara could not have said that she felt one step nearer to her betrothed than she did an hour ago when she half believed he was engaged to another woman, and George had no clearer feeling at this instant than that he was walking with the prettiest girl on the course, and that 'all the fellows' would be envying him when they came to know the truth.

Envying him! And at this very moment Laura was walking back from the Barnesbury telegraph-office, with the words, 'Casserole second! Casserole second!' sounding like a death-knell in her ears. The way was hot and sandy, but she heeded it not. The ragged gum-trees, the parched grass, the dust and the flies, were all unnoticed now. 'Poor George!' – ay, *poor* in every sense, but always the same to her. She could not give him up. Come what might she could not give him up. But supposing he should be driven to give her up! With her head down Laura stumbled on along the rough road. What folly to sob like a beaten child; but there was no one to see, and life would be *so* hard to bear without George.

CHAPTER III

———•———

'Congratulations?'

'I do beseech you – chiefly that I may set it in my prayers – what is your name?' – SHAKESPEARE

If Mrs Cavendish had secret misgivings lest the halcyon days she was now enjoying should end in some violent catastrophe, the news that Sara whispered in her ear, while the attention of the others was fixed upon the ensuing race, might have amply reassured her. She felt as though her highest earthly ambitions were gratified; as though, like Simeon, she would have been content 'to depart in peace,' if there had not been so many new and delightful interests left to live for.

The danger of joining two young people together upon no surer basis than the one that George and Sara had just established would never have occurred to her simple mind. Affinities – physical and moral – subtle sympathies and antipathies, upon which the happiness and shipwreck of so many lives depend, were considerations beyond her mental grasp. She had never heard them discussed in her generation. She did not even know of their existence. To her it seemed the most natural thing in the world that the young people should have 'taken a fancy to each other,' and though Sara had never shown much family affection, Mrs Cavendish had not the smallest doubt that she would follow the natural order of things when she was married, and develop into a very fond wife.

So she wiped her eyes behind her veil, and held her daughter's hand tightly, while she repeated, 'Oh! my dear, my dear!' as the only outlet for an overflowing heart, until Mr Piper, who had guessed how

201

matters stood, by seeing George and Sara return together, inquired 'what was wrong with his sister Bess?'

'Oh, dear! don't ask *me*,' said poor Mrs Cavendish, looking very frightened. 'And there's Sara won't forgive me, I know; but I was taken so sudden, Tom, and I hope you approve, for I'm sure her pa won't sanction anything without you approve.'

'Ah! *I* know all about it,' said Mr Piper; 'they don't make a fool of *me*, do they, squirrel?' turning to Louey, who had been watching the disturbed expressions of the group with grave sympathy. 'You take and kiss your cousin, quick, your sister that's to be, and you tell her from me that I don't think George deserves as good as she, nor as handsome – there now.'

And this was all the revenge that Mr Piper took for being called upon to disburse three thousand pounds. But no one but himself knew the full extent of his riches, and he was rid of a nightmare that had weighed upon him heavily for more years than he could remember.

It mattered little to any one, in the excitement of the moment, that Mr Piper's orders were not literally carried out, and that Louey kissed her cousin Margaret instead of Sara. But that the old-world child had any design in the action would have been impossible of supposition if she had not at the same moment fixed her sweet, solemn grey eyes upon her brother with an earnest, searching look, as though she would have read through his very soul. If George had ever felt like a Judas it was at this particular moment, when he encountered Louey's eyes. But Poppet was a privileged person. So he contented himself by passing his hand across the wistful little face to change its expression, and then turned to his future father-in-law.

Mr Cavendish had only one thing to say, but that thing was of the last importance. He led the young man to the extreme end of the lawn to say it, for it was not a matter to be cried aloud on the housetops, nor to be alluded to otherwise than with extreme caution and delicacy. George made up his mind that it would refer to the question of settlements, or to the necessity of his insuring his life, and he resolved to refer Mr Cavendish to his father. But it had to do with neither of these.

'I am placed,' began Mr Cavendish, clearing his throat, 'in an extremely delicate position. I am quite aware that my dear child's fortune is in no way in conformity with her birth – with her birth, you understand me, my dear sir –'

'Oh! never mind about that,' interrupted George hastily. 'I've more than enough for both, you know.'

'And I could have wished,' sighed Mr Cavendish, unheeding the interruption, 'that all might have been in due proportion – that the fortune on *her* side, and – ahem – you won't mind my saying so – that the birth on *yours*, might have been a – a harmoniously balanced.'

George held his peace. He was afraid now of saying something he might regret, and this man was after all his father's guest, and dependent upon his bounty.

'There is only one way out of the difficulty that I can see,' continued Mr Cavendish, 'pending the discovery of some very important documents, which will throw, I have no doubt, a satisfactory light on your family history – previous, at least, to that little derogation connected with your father's early settlement in Australia; pending this discovery, I say, would you – would you –'

'Would I put off the wedding? Not on any account,' said George shortly.

'No!' replied Mr Cavendish. 'I was not going to ask *quite* such a sacrifice of you. I was going to ask whether you would be obliging enough to adopt the Cavendish crest – to have it used, I mean, for carriages, plate, silver, jewellery – all that kind of thing; in short,' he added airily, 'you see I am not quite *au courant* of the armorial bearings of the Piper family, and it is most essential that there should be no precipitancy in my mode of research. But a wife *may* continue to employ her own crest, and I believe may confer upon her husband the privilege of using it also – at least I will look up the proper authorities on the subject without loss of time.'

'Sara shall do as she pleases, uncle,' answered George, after a moment's reflection. 'She has *carte blanche*, of course, in all matters of that kind.' But before the day was over, he found occasion to inform his cousin of the interview.

'I hope you don't share your father's prejudices,' he said. 'Do you want me to strut about like a jay in borrowed plumes too, Sara? You know I'm a *roturier*, pure and simple, and I should be only ridiculous if I pretended to be anything else.

'Oh, no, you're not,' said Sara, wincing in spite of herself, 'please don't say that; it's nothing to have "roughed it" – isn't that what you call it here? – in the early times, as your father did. And, by-the-by, George, if you don't mind my asking, who *was* your mother?'

'An honest woman – don't laugh, Sara – it was something to be

honest in those days, I can tell you. She was matron, I believe, on
board a convict ship that took a load of convicts to Tasmania – so
she was one of the very few *respectable* females in Hobart – and
occupied a distinguished position in consequence.'

'And is that all you know?' resumed Sara, after a long pause, during
which she had been disciplining herself not to betray her mortification,
'nothing more?'

'Nothing more, excepting that her name was Mary Ann, and that
she died when I was quite a small child'.

Sara made no more inquiries. If her sensations could have been
analysed, something very like resentment towards George would have
been found therein. He need not have been so brutally outspoken in
his answers. He need not have despoiled her so ruthlessly of the last
vestige of an illusion. There have been great and noble ladies who
have undertaken missions to savage countries and who have been
reformers of prisons, too. Why should not the former Mrs Piper have
been allowed the benefit of the legitimate doubt that might have rested
upon the nature of her calling? Sara felt that there was good reason
for the secret irritation excited by her cousin's words. He should
take more account of her well-founded susceptibilities. He should
remember that money was not *everything* . . . But money is a great
deal, as she owned within herself an hour later while enjoying the
luxurious repose of the perfectly-hung landau during the homeward
drive from the races. After all, the matron of the convicts *might* have
been a lady. In all cases she was buried out of sight, and the actual
prospect of buying a trousseau that would realise the most ecstatic
day-dreams might be accepted as a set-off against the doubtful antecedents of a deceased mother-in-law. On the whole Sara was well
pleased with the opening of her first New Year at the Antipodes, and
quite prepared to see the future through the golden haze that had
enveloped her ever since her arrival.

Not so Mr Cavendish. That gentleman was by no means certain
that he was doing his duty as a Cavendish by sanctioning a fresh
mèsalliance in his family. Sara, it is true, was the fruit of a first one,
for which Mr Cavendish himself had been responsible. But whether
this were a reason for being more or less severe in the exercise of his
paternal functions when a second one was threatened it was quite
beyond him to decide. He inclined to the first point of view, when
Mr Piper slapped him on the back as they returned to the house, and
exclaimed that they would 'take and fix the young 'uns off before they

had time to change their minds.' But the evening that wound up the day's festivities, and the undoubted extra superfine quality of the old Burgundy in which the healths of the engaged pair were pledged, inclined him to take a more lenient judgment.

And Margaret? The grave and gentle perplexity that had over-shadowed her countenance ever since the astonishing news had burst upon her gave way to an expression of the most anxious sympathy as soon as she was alone with her sister. 'Dear Sara, it is so sudden!' she said, putting her arms round Sara's neck. 'Have you had time to think?'

'I can't do better, that I can see,' said Sara. 'Every one isn't as romantic as you are, Maggie. One might have a worse husband than George, and I'm not likely to find a richer one.'

'A richer one?' repeated Margaret; 'then it *must* be as I think. Do you know, Sara, I do believe your heart has never been touched the least little bit. Not the least little bit. If it had been you couldn't talk as you do. You couldn't ignore the existence of such things as love and longing so completely. Doesn't inclination count for *anything* in your notions of marriage then?'

'I can't imagine having an inclination for a poor man,' replied Sara, yawning. 'But don't let's argue, for heaven's sake. I'm going to marry George, and I'm going to have just the kind of trousseau I've always imagined I should like. One can get nearly everything in Melbourne, and I can buy the rest when we go home. Uncle Piper wants the wedding to be as soon as possible, you know.'

'And you?'

'*I?* Oh, I don't care. I don't see that there's any particular reason for putting it off. By-the-by, Maggie, I wonder whether Laura Lydiat would care about being my bridesmaid. Of course you and Louey would be the others.'

'She *might*,' said Margaret doubtfully. 'Somehow I don't feel sure. And you know how she and Uncle Piper dislike each other . . . And Sara, dear, it might be as well to leave Miss Lydiat and her brother out of the question – unless – of course – unless things are quite different from what one thinks.'

'What a goose you are, Maggie,' was Sara's only rejoinder, the colour rising to her cheeks as she turned to ring for the maid. 'Who would have dreamed of inviting Mr Lydiat?'

But the question presented itself awkwardly, nevertheless. What if the clergyman chose to take upon himself to play the part of Banquo's ghost at the festival? And ought she to let George have any suspicion of that episode in her life connected with him? The thought was instantly dismissed. As well make her lover declare whether he had ever kissed Miss Lydiat in the course of his existence, and exactly at what point the undoubted flirtation between them had been arrested.

CHAPTER IV

•

Retrospective Musings

'View each well-known scene,
Think what is now, and what hath been.'
                                    – SCOTT

The morning that followed this momentous decision broke over
Piper's Hill as clearly and radiantly as its forerunners. With the
promise of a day of still heat, the luxuriant Murray pines, the golden-
fruited orange and lemon shrubs, the spreading palms and glossy
Moreton Bay fig-trees, gave out the faint, fresh perfume that greeted
George's nostrils as he descended early in the morning, and that
helped to intensify the uneasy remorse that had been weighing upon
him throughout the night. If it is true that *La nuit porte conseil*, the
advice it had brought him cannot have been of a palatable kind,
judging by his appearance as he walked slowly along, revolving it in
his mind. Even the infallible cigarette did not smooth the dark look
from his face. Every plant and every shrub cried aloud to him that he
was a traitor. There was not one that had not been a witness to his
love passages with Laura. Not one that had not seen from the time it
was above ground how matters stood. There on the bench, a few
short months ago, Laura's trusting head had lain upon his breast. And
there, with her arms around his neck, she had combated, for *his* sake
only, his proposal that they should marry immediately. She had wanted
to show her confidence, she had been anxious to brave the perilous
experiment. And he? He had been weak enough to give way. Yet every
sentiment of honour and duty required that he should fulfil his trust.
At the cost of fortune, idleness, luxury – all that had hitherto made
life so easy and (pessimistic philosophy notwithstanding) so pleasant

207

to endure! For the very reason that Laura had trusted him so absolutely, that she had loved him, to the exclusion of every one but their
little sister, from the time that she was herself a little girl; and because
she had loved him wholly, unreservedly, and assuredly, as only a
woman without a creed or, at best, with the creed of a hedonist can
love, his duty pointed in one only direction. In vain he repeated
Laura's own arguments over and over again. His heart cried out to
him that she had been arguing against her own convictions, and
against all her womanly instincts. How many of us indeed discuss
theories that we could never bring ourselves to execute in cold blood?
Had she even for an instant believed in the possibility of his deserting
her when she had advised him to delay their marriage until matters
seemed more favourable for it? But then had she not expressly said
that the existence of such a possibility would have given strength to
her arguments? Situated as she was, she vowed that she could not
and would not hold him by any other bond than by their mutual love,
nor see him cast forth from his father's house. An opportunity for
marriage would come. Perhaps George's father would be made to
listen to reason. Meanwhile, they had continued to put off from day
to day, from week to week, and from month to month, the uncomfortable hour when they should brave him finally, and the months had
gone by, and then the years, and George had been satisfied to direct
the whole of his energies and address towards the miserable end of
saving appearances; and now, in some incomprehensible way, as
though he had been drifting along a current without force to resist it,
he had done the deed which he would have sworn, like Peter, it was
impossible for him to do. And this was how it was to end! Here was
the last chapter of the sybaritism, the fatalism, the utilitarianism, and
all the other convenient doctrines they had upheld! He was little better
than a scoundrel, and Laura was his victim! And this was to be the
end of it all!

But how would Laura take the news of his treachery? To be sure
she was in a measure prepared for it. He had told her that the future
depended upon Casserole, and she had been willing that he should
put their fate to the touch, 'and win or lose it all.' She was tired of
the tension – tired of the false position. There was no longer any
freedom at Piper's Hill. She dared not walk about with George for
her only companion as of yore. She hardly dared to make her old
caustic remarks. The allied party was too strong, and she was the only
one who was not of their kith and kin. George reproached himself

now for not having tried to hold her back when she insisted upon going away. Yet he had felt himself that the position was an untenable one, and that short of a speedy marriage, it had no solution. Well, fate had gone against them, and he was suffering as much as she. Would it be any consolation to her to know how utterly wretched he felt? And who was to tell her, and, once more, how would she take the news?

Under the influence of these disquieting thoughts the peaceful beauty of the morning had little to say to George. Nor did it seem to have had a happier message for another inmate of Piper's Hill, for as he went mechanically towards the bench sacred to his meetings with Laura, he saw a little figure seated there in most unchildlike meditation. His heart smote him when he recognised Louey, and perceived that she must have been crying quietly to herself out of everybody's way.

'Poor Poppet!' George was by her side directly. 'You don't care about me any more, do you? Can't I do the little woman any good?'

'It isn't me,' sobbed the child; 'it's Laura!' and George felt that she was turning away from him. The answer to his inward forebodings was so unexpected, and coincided so exactly with the gloomiest form of them, that George for an instant was at a loss how to reply. In the end he assumed the tender, elder-brotherly, monitor-like tone that had never failed to impress Louey upon the rare occasions of his employing it.

'Look here, Poppet; you must be reasonable. Laura and I understand each other. Laura is like a very dear sister, and perhaps, if your father had chosen, she would have let me be her husband. But as that cannot be, she will still be my dearest sister, next to my little woman here.'

But for the first time in her life under similar circumstances Louey did not slip her little hand into her brother's in token of understanding and acquiescence. She wiped her eyes silently on the small square that Laura used to declare was so 'aggravatingly pathetic,' and after a minute's silence she replied –

'I asked papa might I go and stay a little bit with my new brother – and – and Laura. And papa wouldn't, and then I asked him – oh, *very* much – and he said, 'Yes!' only I must take one of the maids; and he said I was a "turncoat." What *is* a turncoat, George?'

'You're not one, anyhow, little woman, so it doesn't matter; and I'm very glad you're going – very glad,' said George, pulling at his moustache, and looking intently on the ground. 'Now, look here – I'm going to give you a letter for Laura – do you hear? and when you're quite alone with her – *quite* alone with her, mind – you can give it her, and you can stop by her while she's reading it; and you can tell her that I meant every word of it – every single word – and that I kissed you in token of it. You won't forget it, now, will you?'

'No!' said the child earnestly. Then, as though moved by a sudden impulse. '*Must* you marry Sara, George?'

'Yes, I *must*,' said her brother, kissing her again as he put her away from him; 'and that's all you need know about it, Poppet, for the present.'

In terror lest the permission that had been 'coaxed and wheedled' out of him, as Mr Piper termed it, when he descended to breakfast soon afterwards with the squirrel clinging to his arm, should be retracted as the day wore on, Louey slipped the Victorian time-table next to *The Argus* that lay folded by her father's plate, and watched for the result.

'What's that for?' said Mr Piper, half amused and half angry. 'It isn't enough to run away from your poor old father, but you must take and make him fix on a train for you. There's the one you shall have, if you ask *me!*'

He pointed to a blank page with his large, coarse finger, but Louey, standing by his side, with one arm round his neck, turned it over as she said, pleadingly, 'Please, papa, don't be a funny papa this morning. I want so to go *soon*.'

There was a world of unconscious plaintiveness in the utterance of these words. But the full significance of them could only be known to George, whom they arrested in the midst of a grave discussion with his aunt and cousins as to the kind of riding-habit Sara should order, it being clearly out of the question that the *fiancée* of a member of all the hunt clubs and racing clubs in the colonies should not learn to distinguish herself on horseback.

'There's a quarter-past twelve train to Barnesbury,' said George, calculating in his own mind that by six o'clock Laura would be in possession of his letter. The letter, it is true, was still unwritten, and the thought of writing it weighed upon him like a nightmare.

'The quarter-past twelve train!' said Mr Piper. '*That's* too early for you, squirrel! There's the 3.35 'll take and whirl you up in no time. And I daresay your aunt'll drive you into Spencer Street after lunch. Only you must see and send the maid in to meet you.'

Poor Mrs Cavendish hastily declared, with a deprecating glance towards her brother, that, of course, Tom had only to *say* for his orders to be carried out. The control of the household had not as yet accustomed her to the further glory of disposing of the carriage, and it was always with a nervous flutter that she heard the question addressed to her after breakfast, 'Please, ma'am, at what time do you want the carriage brought round to-day?'

Louey's preparations for her departure were as old-fashioned as herself. She hesitated for a long time about her doll, but finally with a little sigh deposited it in its resting-place in her toy-cupboard with the green parasol by its side. As she was searching in the pleasant morning-room where she did her lessons with Margaret for the books that the latter had advised her to take with her, her brother George came in and stood with his hands in his pockets, watching her. Louey felt a little embarrassed. His look was so curiously intent, and yet something seemed to tell her that it was not really directed at her at all, but rather at something that he was thinking of very hard indeed. At last he broke the silence.

'You're a good little soul, Poppet, if ever there was one. Don't you think I don't know why you want to go to Barnesbury. And since you *will* go, I don't see that there's any use in my writing to Laura. Will you tell her I *couldn't* write? She'll understand. And tell her I'm in her hands. She'll understand that too. She'll know what I mean. You need say nothing more. And I'm off to town now. I'm not coming back until this evening. You won't go away without wishing me good-bye, will you?'

The child held up her wistful little face towards him immediately. As he bent down to kiss it, she whispered, 'Is it only because you can't *help* it, George?'

'No, I can't help it,' said her brother vehemently, and with that he left her.

The Piper's Hill carriage was fatally punctual that afternoon. Mr Piper remembered afterwards how he had scolded every one in the establishment to hide his own grief at the squirrel's desertion of him, because Sara had kept it waiting before the door. Ah! if she had kept it waiting only a little longer – just a few minutes – only long enough to let him give full vent to his growing exasperation, and take and put his foot down on the nonsensical whim. But Sara had hurried down at the sound of his loud voice, and Louey had kissed her little hand to him for the last time, and he had slammed the door as he turned back into the house, with a strange impulse that he would have been almost ashamed to own to, to run after the carriage on that broiling January afternoon, and declare that he had made up his mind once for all that Louey should *not* go. But he did not act upon the impulse, or was it only long afterwards, God help him, that he remembered having had it at all?

At the Spencer Street station the train was found to be very full. It was necessary to tack on a couple of first-class carriages at the end, in one of which Louey and her maid found a place. Mrs Cavendish and Margaret waited on the platform to see the last of the little face stationed at the window. And they were careful to tell Uncle Piper that the last words Louey had shouted as the train moved off were 'Love to papa,' and yet again 'Love to papa' until it was out of sight.

CHAPTER V

———•———

'Suspense'

'So, farewell hope.' – MILTON

If the night had been a penitential one to George, it had also brought little solace to Laura. Why is it, I wonder, that a sleepless night, which is surely the blackest of all black nights in the weary prolonging of its darkness, should have come to be called by the French *une nuit blanche?* It is true that its immediate effects are to bleach the countenances of its victims. Laura's bright colour had all disappeared when she came into the breakfast-room the following morning. There were dark lines under her blue eyes, which seemed to be heavy with unshed tears. But, as was her wont, she laughed at her brother's anxious inquiries (a forced stage laugh, without a grain of mirth in it), and rattled on at random about every indifferent subject that presented itself.

'Shall I take you for a drive again to-day, Francis? We might get the butcher's pony to go with this one. It would improve his morals, you know, for he's used to stronger language than "Gee-up" and "Hi;" and I'm sure Mr Marsh's pony never hears anything worse. Isn't he a wonderfully *clerical*-looking cob, this one? I think I could tell a horse out of a parson's stable anywhere.'

'How?' asked her brother, smiling.

'Oh! I don't know. There's a *je ne sais quoi* about his way of standing and looking, a pat-me-down look. I can't describe it to you exactly; you see all horses look much the same to you, excepting for their colour, and this is a very subtle distinction. Perhaps it's only fancy, and because they don't pull up at the public-house so often of their own accord as other horses do.'

'Shall we wait for the letters first?' asked her brother, when breakfast was over.

'Just as you like,' replied Laura carelessly, though her heart turned sick within her at every sound that seemed to herald the approach of the postman.

Her Majesty's letter-carrier, or, to speak more correctly, the letter-carrier of the Victorian Government, being alone in his functions at Barnesbury, the delivery of the morning and evening despatches was a proceeding of a somewhat perfunctory and casual description. Laura had more than once declared that she would like to have the powers of an Eastern potentate for only a quarter of an hour, as the regular time for the morning delivery went by, and the postman still lingered in conversation with the barman at the Junction, and finally turned back with him into the building for an indefinite number of 'drinks.' But this morning, because it seemed probable that her death-warrant was in this same postman's keeping, and because every nerve was strained by the cruellest expectancy and apprehension, she affected the most utter unconcern as to his movements. She seated herself in her accustomed corner of the verandah, looking in the searching morning light like a Dresden shepherdess that might have been left too long on view, and that had begun to fade ever so little in the process, and applied herself to braiding a pair of oriental-looking slippers for her brother, a work of which Francis was wont to watch the progress with a naive admiration and gratitude that amused her openly, and touched her secretly more than she would have allowed.

Truth to tell, Laura was becoming used to the monotonous routine of her life at Barnesbury. Not that she would have tolerated the notion of prolonging it indefinitely. She would have told you that she would have rather died, and she would have quite believed it herself. But as a rest during a great crisis in her life, it was acceptable. Francis's presence seemed to have something healing in it. Certainly she had one fault to find in him, but it was the somewhat paradoxical one of his being apparently *without* a fault. He was never impatient, or idle, or self-indulgent. He never relapsed into the fidgety ways that the absence of anything like a settled occupation had produced in George. He was always thoroughly awake, unruffled, wise, and gentle, and as for thought of *her*, it seemed to Laura that no one had ever been so tender of her as her brother – not even excepting George, in whose case the tenderness was at least returned – and with interest.

'Are you happier than you were in England, Francis?' she asked suddenly. Her eyes had been wandering involuntarily towards the gate, but now she fixed their keen glance full upon him.

'In some ways – yes,' he made reply. 'But life is made too easy for me here. It doesn't seem right or natural.'

Laura laughed her short laugh, and smoothed out the brilliant embroidery upon her lap.

'What self-tormentors you people are, to be sure; and yet you think it's justifiable to reckon upon any amount of impossible, never-ending, undying bliss in a future state. It seems much more logical to take the best in every stage you travel over. What should I have cared, when I was a child, if I had been promised grown up concerts and balls, and been told to think of *them*, instead of amusing myself like a child. It seems such a senseless theory when you come to think of it.'

'That is a large question you are opening,' said Francis, looking at her with his grave half-smile. 'Perhaps we don't mean the same thing at all when we speak of happiness.' Laura snapped her gold thread impatiently.

'I don't know what *you* mean by it, but I know what I mean myself very well. I mean the satisfaction of my actual wants – those that are suited to my mind and body in the present. I don't want to interfere with anybody else's enjoyment, but it seems much juster, and, I must say, much more moderate, to make the most and the best of what one can get here, than to spoil oneself for it all one can, and to spend one's time in thinking of how much more one will get at some future time.'

Francis pondered for a little before replying.

'I think it is very wise philosophy to make the most and the best, as you say, of what we have here; but you are much more fortunate than the rest of the world, Laura, if something is not wanting in your life to enable you to make an every-day practice of it. I think it is generally just the thing that seems most suited to our present wants that somehow eludes our grasp. There it is; just within our reach. We stretch out our hands for itl with infinite longing. And just because we desire it so ardently, it escapes us. But it is not for the finding of mere selfish consolation that we dwell upon the life to come. It is to help and console all our fellow-sufferers around us.'

'But it doesn't console some of them at all,' interrupted Laura, with a half-wail in her voice, for Francis's theories seemed to promise the realisation of the doom she was dreading. 'It hasn't any meaning for them. I don't recognise myself out of my body. Besides you only have to think where you are if you get a knock on the head – or when you get old and worn-out. Nobody has ever answered puzzles of that kind yet.'

'Have you ever heard,' said Francis, 'that curious case of a man who *did* get a knock on the head – as you call it, Laura – only it didn't kill him. He remained senseless for weeks, and when he was restored to himself he took up his thread of thought just where he had dropped it, and was as intelligent and full of life as ever. You see, when the soul is imprisoned in the body it can apparently disappear for a time, but it goes on existing just the same, and comes back itself in the end.'

'And did *you* ever hear,' retorted Laura, 'how that very case is an argument in support of *my* views more than of yours? Supposing the body to be like a machine through which a current of electricity is kept going, the machine being sound, of course; it is easy to understand that when it is out of working order the current is suspended, and when the machine is worn out the current ceases to flow.'

'But the current exists independently of the machine,' said her brother eagerly. 'Only think, Laura –'

But Laura's thoughts were no longer at his command. With a desperate effort to appear unconcerned she was watching the telegraph-boy fasten the bridle of his pony to the gate. As she saw him hand an envelope to her brother a mist gathered before her eyes. It seemed to her that she could hear the quick, painful pulsations of her own heart. Something had happened to George, and she had been thinking of herself alone. Oh, if only *he* were safe she could consent to suffer. She could bear separation, desertion, all, but George must be still of this world, and well.

It is curious that such an eternity of apprehension can be condensed into so short a space. To Francis it seemed hardly a second after the arrival of the telegram before he had handed it to her with the reassuring observation –

'What a pleasant surprise for us, eh, Laura?'

'Yes,' said Laura, with a great sigh of relief, but foreboding that there was something behind the surprise which was not so pleasant

as Francis imagined. 'It is from Mr Piper, I see. He says Louey and
a maid are leaving by the three o'clock express to-day.'

'*There* is an object for our drive,' said Francis gaily. 'The butcher's
pony represents the actual want of your being at this moment, I am
sure. I wonder whether we can gratify it.'

So saying he went away, and Laura, throwing down her embroidery,
ran off to consult with the frightened-looking servant as to the best
means of housing the newcomers. She did not hide from herself the
significance of Louey's mission. But she tried to put away the thought
of it. She had had a reprieve, and she told herself she would make
the most of it.

And there was even a kind of housewifely pleasure in arranging
things for the comfort of the unexpected guests. Despite the scorching
wind, which seemed to blow six days out of seven at Barnesbury, she
hunted bravely throughout the unsympathetic garden for such roses
and heliotropes as maintained a semblance of freshness. And she
turned up her sleeves in the kitchen, and covered her shapely arms
with flour in the preparation of scones for a high tea – thereby
becoming so much of a mere mortal in Jane's eyes that she lost the
fashion-plate prestige that she had seemed to carry with her in the
beginning, at once and for ever.

The Rev. Mr Lydiat's modest ambition was fulfilled. At four o'clock
that afternoon, an hour at which, notwithstanding the prospect of a
gradual decline of a tormenting sun, only brave people venture out of
doors for pleasure on a hot January day, the buggy, drawn by the
butcher's pony in the elevating companionship of 'Mr Marsh's cob,'
was stationed in front of the parsonage door. Laura perched herself
on the high seat, while Francis meekly installed himself by her side.
He had the most respectful and unquestioning faith in his sister's
equine knowledge, and when she purposely aired the horsey phrases
she had caught from George, he listened with the same sense of
awe that an unerudite person might feel on hearing a conversation
conducted in Hebrew. The conjecture that the butcher's pony stood
little more than fourteen hands high; that Mr Marsh's cob had had
his legs fired; that there was a swelling on the off shoulder of the
near horse, conveyed a full and satisfactory conviction of having learnt
something valuable as regarded the science of the stable. He compared
his sister to Boadicea and Jehu, and repeated to her that most moving
poem of Kingsley's concerning poor Lorraine-Loree.

Laura's driving was indeed both skilful and graceful, and she abstained from 'showing off,' as far as was humanly possible, before so naive an admirer as her brother.

His 'new chum' questions were a great source of amusement to her, as she turned off the metal road and drove him over bush tracks past selectors' huts; down towards the gully where the Chinamen were puddling, content if they scraped together some fine grains of imperceptible gold after days of fossicking; through dreary regions of rung gum trees, standing bare in a kind of white-blackness, significant of their life-in-death condition; and finally round the township race-course, where she discoursed learnedly upon the nature of the *jumps*, and held forth upon the relative attractions of steeplechases and hurdle-races.

CHAPTER VI

---•---

Mrs Cavendish Receives A Telegram

'If you have tears, prepare to shed them now.'

It was nearly seven o'clock. The angry sun, that had been glowing like a red-hot copper ball all the afternoon, was sinking in a downy couch of vaporous clouds, an indistinct mass of gold and purple. Laura, flicking away the flies from the backs of her ponies, drove them at a smart trot down the inclining street of Barnesbury and up the opposite hill to the station. She had the triumph of drawing them up in front of it exactly at the moment that the train was descried from the platform, and, calling a man to hold the horses, she pulled down her veil and descended with her brother to meet the travellers.

What was it in the expression of the pale little face at the carriage window that made Laura compress her lips in preparation of the blow that awaited her? As Louey sprang into her arms, quite regardless of the crowd, or her brother, or the dislike that Laura generally professed for demonstrations, there was that in the pressure of her arms round her neck in the close, clinging, absorbing embrace that followed, that seemed to tell Laura all. It was the unconscious affirmation of Mr Piper's favourite truism, that 'blood is thicker than water.' It was the sympathy of sister for sister, the understanding of woman for woman, emanating. Heaven knows how, from the most innocent and childlike little soul on earth. Even while returning Francis's embrace, Louey did not relax her hold upon her sister's hand, but kissed it furtively while her brother was gone to see after the luggage.

219

'Have you a letter for me?' was Laura's first eager question from behind her veil.

'No; George *couldn't* write,' said the child earnestly. 'Perhaps he will; it was all in such a hurry that it was settled yesterday. I think papa *made* him say he would marry Sara, and he told me to say he was in your hands, Laura (kissing them again). He said you would know what it meant.'

To this Laura, however, made no reply. Behind the veil her face was hard and set; but her voice was as composed and not much drier than of wont as she went after Francis with the suggestions that the maid and the 'basket from town' should be sent on to the parsonage in a cab, while room should be made for Louey in the buggy. Francis readily acceded, and the little girl, to whom birth and nature alike seemed to have given the mission of holding together all the contrary elements among which she found herself, was seated, well content, between her brother and sister.

What with the pressure of the thought that was weighing upon her and the veil that Laura persisted in keeping before her face, she did not notice that a change had taken place during her absence, and that, unheeded, perhaps entirely unwatched by the man left in charge, the butcher's pony had been diligently rubbing one of his blinkers against the fence, and that in another instant it would be gone altogether. She was only aware of the catastrophe when, at the top of the hill, the pony made a sudden desperate plunge forward, so terrifying to its companion in harness that he started off at a mad gallop. In an instant, and before any of the occupants of the buggy seemed to have time to realise what it all meant, the two horses were tearing frantically down the hill, and Laura, white as death, though perfectly calm, was directing Francis to pull, and 'pull for his life,' upon the reins. In vain! Before Louey could breathe the prayer that they might be saved – for papa's sake – the nightmare that she had so often seen in a vague, undefined, monstrous kind of shape in her childish dreams was upon her. Sometimes it had been like the hull of a steamer, sometimes like a falling house! Now it had come in living shape before her eyes. It was in front of her, it was upon her! She saw it before it touched her. A mighty, terrific, black, canvas-covered waggon! There was the sense of some powerful shock that made everything round her swim and reel. A wild and confused vision of an infinite number of horses' legs and heads kicking on the ground and in the air all round and about her. Loud voices, and crashing, and noise, and stars shooting through the air. Then darkness and bright spots, and a sudden chill of cold, and darkness again, and then nothing.

How many hours after this could it have been, I wonder, when a telegram was brought into the Piper's Hill dining-room, where the family party was still sitting over the dessert? It had not been a very joyous evening. Mr Piper could not accustom himself to the empty place at his left hand, and Sara had been rendered unusually serious by a piece of news that her uncle had communicated on sitting down to the table. 'You'd none o' you guess it, so you may as well give it up. There's that young Hyde, he that must needs go jackerooing up in the bush. He's lost an uncle and two cousins, and now he's next heir to a baronetcy. If he follows *my* advice he'll take and choose a wife out o' the colonies before he goes home. You're not in the market any longer, Sara, my girl, so we must send him somewhere else for his courting. What do you say if we hand him over to your sister, or that fine piece o' frippery up country, eh?'

Sara smiled, but it was rather a sorry smile. The words uttered in jest were no jest to her. It might be that she had thrown away the one chance of her lifetime, the winning number in the great marriage lottery, to which she was so justly entitled. The recollection of the matron of the convicts came back with poignant force. She dared not encounter the eyes of her betrothed, lest the evident mortification that she was struggling against should be apparent to him. Sara's mind misgave her, indeed, sometimes lest George should be more clear-sighted than he took the trouble to appear. There had been something in his manner since yesterday that she did not understand. It was almost as though a vein of subtle irony ran through his devotion to her. But as this could not possibly be the case, *what* was it that impressed her so uncomfortably in her new relations with him? Was it only her own tormenting recollection of *who* he was and *what* she was? She confessed to herself that Mr Hyde might have behaved in exactly the same way in her cousin's place, and that she might have felt there was nothing to criticise. But a man who owned Mr Piper for a father, and who made it his boast that he had had an 'honest woman' for his mother, could not expect to be measured by the same standard. It was unsatisfactory – and how different everything might have been had she asked for a little time for reflection before commit-ting herself! What a warm glow of hope her uncle's news would have aroused! Whereas now –. Unconsciously Sara sighed audibly, and looked at her plate, whereon Mr Piper's monogram figured in brilliant gilt letters, with a sense of secret exasperation against her surroundings and her fate that she felt to be thoroughly justifiable.

During the pause that ensued the telegram was brought in and handed to Mrs Cavendish.

Now the master of Piper's Hill was in the habit of receiving telegrams by the score, but to Mrs Cavendish the opening of the official brown envelope was a matter for much painful beating of the heart. And this evening, as she performed the operation, every pair of eyes at the table was directed towards her, with a half smile of expectancy, it being evident that the telegram could only give the news of the arrival of the travellers at Barnesbury. The consternation, therefore, was all the greater when Mrs Cavendish, rising from the table with white lips, and the words 'God help us!' carried the telegram straight to her brother, and holding him round the neck, and breaking down into sobs as she tried to speak, besought him incoherently to let them 'be off at once.'

Immediately every one had left his place, to learn the extent of the catastrophe. Mr Piper threw the telegram among them without a word. An instant later he had left the room, and his hoarse voice was heard gasping out an order to 'take and fetch the carriage round at once.' In the meantime, George had seized the missive, and was reading clearly, though with an evident effort, the following words:

'*Barnesbury*. – Accident to buggy. Louey badly hurt. Laura – injuries to face and head. My own arm broken. – FRANCIS.'

It was to Margaret that George turned instinctively during the confusion of bewildered exclamations that followed. Mrs Cavendish had gone to her brother, and was hurriedly putting together a few necessary articles of toilette for herself and him. There was nothing for it but a special train. What George was feeling no one knew. He seemed to forget the presence of every one but Margaret.

'You will come with us?' he said to her, half imploringly.

'Oh, how can you even ask?' cried Margaret, suppressing the choking longing to burst into tears.

No one seemed to remember Mr Cavendish and Sara, who somehow found themselves alone at Piper's Hill only a quarter of an hour after the arrival of the telegram. When the large family carriage drove up, Mr Piper entered it first mechanically. He had no idea but to reach his little girl as soon as might be; he seemed hardly aware of the presence of the others. It was George who handed his aunt and cousin in, and took his seat next to the latter after directing the coachman to drive within half an hour to the Spencer Street station. He had not even time to say good-bye to his uncle or Sara. There was a kind of undefined, vague, horrible feeling that Louey's death would lie at his door. Perhaps he had killed Laura, too. Injuries to face and head! He winced in the darkness as though some fierce blow had been dealt him full and straight upon brows and nose from a prize-fighter's fist, as he repeated the words to himself. He had never felt very deeply before that he remembered; but it seemed to him now that he knew what real suffering meant. Oh! if he could only have taken *all* his little sister's hurt and Laura's upon his own worthless person, and died with his hands in theirs, instead of having the sinister words 'badly hurt' and 'injuries to face and head' beating and burning themselves into his brain with such awful significance.

The journey was performed almost in silence. Mrs Cavendish, holding her brother's hand as she sat next to him in the corner, whispered from time to time such words of hope and sympathy as her pitying heart prompted. He answered never a word. But somehow, when the train reached Barnesbury at last, long after midnight, he was the first on the platform and the first in the waggonette that was there in waiting. And he was the first to hear the driver say that 'there was two doctors in wid 'em,' as he pointed to the parsonage with his whip. There was a bright moon shining, and as the waggonette drove swiftly down the hill the driver pointed to the wreck of the buggy lying on one side of the road, ready for removal on the morrow. How it had run *bang* into the big waggon, and turned *clean over*; how the 'prastely gentleman' had dragged the little miss right from under the heels of the horses, and got a kick that broke his shoulder all to pieces; and how the foine young lady that 'handled the ribbons so well had been all smashed up and kilt entirely,' were graphically narrated. But still Mr Piper said nothing. Only, arrived at the parsonage door, which stood wide open with a kerosene lamp burning on the table in the hall, he rushed past the servant, the doctors, Francis, every one who would have barred his passage, and made his way straight to the room where a little figure was lying, white and rigid, on a bed. And there, on his knees by its side, and with his hands stretched out towards it in a dumb agony of grief and longing, we will leave him.

CHAPTER VII

———•———

Mr Cavendish And Sara Are Left In Charge

'She's beautiful, therefore to be wooed;
She is a woman, therefore to be won.'

There are two ways of feeling sorrow for the misfortunes of others. Mrs Cavendish's and Margaret's way was to incorporate themselves so entirely with the sufferer, and to carry out so genuinely the injunction to 'weep with those that weep,' that they did not even seem to have time to reflect upon the amount of personal grief and discomfort for which they might legitimately shed a few tears on their own account. Mr Cavendish's and Sara's way was to pity themselves fretfully and heartily for having their susceptible nerves subjected to such disquieting shocks. Just on the eve of a marriage, too! – when the whole business of life should have been concentrated in driving about from tailor to *modiste*, and from jeweller to trunkmaker, and in devising all kinds of delicious travelling and *table-d'hote* costumes for the appreciation and envy of real men and women of the world in all the capitals of Europe and the East.

But there was nothing to be said against the outward demeanour of either. Mr Cavendish knew exactly what good taste required of him under the circumstances, and even Sara was impressed by his subdued air of decorous grief when she met him next morning at the breakfast-table. Such platitudes as those which affirm the uncertainty of human affairs and the advisability of not giving way having been duly delivered, Mr Cavendish settled himself with a sigh to *The Argus*. He really did feel a sympathetic kind of shuddering at the thought of broken limbs and bloody heads, and wished that he were not cursed with so finely strung an organisation.

To Sara the morning passed heavily enough. She installed herself with her fancy work in the deserted verandah, and gave herself up to wondering just how much Laura's face was damaged; and why George should have seemed to forget everything in his hurry to get to Barnesbury after the telegram came. Then she reflected upon the possibility of her having to wear mourning (only the thought was so unwelcome from every point of view that she put it away from her), and finally she fell to reproaching George and Margaret and her mother bitterly, and in turn, in her own mind, for not having sent her a telegram by this time of the day.

It was while these unsatisfactory reflections were clouding her beautiful brow that an oblong card was brought to her, bearing the name of Mr Clarence Hyde.

'Did you tell him they were all away?' she asked, keeping her head bent over the card, and uncomfortably aware that she was colouring visibly.

'I told the gentleman you was all away but you and Mr Cavendish, miss,' replied the servant; 'and he said, would you do him the favour to see him an instant in the dining-room?'

'You're sure he meant *me*?' insisted Sara, 'for I think papa is upstairs.'

'He meaned you for sure, miss. He said – would Miss Sara Cavendish see him for a moment, please?'

'You can say I'll come directly,' replied Sara, but she ran upstairs first, and looked in the glass. No – nothing could be prettier than her simple morning dress of white grass-cloth, with its relieving bands of black velvet round the throat and wrists. Her hair, ever so slightly disarranged, seemed to wave towards her brows like a statue's. Her pure skin gave the fullest value to the peculiar richness of colour in eye and lip – more beautiful in the searching morning sunlight than under the brilliant gas candelabra. She could not repress a feeling of exultation as she turned away from the mirror, and first steadying her nerves by remembering that she must announce the news of a terrible family disaster, descended into the drawing-room. Mr Hyde met her with outstretched hand – a hand that was just beginning to lose its aristocratic impress of slenderness and whiteness through the process of 'jackarooing' – and looked at her for an instant with an irrepressible glance of keen curiosity. But that instant was enough. It conveyed the confirmation, and more than the confirmation, of the impression he had carried away. Here was a girl before whom 'professional beauties' – and he knew them all – might hide their heads. Her proper sphere was at the head of London Society. And she might still – who knows – be had for the asking. It was an intoxicating thought for a worshipper of beauty like Mr Hyde, a man who prided himself upon the fastidiousness of his taste, and especially upon possessing a standard so exalted as to be almost impossible of attainment.

'You have heard what trouble we are in?' said Sara in a low voice, as she seated herself upon a sofa, while Mr Hyde was depositing his tall hat, covered with a deep band of black cloth, upon a chair.

'No! I am so sorry. I had no idea. Is any one ill?'

'Oh, worse than that,' said Sara. And then a singular thing happened to her. As she recounted the facts of the accident her voice trembled, and her eyes filled with tears. She could not have said whether it was concern for the sufferers or for herself that moved her. Or whether the sensation was one of mere nervous agitation. To tell the truth, Sara did not possess the 'dramatic instinct,' which enables persons to realise a situation or a sensation with appalling intensity, and it is probable that her imagination had not even outlined the details of the catastrophe until she came to put it into words.

But whatever was the feeling that prompted her it lent a curious charm to her faultless face – such a charm perchance as might have belonged to Galatea when from cold, hard marble, she softened into warm womanhood. It transformed Mr Hyde's sensuous admiration into a stronger more ardent sentiment. It is sad to think that had she been old and ill-favoured she might have wept like a walrus without awakening more than a feeble spark of pity. But as it was, nothing short of passionate sympathy and the entire conviction that this beautiful creature was gifted with exquisite sensibility were the effect of her few natural tears upon her listener, Mr Hyde approached the chair upon which he was seated a little closer to the sofa, and murmured phrases of sympathy. The great point, after all, was that none of the victims had lost their lives. It was because there was so much to do for them that there had been no telegram. Now in his own case there was no room for hope. And then he described how he had received a telegram from England containing in four words the account of an awful fatality in his own family – the deaths of an uncle, a nephew, a cousin, two younger than himself, and one on the point of being married.

Sara kept her eyes fixed upon the ground while she listened. The uncle, cousin, and nephew were such shadowy abstractions. She could not think of them but as impediments that should have been removed a week earlier. It was quite a relief when the luncheon bell rang, and Mr Hyde rose to go, uncertain how he should frame his adieux. But aid came in the person of Mr Cavendish, who at a look from his daughter invited the visitor to lunch. Mr Hyde hesitated, demurred on the score of his being loth to intrude upon their sorrow, but ended by accepting the invitation.

If in the misfortunes of others there is always something not entirely disagreeable to ourselves, Mr Cavendish was now experiencing the compensating side of the family disaster. To do the honours of such a perfectly-appointed table and such unimpeachable sherry to one of his own caste, without any intrusion of the Piper element, and only his own queenly daughter to head the table, was so entirely in accordance with the fitness of things to Mr Cavendish's thinking that he wished, if it could only be managed without hurt to the victims, that there might be a buggy accident every week. Before lunch was half over he had quite established the link, through grandmothers, great aunts, and bishops' cousins twice removed, which connected Mr Hyde's family with his own, and was asking questions about all kinds of people whose names Sara only knew of through seeing them in the London society papers that found their way to Piper's Hill in company with *Punch* and the *Graphic* by every mail.

'And so you are going home! How I envy you!' said Mr Cavendish at last. 'We poor exiles' . . . and he poured himself out a glass of Mr Piper's *Chàteau Lafitte*, with a sigh.

'I shall never regret my glimpse of the colonies, though,' said Mr Hyde, looking at Sara. 'It seems to me you make your exile very endurable in Melbourne.'

'We try to,' said Mr Cavendish resignedly; 'but, my dear sir, there are only two places worth living in for civilised beings. The first of these is London, *and* the second Paris.'

'Is Miss Cavendish of the same opinion?' asked Mr Hyde, looking at her again.

Now Sara had never been to Paris, any more than she had seen the inside of a ballroom before coming to Melbourne; but she was her father's own daughter, and might have been the queen of the preceding London season for the ease with which she replied –

'I'm not *quite* so extreme as papa. Besides, the novelty of Australia is still an attraction; but I fancy I should like *Sydney* better than Melbourne to live in.'

Mr Hyde entirely sympathised with her. He had connections in Sydney who gave him a charming picture of their existence, and he had intended to take a run across before going to England. But his presence at home was urgent, and he allowed it to be understood that his new position as direct heir to a baronetcy was very onerous and responsible. When lunch was over, there seemed to be no pretext for prolonging the visit.

'It is really good-bye, then?' said Sara, as she found herself alone with him for an instant, while her father was gone to get a card that Mr Hyde was to keep 'in remembrance of his newly-found relatives' at Piper's Hill. 'You are really going away by next mail?'

Perhaps she was not aware of it herself. The regret that she could not help feeling at the loss of what might have been so brilliant an opportunity gave something soft and sorrowful to her tone. Besides, as far as she was capable of liking, she felt that she *did* like Mr Hyde. She liked the shape of his head, and his fair moustache; she liked his thin aristocratic nose, and the suave courtliness of his manner. But beyond and above all, she liked his name, and his birthright, and his prospective title. All these likings made up a feeling that rendered his going away very disagreeable to her. But the disagreeableness translated itself, like everything else that belonged to Sara, in the most agreeable way. As it had been with Mr Lydiat, who was, if you please, an exalted enthusiast, so it was now with Mr Hyde, who, for all his youth, believed himself to be an 'old stager' in affairs of the heart. His eyes grew troubled. He breathed quickly.

'There is only one thing that could keep me,' he replied in agitated tones; 'but I hardly dare to say it.'

All this time those wondrous eyes had been fixed upon the young man as Sara stood in front of him next to the open door, but now they were lowered, and he could see nothing but the blue-veined lids, and the exquisite dark lashes that framed them.

What she replied he could not hear, but there was no mistaking the tremuluous half smile of encouragement that flitted across the lips. In an instant he had drawn her behind the door, and in spite of a cooing expostulation it was, perhaps, excusable to disregard, he had pressed his moustache against her face, and was murmuring incoherent words of hope and rapture of which Sara fully understood the purport to be the instant offer of his hand and heart.

'Good God!' exclaimed Mr Cavendish, 'has my daughter gone mad?'

He had entered the drawing-room just in time to see Sara remove her head gently from Mr Hyde's encircling arm. Both the young people were unduly flushed, but Sara's eyes were shining with a light that was by no means that of indignation or anger.

Before Mr Cavendish could give vent to the bewildered wrath that moved him – to tell the truth, he imagined that he had interrupted what he would have justly called 'bar-room amenities,' and his blood boiled within him – Mr Hyde had taken Sara's hand, and was explaining himself in words that left no doubt as to the honesty of his intentions. 'I know it is quite unpardonable to have been so precipitate, but there are uncontrollable sympathies (here he pressed the soft hand that lay in his palm), and knowing I had only two days in Melbourne. I took the only opportunity I might have of asking Miss – Miss Cavendish if she could give me a spark of hope, and – and I understood her to say yes; and if we have your approval, my dear sir, I should be the happiest, the proudest fellow on this earth. I assure you it is no sudden fancy. I have thought of no one else since we first met, but she was so utterly beyond my reach at that time. Only everything has changed since then. I can offer her a position and a fortune that I never dreamed of possessing. I hope you will make every inquiry about me. I beg – indeed, I insist upon it. But I hope you will not debar me from paying my addresses,' and then he turned to Sara. 'Won't you say a word for me?' he added humbly.

It was a perplexing situation. But Mr Cavendish was a casuist. The thought that travelled with lightning speed through his brain was that here was a Heaven-sent wooer, before whom the claims of vulgar clay must give way. All kinds of vague and shadowy recollections of early mythological and Oriental studies – very superficial ones, to speak the truth – rushed upon him, and confirmed the belief that a woman's destiny – yes, the destiny of such women as the mother of a Romulus or a Buddha – is to yield to the instance of the Superior Being, no matter to what extent she may have entangled her destiny with that of a common mortal. What the *Deus ex machina* might be that was to rescue Sara from the uncomfortable complication of being engaged to two men at the same time he was not clear, but he reflected with fervent gratitude upon the fact that Mr Piper had not been able to noise abroad the affair of his son's engagement as yet, and if the worst should come to the worst, why, Mr Cavendish was prepared to play the *role* of *Deus ex machina* himself. He was quite convinced now that with regard to 'that other affair' his consentment had been 'dragged out of him,' and that he would certainly, after a little more time for calm consideration, have withdrawn it. Sara trembled as she waited for her father's answer. She had not dared to enforce her lover's appeal by more than a murmured and hardly audible 'Yes, please, papa,' but she found now that her terror had been needless, Mr Cavendish behaved with admirable dignity.

'Yes, he *must* say,' very genially, 'there had been a little – just a little – precipitancy.' Of course the peculiar circumstances of the case might be pleaded in extenuation – he was the first to admit that – but Mr Hyde would understand that just for the present the matter had better not go beyond the knowledge of those immediately concerned. His connections – that is to say, his wife's connections, under whose hospitable roof they had been spending a few weeks – were in sad affliction, and his dear daughter was overcome by sorrow and sympathy. Mr Cavendish could not find it in his heart to destroy the immense support and consolation that was to be found in the indulgence of so holy and legitimate a sentiment as that which Mr Hyde had had the good fortune to arouse in her. 'But we must not think of ourselves, my dear children; for I feel towards you as though you were my own son,' he interposed, addressing himself directly to Mr Hyde. 'We must be patient and prudent, and we must think of others before ourselves; but God bless you all the same.'

When Mr Hyde had gone away, with the promise of a fresh interview on the morrow, Mr Cavendish came into the drawing-room, where Sara was awaiting him, with an expression in which triumph and shame were curiously mingled. He fidgeted somewhat nervously about the room as he spoke to her. Both father and daughter avoided encountering each other's eyes. 'You quite understand, Sara, why I did not allude to that – that *enfantillage* between your cousin and yourself. For my part, I have steadily ignored it. I cannot sanction any fresh *mésalliances* in my family. But you owe it to Mr Hyde (and I am sure you will agree with me) to be *very* explicit, and without loss of time; you must free yourself immediately from anything like the *soupçon* of an entanglement. You quite understand that?'

'Yes, papa,' murmured Sara, and Mr Cavendish thought she added something about the other affair with George being only a conditional engagement.

'You have a father, child,' he interrupted her sharply. 'If the young man George should have the bad taste to insist, refer him to me. I have had time for reflection. I could not countenance anything so unsuitable. By-the-by, I hope you have not been guilty of the unpardonable folly of committing yourself to writing in any way.'

'Writing? Oh no, papa, I have never had the chance of writing to George.'

'That is right. Of course if you *had* it wouldn't matter with a gentleman. *Noblesse oblige*; but one is never sure of what the Piper breed might be capable. Now, you must be guided by *me*, Sara. Only your father can act for you. *I* will write to my wife's nephew – immediately. I will say that all idea of your uniting yourself with him must be instantly abandoned. He must know nothing of the real state of your affections for the present. You understand?'

'Yes, papa!' said Sara meekly. She was feeling a little stunned by the sudden change in her fortunes, and somehow a silly saying that she had often heard her mother repeat about the danger of falling to the ground between stools was running in her head. Certainly one was a very poor stool – a mere three-legged milking stool, as compared with the other, which seemed to confer almost as many privileges as the legendary *tabouret* in the court of Louis XIV. But even *it* was preferable to the bare boards, let alone the humiliation of the fall. And then Mr Piper was such a formidable figure in the background. Altogether Sara's elation was held in most uncomfortable check, and it was almost a relief when her mind was diverted by the appearance of a maid who entered the room with breathless expectancy, and the announcement 'Oh, please, miss, here's the tellergrum come at last.'

CHAPTER VIII

•

Margaret's Vocation

'When pain and anguish ring the brow,
A ministering angel thou.'

While Mr Cavendish and his daughter are pressing upon their guest
the choicest contents of Mr Piper's cellar, George's eyes are becoming
accustomed to the following vision in a darkened room at Barnesbury
parsonage. The vision of a white curtained bed in the corner, whereon
the indistinct outline of a woman's form is visible. The head and face
are bandaged, but here and there a stray lock of tangled fair hair,
escaping from its confinement, mingles with the lace frills that
surround a slender throat. One white hand, sparkling with costly rings,
is lying on the coverlet. George's gaze is fascinated by this hand. For
every time that there is a nervous contraction of the fingers it seems
to send forth a fresh scintillation from the diamonds and emeralds
that adorn it.

And yet he is not thinking of Laura's rings. Probably it is quite
unconsciously to himself that his eyes follow their successive gleams.
He is thinking of what he will say to the poor mutilated face lying on
the bed there, when it shall first look at him with eyes of recognition,
from out of the mummy-like wrappings that swathe it. That it cannot
so look for some time to come is the reason of his being allowed to
mount guard at the present moment. For in the first pressing into the
service of all the sound people, in behalf of the wounded inmates of
Barnesbury, the functions of sick nurse have been rather promiscu-
ously distributed, and it does not seem strange to any one that George
should be allowed to watch for half an hour in Laura's room, while

232

Mrs Cavendish is making beef-tea, and Margaret is cutting up the food that for the first time since the accident will pass Mr Lydiat's lips.

No! nothing seems strange in face of the sudden and awful change that such a trifling incident as the rubbing off of a blinker by the butcher's pony has brought about. There is no time to think of conventionalities. The only thing that presses is to help and relieve the sufferers. For, thank God! there are none of them yet quite beyond the reach of earthly help and relief. What might have passed for death in Louey's immovable pose is the forerunner of concussion of the brain. The great Melbourne doctor, to whom Mr Piper telegraphed on the night of his arrival, has affirmed it, and though there have been whispered rumours of paralysis of the spine on the part of the two local doctors, who took it upon themselves to prepare the father 'for the worst,' there is yet the breath of life in the frail little body, and to that feeble breath Mr Piper clings with the same dogged, desperate tenacity that he has carried into all the other purposes of his life. What superstition moves him it would be impossible to say; he does not explain it to himself. But all his thoughts, his hopes, his most passionate desires, are concentrated now upon the one object of keeping that spark of life from going out. He does not eat or sleep. I cannot say that he renders himself very useful either; but he *longs* with a frantic longing. And though he cannot act upon the Catholic theory of propitiating some pitying saint by a magnificent bribe, he does cherish the idea of making all manner of wild sacrifices if Heaven consents to give him back his little girl.

There is no one who can approach him now with such under-standing as Margaret. For he knows that Margaret loved her. But Margaret, though she is Louey's sole sick nurse, and carries out every separate instruction of the doctor with the deftness that her inherent womanliness confers upon her, is yet often called away for other offices. Poor half-conscious Laura has to be rebandaged and soothed, and Mrs Cavendish has discovered that unless she prepares with her own hands all the sickroom potions, the unhappy sufferers will be nourished upon greasy, peppery water instead of broth. So after a hurried consultation with Margaret, it is decided that the incapable Jane should be relegated to the sole task of cleaning up – while Mrs Cavendish, aided by the Piper's Hill maid, becomes the responsible cook of the establishment. It is good to see her Norma-like brows gather wrathfully over Jane's saucepans, that bear such unequivocal signs of never having been 'properly scoured.' She discards them at once, and makes out a list of all that is necessary, to be bought in the township. Even in the midst of her absorbing sympathy and pity the instincts of the true housewife are strong within her, and she cannot refrain from a 'Did you ever?' to Margaret as she holds up the condemned saucepans to her daughter's view, when the latter comes to see whether Mr Lydiat's dinner is ready.

For, strangely enough, Fate will have it that Francis, who only yesterday seemed such miles away actually and metaphorically, is now brought as close to Margaret as though he were her very child. She has heard the entire tale of his prowess – not from himself though – and in the midst of the never-ending demands upon her pity she still finds room for an exultant sense of rejoicing at the thought that her hero has been worthy of her belief in him. The driver of the waggon with which the buggy came into such fatal collision has been up at the parsonage that morning, and has described to Mrs Cavendish all the details of the accident. The little girl, it appeared, had been thrown out on her head, and had fallen somehow right between the horses, that were struggling furiously on the ground in a tangle of traces, reins, and broken pole. Mr Lydiat had gone over with the buggy – but was on his feet in an instant, and he seemed to leap right over the prostrate horses in his attempt to drag the little girl from certain death. He had received a kick that the waggoner considered quite enough to kill him, but it had only fractured his arm, and he had been able to make use of his left to lift the senseless child from the ground, and to carry her away to a place of safety. Meanwhile Miss Lydiat was lying unconscious on the ground on her face. It seemed that her wrists had caught in the reins, and in falling she had not had time to throw out her arms in self-protection. And then help had come, and Mr Lydiat had walked back to the parsonage with the men who carried the ladies upon impromptu litters, and the two doctors had been quickly on the spot, and no one knew that the clergyman was hurt (for he never 'let a word or groan out of him') until the others had been attended to. And the doctors had been heard to say that he was one of the gamest fellows they had ever come across – an expression which in the mouth of a colonial country medico is tantamount to saying that a man has nerves of iron. And Margaret treasured up every single word of this account, and wonders why – when she is so proud of it – she cannot think of it without an inclination to cry.

But crying is a luxury not to be indulged in now. There is no time for it. Margaret must go the rounds of her hospital wards with her tray, and first, kneeling by her uncle's side, she must constrain him with words of loving encouragement to break his fast by Louey's bed.

'Dear uncle, she must see you looking the same as always when she comes to herself. It is for *her* sake you must force yourself to eat a little.'

And then there is George to be gently admonished as he creeps with jaded face out of Laura's room. That it should require so violent a remedy to bring some people to their reason! George may well look jaded, considering the nature of the thoughts that have been occupying him during his vigil. One by one the spectres of his own misdeeds have risen by the side of the white-curtained bed in the corner, and called him to account. And before each in turn he has been dumb. He had not thought himself much worse than most other young fellows until now. On the contrary, he had a notion that he was rather better. He disliked coarse excesses of any kind. He did not drink or cheat, and was never averse to doing a good turn for a friend at his father's expense. But there the list of his merits might close.

And now as for the rest! What an utterly aimless, futile, useless existence he had been content to lead; with an undercurrent of something that severe moralists might consider little short of crime. Laura had not been quite fifteen when his young man's fancy lightly turned to thoughts of love in her direction. She was such a brilliant-hued, petulant, daring, ignorant, impossible being. How it had begun now he could hardly remember. Who can say how such things begin? He had won her whole heart – then, and for ever. They had been both little more than children. But it is a mistake to affirm that mutual respect is a necessary condition of enduring love. Paolo, we may be sure, cherished Francesca throughout the torments of eternity none the less that they had fallen together upon earth. Laura fortified herself with the strongest philosophy she could find among the works of the French *encyclopedistes*, but nothing could prevent her from growing hard and bitter. Sitting in the darkened room with the nightmare of the stained bandages and the yellow hair in front of him, George shuddered at himself. It seemed to him that up till the present moment his only aim in life had been to avoid disagreeable sensations. But what a lifetime of remorse he had been unwittingly preparing for himself. Who could say, if it had not been for this accident, whether he might not have consummated the disloyal act of treachery to which he stood committed?

But now the scale had fallen from his eyes. If he could betray Laura while she was in possession of her health and beauty, and reckless 'don't care' principles, he must return to her now that she would have such need of him. It was curious how Sara's radiant image faded into nothingness compared with the vision of Laura lamed and disfigured. What a poor and worthless thing the mere dazzling of the imagination proved set against the gush of tender, pitying, longing love that welled up at the thought of shielding that poor mutilated face against the world! Ay, at the expense of being turned adrift by his father, and having to offer Laura a selector's hut as the home to which he must conduct his bride. But what would Sara say, and how should he explain his utterly disgraceful conduct? No wonder he looked humbled and heart-sick as he met Margaret in the passage.

'How is she?' says Margaret gently.

'I *can't* stand her groan!' he replies in a hoarse whisper. 'Can't you do anything for her, in God's name?'

A minute later Margaret returns with consoling assurances. 'She is only in a feverish sleep, George. I don't think she is conscious of much suffering. Don't give way. The doctor says the fever is the natural consequence of the shock and the hurts, but there is no internal injury – he is sure of that. She will soon be on foot again.'

'Do you think,' asks George, always in the same intense whisper, 'that she will be very much disfigured?'

'It was a cruel blow,' says Margaret softly. She has seen so much more than poor George, and she knows that a cheek laid open, and front teeth broken, mean a very serious disfigurement; 'but indeed it might have been so awfully much worse than a scarred face.'

George accepts the consolation with a somewhat despondent shake of the head, and Margaret hurries on to her next patient.

Mr Lydiat is installed on a couch in the sitting-room, with his right arm in splints, and his face pale with pain. No one has had time to attend to him this morning, and it is evident that the sense of his own helplessness at such a time of need is a great trial to him. But Margaret's entrance is like a ray of light. No faith-inspired Sister of Mercy could carry a serener influence of helpfulness and hope. All thought of self is completely gone, as happens in every instance where a woman is a born nurse. All her patients become impersonal beings (not mere 'cases,' as from the doctor's point of view), but suffering fellow-creatures without sex or age, whom it is her mission to help and soothe.

Francis has never realised before the wondrous influence of a woman's presence in a sick-room. He lets himself be tended like a child, as she brings cool water to wash his face, and wipes his awkward left hand with a towel. And before he knows it his room is straight, and his pillow feels different, and he has a refreshed sensation that makes the tray, with the snow-shite napkin and the dainty wing of fowl, put on quite another aspect. And all the time she divines just what he is craving to know about his fellow-sufferers, and gives him fullest details concerning each in turn. And in the very tones of her voice there is such hope and consolation, that despondency cannot endure long in her presence. Still the fact remains that Louey is in grave danger.

'And yet,' says Margaret with a trembling voice, 'I cannot help hoping and believing that you did not risk your life for nothing.'

'Oh, that is nothing,' replies the young clergyman, reddening. 'Anybody would have done as much.'

'*Would* they?' she cries vehemently. 'The waggon man who came this morning said he considered you a dead man when he saw what you were going to do. Only I see you don't like my talking of it. But I can't help saying only this once how we all honour, and worship, and love you for it – there. And now I won't speak of it again.'

The tears are streaming from her eyes as she sweeps up the tray, and leaves the room precipitately. Mr Lydiat has never seen her moved to this point before. Perhaps if he had been asked yesterday, he would have said that the elder Miss Cavendish (an excellent girl as far as he knew) was somewhat quiet and impassible. Margaret impassible! So much for the judgment of a man bewitched! But if there be any truth in the saying that 'Love is blind,' the young clergyman was hardly responsible for the want of clear-sightedness that had distinguished him until now. Perhaps it is a defect that the violent shock which has shaken him, in common with all his relatives, out of their *assiette*, may tend to remove. At any rate his face wears a curious half-puzzled expression as he looks after Margaret's retreating figure. And then his eyes soften, and he goes gently out upon his slippered feet to hang about the doors of his sisters' rooms, and learn the latest reports of the doctors upon their condition.

CHAPTER IX

———•———

George Repents Himself

'Calamity is man's true touchstone.' – BEAUMONT and FLETCHER

That men in the heyday of life, with strong, active limbs, should have been placed in the cruel old times in cages too small for them to lie down in, or to sit in, and that they should have adapted themselves to the hideous conditions of this unnatural torture so far as to retain their lives and their senses, and to drag out many terrible years of existence afterwards, is a fact to which many chronicles attest. Small wonder then that in a lesser way human beings are every day learning the lesson of 'getting used to it,' whatever *it* may be – some slowly, some readily, some with a good grace, and some with a bad grace, but all accomplishing the disagreeable task of accommodating themselves to the cramping conditions in the end.

To certain among the new inmates of Barnesbury parsonage the lesson is a hard one. To Mr Piper, sitting in gloomy misery by Louey's bed; to George, torn by pity and shame and remorse, the first day under the unfamiliar roof seemed to cover in its dreary length more than time sufficient to furnish a whole weekful of ordinary days. Not so to Mrs Cavendish and Margaret, who would willingly bid the sun halt until they have completed the thousand and one arrangements that the housing of a set of helpless men and sick people in a habitation originally devised for two people entails upon them. George is made to hear reason at last and to take a bed at the hotel. Mr Lydiat is accommodated with the 'parlour.' For poor obstinate Mr Piper, as comfortable a bed as can be contrived is made up at night-time at the door of Louey's room, while Mrs Cavendish and Margaret agree to take it turn about to snatch a few hours of rest alternately on a sofa stretched on the floor of Laura's room – the same apartment that she had originally handed over to Francis on the score of his not 'minding where they put him.' But before all can be arranged the long January day has closed in, and it is by the light of the kerosene lamp that Margaret does her final rounds with her tray of tea and toast. The doctors pay their third and last visit, and goad Mr Piper to inarticulate despair by their manner of consulting each other over Louey's unconscious form. As their professional shibboleth tells him nothing he dogs their steps until they are on the point of going away, and arrests them to assure them for the hundredth time that they shan't lose by it if they'll only take and do their best for his little girl. In face of his suffering eyes, they pardon this unconscious insult to the profession. They can say nothing certain, they tell him; but they are more hopeful than in the morning, and with that consolation to rest upon, and seeing Margaret posted by Louey's bed to act as night nurse, and knowing that she will carry out every minutest direction of the doctor, the poor unhappy father consents to lie down on the couch prepared for him and falls into a dull heavy sleep.

Is it a time to think of marrying or giving in marriage? If Mr Piper knew what George was writing at this instant from his solitary bedroom at the Junction Hotel, I doubt whether it would move him to any expression of wrath or disappointment. Since yesterday the entire world has changed. Can you imagine the sensations of a man who, towards the close of a long voyage, is shipwrecked the very night before he reaches port? How much thought do you suppose he will bestow upon the plans that filled his brain to overflowing when he sought his berth the evening before? I answer for it that he will not even remember them. He has no time to consider anything but the saving of his life, and if he is thrown on a barren coast, he will be elated if he can scratch together a few shell-fish to serve in lieu of the champagne luncheon that was to celebrate his return. His mental focus has been violently jerked out of place, and the things that seemed to make life worth living the day before are all forgotten. So it is now with Mr Piper. All the hopes and ambitions, all the grievances and grudges that have filled his thoughts for so many years past, seem suddenly to sink into nothingness. That George should leave the home of his betrothed, and hang about Laura's room with a white, woe-begone face, does not even excite a feeling of surprise in him. It seems natural that every one should concern himself for the victims

of the accident; and Mr Piper's vindictiveness has never gone to the
length of wishing Laura any worse fate than that she should 'keep
herself out of the way of *him* and *his*.' Though it is impossible to say
what his feelings might have been, if Laura had been the only sufferer.
I am afraid it needed a mighty thrust into the very kernel of his
affections to arouse even the understanding of grief in him. But it has
been aroused effectually this time, and though Mr Piper does not
know it, he is learning a lesson compared with which the one of
making his mark in life was as nothing in its influence upon his better
nature, which, after all, is the first we have to consider.

But Mr Piper is not the only person who required a violent shock
to open his eyes. George wonders now when he contemplates himself
in the light of his past conduct. He has yet another ignoble action to
accomplish before he can even think about getting back his self-
respect, but that bitter pill swallowed, he may turn over a new leaf,
and learn to hold up his head like a man among men. The offer to
his cousin, the promise to his father – all *that* is connected with a
short and shameful phase of madness, which his own past self-indulgence, and perhaps Laura's arguments too, have helped to produce
in him. But he will confess his shame and his weakness. He will throw
himself upon Sara's mercy, and let him appear in ever so contemptible
a light before her, he may yet begin a clean and honest career, instead
of sinking into a slough, in which he would have lost every vestige of
manhood and honourable feeling.

But the letter is hard to write, all the same. Not that George believes
that Sara's heart will have much to suffer. But it is not an easy matter
to write to a beautiful woman whom you are pledged to marry in a
few weeks time, that you have been a fool and a knave, and that you
beg to retract your offer. And that, as George told himself more than
once, was the plain English of his epistle. And then he is in the sorry
plight of being utterly unable to hint at his desire that whatever was
to have been settled upon Sara at the time of the marriage should
still be so disposed of in her favour. For he has nothing – nothing,
that is to say, but his debts.

As regards these, he does not doubt that his father will pay them
in the long run, and as regards the question of money he does manage
to convey to Sara his impression that the immediate consequence of
the step he is now taking will be that his father will disinherit him,
and that Sara will thereby be very considerably the gainer from a
pecuniary point of view. But the letter, as I have said before, is not

an easy one to write, and midnight is long past ere George seeks his unfamiliar bed, and falls into troubled dreams, in which he sees Laura's back bending over a wash-tub, round which she slowly revolves, as he makes frantic endeavours to catch a glimpse of her face.

It is late when he wakes, and the first object that catches his eye is his letter of the night before. There is no test like that of reading over in the cool morning light the heated compositions of the preceding evening. But even before this ordeal George's letter is allowed to stand. It is weak, it is *mean* – but there is no mistaking the purport of it, and it represents the first step in that hard upward path he is now resolved to climb.

After breakfast he gives his letter to the barman, who undertakes it shall be posted in time for the ten o'clock clearance, and sets out for the parsonage. The chemist's boy is dismounting from his rough horse at the gate as he arrives, and from him he learns that the 'doctor from Melbourne is along o' the ladies.' Although it is still so early, the place seems as orderly and sweet as a real model hospital, and Margaret greets him with her usual sweet tranquillity.

'Laura has had a good night,' she assures him, 'and has been talking a little this morning. Mr Piper insisted that the Melbourne doctor should see her, and Mr Lydiat, too, after he had been to Louey. Oh, George, he thinks, please God, we may save our little darling yet. She is delirious now – we have been shaving her head – and there cannot be a change for a long time. It *is* concussion of the brain, but there is room for hope – if there are no complications. But you must help me with your father. And I see there is a letter for you from papa – you will find it on the hall table.'

As though by tacit consent there had been no mention of Sara on the part of any one since the accident. George winced nevertheless at the mention of the letter, though with a slight feeling of wonder that Mr Cavendish should have written to him. As he seated himself in the verandah, and opened it hurriedly, his wonder increased with the opening line.

'MY DEAR SIR, –'
'What a formal prig he is, to be sure!' thought George. 'Why can't he say my dear George, or my dear nephew? Well! we'll see what "my dear sir" brings us to.'
'I need hardly say with what a sense of relief and gratitude we

received the telegram yesterday, informing us that our dear sufferers were progressing as well as could be expected. Assure your worthy father of my most hearty sympathy in his great trial. I learned yesterday that Dr. B. had been summoned from Melbourne. If I mistake not, he is a cousin of Sir Wilkins B., formerly physician-in-chief to the Duke of V. It is a most satisfactory connection. Sir Wilkins was an eminent scientist and man of the world, and I have had many a pleasant rubber with him in bygone days.

'*Apropos* of the preference with which you have honoured my youngest daughter, I am obliged – very much against my will – to consider my duty as a father, and say a word in season. Your worthy father is so (pardon me the expression) so impetuous, so precipitate that he carries us along with him as by storm. But since he left us I have taken the opportunity of sounding my daughter's heart. I find that she is full of cousinly – nay, to use a stronger term – full of sisterly regard for you. But the consent which was wrung from her was prompted more by her sense of all the amiable attentions she has received from your father and yourself than by any wish to give away her maiden affections irrevocably. Believe me, my dear young friend, we have all been too hasty. I appeal to you now as a man of honour to give her back her unconditional freedom – and since the matter has not even had time to take shape or substance we will refrain from alluding to it. I shall be obliged by your informing your father – when he is in a condition to hear it – of my daughter's decision, and I feel sure I may reckon on his discretion as on yours.'

After the usual ending there was a postscript in Sara's hand:

'MY DEAR COUSIN, – Papa has said for me all I wanted you to understand since the day before yesterday; when you paid me that compliment which I really did not believe you intended me to take quite *au sèrieux*. I trust we shall remain as good friends as ever. – Yours very sincerely,

SARA CAVENDISH.'

George read this little addition in Sara's hand with a curious pricking sensation in his face. His first action was to snatch up his hat, thrust his letter into his pocket, rush to the gate where the horse of the chemist's boy was still standing (no one hurries himself very much in Australian townships), jump into the saddle without so much as a by your leave, and tear at full gallop down one hill and up another to the Junction. The messenger had already gone with the letters. George urged on his horse at the same mad pace to the post-office, where the man from the hotel was lazily inspecting the addresses of the various letters as he dropped them into the box.

'Stop,' shouted George hoarsely, 'there's a mistake – it's not true – I want my letter back.'

He was just in time. The man handed him the remaining bundle of letters he held in his hand, and first in the number was his letter for Mr Cavendish.

'That's all right, and here's a shilling for you,' said George. He put the letter into the same pocket with the one he had just received. The coincidence seemed to him little short of providential, and it was with an almost tumultuous sense of triumph that he rode back to the parsonage. How easy it seemed to write to Mr Cavendish now! With what quiet dignity and resignation he could bow to Sara's decision. In the first feeling of gratitude at his escape, he forgot to wonder as he did afterwards at the promptness with which father and daughter had dismissed him.

He could think of nothing but the miracle of their having forestalled him. He met the disconsolate chemist's boy walking down the hill with a countenance that was nothing if not 'sulky,' and brought it back to its normal expression of happy-go-luckiness by a handsome 'tip.' He felt now that if his poor little sister (whose death would lie at his door, if death should be the end) could only smile on him again in her sweet wistful way, he could brace himself up to lead a happier as well as a better life. As for his father he would act very differently by him henceforth, and so should Laura. George had dismounted when he met the owner of his steed, and whether it was the smart walk up the hill, or the morning sunshine, or the earnestness of his own resolving, it is certain that there was a curious moisture in his eyes as he swung open the little gate and approached the parsonage for the second time that morning.

PART VI

CHAPTER I

———————•———————

Sick Unto Death

'The purest ore is produced from the hottest furnace.' – COLTON

Three weeks have gone by at Barnesbury parsonage since the night of the great disaster. Three strange terrible weeks, during which the ordinary course of time seems to have been all altered and upset. The outer world, indeed, has not changed. The January days have shed their accustomed dry glare upon the landscape. The smoke of the distant bush fires obscures as usual the summits of the low-lying hills round the township. Mr Marsh's grass-plot, which he calls the 'parsonage lawn' in his letters to friends in the old country, is all shrivelled and yellowed by the fiery breath of the fierce north wind; and the few rose-bushes that grow against the rough, verandah-posts are covered with a coating of fine white dust, blown across the road from the heaps of overturned quartz near the deserted claims. The Australian summer runs its ordinary course, but the world within – the world of Mr Piper and Mrs Cavendish, of George and Laura, of Mr Lydiat and Margaret – has changed. For some of them it has become a world of hushed darkness, of closed venetians, of light footsteps and low voices. And for others, a world of active service and never-ending devotion. But for all alike a world in which one common anxiety knits them all together, as they have never been knit before, and forces each to put aside all thought of personal hopes, and longings, and disappointments, in the face of the over-mastering suspense that holds them all in thrall.

For Louey lies sick unto death in the room into which she was brought, unconscious, on the fatal evening of her arrival. She knows no one, not even her father, who sitting night and day in the darkened atmosphere, waits in vain for some sign of recognition from his squirrel. If the little form lying there in the dim light, with the close-shaven head and unnaturally bright eyes, that seem already to shine with the strange imprint of another world, is difficult to identify as Louey's, the form of her watcher is difficult to recognise as that of Mr Piper. All the inflation, the unconscious self-glorification, of the self-made man are gone. Nothing is left but a poor, dependent, heartbroken father, who hangs humbly upon the doctor's words, and questions the faces of every one who passes in and out of the sickroom, like a condemned criminal seeking for a sign of reprieve in the countenances of his jailers.

These three weeks have aged Mr Piper beyond all belief, though to those who know how he spends his time the wonder is that he is not laid upon a sick bed himself. He can never be induced to lie down for more than two or three hours at a stretch. He is too awkward and inexperienced to take the post of nurse, but he will not absent himself from the sick-room for all that. In the still night, when the mosquitoes whine round the little bed, guarded by its transparent curtains, he insists upon keeping solitary watch by its side. He is not an imaginative man, but love and fear evoke visions that make him cry like a child at these times. How Louey would kiss away those tears, and how many of her own she would mingle with them, if she could imagine a catastrophe so unheard of and heartrending as that of Papa crying! But Louey is not even aware of his presence. She is not at Barnesbury at all. She is in the Piper's Hill garden, or up in the tower, or more often in that pitfall for unprotected papas and sisters – the dreadful Collins Street crossing. And about all these places she raves and mutters in the vibrating voice of delirium, until her father is fain to creep out of the room on his heavy slippered feet, and wake his sister or Margaret to reassure him in his helpless terror and anguish.

When he is left alone again (for he resents all entreaties that he should give up his night watch, excepting to George, who would gladly take it entirely), the visions return. The most persistent is the one which portrays the going back of all the party to Melbourne. *All* the party? Alas! the most prominent object is a little coffin, that somehow has come to look like Louey herself by dint of picturing it so often. Mr Piper never has this vision without an accompanying sensation of a great tightening pain in the throat, and the unheeded impression of a warm salt flavour between his lips. He hungers so for the feel of the slender little arms round his neck; for just one more look of wistful love from the sweet eyes.

No wonder he looks thin and haggard. There is not an expression of pain or disappointment he has ever called forth in the dear little face that he does not recall now with a passionate longing to efface all trace of it. How often he has seen her lips quiver when he called Laura names! Why, he would call Laura one of God's angels, and treat her as such, if he could bring one smile of recognition into his darling's eyes. Ay – no wonder he looks haggard, torn by emotions like these. And there is no one to whom he can sob them forth – not even his sister, whose heart nevertheless bleeds for her brother Tom. But I believe that a great many of his fears are better understood and shared by Mrs Cavendish and Margaret than either of them would dare to admit. Have not dreary visions of the desolateness of the great Piper's Hill mansion, bereft of the light of the sweet child face and shining auburn curls, thrust themselves upon *their* minds too? And indeed upon the minds of all the rest of Louey's belongings at Barnesbury; who come softly at intervals to gaze upon the fever-tossed form, and to listen with sick hearts to the incoherent mutterings and rapid breathing that sounds in their ears like the panting of a hunted animal.

Mrs Cavendish confides to her daughter that she is at her 'wit's ends' in respect of Uncle Piper's condition. 'If I could only get him to take a bit!' is the invariable conclusion of her confidences. In the midst of all the distracting anxieties that encompass her – doctors coming and going – a patient in every room in the house – Sara writing from Piper's Hill that she has reconsidered her cousin's proposal, which her mother translates into signifying, 'in plain English, that she's thrown him over' – Mr Cavendish demanding in two successive letters an explanation of the singular circumstance that his weekly 'loan' has not been forthcoming as usual – in the midst, I say, of all this accumulation of worry and distress of heart, Mrs Cavendish always has a bit, and a tempting bit too, ready for every emergency.

It is quite a sight to see her in the little parsonage kitchen, among the renovated pots and pans. Everything that money can purchase is at her command, but the life-long habit of economy still holds good in this land of plenty. To the Australian Jane (now deposed to the post of scullery-maid), who has been wont, upon Australian principles, to cook a joint and throw half of it away next day, the saving of bones and scraps for broths and *rechauffés* is a matter for mingled wonder and contempt. It is an undeniable fact that, with a butcher's bill not perceptibly increased, there is always a stock of the most appetising of broths and jellies ready at an instant's notice. The milk, too, has lost its tendency to 'go sour' so unaccountably, and the fowls and fruit puddings that are sent into the parlour for the *tête-à-tête* dinner of George and Francis are such as have never been known to issue from the Reverend Mr Marsh's kitchen before.

Perhaps in all that sad household Mrs Cavendish, divided between the cares of straining beef-tea and examining into the condition of Jane's saucepans, is really one of the least to be pitied. Heaven knows there is room enough in her large heart for sorrow and apprehension in plenty, but when grief is in us and about us, it is a merciful thing to have work at hand every day and all day into which we must needs throw ourselves. All Mr Piper's gold could not have bought the real service which Mrs Cavendish renders during this crisis. Margaret cannot refrain from a smile of tender sympathy every time she comes into the kitchen for the broth for her various 'wards.' There is something in her mother's face that touches one of those inner chords which seem to vibrate to tears and laughter in the same instant. She has to listen to many a confidential 'aside,' in which Mrs Cavendish imparts her 'sure and certain conviction' that Jane has 'made away' with a whole half-pint of chicken broth; or, worse still, substituted a *bought* egg for the fresh-laid one she brought in with her 'own hands' from the fowl-house before breakfast. Another time she finds her mother surveying almost regretfully a pair of tender spring chickens 'boiled to a hair,' and destined for the 'parlour.' 'I was thinking,' says Mrs Cavendish, as she pours a creamy-looking sauce over the dish, 'I was thinking, my dear, how I'd like to set 'em before your pa.'

Margaret, however, has work that leaves scant time for interesting herself in the chronicles of the kitchen. The entire charge of the invalids (for poor Mr Piper is rather a hindrance than a help) seems to have fallen upon her shoulders. From the very outset she and her mother have declared that they would not have any extra assistance. 'There is hardly room to turn as it is,' she observes; so with a good laundress and Jane for the rough work, these two women toil through the long burning January days, in the face of all the untried miseries of an up-country midsummer in Australia. The armies of flies and mosquitoes, the hordes of invading ants, the blasts of sultry dust-laden wind, the hideous buzz-flies that scatter corruption wherever they can 'settle' for an instant, the low roofs and small rooms, render their task one of devotion indeed.

To poor Mrs Cavendish to struggle against discomfort of all kinds comes so naturally that she accepts the new order of things as though it were her rightful lot. If a sudden vision of the cool palace of Piper's Hill comes before her, when she retreats for breath from the scorching colonial-oven into the sultry atmosphere of Mr Marsh's yard, it is only to rejoice that 'your pa' and Sara are safe within that celestial haven. As for Margaret, has she not the responsibility of helping and guarding nearly all she loves on earth? It is to her the doctors give their directions. It is to her that they look to measure the drops for their 'case of fever,' to plaister Laura's 'flesh-wounds,' and to bandage Mr Lydiat's broken arm. They are loud in their praises of her as they leave the parsonage every morning and evening. The curious questioners, who waylay them for the latest details and ply them with 'drinks' after the manner of Australian township folk, are always hearing of her merits. 'She is a regular brick,' say they, after which the company proceeds to speculate, with an air of mysterious impressiveness, upon the extent of 'old Piper's tin.' The great Melbourne authority has been heard to say, going down in the train, that 'that Miss Cavendish is quite an exceptional woman. She's got a head.' But it is Margaret's heart that is the motive power, if the doctor only knew it.

I think, however, that some one else is beginning very slowly to find it out, and to wonder, perhaps, why he should have been such a long time in making the discovery. Francis's nature is not one to remain unmoved in the presence of any kind of beauty, and what is more beautiful than genuine unselfishness? He possesses a great fund of enthusiasm, and though he has lavished it upon the outcasts of London for so many years, and upon Sara's magic loveliness for so many months, it is not by any means expended, and is quite ready to revive under the influence of such qualities as those of which Margaret gives unconscious proof now. It is true that enthusiasm is not love, but it is at least as akin to it as pity, and who knows but that it may lead *up* to love in the end, whereas pity can but lead *down* to it?

However, I declare that during these terrible weeks, there is no time for the indulgence of any kind of dwelling upon the 'might have been' for either Mr Lydiat or Margaret. There is too strong a call upon their sympathies in other directions. Margaret has her maimed and her lamed to look after, and Francis has to help her in his own way. Despite his broken arm, there is a power in his strong, calm presence, whether he brings it into the room where Mr Piper sits by his little girl's bedside in moody misery, or into the darkened corner where poor Laura lies with her disfigured face, or into the hot veranda where George is mostly to be found in a very low condition, or into the stifling little kitchen where Mrs Cavendish's portly figure and Juno-like face may be perpetually encountered, there is a promise of hope in his voice that always brings a certain courage and consolation. And the good work that he and Margaret are doing together unconsciously brings them closer to each other than all the months they spent on the *Henrietta Maria*, when the Rev. Mr Lydiat's eyes were so dazzled by the light of one beautiful countenance that he had no sight left for the reading of another.

Perhaps, too, the deft way in which Margaret bandages his arm – for priests are human after all – contributes a little to swell his newborn admiration of her. She performs this office in a very matter-of-fact way, with a great amount of demureness – a little more demureness perhaps than the occasion warrants, but then she is intensely conscious that it is very different from bandaging anybody else's arm – Uncle Piper's or her cousin George's, for instance. And there is a kind of subtle sense that Francis likes to be tended by her, which increases the demureness a hundredfold. The operation does not always finish either with the bandaging of the arm. The Rev Mr Lydiat is very grateful when she ties his clerical stock for him and fastens the solitary stud in the sleeve of his undamaged arm.

Though only a few words are exchanged upon these occasions, terminated by a simple 'Thank you,' Margaret's fingers thrill to the very tips, and she is glad to escape to Laura's couch, where she lavishes such an amount of repressed tenderness and loving care upon Francis's sister that the girl is moved one day to make a kind of response. For the most part Laura turns her face to the wall – like the king in Scripture – and remains plunged in a kind of dreary torpor, thinking Heaven knows what dreary thoughts – when she thinks at all. For here is the end of all the thoughtless, selfish, reckless, butterfly life! The man to whom she had given her whole being, to abandon her – she herself to become a poor deserted, disfigured old maid – and the only creature who loved her on earth and whom she herself loved after George – her little sister – to die a miserable death through her agency!

And George, who, when he is not going upon errands to the

chemist's, or writing Francis's letters for him, or mounting guard in Louey's room, sits, as I have said, in dreary silence, with his hat over his head, in the verandah – George gives way for the most part to reflections that are little less cheerful than Laura's. He has escaped from the committal of one great wrong, and he has escaped with honour. But what prospect does the future hold out? How is he to uphold and support poor Laura, to whom his heart goes out with a passionate tenderness, all the stronger for his short desertion of her, and his knowledge of her suffering and her disfigurement? How is he to console his father if that dear little soul (who seems now to have held them all together) should disappear from among them? And what kind of consolation will it be to offer Laura to him as his new daughter? For George is determined, once for all, that no matter what may be the consequences, his first duty is to make Laura his wife.

All these reflections, and a hundred others, in which shame and remorse play a considerable part, pursue him unceasingly. Perhaps it never occurs to him, any more than it does to Laura, to think how much they both needed an awakening of this kind. Neither perhaps are Mr Piper and the Rev. Mr Lydiat aware that each is learning a lesson it behoved him to learn. But, as Longfellow says, 'though the mills of God grind slowly, yet they grind exceedingly small.' The inmates of Barnesbury parsonage present a mournful picture enough, judged by their bodily and mental sufferings, but I am not sure whether an examination below the surface a few weeks ago, when the Piper's Hill party seemed at the zenith of their prosperity, would not have disclosed a sadder one still. Whatever furnace of affliction they are passing through now, one may be sure at least that it is a purifying one.

CHAPTER II

───────────●───────────

The Rev. Mr Lydiat Is Called To The Rescue

'More things are wrought by prayer than this world dreams of.'
                                                        – TENNYSON

One morning, a cool cloudy morning, such as the blessed sea-breeze will sometimes send far up country even through the stifling atmosphere of a Victorian midsummer, an ominous change took place in Louey's condition. It was the twenty-first day since the fever had declared itself, and all that time it had held her in its fierce clutch, until the poor little frame was worn and wasted to a shadow. Now the strength to battle any longer seemed to have gone. The fever had taken its departure, but what of vitality was left appeared to have gone with it. The spark of life that yet remained flickered so feebly, it seemed every instant on the point of extinction.

This morning the great Melbourne doctor did not return to town according to his wont. On the contrary, he proposed of his own accord to remain by the bedside of his patient; a concession which, as he had never been known to make anything approaching it before (excepting in the case of a foreign duke who had fallen a victim to quinsy on a back-block station), created a vast amount of agitation among the inmates of the parsonage. Mr Piper was the most difficult to calm. He had a presentiment that the end was approaching, and all the climax of his grief showed itself in a kind of jealous suspicion of all who came nigh to his little girl. It needed all the loving tact of Mrs Cavendish and Margaret to persuade him that the doctor was to be trusted. If they could only have assured him that he would yet bring back Louey from the brink of the grave! But they dared not hold out more than the slenderest thread of hope, her utter prostration was too plainly visible, even to their inexperienced eyes, and they could see that the doctor himself was of opinion that he was leading a forlorn hope. She had sunk into a kind of lethargy, so like death that it might easily have been mistaken for it. Still it was not actually death as yet, only 'his brother sleep,' and a brother that mightily resembled him.

The first condition of the great authority's taking up his post in his patient's room was that every one else should be turned out of it. Even the desperate father was obliged to submit. What with grief and fatigue, poor Mr Piper would sometimes groan as he breathed, quite unconsciously to himself. Now utter silence – a silence like that of the grave, whither the patient seemed tending – was a paramount necessity. Therefore Mr Piper had to go. Then the door was closed, and the window opened at the top. A guard was set to prevent any cart from approaching the house. All noises indoors were forbidden, and nothing but the drowsy hum of the bees and bluebottles in the garden, and the pecking and perking of the tiny shell parrots strutting about the gravel paths, penetrated faintly into the sick chamber. If expectant Death, hovering about the couch of the sinking child, had already carried her away to his shadowy kingdom, the silence could hardly have been more complete.

How the doctor passed his time in Louey's room belongs to the secrets of the profession. He had provided himself with manuscripts for his private perusal, so it may be surmised that he did not spend the entire day in watching the countenance of his patient. He had promised that, if death should become imminent, he would apprise the child's father – but that he did not as yet entirely despair might be gathered from the fact that he had drawn in her behalf upon Mr Piper's most valued stock of old brandy – that glowed like pale amber when it was poured out. It was of the kind which, according to the popular phrase, might well 'restore the dead,' and in this supreme hour its virtues were to be called into requisition to attempt the miracle of bringing back a life well nigh extinct.

What the rest of the household endured during these hours of suspense passes description. Even Margaret found the tension almost beyond the power of her nerves to endure. Mrs Cavendish, with careful forethought, had made all her domestic preparations early in the morning, and although an occasional flash of apprehension on the score of the potatoes (the only eatables she allowed the incompetent Jane to cook on her own responsibility) *would* intrude itself now and then, she had all her time and thoughts free for her 'brother Tom.'

There was, as I have said, a southerly breeze, and fortunately the oven-like verandah was cool enough to sit in. Margaret had placed all the available chairs in the shadiest corner, and she and her mother strove their utmost to keep the unhappy father in this quiet spot, away from the unnerving spectacle of the closed bed-room door. But after three long, dragging hours, during which they had led him on by gentle questioning to tell them, in his broken voice, and perhaps for the hundredth time, all about the early 'roughing it' in the colonies, and how he had first made up his mind to wed Louey's mother, and what a 'downright good wife she had been to him,' and what a 'born lady,' and how Louey 'took after her,' Margaret began to perceive that he was growing restless. The old dogged determination 'not to be crossed,' that seemed to have faded out of his expression of late, was creeping into his eyes. He was grumbling, too – a sign that always augured mischief. He 'misdoubted' that doctor. What business had he, if you came to that, to 'take and turn him out?' He supposed he had as good a right to look after his own child as *him*. Margaret trembled for the consequences of her uncle's unreasoning grief. In another minute there would be no withholding him. She exchanged a half-despairing glance with her mother, and went for counsel to the Rev. Mr Lydiat.

Francis was not long in finding a suggestion, though he made it hesitatingly and half-apologetically. 'I can't bear to give an impression of improving the occasion,' he said; 'it might do more harm than good. But here we are all suffering, and sorrowing, and trembling, and hoping together. Don't you think you could persuade your uncle to come in here with the rest of them, and let me read a little and pray a little? If it could only help to give him heart for what he may still have to bear! I am sure George and my sister would come. Poor Laura! I was with her this morning – I am sure she would come. And then – and then – one can't help feeling there have been fancied grievances and bitternesses that might melt away in the shadow of this common trouble. Don't think it is professional zeal, Margaret,' he added. 'God knows whether the mystery of the unknown presses upon me too at times. But I want so much to help you, and I can't think of any other plan.'

'It is a very good plan, I think,' said Margaret, simply, 'if the others will agree to it. I will try to make them come.'

As she went upon her mission a hundred unbidden thoughts, suggested by Francis's words, rushed into her mind. Was it possible that even for *him* the hope of answer was still 'behind the veil' – that veil which seemed to turn into a wall of adamant when she essayed to peer ever such a little distance through its dark folds? The idea seemed somehow to bring him nearer to her than before. Had he noticed that he had called her 'Margaret' for the first time? Had he done it on purpose? 'Margaret, Margaret?' It had never struck her as being such a pretty, soft-sounding name before. ... Then came a sudden rush of self-reproach for allowing the intrusion of such thoughts at a moment when death was stalking through the house – and a vividly returning vision of the poor little wan face, with its dying eyes. Pity and sympathy flooded Margaret's heart afresh, and shut out the image that so often took possession of it. She went straight in search of her uncle, and succeeded, to her surprise, in obtaining his consentment to Francis's proposal.

A great heart-trouble or apprehension is more like physical pain than people suppose. It has its long, dreary, gnawing phases, its moments of almost intolerable torture, and its curious periods of numbness, when the mind seems stolid and almost indifferent, but is perfectly aware that in a very short time the anguish will begin again, all the sharper and keener for the unnatural calm that precedes it. Mr Piper was in this mood of stolidity when Margaret brought him Mr Lydiat's message. He had talked (and cried between whiles) as he went over the past until he had worn himself out. As they would not let him go to his little girl he had no objection to 'giving the parson a hearing.'

Still it was with many misgivings and an almost deprecating air that Margaret led him into the little parlour, where the rest of the household was already assembling itself, in compliance with Mr Lydiat's request.

There is no more subtle quality than the one which belongs of right to the born orator, and that for want of a better name we call by that of magnetic sympathy. Francis possessed this gift to a remarkable degree. If he had been 'clairvoyant' he could not have seen more clearly into the minds of his hearers. He was perfectly aware that Mr Piper's attitude was one of sullen, half-ashamed acquiescence and resentment, and that Laura cherished a secret aversion to what she would have called the 'whole performance.' As for George, his face wore such an expression of well-bred imperturbability that there was no making anything of it at all. It was only when Laura (who left her room for the first time this morning) made her appearance in a black stuff gown, with a bandage across her eye and cheek, and nothing visible but a knot of fair hair and two very tightly-closed pale lips, that it changed. He jumped up immediately and led her unresistingly to the shabby little sofa against the wall, where he seated himself by her side, and glared round at the assembled company with a kind of moody defiance, as though he would have challenged the right of any one present to take her from him.

Mrs Cavendish sat next to her brother with a feeling of being at church, and the same simple faith in the propriety of the proceeding that she took with her to morning service on Sundays. There was only Margaret whose whole heart was going along with the young clergyman in his effort; and even she was fearful lest he should but succeed in awakening the dissonance that the presence of so many discordant elements seemed to render inevitable. But she need not have been afraid. She had not measured as yet all the power of real eloquence. The subtle sympathy that enabled Mr Lydiat to divine the mingled sensations of each individual mind taught him at the same time to strike in each the responsive note that helped to create one great harmonious chord. Eloquence is only the calling into action of latent emotions that we all possess to a greater or less degree. Sometimes it seems to operate miracles more wonderful than that of Moses's rod, which caused the water to rush forth from the dry rock. But that is because we so rarely meet with it in its true form; many indeed go through life without once encountering it.

What makes it appear like inspiration is that it is not always within the grasp of the one who possesses it. It will not come infallibly at his bidding, and unless he can put away all thought of self, it will sometimes refuse to come at all. Francis had known this misery in his young and nervous days of public preaching, but his long years of earnest labour among the reckless and the wretched had taught him to speak straight to the heart, and from the heart. He felt now, and understood to its fullest extent, just the kind of suffering he had to deal with. And he must show that he understood it before anything he could say in the way of support or consolation could be of the least avail.

He began, therefore, by giving, very simply, his impressions of

Louey's character, and of what she would wish all her loved ones to do now. It was so true, and seemed to bring them all so near to her, that Mrs Cavendish ventured to place her hand in her 'brother Tom's,' and hold it all the time Mr Lydiat was speaking, while she wiped her eyes with the other. How was it possible that Francis should have divined the little girl's nature so well, thought Margaret. True, they were both born of the same mother, and it sometimes happened that a certain inflexion of the voice, a something appealing and pathetic peculiar to Louey's way of speaking, might be detected in her brother's tones. But it was in the spirit of his words that Francis most proved his kinship with her. It was almost startling. It was as though poor little Louey herself, with all her life's longing for the establishment of peace and mutual goodwill among those to whom she clung with the whole force of her child's heart, were speaking through his lips. And yet he did not make a single allusion that could be interpreted into a reproach addressed to any individual member among his listeners. Only, as he spoke, the vision of a nervous child face, and two pitiful, pleading eyes, seemed to rise before each. They had been cruelly regardless of that sensitive nature. They had said and looked bitter things at each other when she was by. They had tried to wound each other all they could without ever taking into consideration that they were stabbing right through her tender little heart. And now it was too late to make amends. They could never make amends.

And yet – thanks always to that marvellous gift of eloquence of which I have spoken, Mr Lydiat knew how to illumine even such despairing reflections as these. There was no hint of sectarianism in his words. They might have poured balm into the sorrowing hearts of Pagan mourners in any period of the world's history, just as well as into that of poor Mr Piper, who paid fifteen guineas a year for his sitting at St Peter's and slumbered therein every successive Sunday with the most exemplary regularity. But there was wondrous understanding in them. It seemed as though his perfect knowledge of his little sister gave Francis a right to speak which no one else possessed. When he expressed his firm belief that the same power which had created that gentle spirit could also prolong it and take care of it, and cause it to animate some higher form than any we can conceive in this earthly stage of being, his words carried quite a different weight from the one we give to ordinary pulpit assurances. Even George and Laura listened with a vague sense of having been too positive in their materialistic conclusions, and could have said, like Felix – 'Almost thou persuadest me to be a Christian.' 'After all,' thought Laura, 'when we make our physical conformation responsible for *everything* we feel and do – as George and I have always done – there is no point in wanting to prolong our individualities. In fact, it would only mean wanting to live on with our earthly bodies indefinitely, which is out of the question. But I can just fancy how people like my brother and poor little Hester (I mustn't call her that, any more, by the by) – I can just fancy how people like those – who are differently constituted from us, perhaps – must long for, and believe in, a prolongation of their beings. They overcome the tendencies, whatever they are, to self-indulgence. I suppose it costs them an effort, too. At any rate they *feel* it's an effort, so I suppose it's the same as though it really *were* one. And if they get their bodies and thoughts under spiritual control, it's quite natural and reasonable that they should expect to glide out of them into some fresh form, that they can go on moulding, and overcoming in the same way – until – until *what*? Yes, there one gets lost again, but meanwhile what George and I feel need not be a reason for scouting what better people than we feel. Perhaps they really *may* go on, while we –'

But at this point the music of her brother's voice aroused Laura's attention once more. He was still speaking of the hereafter, and as he went on, the present seemed somehow to dwindle away into the proportions of an uneasy nightmare, and the great, mysterious future, flooded with light and peace, became half unveiled. For an instant it seemed as though it would be almost a wrong to the child's pure spirit to wish to force it back into the atmosphere of the small earthly circle, so full of bickerings and discontent, that had surrounded it. And now there was no backwardness in kneeling down in obedience to Francis's request, and letting him say 'Thy will be done.' There was not even room for the intrusion of those incongruous and grotesque fancies, or for the disagreeable sensation of being out of sympathy and in a false position, which such an unusual proceeding as that of a prayer-meeting in an ordinary room on a week-day must otherwise have aroused.

The prayer being over, Laura suddenly left her place on the sofa next to George, and crossed over to where Mr Piper was standing near the window. It was the first time he had met her since the accident. Two of her teeth were knocked out, there was the mark of a half-healed scar that seamed her cheek, the upper part of her face was covered by a white bandage, but from what still remained visible, it might be seen that all her bright colour was gone. Her gay plumage was gone also. Even in the midst of the weight of sorrow that oppressed him, Mr Piper was conscious of a vague feeling of curiosity and wonderment as he regarded her. The 'painted hussy' of a few weeks ago was gone for ever.

'I want to say, Mr Piper,' said Laura with a mighty effort, and her lips trembling very much, 'that I have to ask your forgiveness for the way I've always behaved to you, and now, and now,' with a suppressed sob, 'you must wish me dead! I am sure – I should – in your place.'

She broke down at this point, and Mr Piper did not answer for an instant. Then he held out his hand, and his own voice was not much firmer than Laura's as he replied, 'Don't you take on about *that*, my girl. It's a bad job for all of us, but it might have happened to any one else the same as you. I'm sorry to see you in such a condition, and we'll let bygones be bygones. There, take and shake hands upon it. You was always fond of the little one.'

'I wish I were in her place,' sobbed Laura passionately, as she took Mr Piper's hand.

'So do I,' said George, suddenly springing up and appearing by Laura's side. 'Her life's worth more than mine to my father.' Then turning to Mr Piper, the young man continued in a low, hurried, but distinctly audible tone, 'I've been awfully to blame, too, sir, only I didn't like to say it. I see it all now, and I ask your pardon, and I ask yours too, aunt,' he added, addressing himself to Mrs Cavendish. 'I had no right to propose to my cousin, and she's treated me just as I deserve. I've been engaged to Laura here ever since we were children, but it's not the moment to speak of that now –'

'I think Mr Lydiat has something more to say,' interrupted Margaret, in an agony of fear as to the result of this avowal on her uncle, and Francis, quick to take the hint, asked leave to read the story of the ruler's daughter in conclusion.

The ruffled faces composed themselves once more, and Francis had just reached the passage, 'Give place, for the maid is not dead, but sleepeth,' when there was a low tap at the door, and the Melbourne physician made his appearance. Mr Piper's ruddy face turned a curious ash colour, and he almost unconsciously wrung his sister's hand. All were more or less prepared to see in the doctor the messenger of doom, and even Mr Lydiat felt that he needed to brace himself up to receive the dreaded tidings. But there was something in the physician's face that turned the agony of expectancy which held all the hearts into a tumultuous hope. Margaret did not even give him time to speak before she full upon her uncle's neck with a half-hysterical cry of 'Oh, thank God! thank God!'

'No, she is not dead,' said the doctor, paraphrasing the words he had heard on entering. 'The crisis is over, and unless there is any new complication, which I must say I do not look for, I think I may affirm that she is saved. She has asked for her father, and now, my dear sir,' and the doctor turned to Mr Piper with great solemnity, 'if I allow you to come in for *one* instant to kiss your little girl, remember, I entreat you, that it is as much as her life is worth to agitate her in the very smallest degree. You must walk in softly, kiss her quite calmly and naturally, as though you had just been out for an airing, and then come away.'

The manner in which poor Mr Piper attempted to carry out these instructions would have been ludicrous if it had not been so touching at the same time. After blowing his nose elaborately – for which operation he had previously closed the parlour door – he put away his handkerchief, but was forced to bring it out again before he had got half-way down the passage. His attempts to walk gently produced the effect of a ponderous shuffle, which set the common candelabras, with the prismatic pendants that adorned Mr Marsh's mantelpieces, all ringing and jingling. It was with a mighty effort that he restrained himself as he got up to the little bed, whence two white, transparent arms of terrifying thinness emerged from the loose, broidered sleeves of a nightdress, and essayed to lift themselves up towards him.

Mr Piper was down upon his knees – he was in practice that morning – with a rapidity remarkable in an elderly gentleman of undoubted obesity. He dared not trust himself to say more than 'There, there now!' in a very husky whisper, but the child understood him as well as though he had poured forth in a torrent the whole long history of his love and his suffering. The old fond look came back into her eyes, and as he perceived her lips moving, and placed his ear close to them, he could just distinguish the words, 'I've come back to you, dear papa – I *would* come back.'

'Bless you, darling,' said Mr Piper, in a whisper of appalling intensity; and at this point the doctor came up gently and drew him away.

CHAPTER III

---•---

A Readjustment

'Love sought is good, but given unsought is better.' – SHAKESPEARE

It was about a fortnight after this that Mr Piper was seated, one Sunday forenoon, next to the bed of the now convalescent Louey. To compare his broad florid face with that of one of Lucca della Robbia's *faïence* songsters may seem a trifle far-fetched, but it is certain that it wore the same expression of helpless, almost inane beatitude as that of certain among those children of light; the sole reason being that he had been engaged in watching, open-mouthed, the slow but sure consumption of a bowl of chicken-broth by the invalid. I think that the last four spoonfuls cost Louey something of a struggle, if the truth were known, but in the face of that expression in her father's eyes, and the tender triumph depicted in her Aunt Cavendish's countenance, as she stood watching the performance, what could a grateful little girl do but 'make an effort' *à la* Mrs Chicks?

The last drop having been swallowed, Mrs Cavendish bore the basin away with indescribable elation, tremulously observing that there was 'chicken broth *and* chicken broth,' and she *did* wish (almost plaintively) she could have shown her brother Tom what she had served to their precious little lamb before heating it – a firm jelly as clear as crystal, and the loveliest colour you ever saw.

Mr Piper patted his good sister's back with moist eyes, and re-seated himself by the bed. He had become quite fond of the little room, and was perfectly satisfied to doze away in it by the hour together, while Louey slept the restoring sleep of childhood. The father required to recoup himself almost as much as the child, for the wear and tear of those three weeks of overwhelming anxiety and watching had told upon his frame, and his sister insisted upon it that he needed rest and 'feeding-up.' He took kindly enough to both prescriptions, and Mrs Cavendish outdid herself in the concocting of dainties for the tempting of the returning appetite of her charge.

It was George's pleasure to go down to Melbourne to forage at her bidding for impossible qualities of rice and rusks. The news of a threatened European war did not affect her half so much as any delay in the arrival of the supply of ice in which she was to 'set' her creams and her jellies; and despite her ingrained spirit of economy she would think nothing of telegraphing to the fishmonger twice a day to remind him that the Murray perch was to be *stopped* on its passage down to the Melbourne market in order that she might have the choice of the freshest.

Surrounded by this atmosphere of coddling, Mr Piper and his little girl grew daily more and more like their former selves, and on this particular Sunday morning, all the household excepting Aunt Cavendish being at church, they waxed quite communicative. It was now well on in February. The French windows were wide open, and the intense sunshine flooded the little parsonage garden.

The thinly-clad gum tree, the dark, evergreen shrubs, the stiffly-arranged gladioli seemed one and all to rain down light upon the white gravel paths. A belated magpie that had evidently been 'taking it out' this Sabbath morning, was pouring forth its full, sweet cry from a neighbouring lightwood tree. Louey could see across the gorse hedge to the yellowing hills and lines of post-and-rail fencing that stretched away towards the misty horizon. Misty with heat, alas, for overhead the sky blazed like a huge sapphire dome, and there was not a fleck of white to be seen. But here in the invalid's room everything that love and money could contrive to temper the atmosphere had been effected. George had constructed a punkah; Laura had devised web-like curtains for the keeping out of the flies; Margaret had actually assisted Jane to place a huge sailcloth on the shingle roof, upon which the hose being constantly turned, the upper stratum of air was kept deliciously cool.

It was evident that Louey was to be coaxed back into health. But it was not only the physical atmosphere about her that contributed to bring the returning light into her eyes. Before she was strong enough to speak, an instinctive feeling that there was peace among her surroundings had crept upon her tired soul. She had not even formulated the thought to herself. She was too weary and confused to think. But her sensitive organisation felt all the influence of the heavenly calm. Everybody seemed to love her and each other. And she lay in drowsy, contented bliss for several days after the great crisis, apparently indifferent to all that went on around her, but in reality mending fast in body and mind.

Hitherto she had said very little, but on this especial Sunday morning the quality that had made her companionable to her father from the time she could frame her first baby sentences began to manifest itself again.

'I *would* come back to you, papa,' she said, perceiving that Mr Piper was watching her intently.

'Come back from where, my pet?' said her father, in a voice from which he strove to eliminate the slight admixture of awe which Louey's words had infused into his satisfaction.

'Oh, from *so* far,' said the child. Her voice still had the quaver of weakness, but its clear pathetic *timbre* was the same as ever. 'I don't know exactly, but I think it was very far. It was one day, papa. It had been very dark for a long, long time, and when I woke I thought I was in bed, only I wasn't in bed, and it wasn't dark. It was so *lovely!* I was going along somewhere – I didn't know where – but I wasn't frightened. I didn't care to look about me. I felt so safe. By-and-by I opened my eyes just a little, and then I saw mamma's face – just the same as in your locket. And what do you think, papa? She was taking me along, and there was a lovely soft wing all covering me. It was like floating, and I wasn't a bit frightened. It was lovely. And there was all soft air everywhere. I don't know where we were going. I know it was to some lovely place, and I wanted to get to it. Mamma cuddled me so close, just like you. I wanted to go with her. Then all of a sudden I remembered you. I said, "Oh! papa wants me *so* much!" Then mamma said, "We will bring him some day, too." But I said, "Oh! he wants me *now*;" and you did, didn't you papa? Mamma smiled, but I think she was a little sorry to turn back. Then the next thing I remember it was all dark again and by-and-by I woke up in this room. I didn't know it a bit, only you came and knelt by me, papa, and I told you how I had come back to you, and you kissed me, don't you remember?'

Louey stopped, exhausted. Mr Piper had listened to the entire narrative with profound and respectful attention. It was evident that to the little girl it was quite a real experience, and her father would not dispute it. Who could say what force of will, inspired by her love for him, had helped to bring her back from the border of the mysterious land into which she had so nearly passed? So his only answer was to take the frail little hand into his own and to kiss it in recognition of her having come back to him of her own accord.

After a long pause Louey spoke again, and this time her voice had a very pleading tone.

'You won't take George away from Laura, will you, papa?'

'I won't take nobody from anybody, my little darling pet,' said her father with incoherent promptitude. 'You shall settle it all your own way, and you shall take and pair 'em all as you please, only make haste and get well. I can't get along without my squirrel to advise me.'

This point being settled, Louey closed her eyes in utter peace, and I will not answer for it that her father did not follow her example.

Meanwhile two couples, at a very safe out-of-hearing distance the one from the other, were toiling up the sandy township street on their return home from church. The little building had been unusually crowded – in fact, there had never been so many people in it since its first consecration by the bishop – for the already renowned Mr Lydiat was to mount into the pulpit with his arm in a sling, and to preach his first sermon since the accident. Local politics and mining interests being rather quiet at that time, the 'great buggy accident' had excited an immense amount of public interest and sympathy. The scene of the disaster had been visited and revisited. The 'locals' had published daily bulletins concerning the progress of the victims. Strangers of all conditions and classes waylaid George on his way to and from the station, and begged to know how his people were getting on. Even the fact that no one was to die, after all – the whole buggyful having been killed on the spot in the popular imagination under the first excitement of the disaster – did not abate the public interest.

The foremost couple was very unlike the pair of matinal lovers that Mr Piper had descried from the top of his tower a few months ago. Laura seemed to have adopted the same resolution as that of the modest Jenny Wren, who promised 'to wear her brown gown and never dress too fine.' But this was not the only change. Behind the gauze veil that covered her face, the mark of a deep cut, extending in a white furrow right through her eyebrow and down her cheek, was plainly visible. The teeth were replaced – (she still cried when she took out her false ones at night) – but nothing could replace the delicate bloom that had made Sara imagine Laura must be painted when she first encountered her. *That* was gone for ever.

And yet Laura was infinitely more attractive than she had been in her hard and brilliant epoch. It was wonderful to see how her eyes had gained in expression now that their bright china blue was softened by the feelings that had been working in her so strongly of late. Certain tight lines around her lips seemed to have disappeared as well. To be sure, she was irretrievably spoiled in her own estimation, but then a woman is not always the best judge in these matters. Sara might have agreed with her, perhaps, but her brother and Mr Piper, and even George, who, like Geraint, had always been 'satisfied' with his love just as she was, would not have been at all of Sara's way of thinking.

They had been walking for some time in silence, swiftly notwithstanding the heat, for the curious glances cast in their direction by the township folk seemed worse to bear than the hot sun, when they found themselves passing before the doors of the Junction Hotel. Laura turned her head away. The yard was full of carts and bush buggies, into which the wives and daughters of selectors and cockatoo farmers were climbing. The men were harnessing the horses and talking about the qualities of their 'mokes,' though more than one among them was emerging from the back entrance to the hotel after exchanging a friendly 'drink' with a neighbour. But all stopped as George and Laura passed by, and pointed out the pair to each other.

'It's a place I've good reason to remember,' said George in a low voice. 'Lord! what a miserable wretch I felt that night when I was writing to my cousin to break off our engagement.'

'I wish you'd kept that letter,' said Laura meditatively.

'I can tell you every word of it,' cried George eagerly.

Then, as they continued their way along the dusty country road, all baked and cracked by the dry glare of the Australian midsummer sun, the young man poured out the full confession of his past weakness. How *mean* he had felt himself after proposing to Sara! How he had despised himself and her, and how difficult it was to look upon the whole affair as anything but a kind of comedy – a piece of acting which 'took in' neither her nor himself. Still, the comedy had threatened to turn into dreadful earnest at one time. What an unspeakable relief it had been when he was suddenly released without dishonour from the situation into which he had plunged so heedlessly in a moment of reckless frenzy!

'It seems to me as though you were both a little mad on the whole,' panted Laura – the ascent to the parsonage was *very* steep. 'But there is a method in Sara's madness, at least.'

George gave vent to a short meaning laugh. 'She'd throw the new one over to-morrow if a richer fellow proposed to her. I don't believe she's more heart than this stone' – kicking a lump of quartz into the hedge as he spoke.

'How did you know about Mr Hyde?' asked Laura.

'Why? Didn't I tell you? Last time I went to Piper's Hill I dropped upon him in the drawing-room, saying goodbye to my cousin. Of course, it was no business of mine; but they had not expected me; and it was so evident, you know, that they hadn't, that Hyde wouldn't let me go without telling me at once that they were engaged.'

'What did Sara look like? Did she look at you?'

'Yes, partly. I could have laughed if I had dared. But I didn't. I congratulated them with the greatest gravity and *sang froid*. I think I scored one in Sara's estimation for not looking more surprised.'

'What will Mr Piper say?' said Laura, after a long pause.

'We'll manage it, never fear!' said George, with assurance. 'Leave that to me. I don't say the governor will do more than pay my debts at first. But he's bound to do *that*. And then, if it comes to the selection after all – how often we used to joke about it, do you remember? – you'll see whether I can't keep a decent roof over your head.'

'And give me a Sunday bonnet like the one in front of us to-day?'

'What bonnet? What a woman you are! I'll be bound Margaret couldn't tell what kind of a bonnet was in front of us.'

'Margaret's not a woman,' said Laura. 'She's a saint, and I'm only just beginning to forgive her for being one. By the by, where is she? Oughtn't she to be behind us somewhere?'

'Oh, she's all right! She's with another saint. They don't want *us*.'

'George! And to think you should have been the first to find it out! But to go back to the selection –'

'When a little farm we keep,' hummed George, interrupting her.

'Yes, when a little farm we keep. Never mind the rest. Do you think you will ever *really* be able to settle down to work?'

'I mean to try my level best anyhow. If I could only think that *you* wouldn't repine.'

'I!' cried Laura, vehemently protesting, but she checked herself as suddenly as she had begun. Perhaps because she was afraid of saying too much.

Meanwhile the couple alluded to by this pair of reprobates was slowly ascending the dusty hill towards the parsonage. Not arm-in-arm like the reprobates, for Mr Lydiat's right arm was in a sling, and Margaret chose to walk by it, having come somehow to feel herself responsible for its safety.

'What a new world! What a new life!' says Francis with a half sigh. 'You and I had never met then. Can you understand that?'

Margaret feels that his eyes are turned towards her. She can imagine their expression almost as well as though she had returned the look. But she does not dare to return it – as yet. That particular look is meant for Sara not for her. If she should raise her own timid, flushed, adoring face to his, the look might change or die away. Margaret does not know what envy means, but if it were possible to array herself for just one hour in Sara's body, she thinks she would feel more confidence, and it would be a very happy thing to have Francis speaking to her in that tone, and to feel no misgivings or self-consciousness.

'No, we had never met,' continues the young clergyman musingly; 'indeed, it often seems to me that we never met properly until quite lately, though at other times I could fancy I had known you all my life. It is very strange – but it was all my own fault – I have been of those who have eyes and see not.'

'What do your eyes see now?' asks Margaret gently. There is a half smile on her flushed face, but she is still looking at the ground, and in her heart of hearts she is trembling at her own boldness.

But Francis does not think her bold. The opportunity that she holds out is the very one he has been seeking for days past. Small wonder, then, if he rushes upon it precipitately.

'What do my eyes see now? Oh, Margaret, may I really tell you what they see? To begin with, they see the best and sweetest woman I ever dreamed of –'

'Oh, *please*,' cries Margaret, interrupting – she is certain she will break down if this is to continue. '*Don't*, pray; I've never been used to it, and I don't know how to take it – and besides it isn't so at all – and – and – you will make me so vain.'

Anything to gain a little mastery over the confusion and the happiness that Francis's praise has awakened. For Margaret is not Sara, to whom admiration of any kind seems to come as naturally and to leave as unmoved as the Madonna herself. But Mr Lydiat is not going to spare his victim this time. He has more to say, and he will not be cheated of saying it by any deprecating protests of any kind whatever.

'You vain! You could not be vain if you tried. There is no room for it in your nature. There is no room for even a thought of yourself. You are like your own name, Margaret, a pearl that hides itself in the depths of the ocean. But when you are brought to light you can't help revealing all the preciousness and purity that belong to you.'

'All this because I can "turn to" for a little, as mother calls it, when there is need,' interrupts Margaret in a trembling voice. 'I cannot bear you to overrate it so much.'

'I am not overrating it,' replies Francis with decision, 'but I was not thinking just then of all you have been doing during these past weeks. I was thinking more of all the unconscious good you have been operating. The healing balm you have been distributing everywhere. You can't imagine what I felt like when I came here – how sick and sore at heart! My whole world seemed out of joint.'

'About Sara?' interposes Margaret in scarce audible tones.

'Yes, about Sara. It was not the knowledge that she was out of my reach. That did not affect my blind worship of her. I could have accepted the certainty that she could never be mine, and kept an honest, chivalrous, love for her, and she would have remained on the pedestal to which I had been foolish enough to lift her, to the end. It was not that – I don't know whether I ought to tell you, but I want to tell you *everything* – it was the way in which I was treated. The uncertainty, the longing, the look which bid me hope, and then the cold rejection – the *torment* of it all. Then you came, and little by little all the rankling pain seemed to be drawn out of my heart. My eyes were opened as they had never been before. I saw quite plainly that the sentiment I had had for your sister was creature-worship in its intensest form. And I had had what I deserved. ... Perhaps the punishment would have endured all my life, I can't say how that might have been, if it had not been for you. But since I have known you – for I *do* know you now, Margaret – and all your worth and sweetness, it is all so different. It is inconceivable ... but I feel I may tell you all about my madness, and what I felt then, and what I feel now, ay, dear Margaret, and ask you to be my wife, and to let me love and cherish you. I *may* say it all, may I not? You understand me and you believe in me, don't you?'

Oh, the humility of the appeal! It went to Margaret's very heart.

She to be petitioned for faith in her idol! Why, what happier mission can she conceive than the one of smoothing away by the tenderest, deepest love that woman can conceive for man, the scathing impression of Sara's image? Love like this has no reticence. It is with simple fervour that Margaret replies quietly, 'I am very happy.'

'Are you happy, darling?' Francis's tone is inexpressibly tender. 'Then I have much more happiness than I deserve. How we shall work together in this happy land!'

'I will help you all I can,' responds Margaret earnestly; 'and oh, how many things there are hidden away to ask you about. I never liked to, on board, you know, because – because – but I have kept note of them all – and all the difficulty of believing things – and the need for keeping hold of certain truths, and working upon them.'

They had reached the gate by this time, and can descry George and Laura sitting in the verandah to recover themselves after their climb in the noon-day heat. They are just in time to hear Mr Piper call to the pair to 'take and hurry indoors – the little one wants to give 'em a talking-to.'

'May we come, too?' cries Margaret, breathless. Her face is so radiant with joy that her uncle cannot but detect the change in it; and it is with a portentous chuckle and a sidelong wink, which, fortunately, misses fire in the quarter for which it is intended, that he bids his niece 'Come on, and fetch her young man along with her.'

So the two couples defile down the little passage that has echoed so much coming and going since the night when the victims of the accident were borne down its narrow length, and pass into the fragrant room, where returning health and hope seem to hover round the couch. Louey is sitting up now, for she has been expecting the visit of her 'family,' as Mr Piper has christened the Barnesbury household. She has put a blue riband around her fast-growing hair, and the far away look so alarming to her father is exchanged for one of joyous anticipation. For as George and Laura come in and kiss her, she throws her arms round the necks of each simultaneously, and includes them in a general embrace which conveys a world of meaning.

'But kissing ain't bread and butter,' remarks Mr Piper sententiously, 'though some folks think they can live on it. Wait till we take and put 'em on a back-block, squirrel, and see how soon they'll find it out.'

But even this dreadful threat does not discompose the betrothed pair, who retreat to make way for the other couple who next approach the bed.

Louey was preparing discreetly to embrace each in turn, when Mr Piper, to the astonishment of all, and especially of those attacked, suddenly pushes forward Margaret and the young clergyman in the same instant towards Louey's extended arms.

'There! you may take and hug 'em all round, and wish 'em joy as soon as you like.'

It is not a very dignified way of announcing an engagement to the public, but the accused pair are saved the trouble of revealing it for themselves, and Mr Piper is so elated by the conviction of his own 'knowingness,' and Louey is so radiant with delight at this new cementing of all the affections she cherishes, that there is nothing left for the victims but to laugh and comply. So the first time that Margaret is embraced by her affianced husband is within the encircling arms of tender and innocent childhood. My Lydiat feels that there is something typical of the nature and sanctity of his projected union in this. What different feelings that other kiss in the tropical atmosphere of the conservatory, with Sara's bare, white shoulders and heaving bosom, had aroused and left behind it.

CHAPTER IV

•

Sara's Last Appearance

'Oft expectation fails, and most oft there
Where most it promises.' – SHAKESPEARE

However much of a contradiction it may seem to betake oneself to
town at the end of the summer, in quest of cool lawns and waving
boughs, it is certain that Piper's Hill seemed a very oasis of green
after a two months' experience of the parched landscape round
Barnesbury. As our tired travellers drove through the wide-open iron
gates, and descended under the great portico, where Mr Cavendish
and Sara were waiting to receive them, the size and magnificence of
their colonial home came upon them all with a kind of surprise. It
almost seemed as though it had been growing during their absence,
as though the great carriage-drive were broader, the shrubs bigger,
the lawns greener and ampler – even the tower taller than before. Mr
Cavendish and Sara seemed likewise to have participated in some
curious, intangible way in the change; Mr Cavendish especially, for
the dignified grace with which he received his relatives, and flourished
his faintly-perfumed handkerchief of Indian silk, gave Mr Piper the
curious sensation that his brother-in-law was doing the honours of
Piper's Hill to its actual proprietor. ·

Possibly Mr Cavendish, in his sense of the 'fitness of things,' had
forgotten that even the subtly-refined perfume he affected was paid
for out of Mr Piper's pocket. However that might be, he welcomed
the arrivals with an impressiveness suited to a party of prodigal sons,
and bestowed upon each the exact amount of effusion that the occasion
required. He embraced his wife and daughter with forbearing affec-

tion, that matter of the non-appearance of the weekly loan on two distinct occasions had yet to be inquired into; he shook hands with George and called him 'my dear nephew,' and asked permission to kiss Laura on the cheek. To Mr Piper he held out both hands, with the very gesture of a gentleman of the old school in a modern play. Perhaps the sincerest feeling that moved him next to his salutation of Mr Lydiat, as to whose great-great-grandfather he had received a most satisfactory *éclaircissement*, was the kiss he bestowed on Louey. 'And how you have grown, my sweet child, to be sure! Dear, dear, and to think you should have been the heroine of such an adventure! And we have been quite lost without you. Sara there will tell you how dull we have been. We have been actually moping like a pair of owls. Haven't we, Sara?'

'Of course we have,' replied Sara dutifully, but she did not enlarge upon the circumstance. She was occupied in wondering how her two discarded lovers felt. Both George and Francis had greeted her with a calmness which was disconcerting, to say the least of it. Granted they were both engaged, and she as well, had they not each of them sworn, only a few weeks ago, that they adored her and desired her? Out of mere self-respect, if not for the 'pangs of disprized love,' they might have worn the willow just a little longer. It was hardly proper, and for a clergyman, too! Of course her sister and Laura were welcome to her cast-off admirers, but really, if it were not for Mr Hyde, it might have been almost worth her while to test how far all this new-born allegiance, diverted from herself, was worth.

It was worth at least, in Mr Piper's eyes, the ordering of two wedding-cakes of great splendour. The double marriages had been fixed to take place on the same day, some six weeks after the return to Piper's Hill, and George's father, having once given in, was of opinion that the thing should be done 'in style.' George himself, and all the others who stood committed to matrimony, were eager that the ceremony should be as simple and private as possible, and for once Mr Piper found that even his own 'flesh and blood' could rise in rebellion against him. As there seemed to be a conspiracy to overthrow the kind of wedding-breakfast he had imagined – with plentiful carriages and white favours, and a string of waiters from town – he was fain to throw his interest into the purchase of the trousseaux and the choosing of the furniture for Margaret's home. But here, again, he declared that they were 'all against him.' Laura had assumed a new *role*, into which she threw herself quite as energetically as into her former one.

'A back-block means a log hut, my dear,' she would say to Margaret. 'A sun-bonnet and a strong riding-habit are the kind of thing *I* must look for!' Margaret would declare that, for the wife of a poor curate, nothing was more befitting than plain stuff gowns, with perhaps *one* black silk for great occasions; and the two conspirators, or conspiratresses, if such a word may pass, would set off with light purses and lighter hearts for the unfashionable shops of Collingwood, in search of cheap hosiery and aprons.

But Margaret was circumvented, after all, in the matter of the furniture, for Mr Piper pressed Mr Cavendish into the service, and received a willing ally. 'It must be remembered,' said the latter, 'that my son-in-law to be is the scion of an undoubtedly ancient house, and as such, entitled to refined surroundings;' and backed by Mr Piper's authority, he actually went in his own person to choose the new art-carpets and couches that were to figure in his daughter's drawing-room. By dint, indeed, of choosing and ordering, he had to come to look upon the gift of household goods to the young couple as proceeding from himself, and was very magnanimous in his determination to provide all of the *very* best. They might trust him entirely, he assured them, with respect to the drawing and dining-room appointments. He flattered himself that he knew exactly what ecclesiastical taste required. He had even now a vision of his brother, the Bishop of Blanktown's sanctum before his eyes – the massive bookcase of carved oak, and the wonderful collection of South Sea curios presented by the delegates of the various missions! Of course old oak was not to be had in the colonies, but he would get the nearest approach to it, and everything should be subdued in tone, chaste, tender, with just a *soupçon* of devotional decoration, copied from the Byzantine churches, to relieve it.

Margaret's alarm at this announcement was so great that she went immediately to her uncle to entreat him to retract the *carte blanche* permission he had extended to her father. But Mr Piper only chuckled upon hearing her story: 'It'll take a deal more than that to ruin *me*,' he said, as he patted her on the shoulder with his broad hand. 'I'm going to let your father have his head a bit longer. I'll know when to take and pull him up, never fear. And mind you, it ain't *my* present, nor yet your mother's; it's the little one's. And she don't do things by halves any more than me. We don't do things by halves out here, do we, squirrel?'

Louey's only reply was to hold up her face to be kissed alternately by her father and her cousin. It was the first time she had heard of the present she was conferring, and the easiest way out of her embarrassment was to kiss everybody concerned and to run away. After that, the preparations for the weddings were the theme of a great deal of mysterious conversation between herself and her father. They would stop talking when George or Laura came into the room, and look at each other meaningly. Sometimes they would go upstairs and plot in the tower, for Mr Piper would hardly allow his little girl out of his sight since her illness. The doctors had told him that she was a delicate subject, and what with the increased height and pallor she had gained, and the upstanding aureole of soft auburn hair, that made her look like one of Burne Jones's watching seraphs, there was something in her aspect that almost justified his vague alarm lest she should fall ill again suddenly, and fly away from him this time for good and all.

But she was well enough and happy enough when the great day came round at last. Margaret and Laura had carried their point, and only Sara and Louey were to accompany the wedding party to church. The brides had arranged to dress alike, in soft grey cashmeres and bonnets, their own choice, to be used as future visiting toilettes. Sara had arrayed herself in her raceday splendour, and was fidgeting about the room in which her sister was dressing, with an expression which argued that she was not entirely pleased. These past six weeks had been somewhat trying to Sara. Every one was so selfishly absorbed in his and her particular concerns, that they seemed to have lost all interest in hers. And here was mail day come round, and the letter she had been reckoning upon from Mr Hyde (who *must* have reached Colombo in plenty of time to write) was not forthcoming. And her uncle had actually made her the subject of one of his vulgar jokes, and told her 'to have a care her young man didn't serve her the same as she'd served George,' and then reminded her that there was a man-of-war coming in with a lot of swells on board – some of 'em with tails to their names.

She had run upstairs with her heart beating loud with indignation. It was unpardonable in her betrothed to be so neglectful, and hateful to be at the mercy of such a vulgar old wretch as her Uncle Piper. Though it was impossible to help speculating, too, upon the amount of truth that might have been embodied in his last communication. A man-of-war, and opportunities, no doubt, without end! Well, if Reginald did not explain everything in the most clear and satisfactory way by the very first mail from home, there could be no earthly reason for debarring herself anything when the man-of-war arrived. Meanwhile it *was* a little aggravating to see Margaret, with that 'good-little-girl' kind of expression in her face, tying her bonnet before the glass, as though it was the most virtuous thing in the world to go and get married – to a man, too, who would have sold his soul a few weeks back to win the sister of his bride. In short, when Sara came to reckon up all her various grievances, she felt justified in coming to the conclusion that she had been very badly treated.

'It is curious – isn't it?' she remarked slowly, as she continued to watch the tying of the bonnet-strings.

'Curious! What is, dear?' rejoined Margaret abstractedly. For the first time in her life she was thinking more of her own appearance than of Sara's. Perhaps she could hardly have said, indeed, what the latter was wearing.

'Very curious,' replied Sara. She had thrown herself back in an easy-chair, with her gaze, however, always fixed upon her sister. 'I am going to see two weddings to-day, and I might have been in the place of both the brides if I had chosen.'

'Not both at once, I hope,' said Margaret, essaying to joke, but wincing a little nevertheless.

'How silly you are, Margaret!' There was decided anger in Sara's tones now. 'It *is* curious when one thinks that both the bridegrooms begged and prayed me to marry them three months ago. I don't care what any one says – *that* will always remain a fact.'

Margaret was silent. There was no denying the truth of her sister's words. Whatever might be Sara's motive in insisting upon it at this moment, it had the effect of casting a chill upon her joy.

But her mother arrived opportunely at this moment in a new gown, and Louey made her appearance with two fragrant bouquets of orange-blossom, which were still the only orthodox flowers for a bride, and Mr Piper's heavy step, accompanied by the discreet creaking of Mr Cavendish's elegant boots of patent leather, was heard below. There was no time for the rejoinder that Margaret felt tempted to make. And perhaps she was glad she had not made it an hour later, when she left the altar by Francis's side, to have and to hold him from that day forward without fear or misgiving. She had followed the service in its most literal sense with all the earnestness of her nature, and would have had no sympathy with the half-perceptible gleam that might have been detected in Laura's eyes at being called upon to *obey* George. Mr Piper gave his step-daughter away with a loyal resolution to take back all the hard things he had said of her in the days when she had deserved them, and Mr Cavendish handed over *his* daughter to the Rev. Mr Lydiat with pleasant inward speculation upon the possibility of becoming father-in-law to a bishop as well as brother to one. Mrs Cavendish was found at home just lachrymose enough to temper her brother's effusive hospitality, which took the form of insisting upon such an amount of health-drinking in Pommery and Greno, that Mr Cavendish reaped therefrom a violent headache, and said many bitter things to his wife before the end of the day about the drawback of being entertained by a *nouveau riche*.

But none of these circumstances affected the happiness of the heroes and heroines of the day; not even Sara's dark looks, which made her appear like a wrathful goddess, with no other result than that George confided to Laura later in the day, that he 'shouldn't wonder if his cousin had a temper of her own,' while Mr Lydiat marvelled that he should have lived so long in the society of the two sisters and never discovered how immeasurably superior his own wife's expression was to Sara's. There was a surprise in reserve for the wedding party, which had been a great success. An envelope was discovered next to Laura's plate addressed to Mrs George Piper. The superscription was in Louey's hand, and the envelope on being opened disclosed a neatly-folded slip of paper with the following words: 'For a year's travel in Europe before going to the back-block.' Laura opened it with trembling fingers, when out fell a cheque for a thousand pounds, signed by Mr Piper. In presence of all the company she left her seat and went round to kiss her father-in-law, then handed over the cheque with something of a stage effect to her husband.

To bring a narrative to a close with a wedding is only possible in very exceptional cases. But no one could look at Francis and Margaret and pretend to see in them the stuff for post-nuptial adventures. Francis has lived though his mistake, perhaps he has lived through his romance as well; for infatuated worship such as he had bestowed upon his ideal after clothing it in Sara's regal form does not manifest itself twice in a lifetime. At any rate, he is safe now, as sporting people say, to make a fond and faithful husband for all time. As for poor Margaret, she has realised her romance, and will continue it until she is a grey old woman, if she should live so long. I am not so sure about the future of George and Laura, though George is of opinion that they have 'bought their experience,' both of them. But I am sure that whatever may befall them the world will never be large enough to afford them separate living room, and that they will stand or fall together.

As for Sara, the last we see of her is some six or seven months after her sister's marriage. She is still wont to carry her triumphs and her troubles to Margaret, and thinks it extremely selfish of the latter to let her attention wander to such trivialities as her husband's supper or the coming baby. On this particular afternoon she has run in upon the pretext of asking for a cup of tea – Margaret has an enchanting little tea-service, Louey's veritable present – but in reality to unburden herself of the multifarious grievances which weigh upon her existence.

Margaret listens with her grave smile of sympathy to the entire list. How insufferably rude Uncle Piper has been, how mamma actually forces that chit of a Louey to take the grown-up place in the carriage, and expects Sara to sit with her back to the horses, how frightfully dull the evenings are, with her mother and Uncle Piper playing backgammon all the time, and how dreadfully offended papa was – and no wonder! – when he was actually refused the right of inviting his old friends to dinner.

'But what about Mr Hyde?' asks Margaret. 'If you are as happy in your married life as I am, Sara, dear, you will soon forget these trifling worries.'

'Trifling do you call them?' interrupts her sister indignantly, 'I only wish *you* could feel them. But you were always like that, Maggie. Unless a person were literally to knock you down and trample upon you, you wouldn't mind. I only wish *I* were as thick-skinned!'

'And Mr Hyde?' says Margaret once more. She does not even feel tempted to make a rejoinder to her sister's words. With the consciousness of being loved and valued beyond anything she could have conceived, what can it matter that Sara should call her thick-skinned – 'And Mr Hyde?'

'Mr Hyde? Oh, I don't know. Somebody's been making mischief, I'm positive. That's another worry. If I hadn't been engaged, I wouldn't have hesitated when the *Melpomena* was here. However, she's coming back, thank goodness, and this time I *will* listen to Lord Lennox. He was only waiting for me to say "Yes," you know.'

'I can quite believe it,' says Margaret. Her tone is grave almost to sadness. But Sara is too taken up with her own reflections to notice it.

'And this time,' she continues, 'there's a Russian Prince on board. Only fancy, Maggie, a real prince, and a Russian. Well, good-bye, and mind you come up this evening. We're not going anywhere, and it's too deadly dull to be endured.'